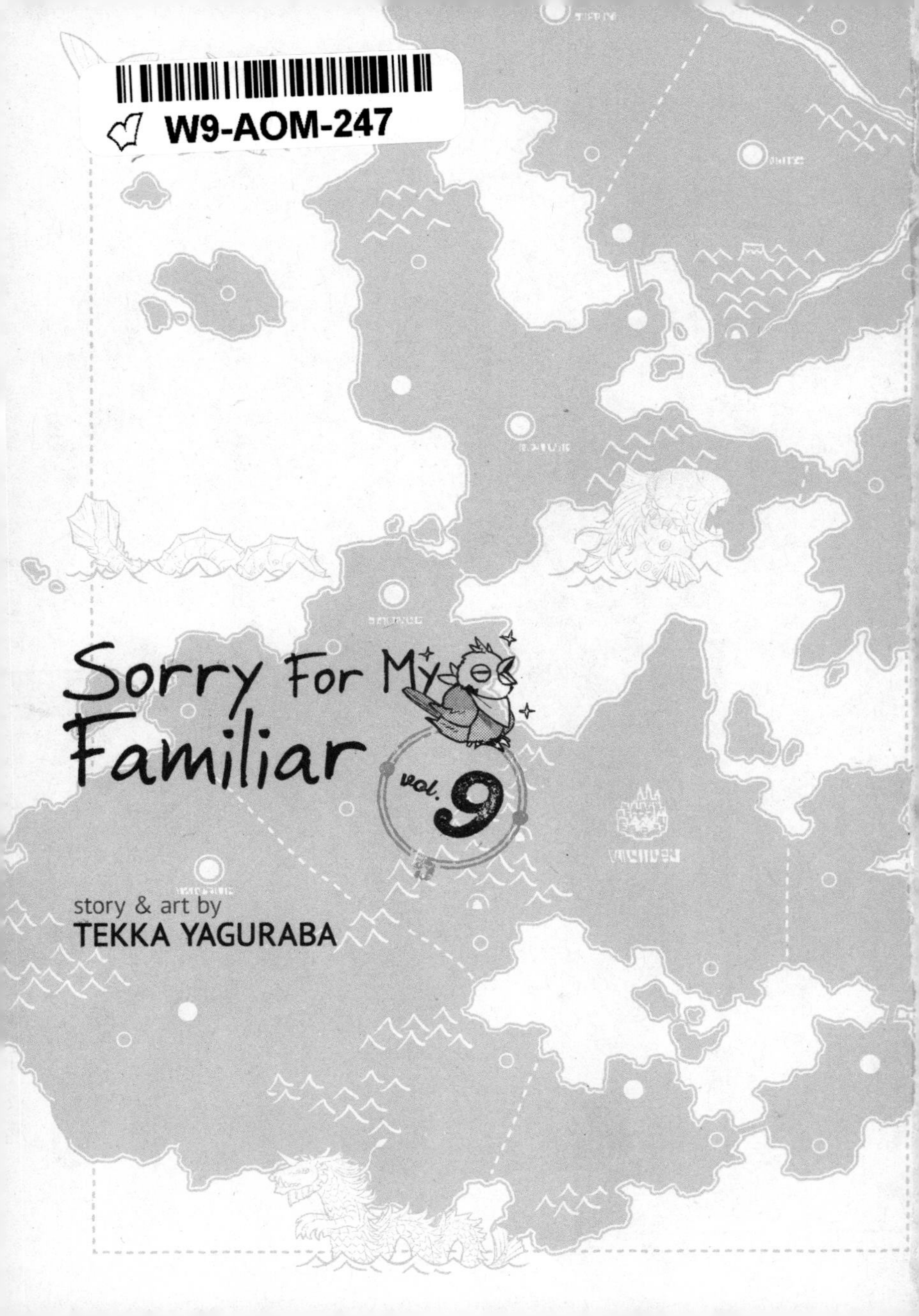

Sorry For My Familiar

vol. 9

story & art by
TEKKA YAGURABA

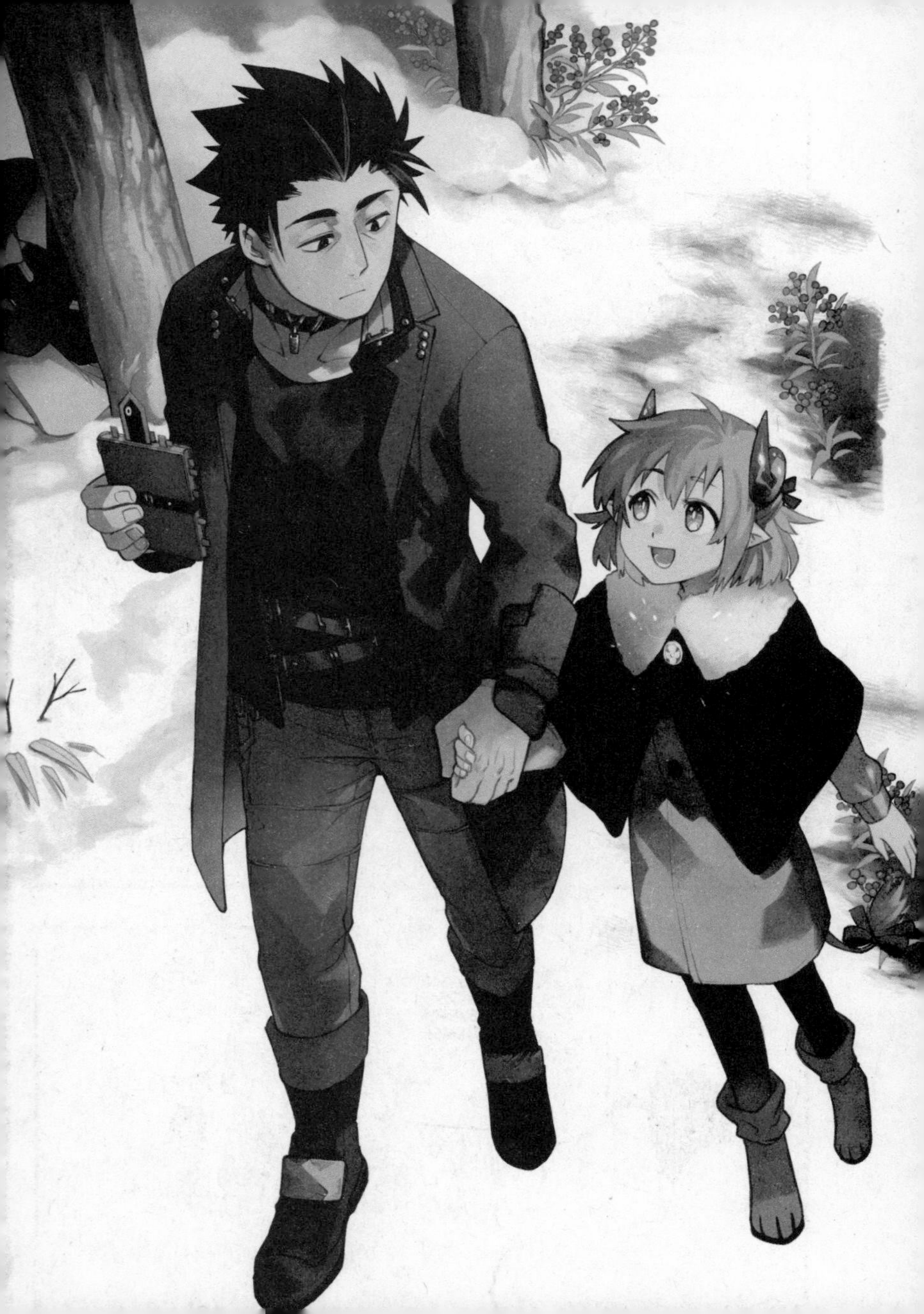

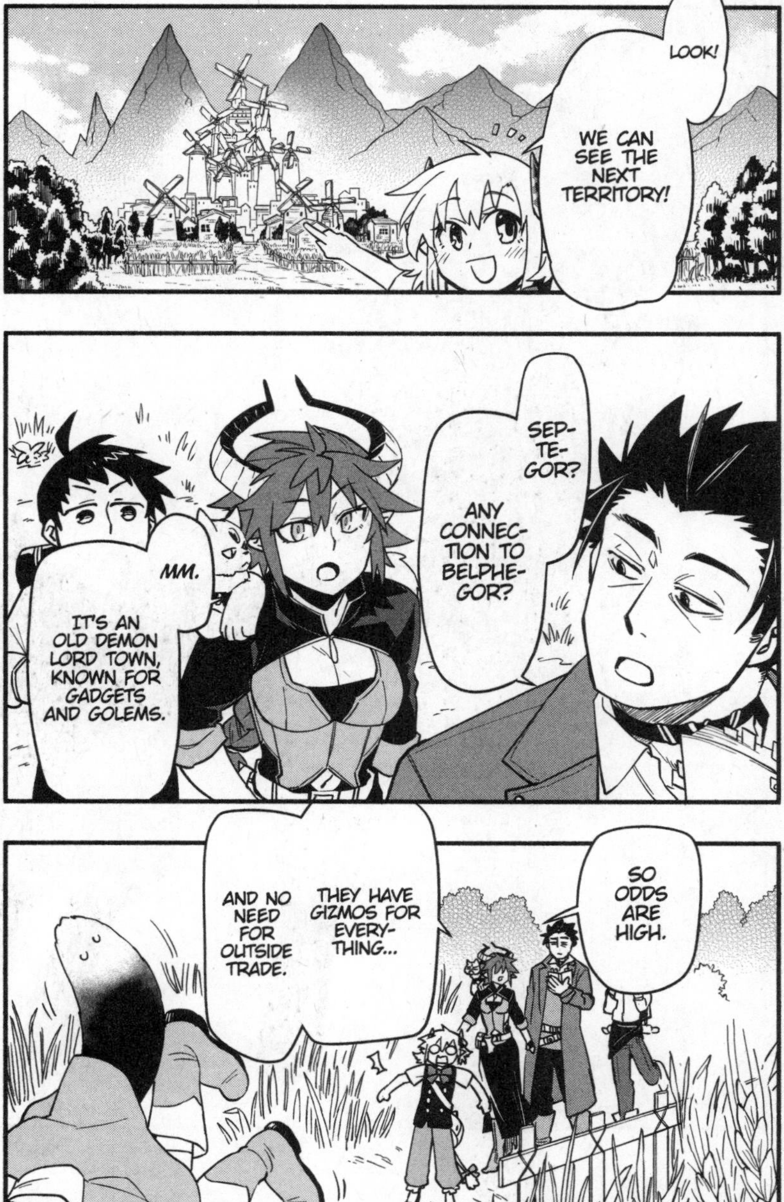
LOOK!
WE CAN SEE THE NEXT TERRITORY!
SEPTEGOR?
ANY CONNECTION TO BELPHEGOR?
MM.
IT'S AN OLD DEMON LORD TOWN, KNOWN FOR GADGETS AND GOLEMS.
SO ODDS ARE HIGH.
THEY HAVE GIZMOS FOR EVERYTHING...
AND NO NEED FOR OUTSIDE TRADE.

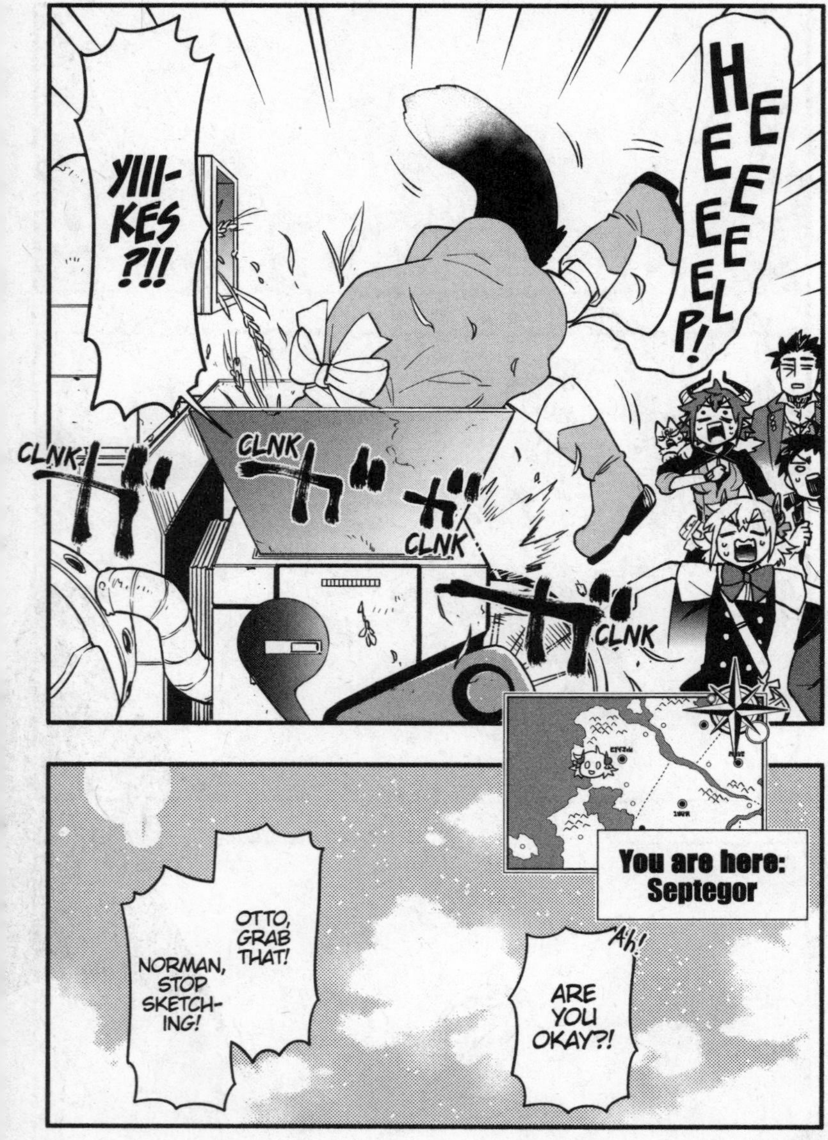
HEEEEEELP!
YIIII-KES?!!
CLNK
CLNK
CLNK
CLNK
You are here: Septegor
Ah!
ARE YOU OKAY?!
OTTO, GRAB THAT!
NORMAN, STOP SKETCH-ING!

FILE 57: Septegor

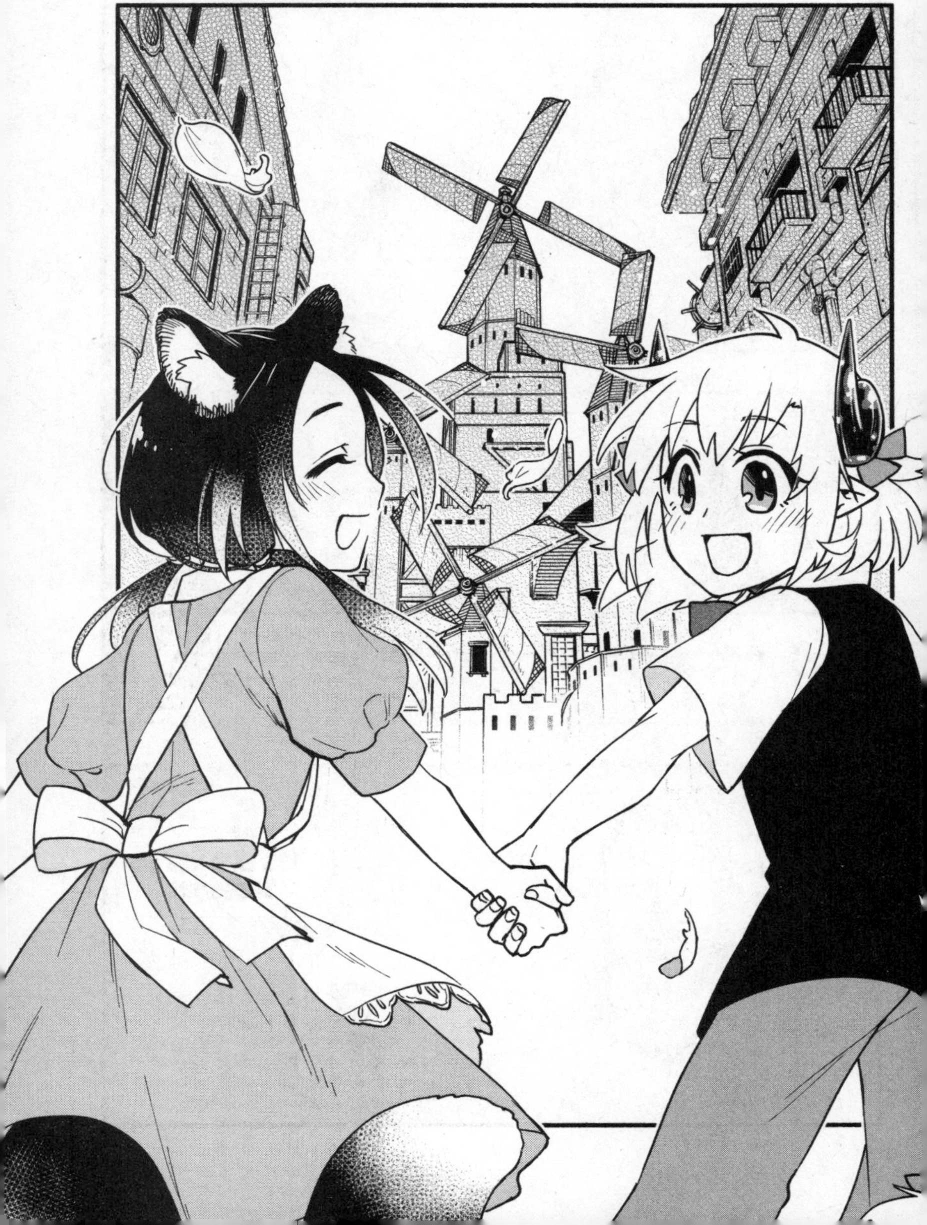

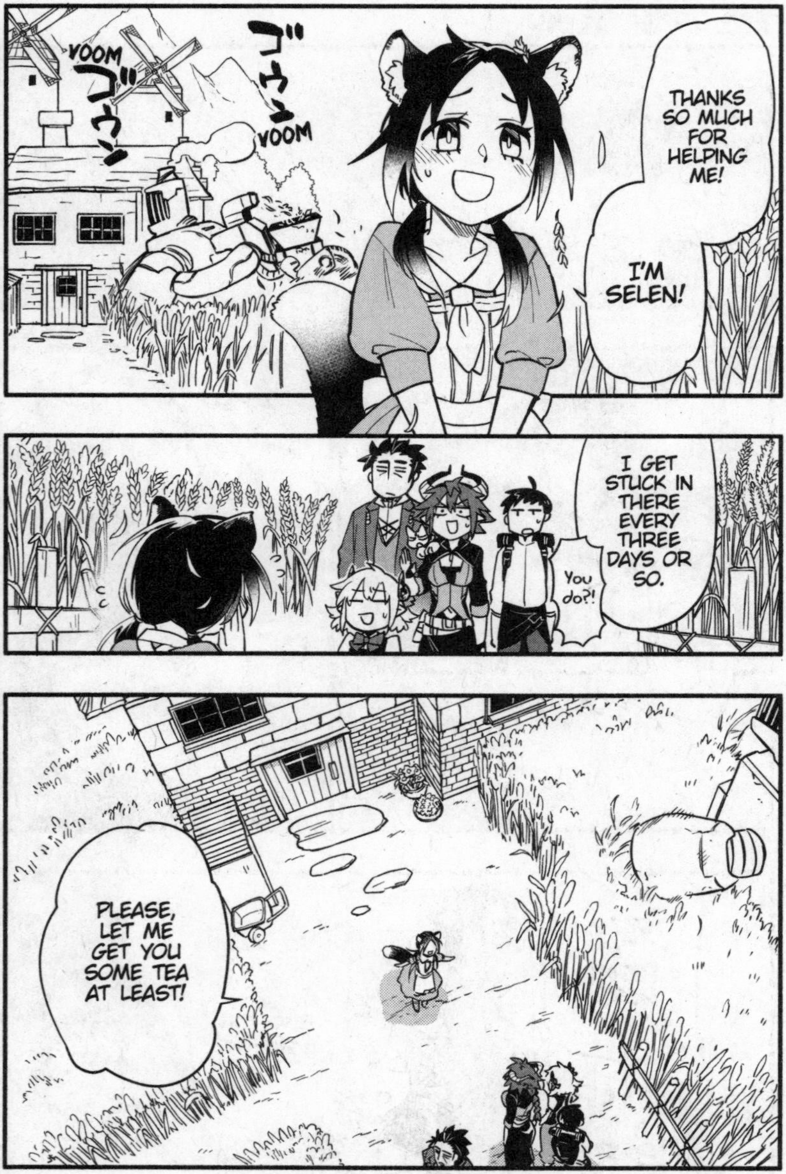
THANKS SO MUCH FOR HELPING ME!
I'M SELEN!
ゴウン VOOM
ゴウン VOOM
I GET STUCK IN THERE EVERY THREE DAYS OR SO.
You do?!
PLEASE, LET ME GET YOU SOME TEA AT LEAST!

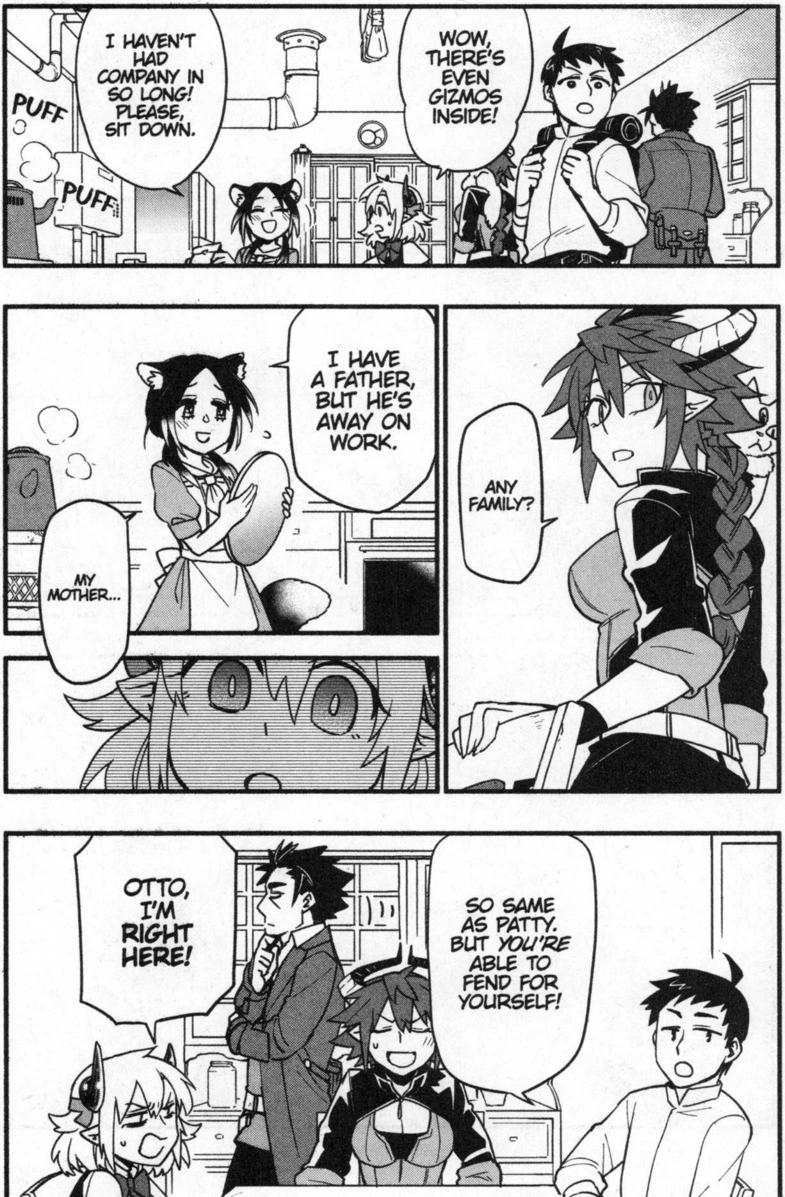
WOW, THERE'S EVEN GIZMOS INSIDE!
I HAVEN'T HAD COMPANY IN SO LONG! PLEASE, SIT DOWN.
PUFF
PUFF
ANY FAMILY?
I HAVE A FATHER, BUT HE'S AWAY ON WORK.
MY MOTHER...
SO SAME AS PATTY. BUT YOU'RE ABLE TO FEND FOR YOURSELF!
OTTO, I'M RIGHT HERE!

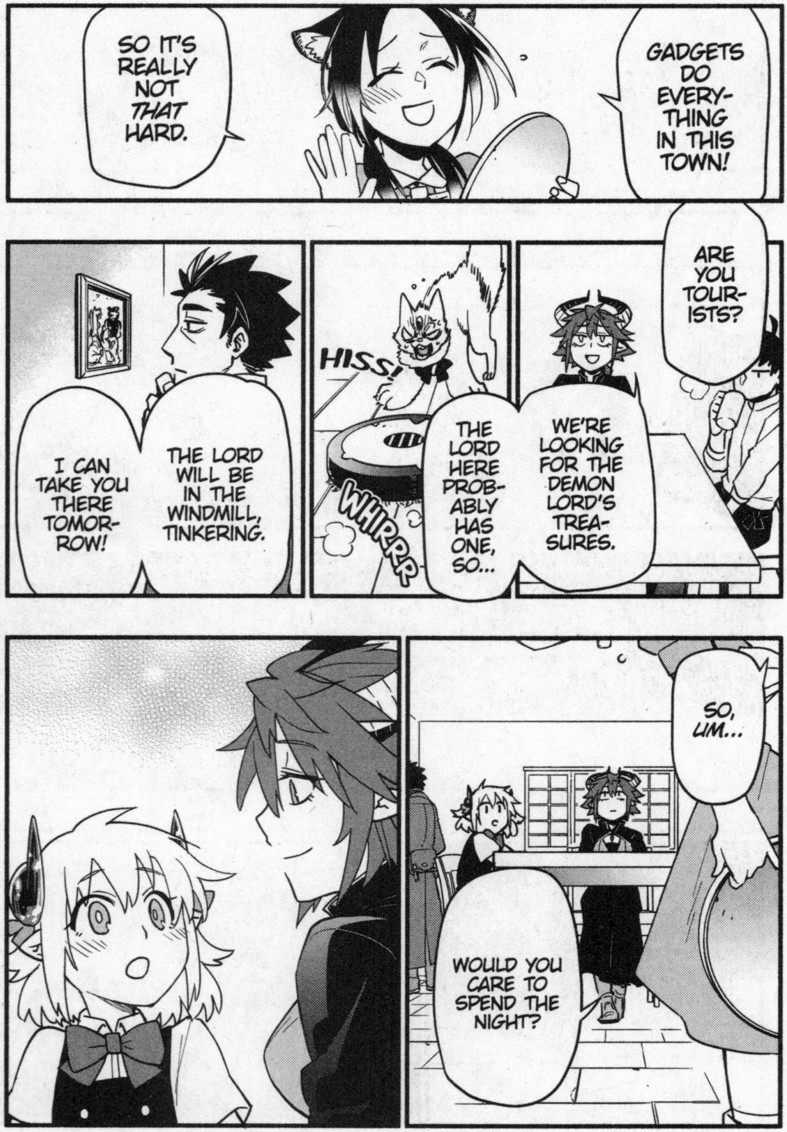
GADGETS DO EVERYTHING IN THIS TOWN!
SO IT'S REALLY NOT *THAT* HARD.
ARE YOU TOURISTS?
WE'RE LOOKING FOR THE DEMON LORD'S TREASURES.
THE LORD HERE PROBABLY HAS ONE, SO...
HISS!
WHIRRR
THE LORD WILL BE IN THE WINDMILL, TINKERING.
I CAN TAKE YOU THERE TOMORROW!
SO, UM...
WOULD YOU CARE TO SPEND THE NIGHT?

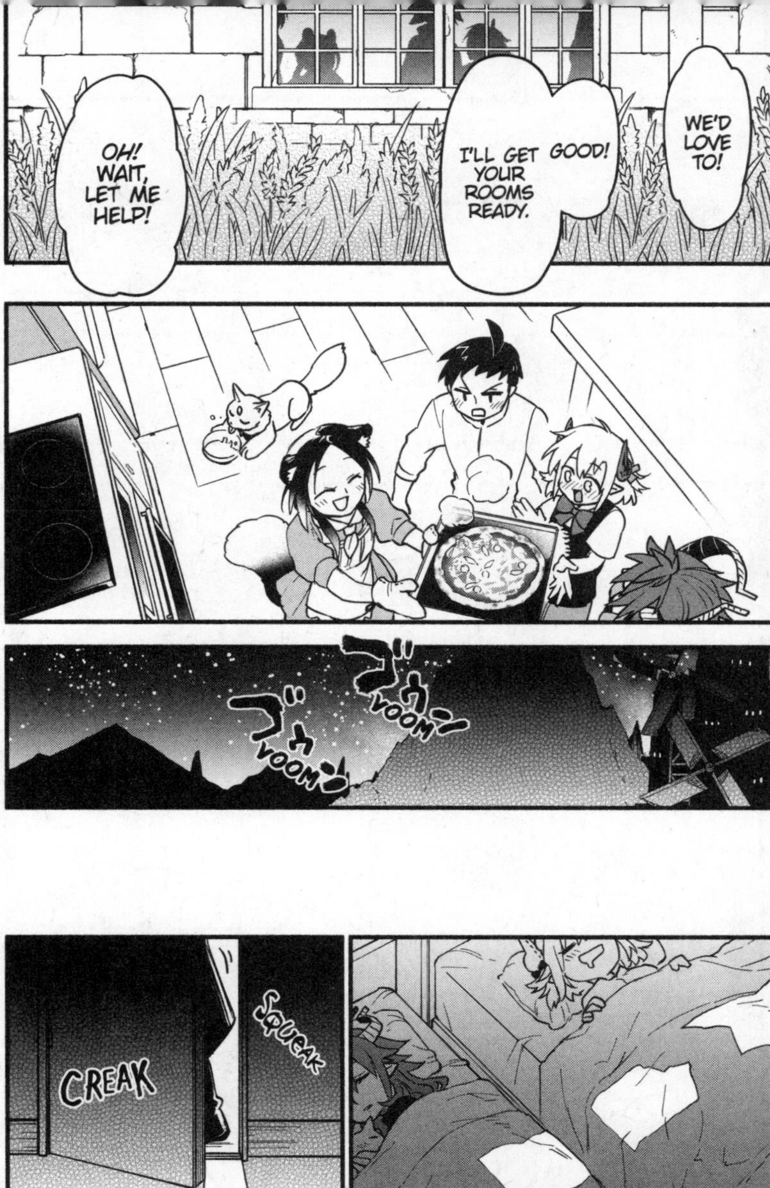
WE'D LOVE TO!
GOOD!
I'LL GET YOUR ROOMS READY.
OH! WAIT, LET ME HELP!
VOOM
VOOM
SQUEAK
CREAK

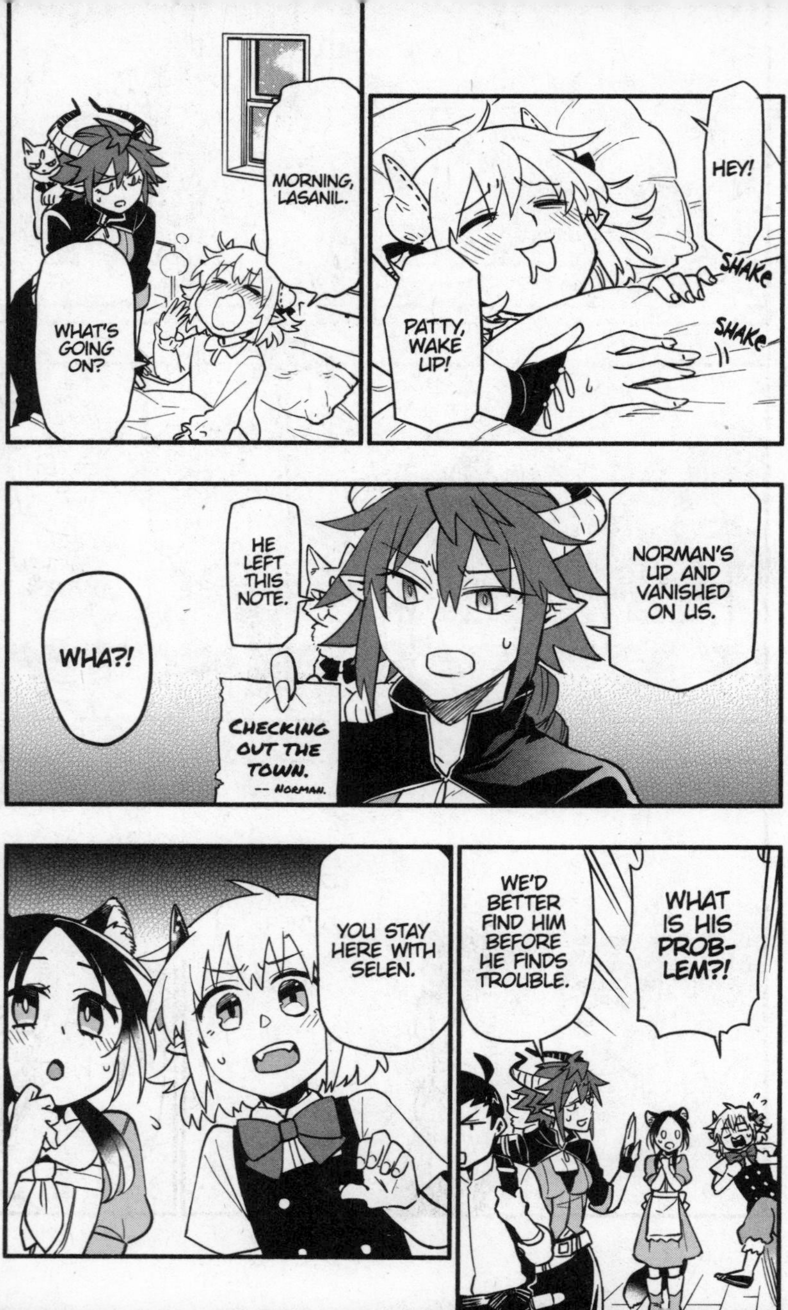
HEY!
SHAKE
SHAKE
PATTY, WAKE UP!
MORNING, LASANIL.
WHAT'S GOING ON?
NORMAN'S UP AND VANISHED ON US.
HE LEFT THIS NOTE.
CHECKING OUT THE TOWN.
-- NORMAN.
WHA?!
WHAT IS HIS PROB-LEM?!
WE'D BETTER FIND HIM BEFORE HE FINDS TROUBLE.
YOU STAY HERE WITH SELEN.

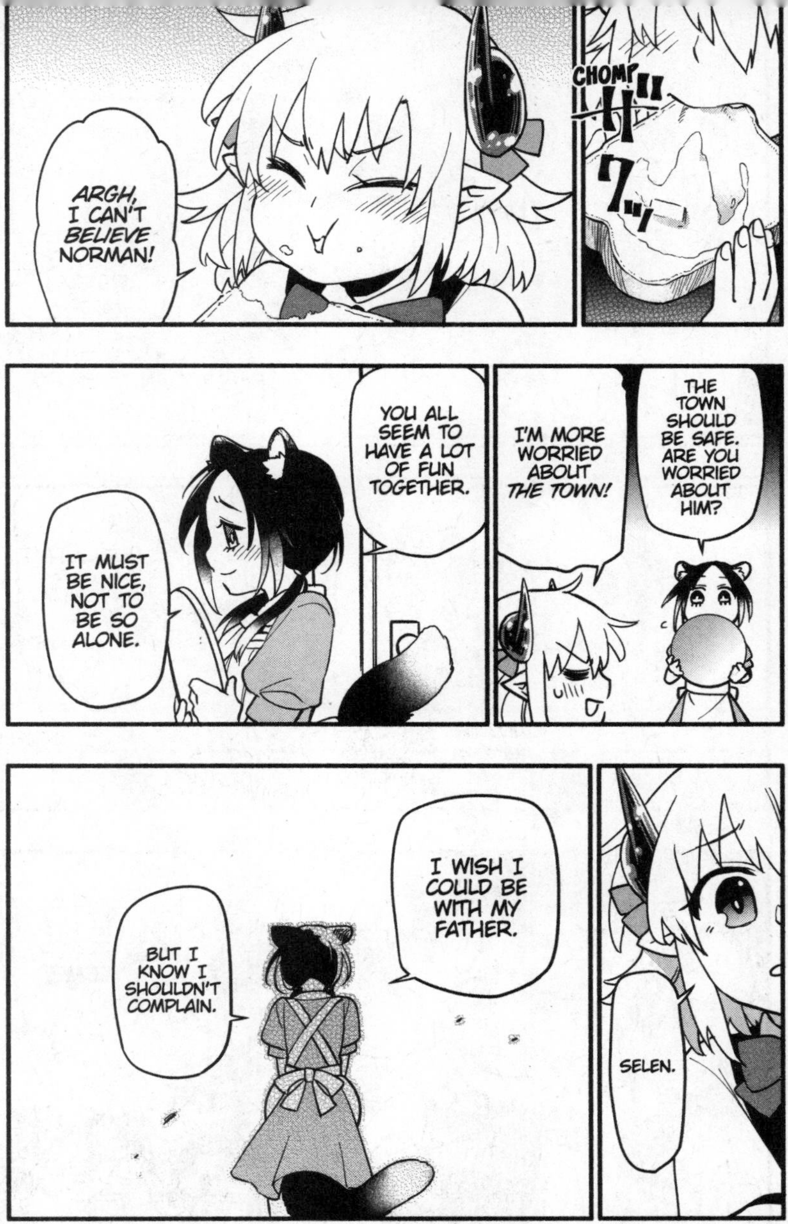
CHOMP!!
ARGH, I CAN'T *BELIEVE* NORMAN!
THE TOWN SHOULD BE SAFE. ARE YOU WORRIED ABOUT HIM?
I'M MORE WORRIED ABOUT *THE TOWN!*
YOU ALL SEEM TO HAVE A LOT OF FUN TOGETHER.
IT MUST BE NICE, NOT TO BE SO ALONE.
SELEN.
I WISH I COULD BE WITH MY FATHER.
BUT I KNOW I SHOULDN'T COMPLAIN.

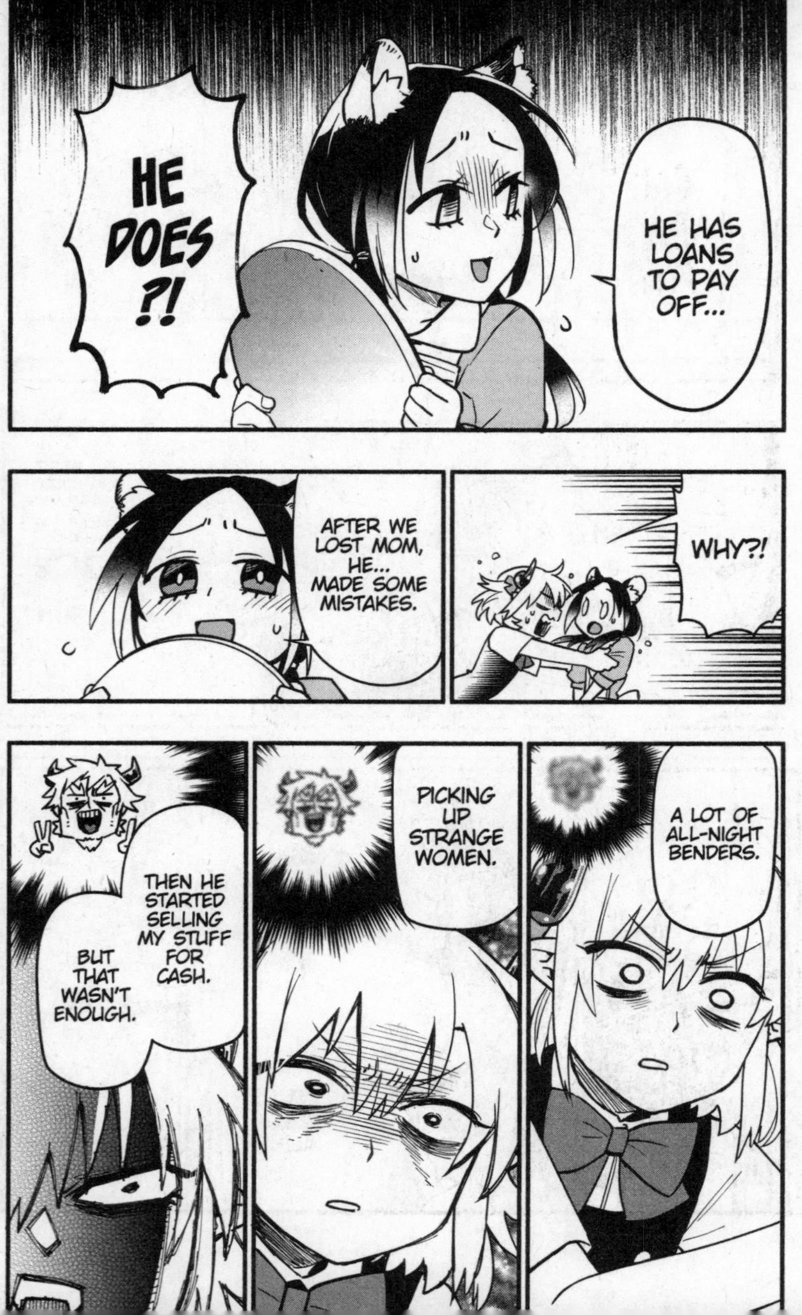
HE HAS LOANS TO PAY OFF...
HE DOES ?!
WHY?!
AFTER WE LOST MOM, HE... MADE SOME MISTAKES.
A LOT OF ALL-NIGHT BENDERS.
PICKING UP STRANGE WOMEN.
THEN HE STARTED SELLING MY STUFF FOR CASH.
BUT THAT WASN'T ENOUGH.

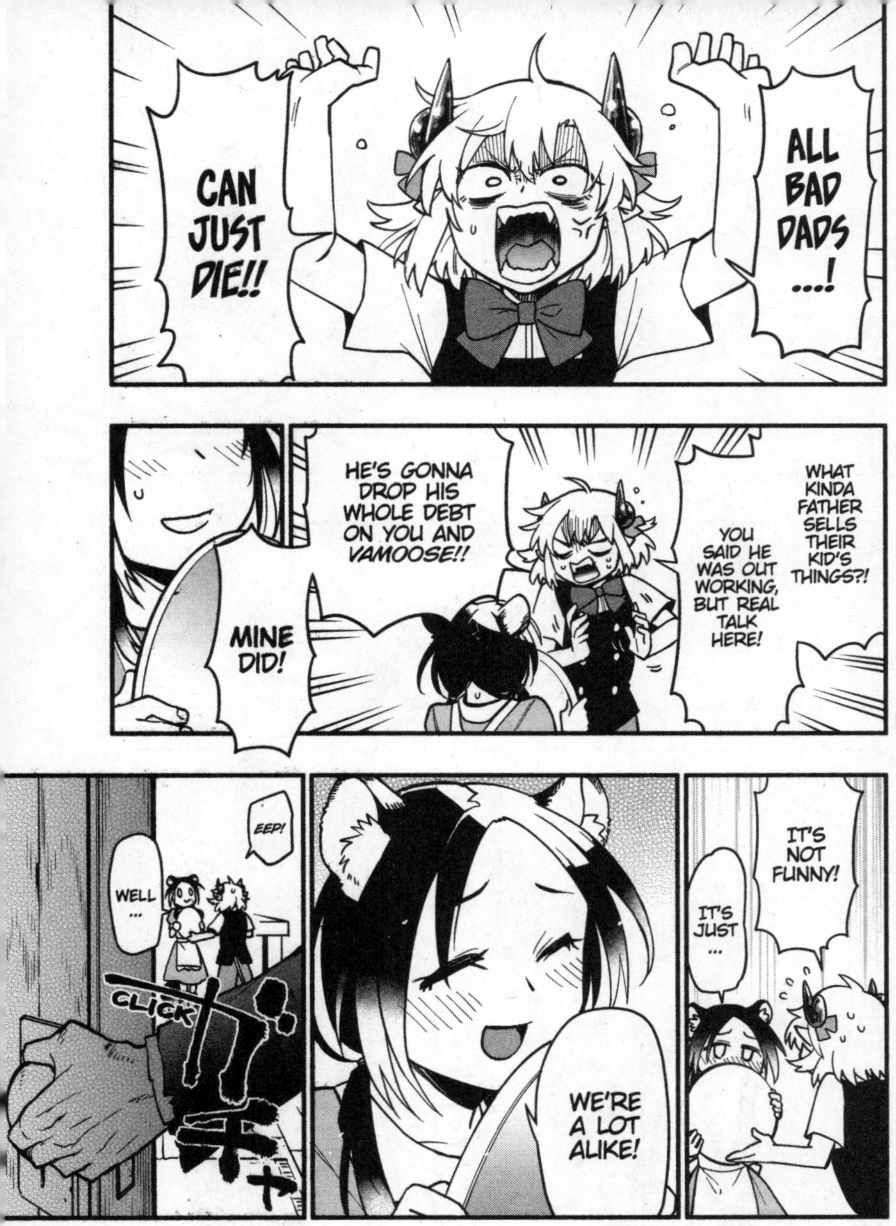
ALL BAD DADS ....!
CAN JUST DIE!!
WHAT KINDA FATHER SELLS THEIR KID'S THINGS?!
YOU SAID HE WAS OUT WORKING, BUT REAL TALK HERE!
HE'S GONNA DROP HIS WHOLE DEBT ON YOU AND VAMOOSE!!
MINE DID!
IT'S NOT FUNNY!
IT'S JUST ...
WE'RE A LOT ALIKE!
EEP!
WELL ...
CLICK

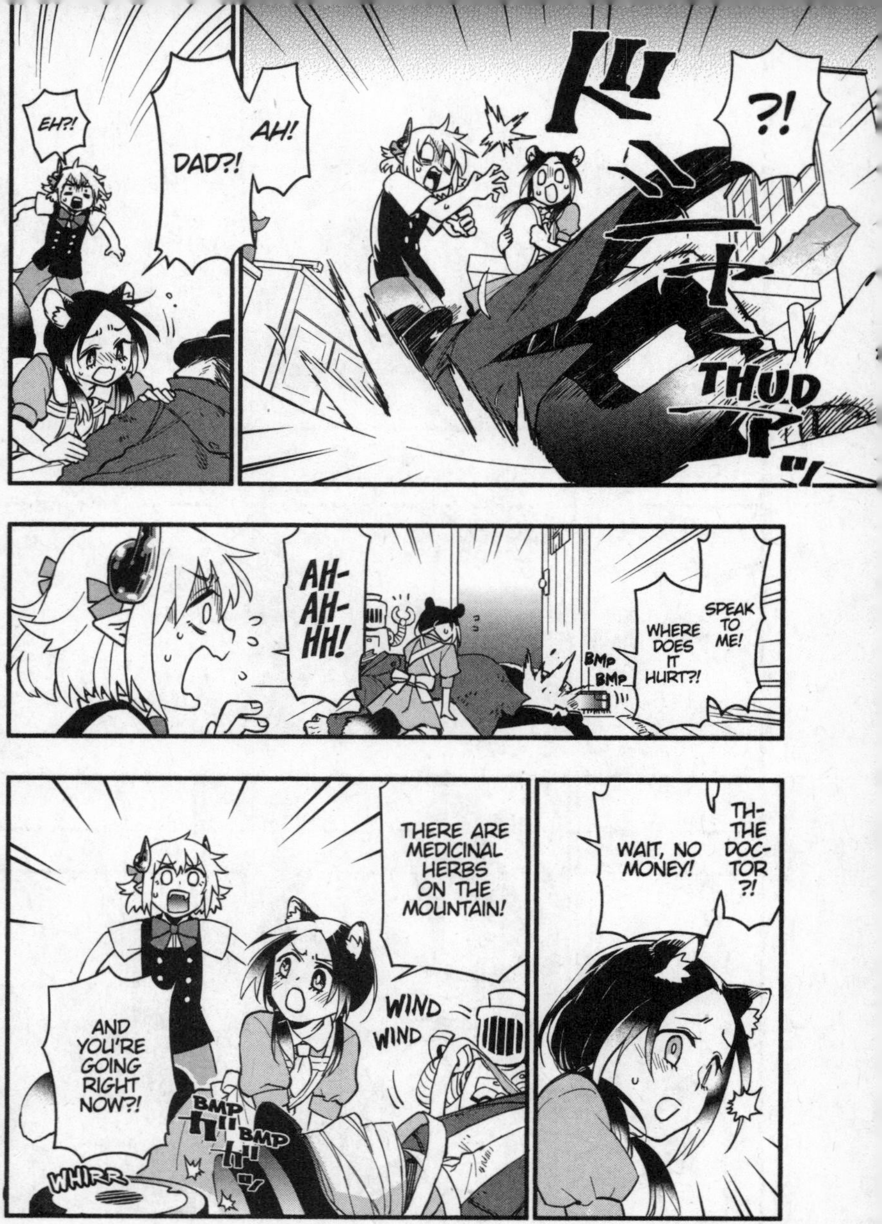
?!
THUD
AH! DAD?!
EH?!
SPEAK TO ME!
WHERE DOES IT HURT?!
BMP BMP
AH-AH-HH!
TH-THE DOCTOR?!
WAIT, NO MONEY!
THERE ARE MEDICINAL HERBS ON THE MOUNTAIN!
WIND WIND
AND YOU'RE GOING RIGHT NOW?!
BMP BMP
WHIRR

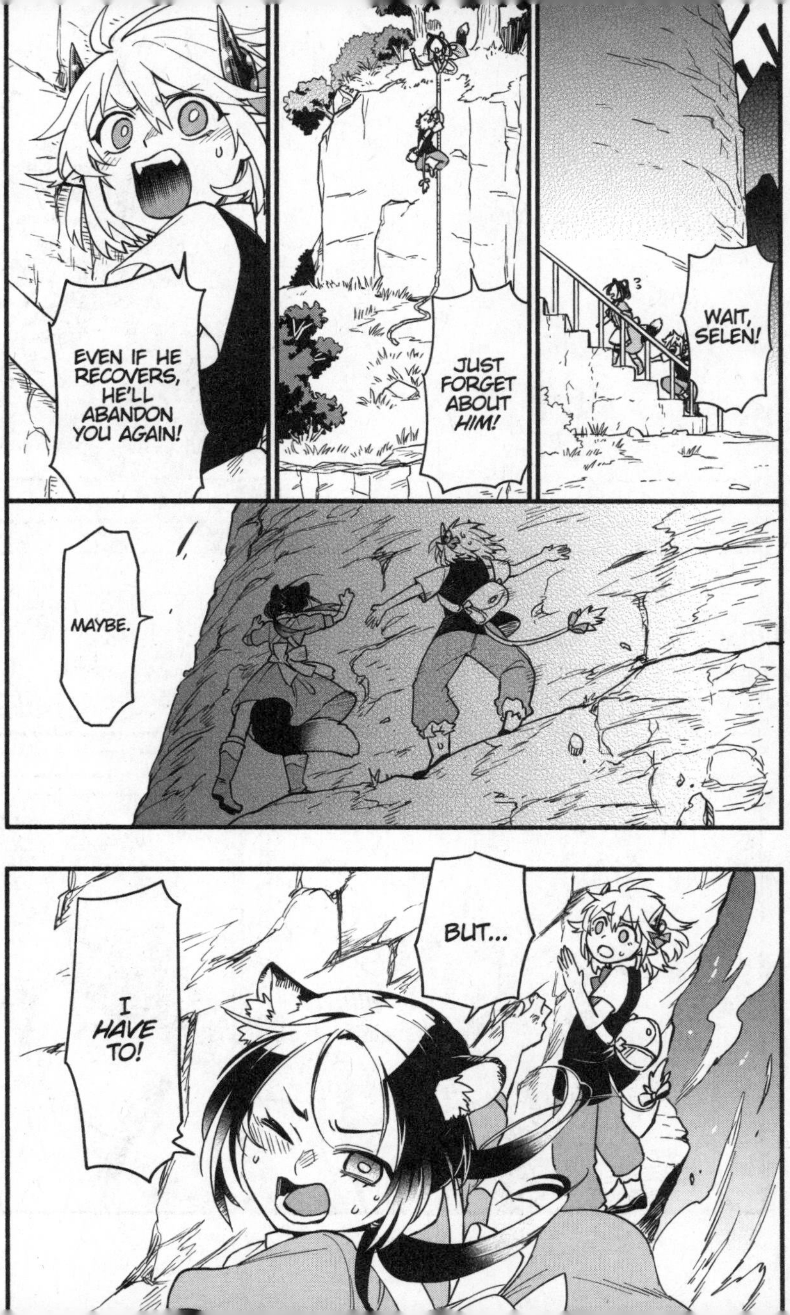
EVEN IF HE RECOVERS, HE'LL ABANDON YOU AGAIN!
JUST FORGET ABOUT *HIM!*
WAIT, SELEN!
MAYBE.
BUT...
I *HAVE* TO!

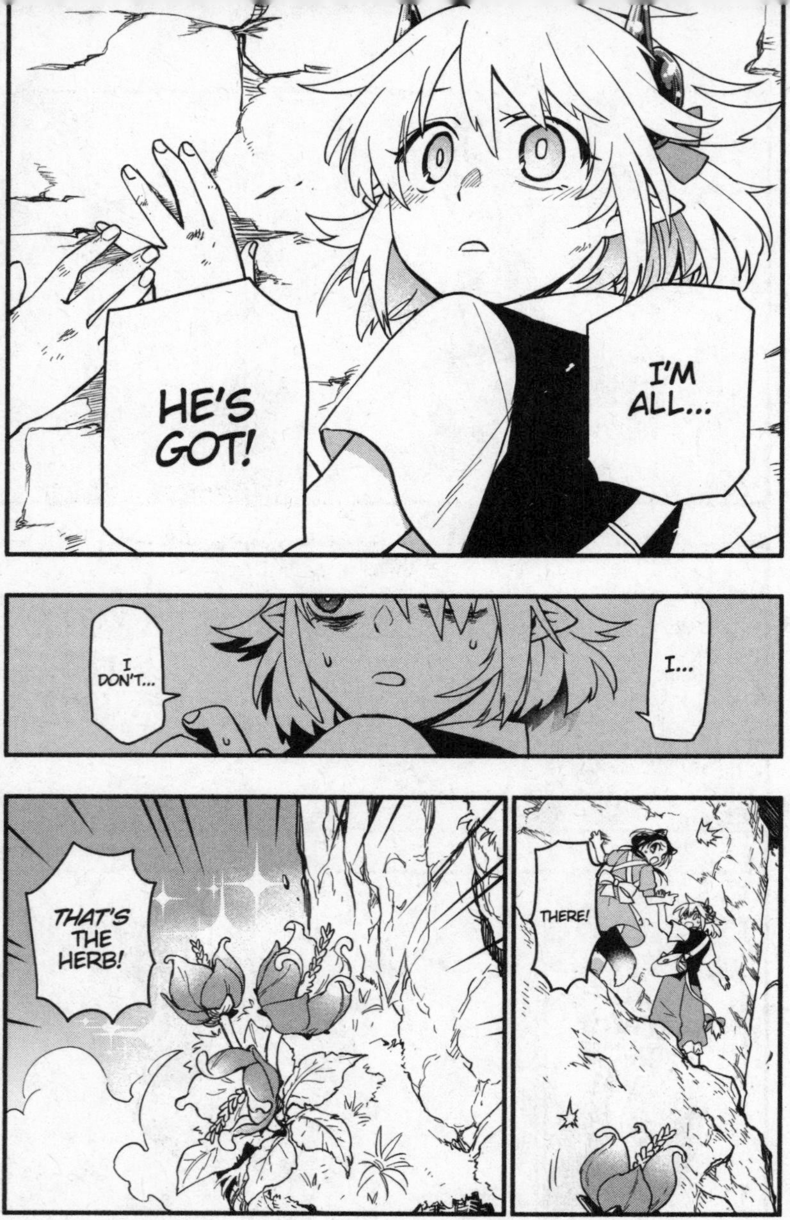
I'M ALL...
HE'S GOT!
I...
I DON'T...
THERE!
THAT'S THE HERB!

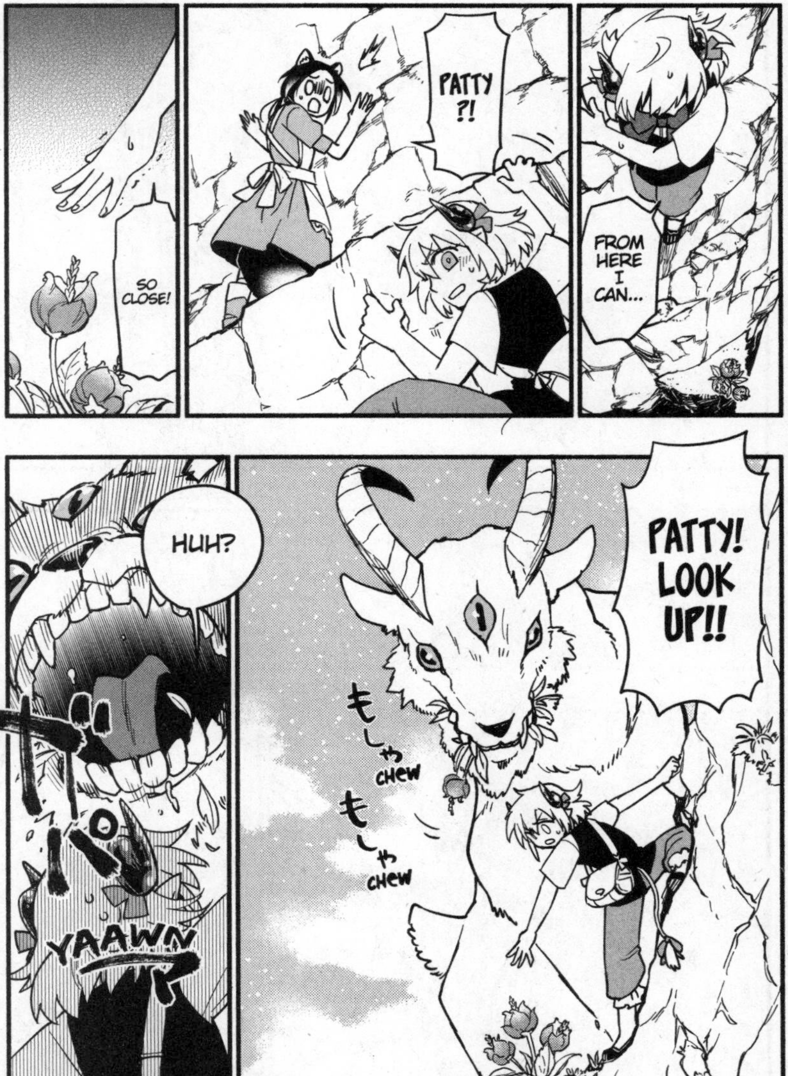
SO CLOSE!
PATTY ?!
FROM HERE I CAN...
HUH?
YAAWN
PATTY! LOOK UP!!
もしゃ CHEW
もしゃ CHEW

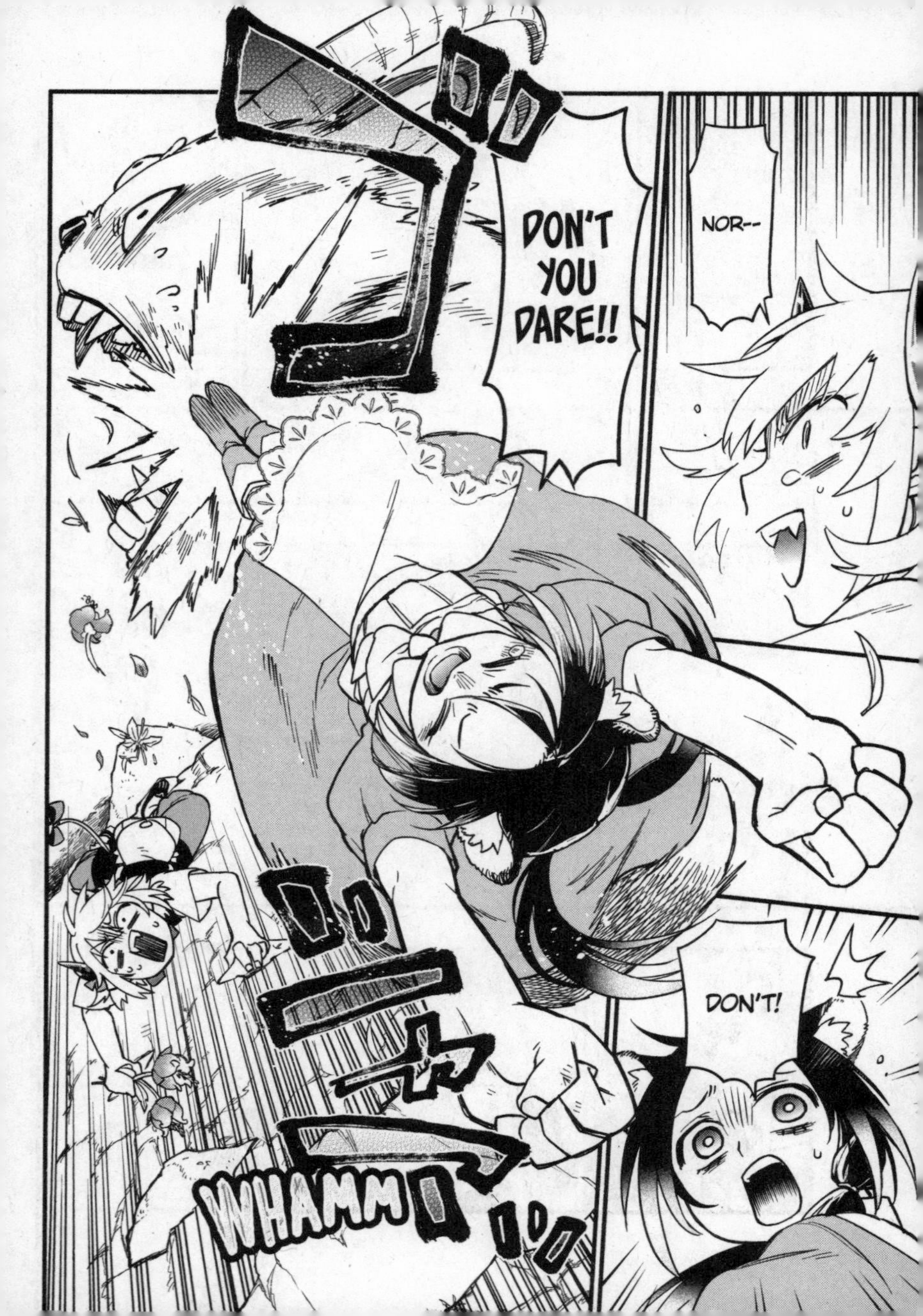
NOR--
DON'T YOU DARE!!
DON'T!
WHAMM!

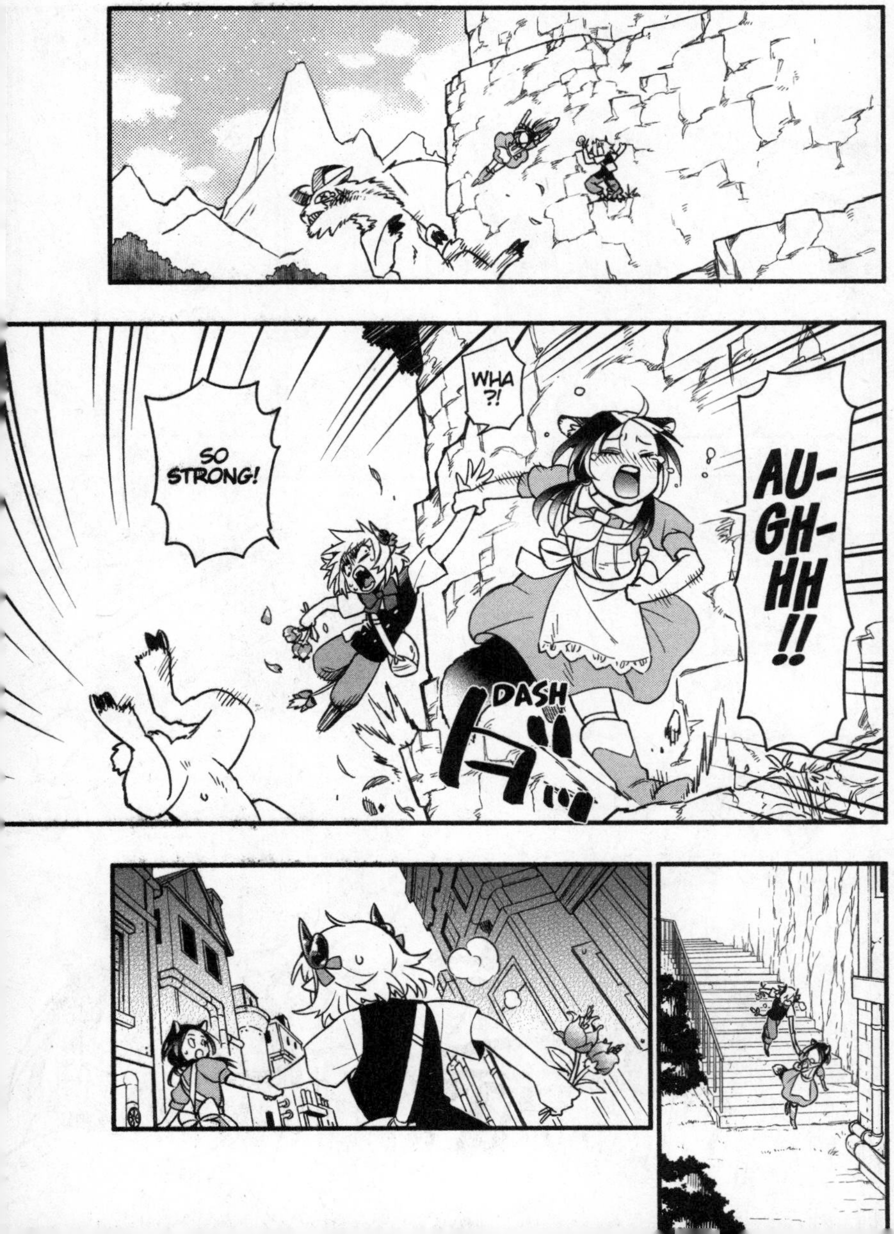
AUGH-HH!!
WHA?!
SO STRONG!
DASH

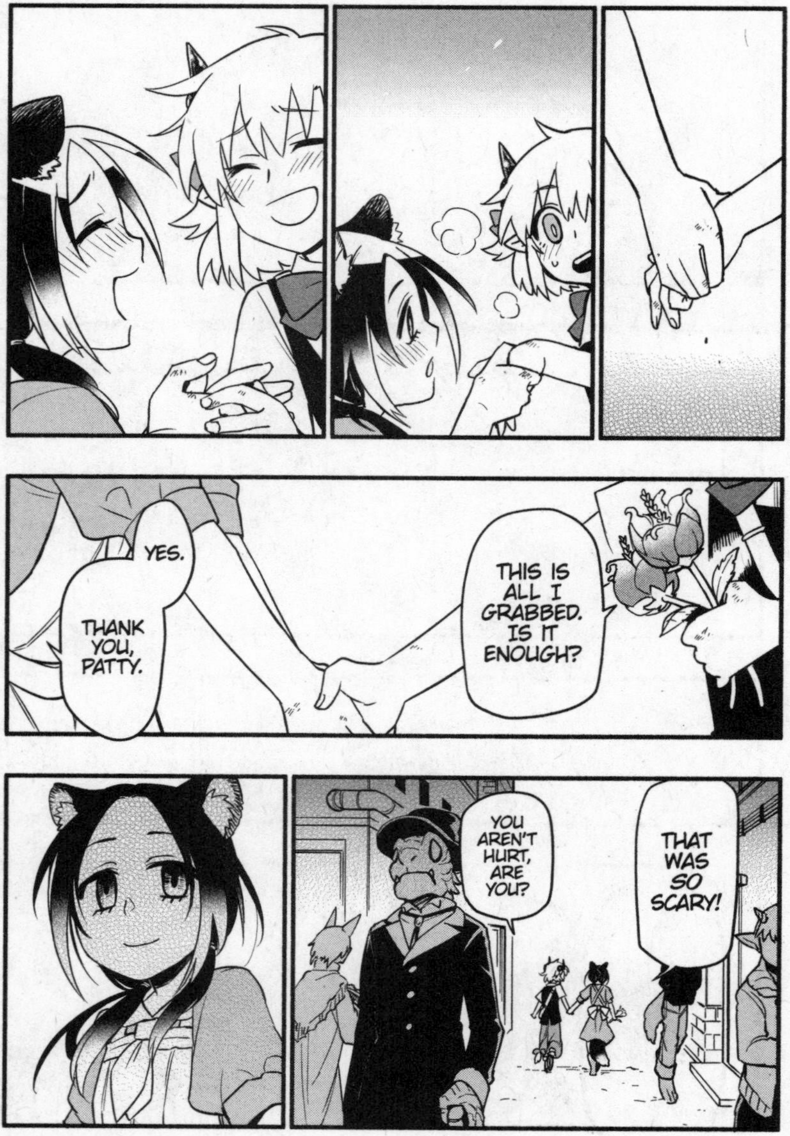
THIS IS ALL I GRABBED. IS IT ENOUGH?
YES.
THANK YOU, PATTY.
THAT WAS SO SCARY!
YOU AREN'T HURT, ARE YOU?

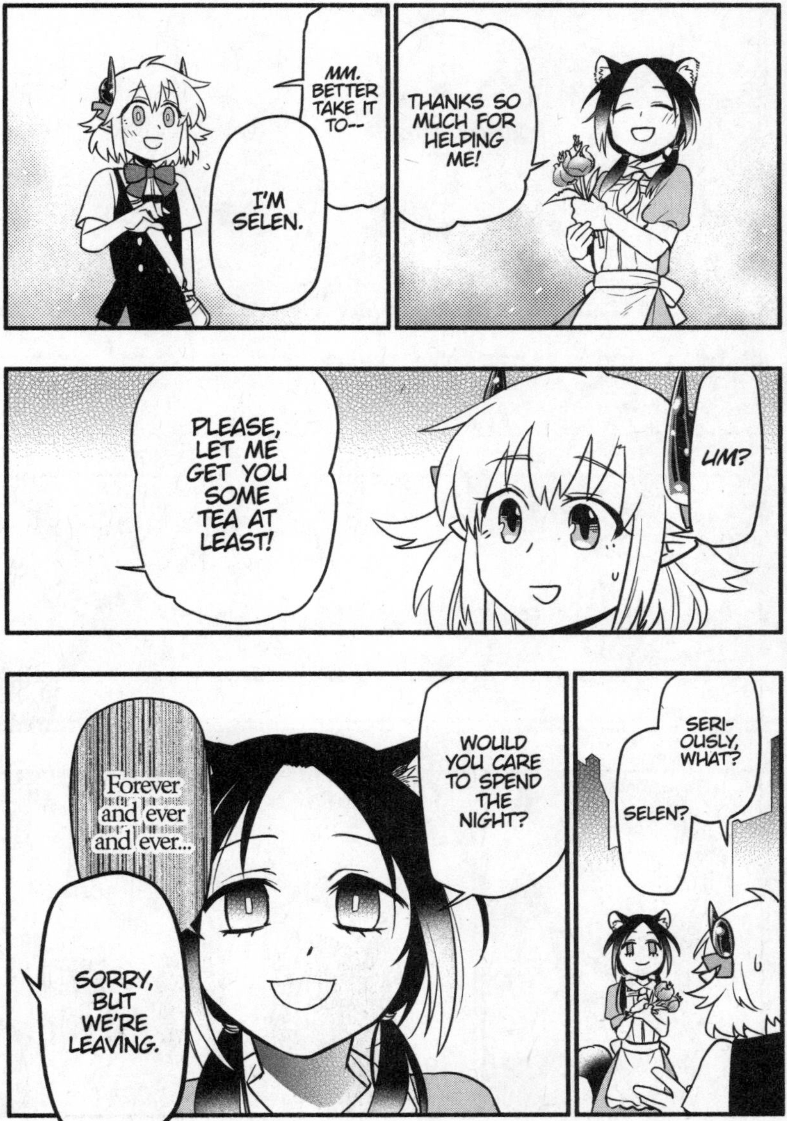
MM. BETTER TAKE IT TO--
I'M SELEN.
THANKS SO MUCH FOR HELPING ME!
PLEASE, LET ME GET YOU SOME TEA AT LEAST!
UM?
Forever and ever and ever...
SORRY, BUT WE'RE LEAVING.
WOULD YOU CARE TO SPEND THE NIGHT?
SERIOUSLY, WHAT?
SELEN?

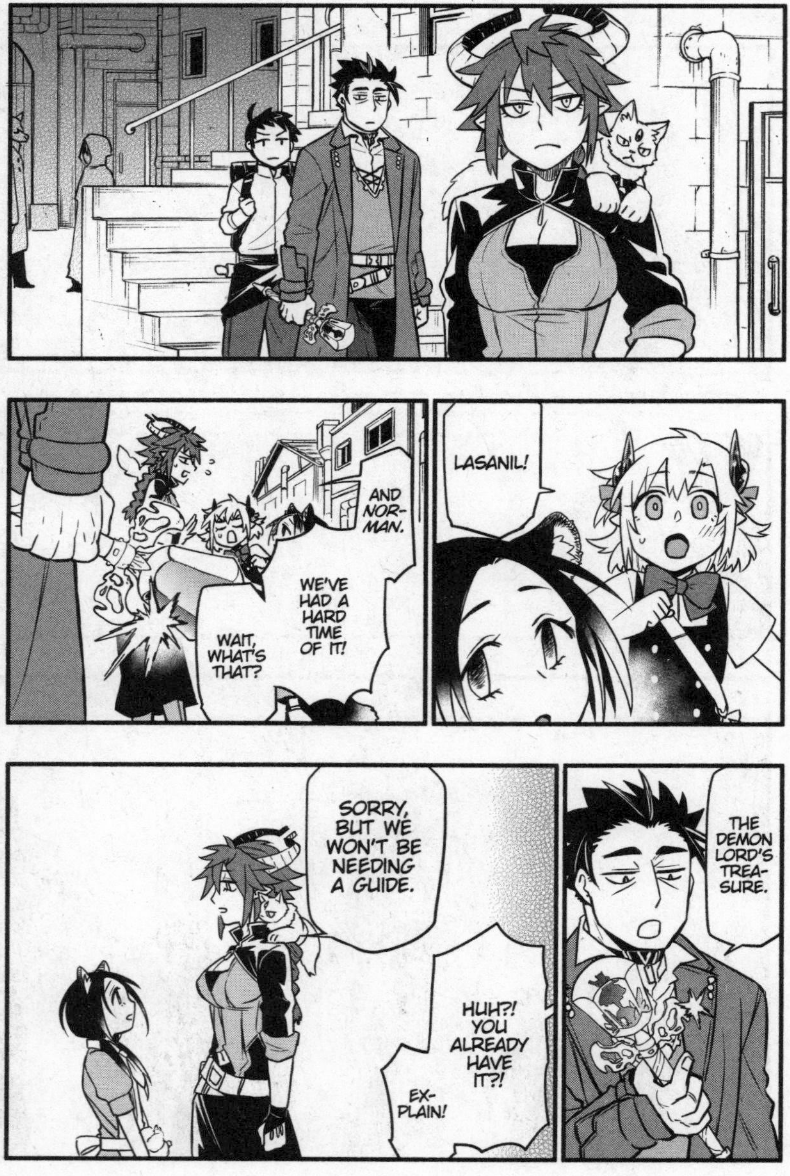
LASANIL!
AND NOR-MAN.
WE'VE HAD A HARD TIME OF IT!
WAIT, WHAT'S THAT?
SORRY, BUT WE WON'T BE NEEDING A GUIDE.
HUH?! YOU ALREADY HAVE IT?!
EX-PLAIN!
THE DEMON LORD'S TREA-SURE.

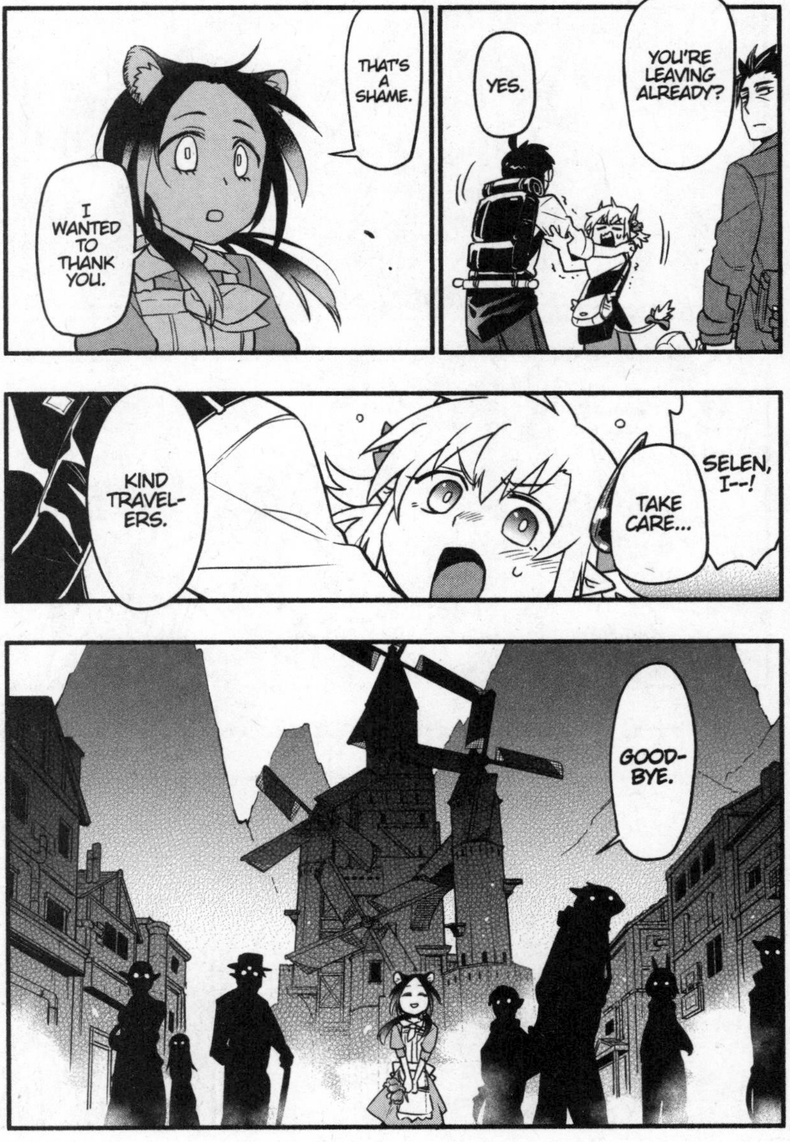
YOU'RE LEAVING ALREADY?
YES.
THAT'S A SHAME.
I WANTED TO THANK YOU.
SELEN, I--!
TAKE CARE...
KIND TRAVEL-ERS.
GOOD-BYE.

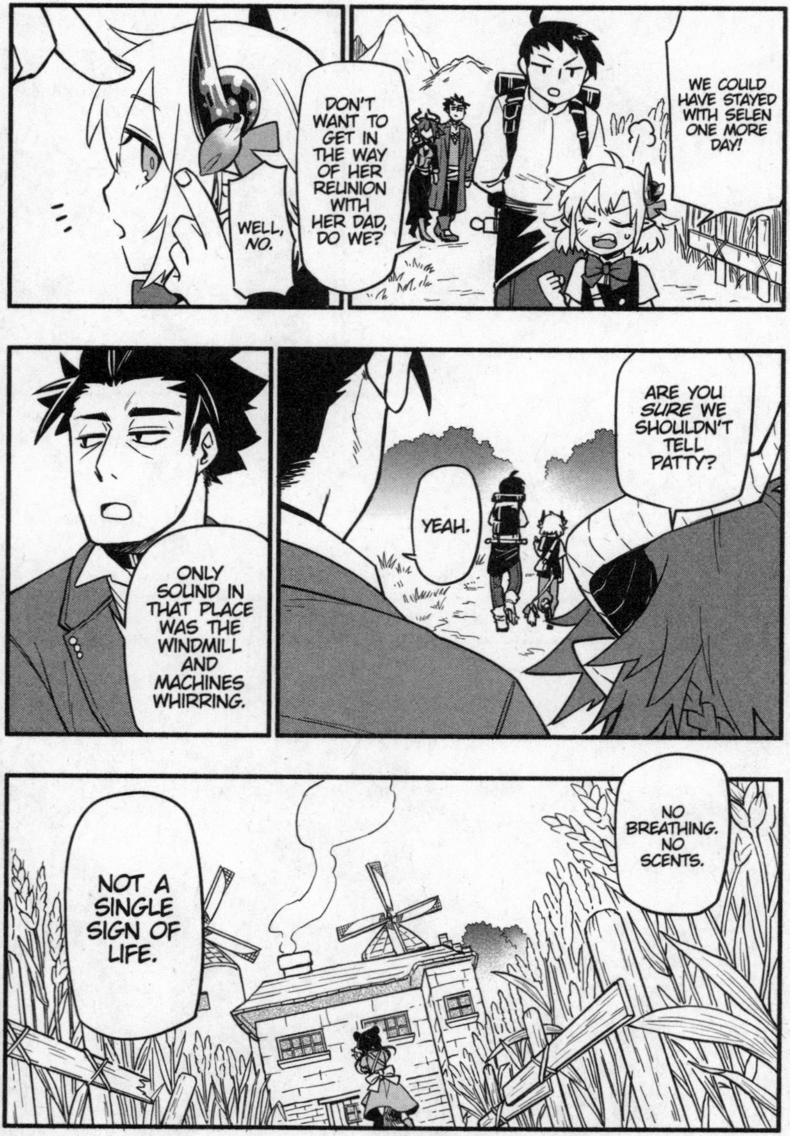
WE COULD HAVE STAYED WITH SELEN ONE MORE DAY!
DON'T WANT TO GET IN THE WAY OF HER REUNION WITH HER DAD, DO WE?
WELL, NO.
ARE YOU SURE WE SHOULDN'T TELL PATTY?
YEAH.
ONLY SOUND IN THAT PLACE WAS THE WINDMILL AND MACHINES WHIRRING.
NO BREATHING. NO SCENTS.
NOT A SINGLE SIGN OF LIFE.

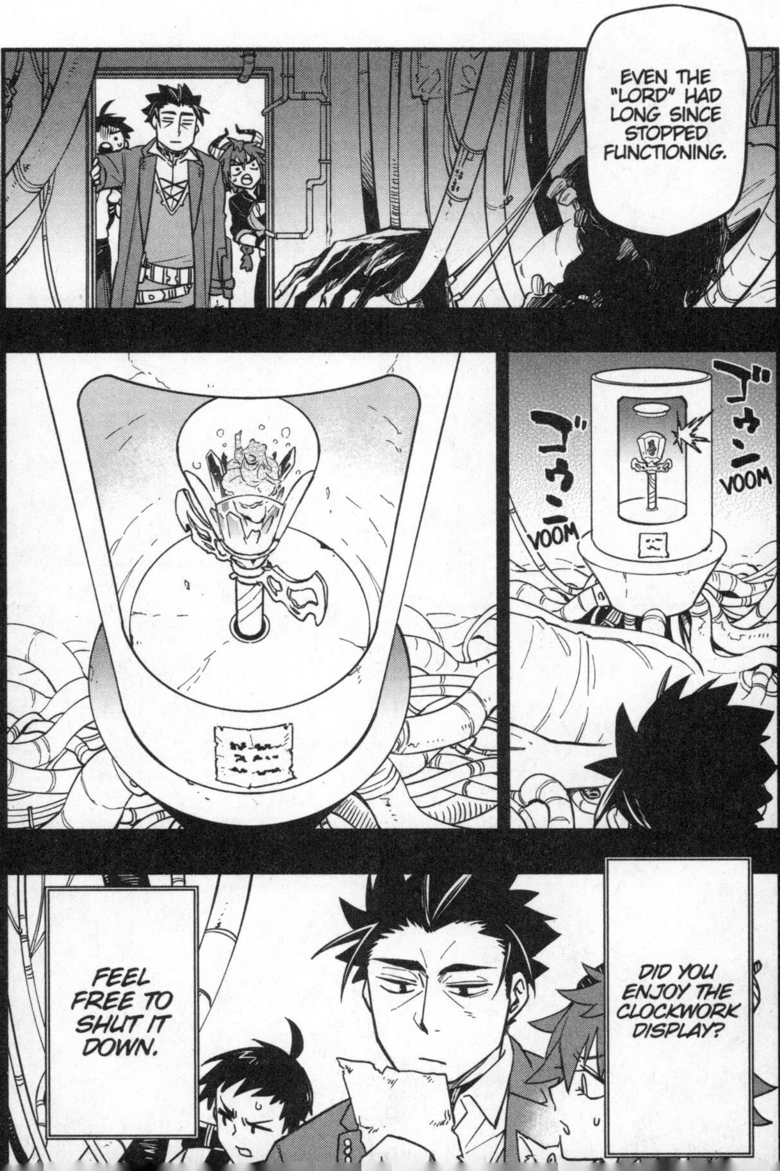

EVEN THE "LORD" HAD LONG SINCE STOPPED FUNCTIONING.
VOOM
VOOM
DID YOU ENJOY THE CLOCKWORK DISPLAY?
FEEL FREE TO SHUT IT DOWN.

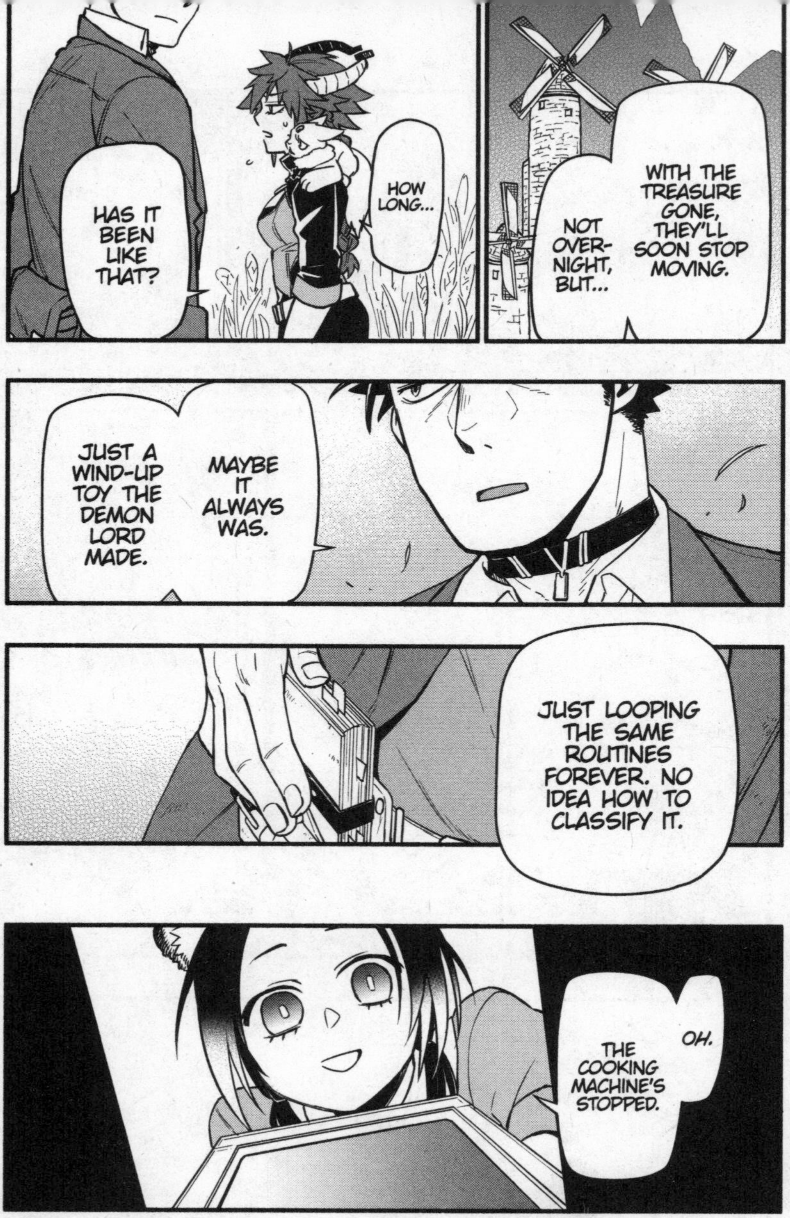
WITH THE TREASURE GONE, THEY'LL SOON STOP MOVING.
NOT OVER-NIGHT, BUT...
HOW LONG...
HAS IT BEEN LIKE THAT?
MAYBE IT ALWAYS WAS.
JUST A WIND-UP TOY THE DEMON LORD MADE.
JUST LOOPING THE SAME ROUTINES FOREVER. NO IDEA HOW TO CLASSIFY IT.
OH.
THE COOKING MACHINE'S STOPPED.

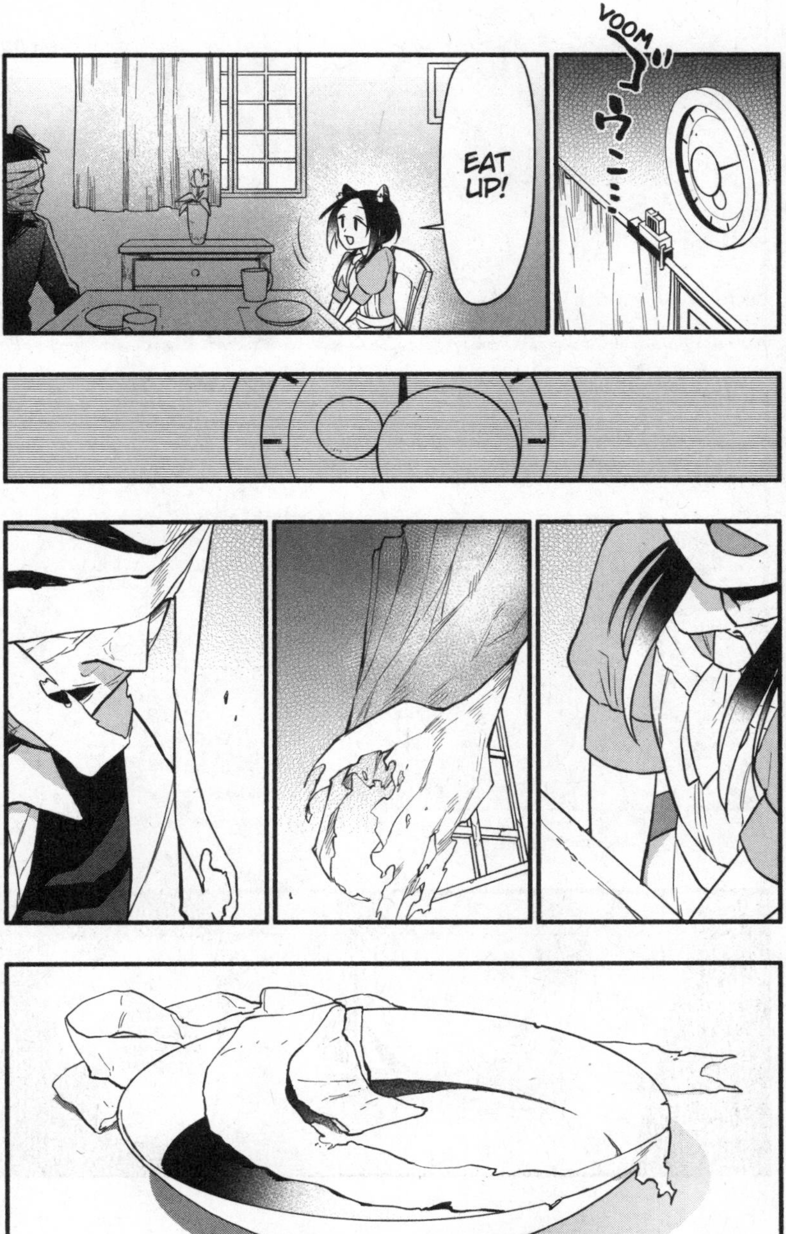
VOOM
EAT UP!

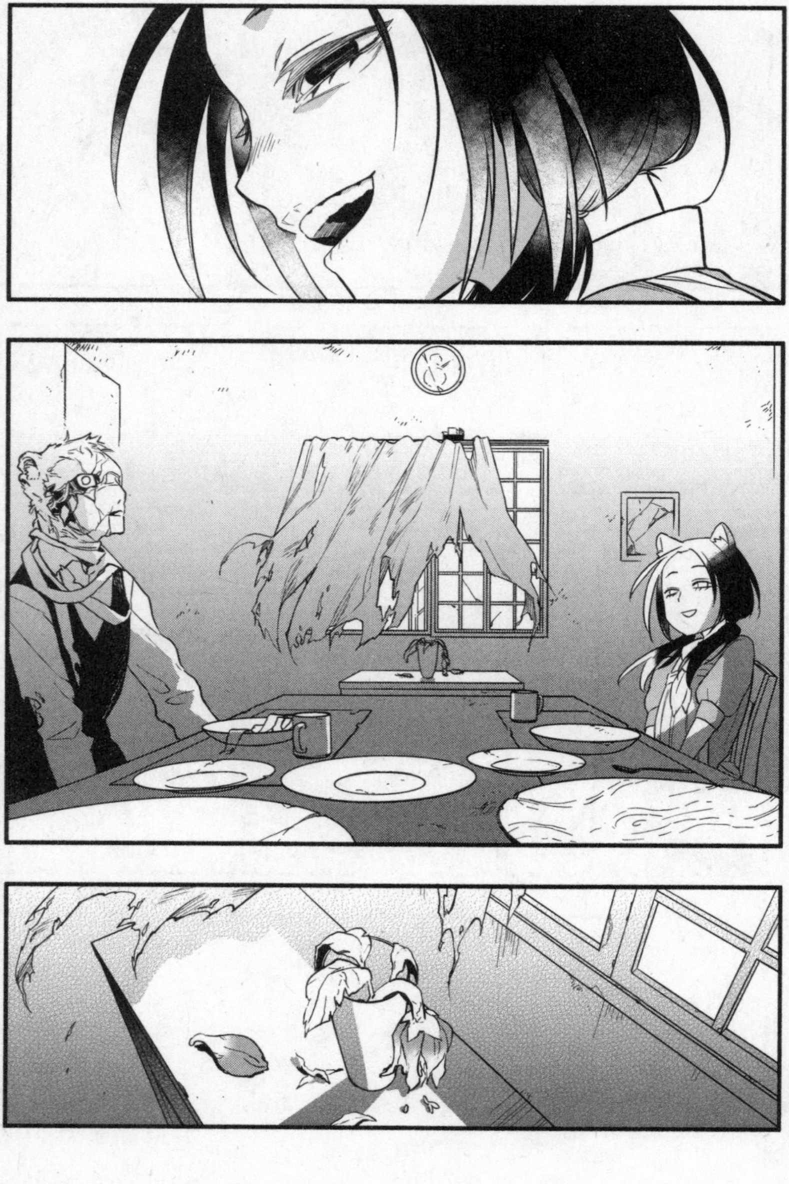

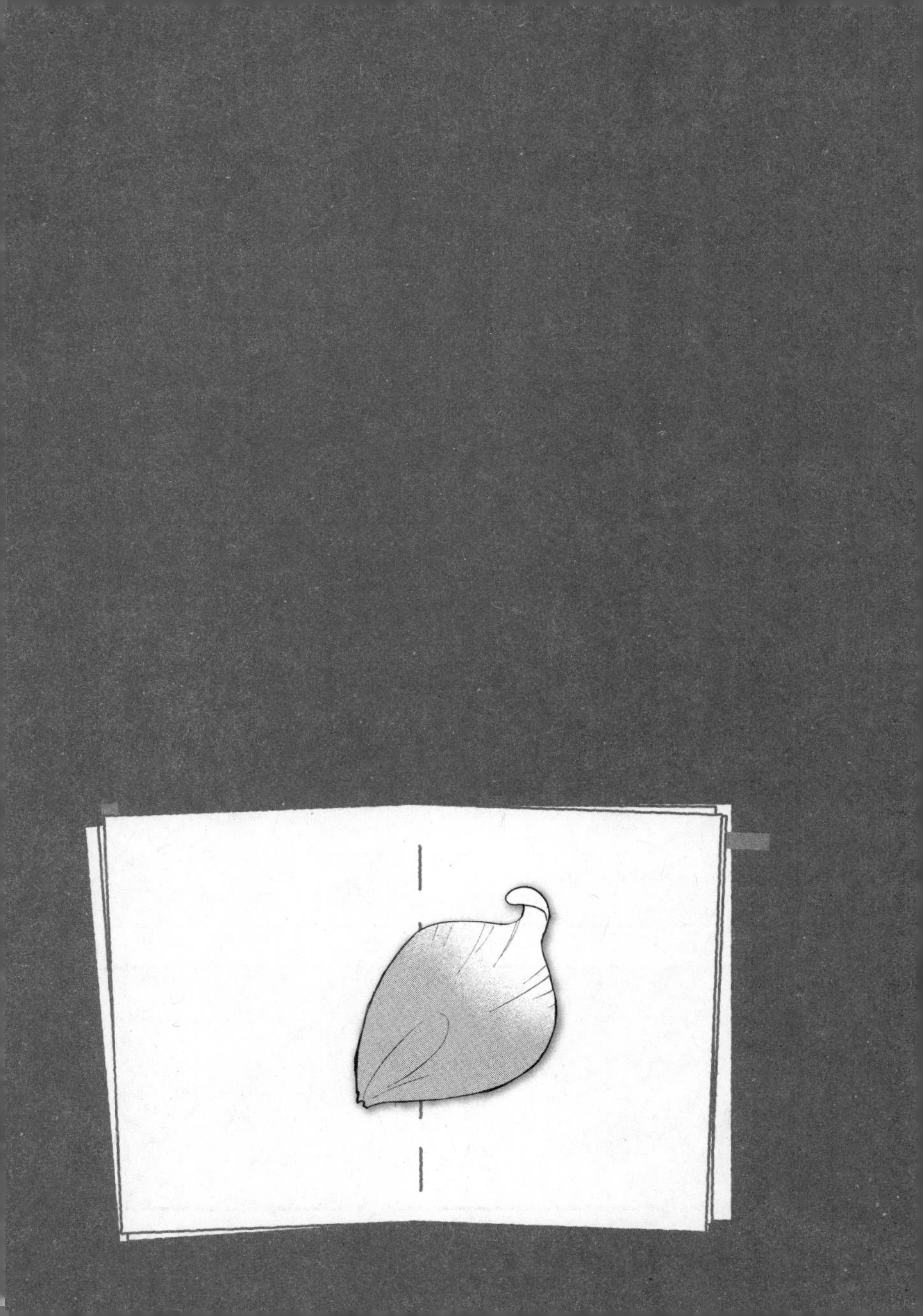

Sorry For My Familiar

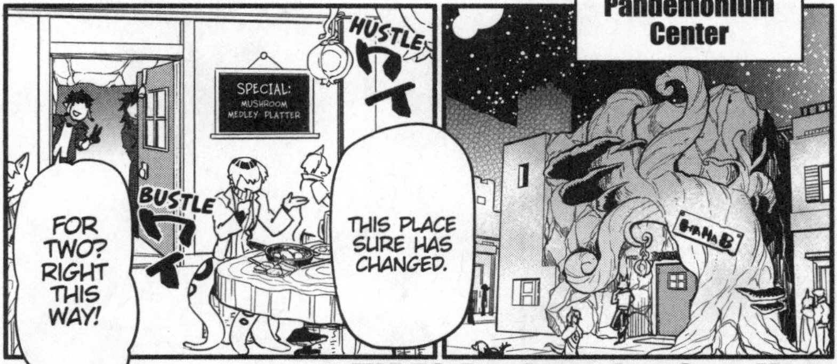
SPECIAL: MUSHROOM MEDLEY PLATTER
HUSTLE
BUSTLE
FOR TWO? RIGHT THIS WAY!
THIS PLACE SURE HAS CHANGED.
Pandemonium Center

FILE 58: Pandemonium Once More

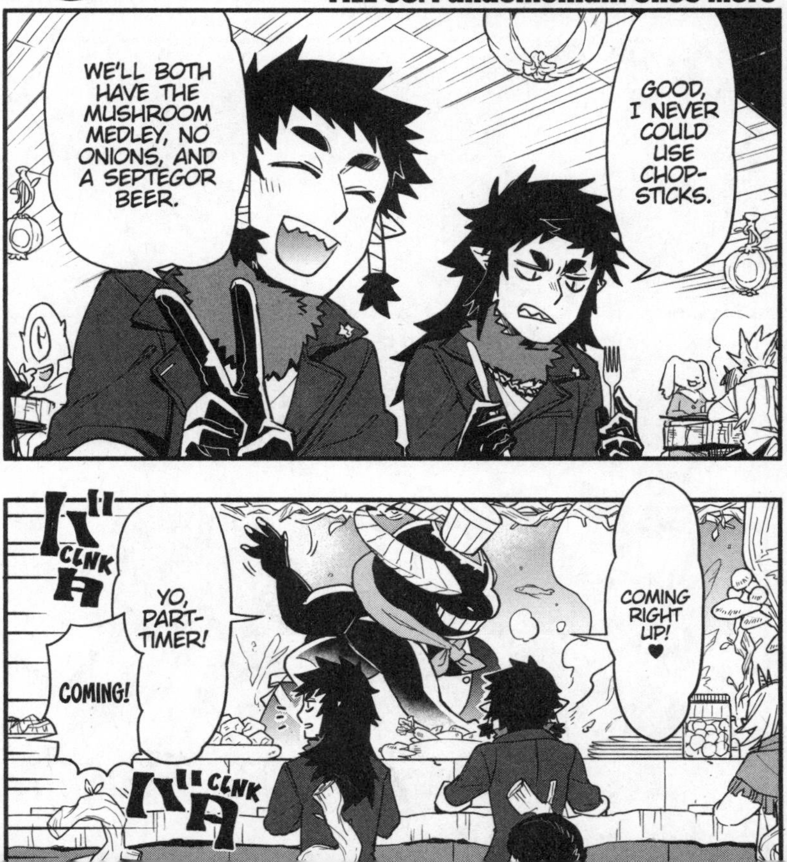
WE'LL BOTH HAVE THE MUSHROOM MEDLEY, NO ONIONS, AND A SEPTEGOR BEER.
GOOD, I NEVER COULD USE CHOP-STICKS.
CLNK
YO, PART-TIMER!
COMING!
COMING RIGHT UP! ♥
CLNK

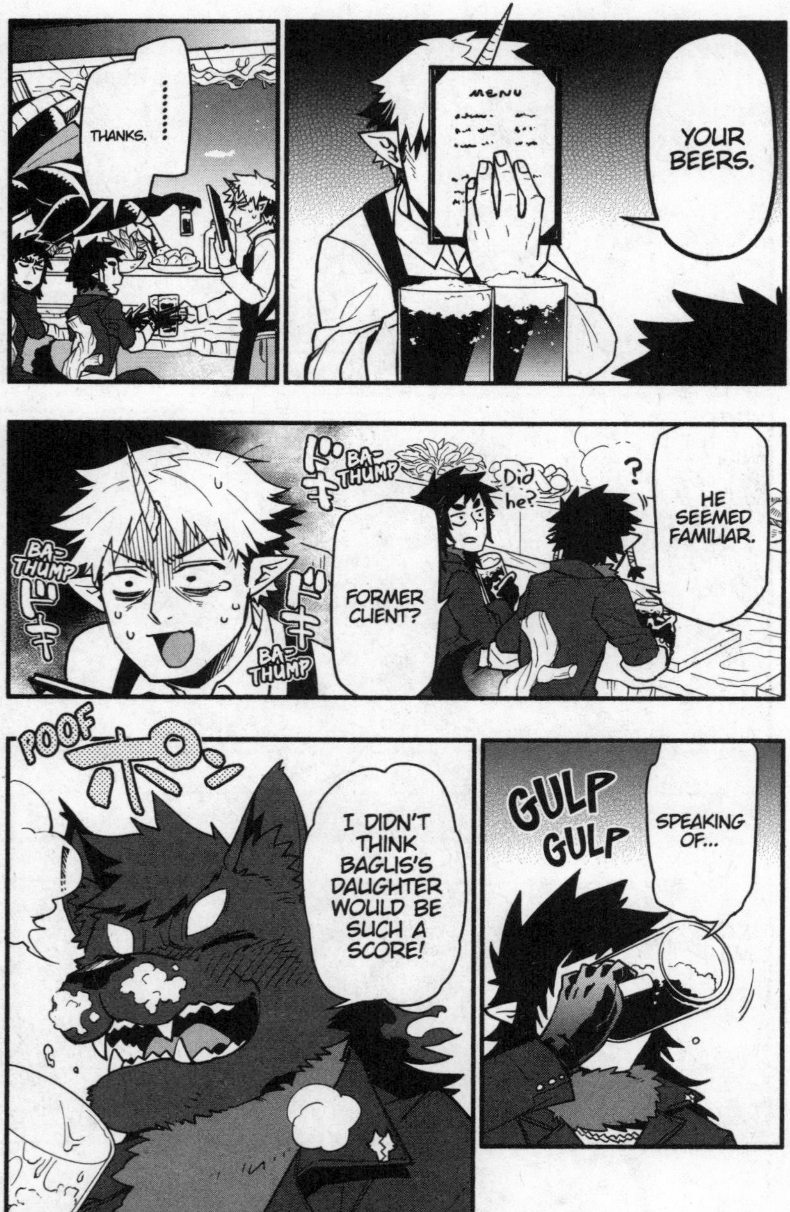

YOUR BEERS.
......
THANKS.
HE SEEMED FAMILIAR.
?
Did he?
BA-THUMP
FORMER CLIENT?
BA-THUMP
BA-THUMP
GULP GULP
SPEAKING OF...
POOF
I DIDN'T THINK BAGLIS'S DAUGHTER WOULD BE SUCH A SCORE!

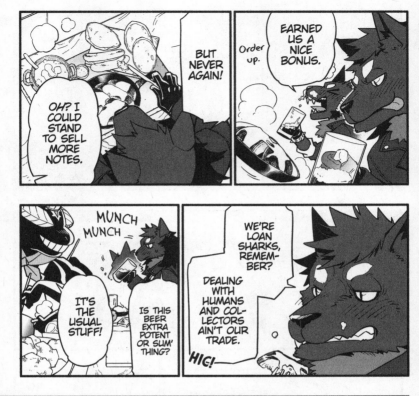

EARNED US A NICE BONUS.
Order up.
BUT NEVER AGAIN!
OH? I COULD STAND TO SELL MORE NOTES.
WE'RE LOAN SHARKS, REMEMBER?
DEALING WITH HUMANS AND COLLECTORS AIN'T OUR TRADE.
HIC!
IS THIS BEER EXTRA POTENT OR SUM' THING?
IT'S THE USUAL STUFF!
MUNCH MUNCH
BAGLIS AIN'T THE ONLY PAIN IN OUR SIDES. HIS DAUGHTER AND HER FAMILIAR ARE JUST AS BAD!
THAT NORMAN CHUMP MADE FOOLS OUT OF US EVERY TIME!
YEAH, I'M DONE DEALING WITH HIM.
NOR-MAN?

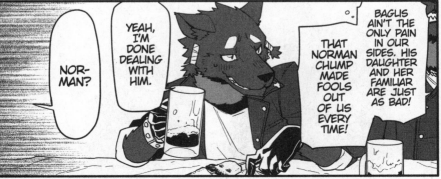

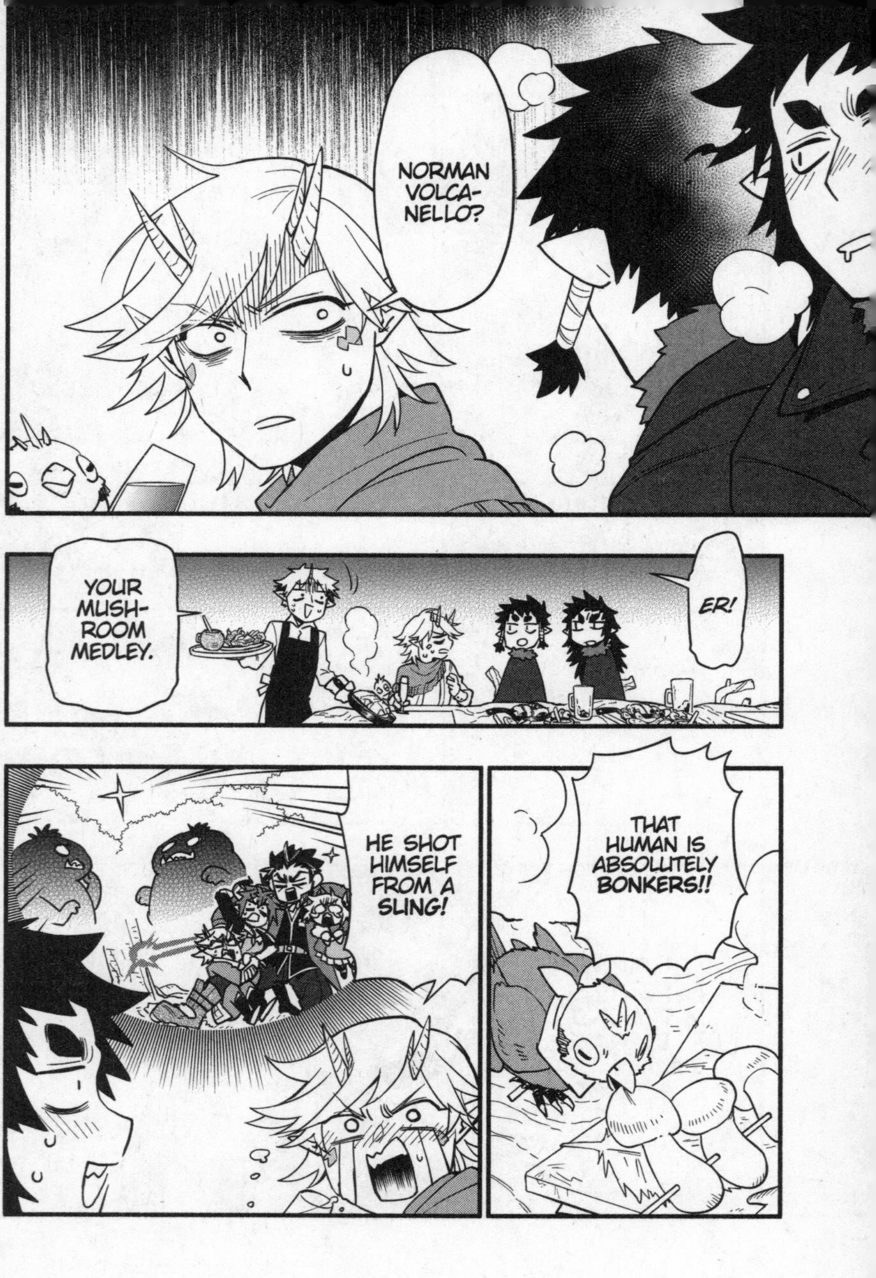
NORMAN VOLCA-NELLO?
ER!
YOUR MUSH-ROOM MEDLEY.
THAT HUMAN IS ABSOLUTELY BONKERS!!
HE SHOT HIMSELF FROM A SLING!

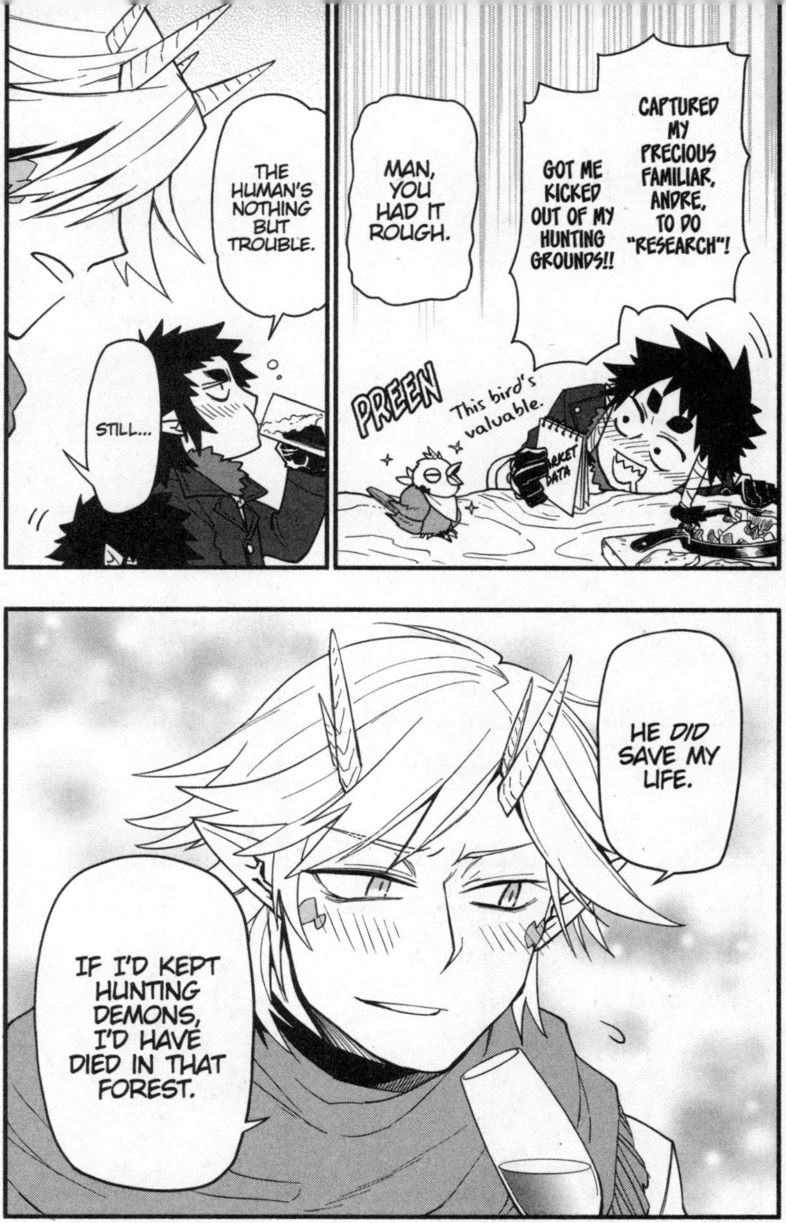
CAPTURED MY PRECIOUS FAMILIAR, ANDRE, TO DO "RESEARCH"!
GOT ME KICKED OUT OF MY HUNTING GROUNDS!!
PREEN
This bird's valuable.
MAN, YOU HAD IT ROUGH.
THE HUMAN'S NOTHING BUT TROUBLE.
STILL...
HE *DID* SAVE MY LIFE.
IF I'D KEPT HUNTING DEMONS, I'D HAVE DIED IN THAT FOREST.

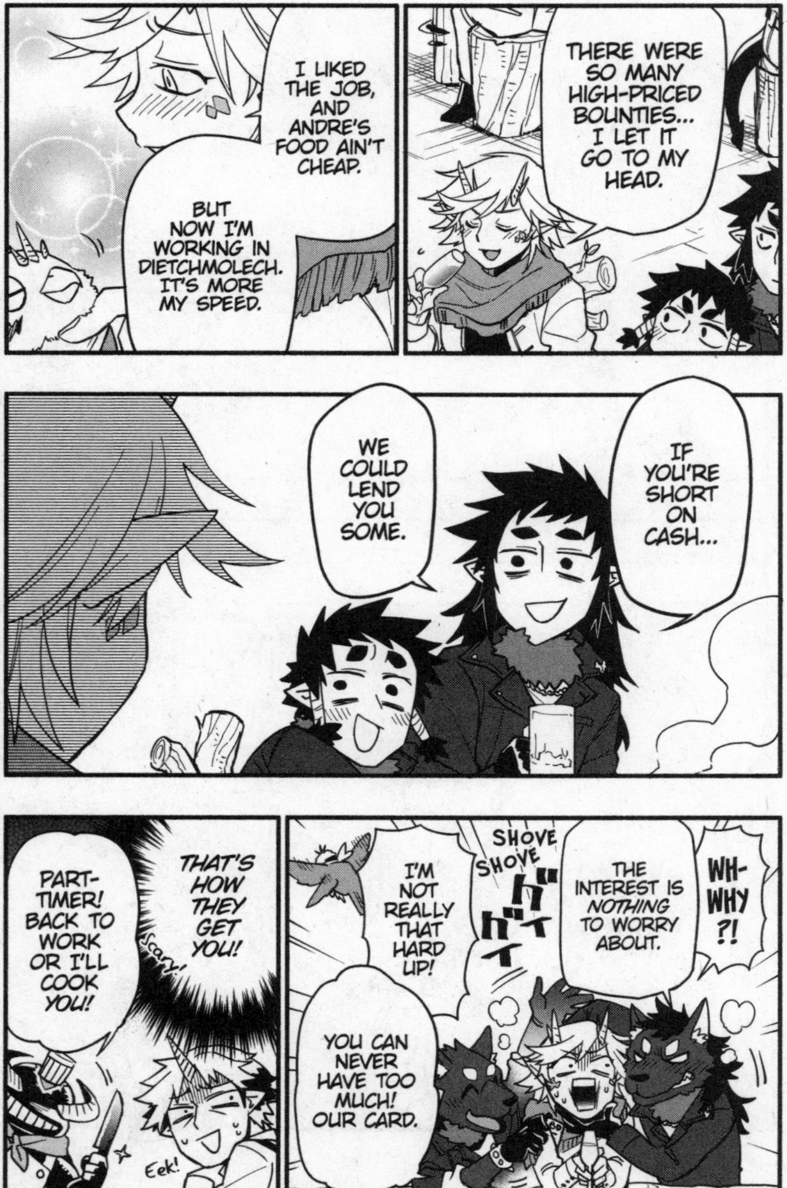
THERE WERE SO MANY HIGH-PRICED BOUNTIES... I LET IT GO TO MY HEAD.
I LIKED THE JOB, AND ANDRE'S FOOD AIN'T CHEAP.
BUT NOW I'M WORKING IN DIETCHMOLECH. IT'S MORE MY SPEED.
IF YOU'RE SHORT ON CASH...
WE COULD LEND YOU SOME.
WH-WHY?!
THE INTEREST IS *NOTHING* TO WORRY ABOUT.
SHOVE SHOVE
I'M NOT REALLY THAT HARD UP!
YOU CAN NEVER HAVE TOO MUCH! OUR CARD.
THAT'S HOW THEY GET YOU!
Scary!
PART-TIMER! BACK TO WORK OR I'LL COOK *YOU!*
Eek!

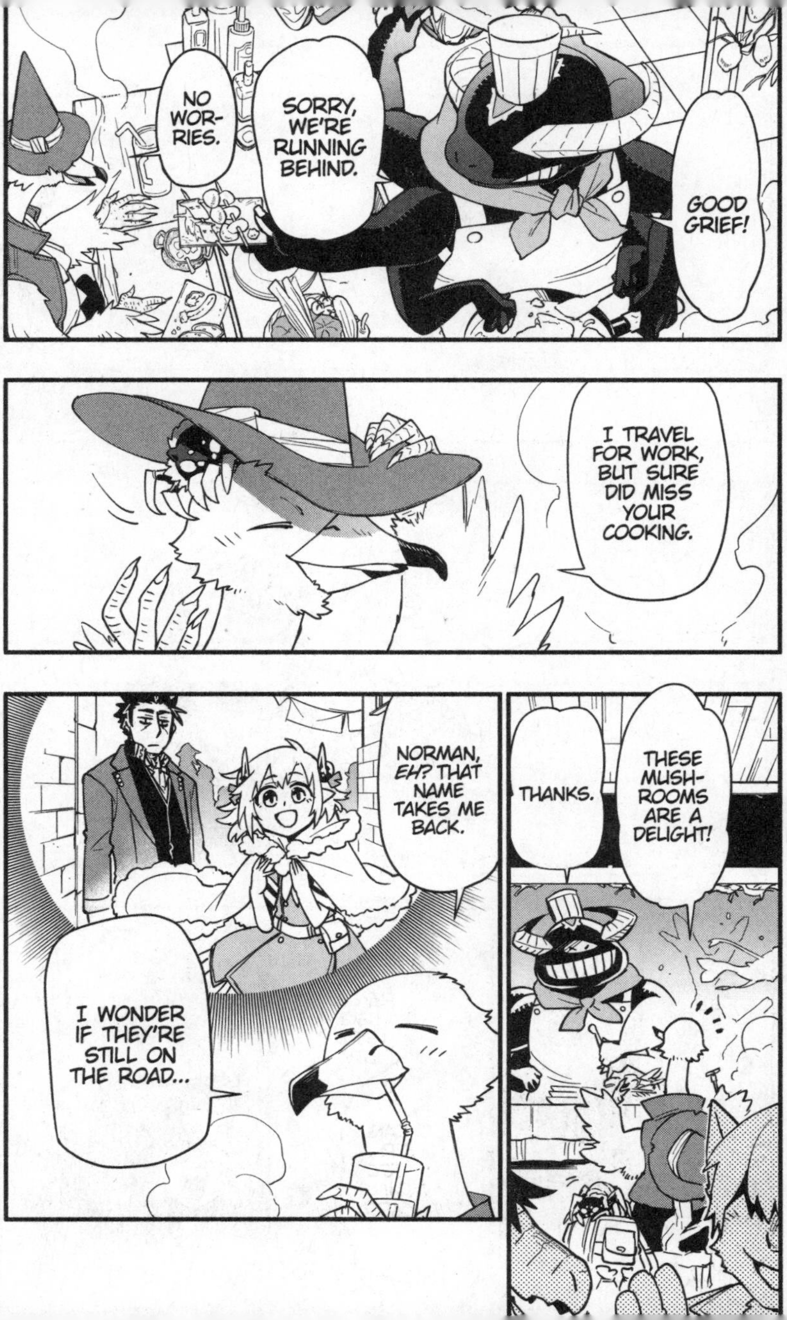
NO WOR-RIES.
SORRY, WE'RE RUNNING BEHIND.
GOOD GRIEF!
I TRAVEL FOR WORK, BUT SURE DID MISS YOUR COOKING.
NORMAN, EH? THAT NAME TAKES ME BACK.
I WONDER IF THEY'RE STILL ON THE ROAD...
THANKS.
THESE MUSH-ROOMS ARE A DELIGHT!

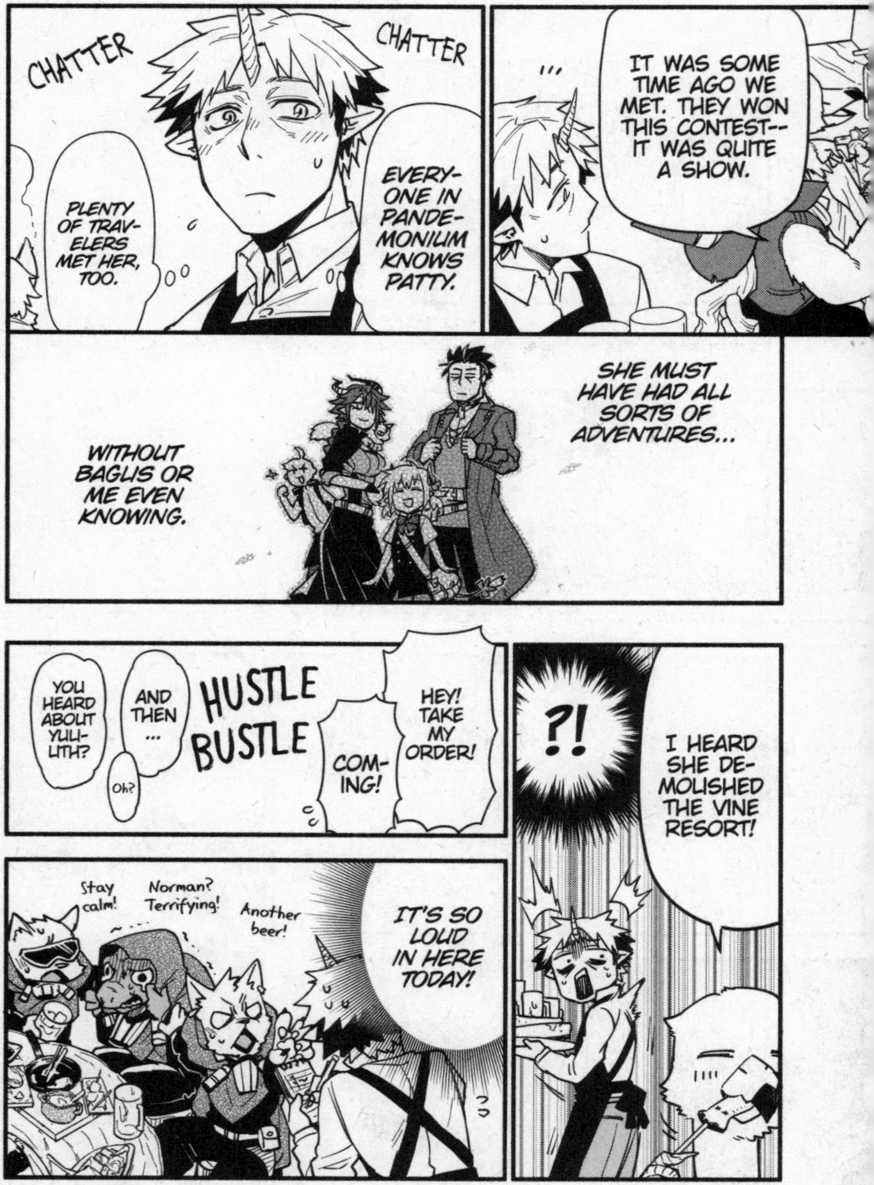
IT WAS SOME TIME AGO WE MET. THEY WON THIS CONTEST-- IT WAS QUITE A SHOW.
CHATTER
CHATTER
EVERYONE IN PANDEMONIUM KNOWS PATTY.
PLENTY OF TRAVELERS MET HER, TOO.
SHE MUST HAVE HAD ALL SORTS OF ADVENTURES...
WITHOUT BAGLIS OR ME EVEN KNOWING.
I HEARD SHE DEMOLISHED THE VINE RESORT!
?!
HEY! TAKE MY ORDER!
COMING!
HUSTLE BUSTLE
AND THEN ...
Oh?
YOU HEARD ABOUT YULILITH?
IT'S SO LOUD IN HERE TODAY!
Another beer!
Norman? Terrifying!
Stay calm!

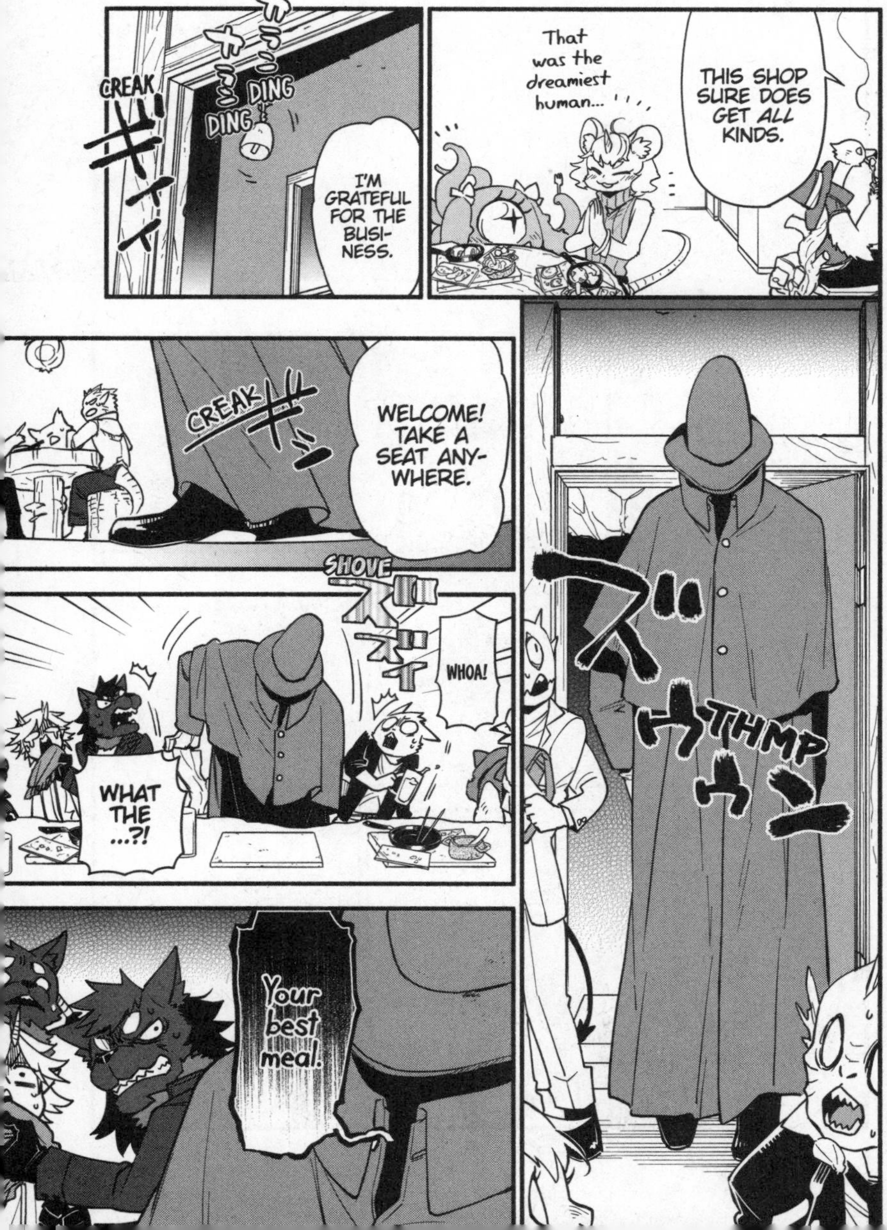

THIS SHOP SURE DOES GET ALL KINDS.
That was the dreamiest human...
CREAK
DING DING
I'M GRATEFUL FOR THE BUSI-NESS.
THMP
CREAK
WELCOME! TAKE A SEAT ANY-WHERE.
SHOVE
WHOA!
WHAT THE ...?!
Your best meal.

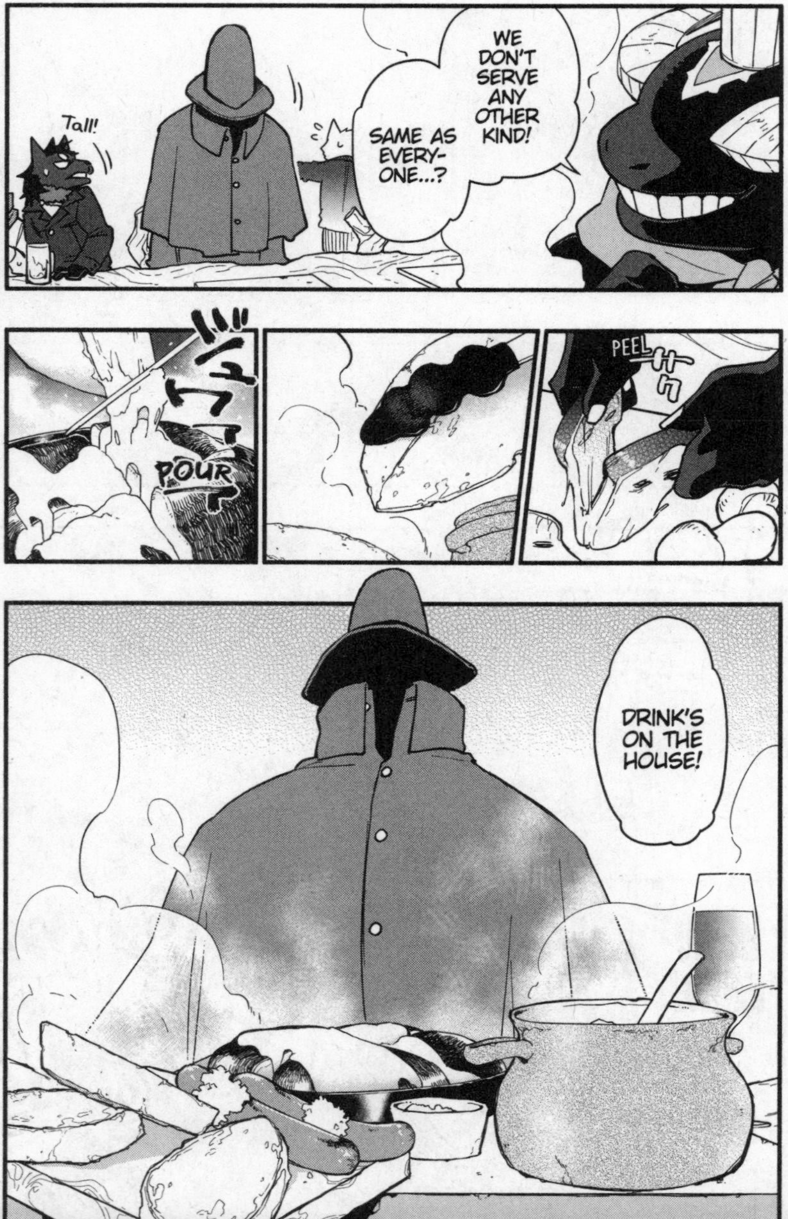
SAME AS EVERY-ONE...?
WE DON'T SERVE ANY OTHER KIND!
Tall!
PEEL
POUR
DRINK'S ON THE HOUSE!

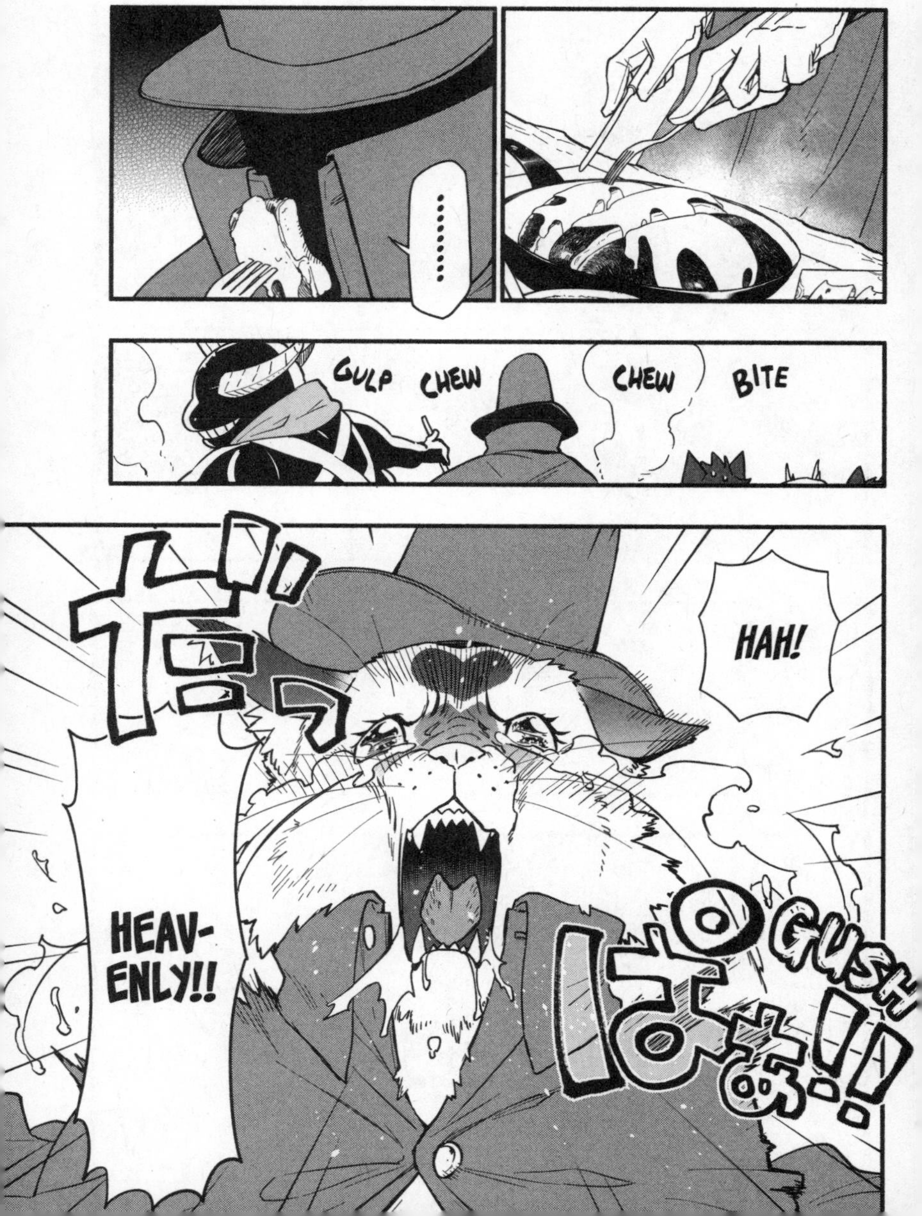
....
GULP
CHEW
CHEW
BITE
HAH!
HEAV-
ENLY!!
GUSH
ぱぁ!!

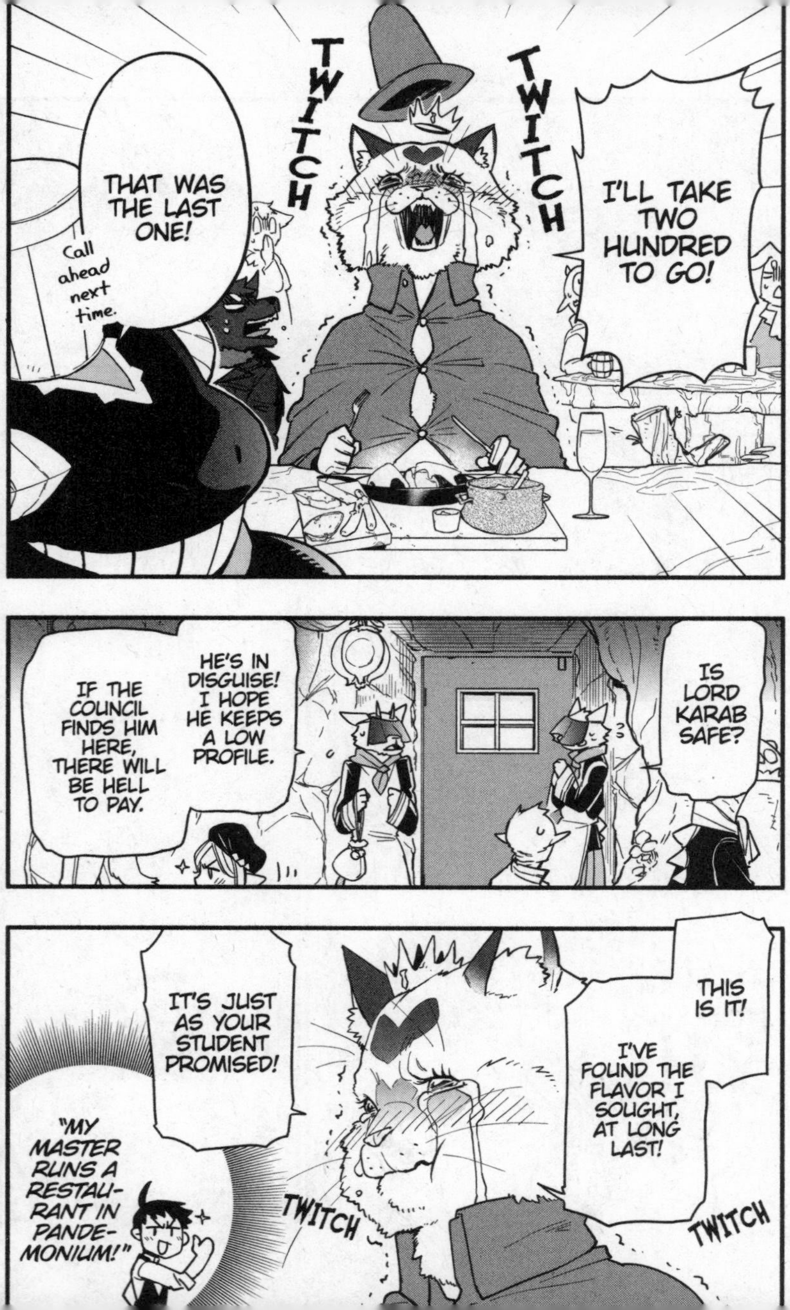
I'LL TAKE TWO HUNDRED TO GO!
TWITCH
TWITCH
THAT WAS THE LAST ONE!
Call ahead next time.
IS LORD KARAB SAFE?
HE'S IN DISGUISE! I HOPE HE KEEPS A LOW PROFILE.
IF THE COUNCIL FINDS HIM HERE, THERE WILL BE HELL TO PAY.
THIS IS IT!
I'VE FOUND THE FLAVOR I SOUGHT, AT LONG LAST!
IT'S JUST AS YOUR STUDENT PROMISED!
"MY MASTER RUNS A RESTAU-RANT IN PANDE-MONIUM!"
TWITCH
TWITCH

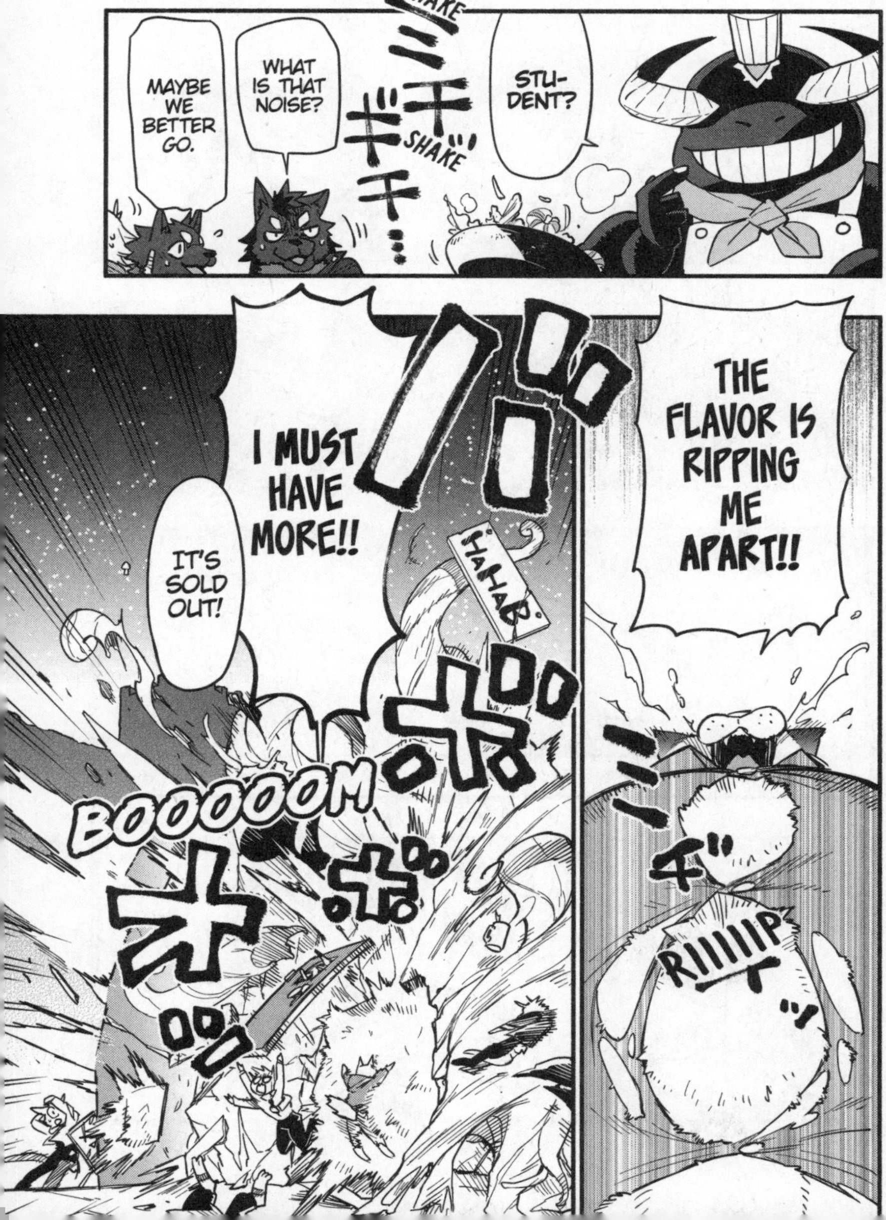
STU-DENT?
SHAKE
SHAKE
WHAT IS THAT NOISE?
MAYBE WE BETTER GO.
THE FLAVOR IS RIPPING ME APART!!
RIIIIIP
I MUST HAVE MORE!!
IT'S SOLD OUT!
BOOOOOOM

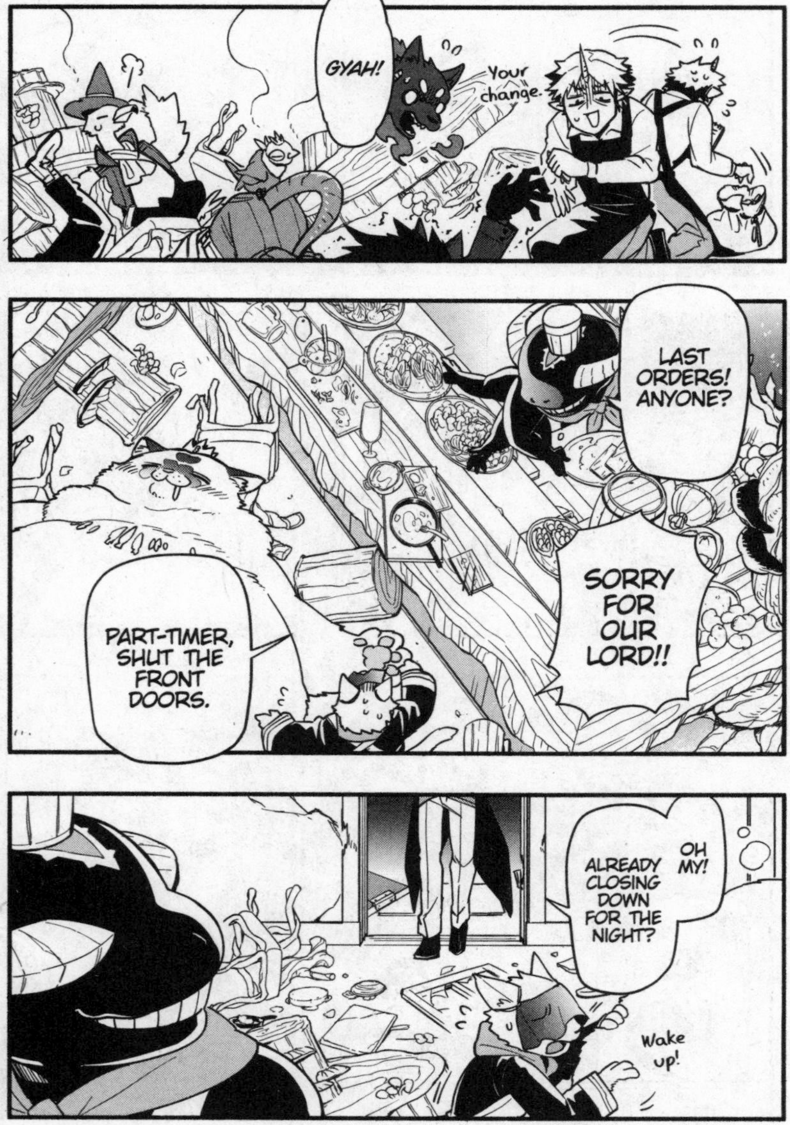
GYAH!
Your change.
LAST ORDERS! ANYONE?
SORRY FOR OUR LORD!!
PART-TIMER, SHUT THE FRONT DOORS.
OH MY!
ALREADY CLOSING DOWN FOR THE NIGHT?
Wake up!

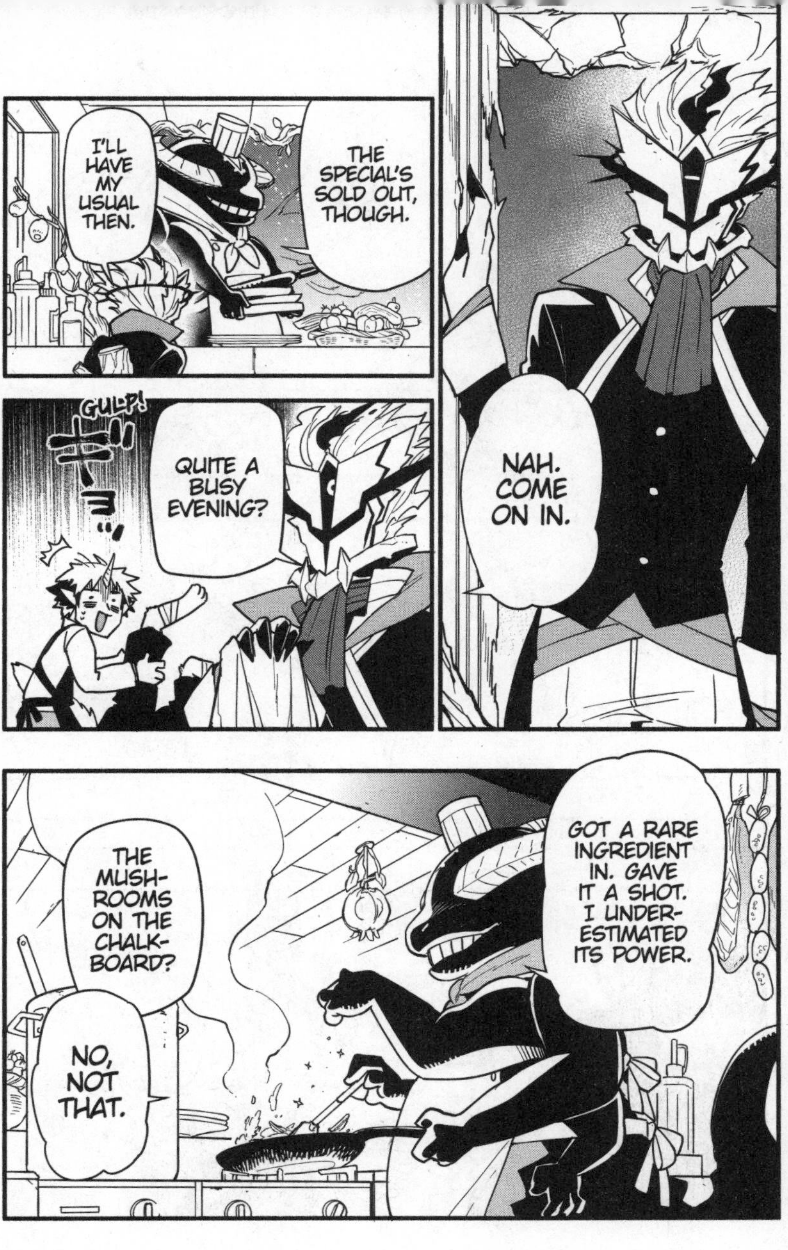
NAH. COME ON IN.
THE SPECIAL'S SOLD OUT, THOUGH.
I'LL HAVE MY USUAL THEN.
QUITE A BUSY EVENING?
GULP!
GOT A RARE INGREDIENT IN. GAVE IT A SHOT. I UNDER-ESTIMATED ITS POWER.
THE MUSH-ROOMS ON THE CHALK-BOARD?
NO, NOT THAT.

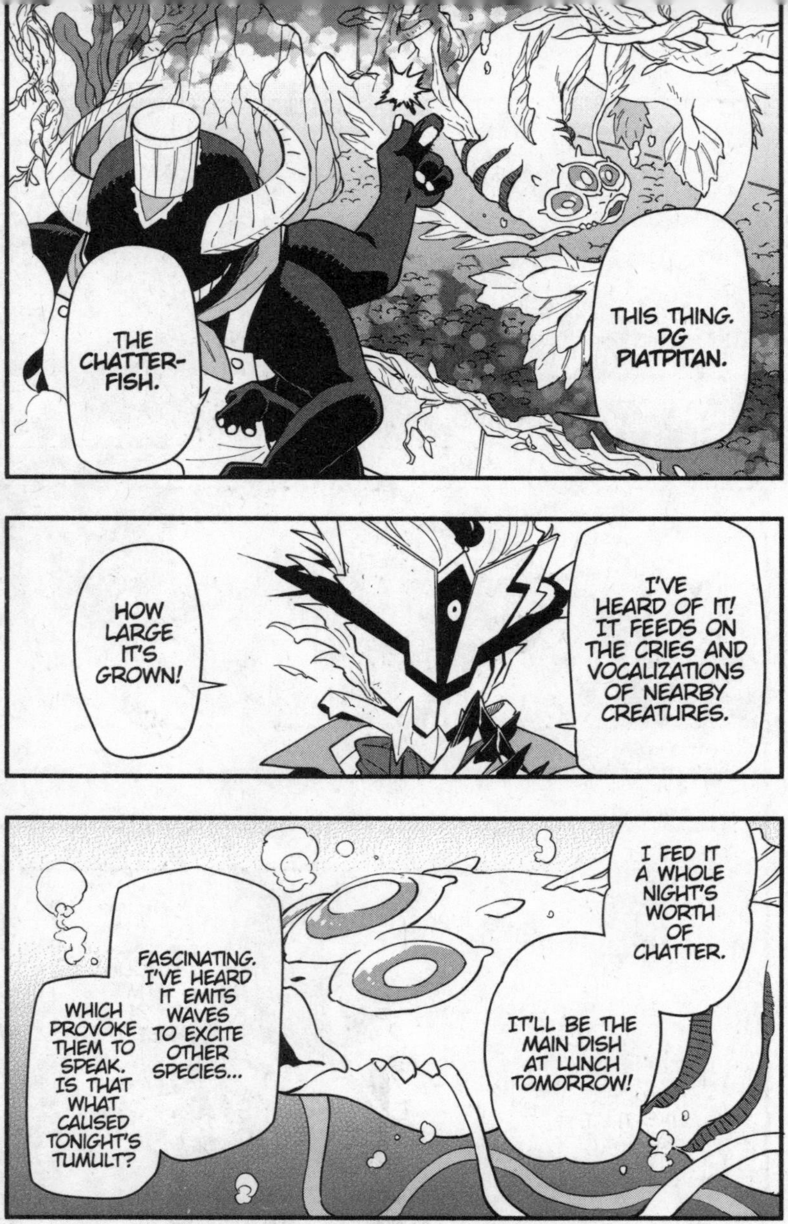
THE CHATTER-FISH.
THIS THING. DG PIATPITAN.
HOW LARGE IT'S GROWN!
I'VE HEARD OF IT! IT FEEDS ON THE CRIES AND VOCALIZATIONS OF NEARBY CREATURES.
I FED IT A WHOLE NIGHT'S WORTH OF CHATTER.
IT'LL BE THE MAIN DISH AT LUNCH TOMORROW!
FASCINATING. I'VE HEARD IT EMITS WAVES TO EXCITE OTHER SPECIES...
WHICH PROVOKE THEM TO SPEAK. IS THAT WHAT CAUSED TONIGHT'S TUMULT?

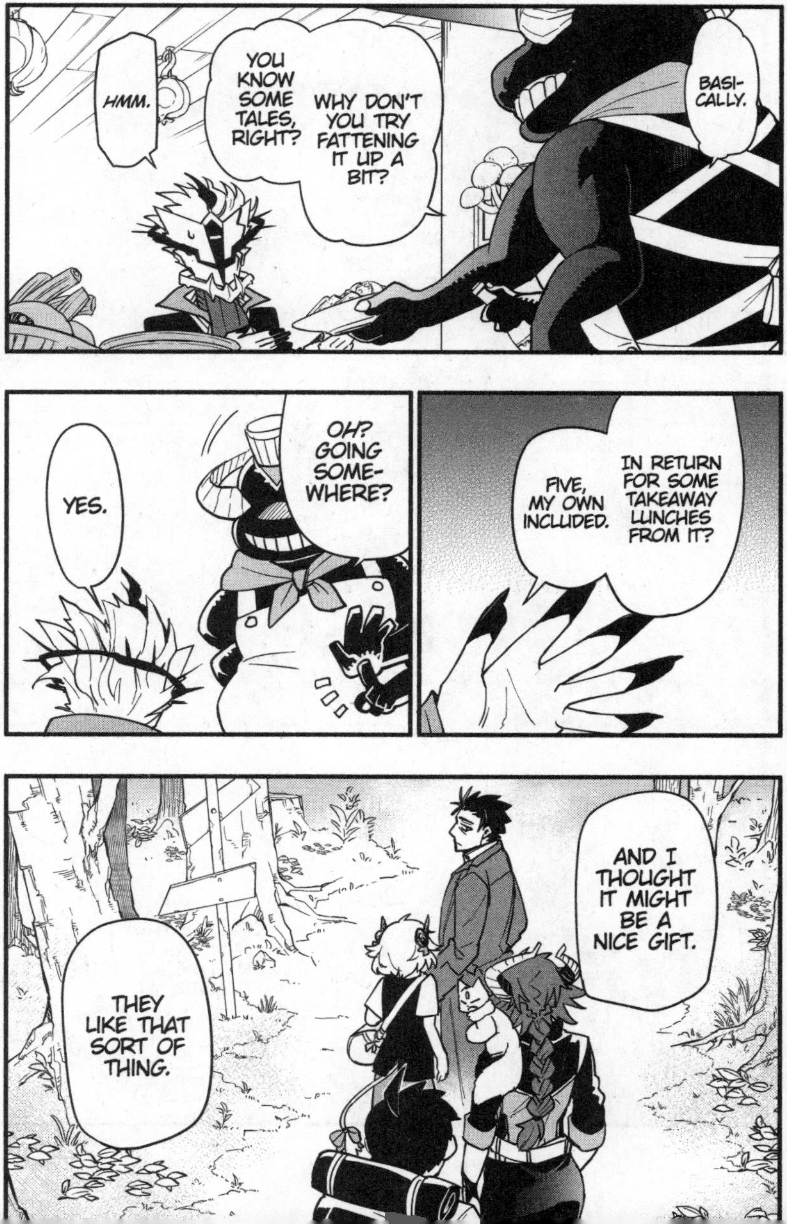
BASI-CALLY.
WHY DON'T YOU TRY FATTENING IT UP A BIT?
YOU KNOW SOME TALES, RIGHT?
HMM.
IN RETURN FOR SOME TAKEAWAY LUNCHES FROM IT?
FIVE, MY OWN INCLUDED.
OH? GOING SOME-WHERE?
YES.
AND I THOUGHT IT MIGHT BE A NICE GIFT.
THEY LIKE THAT SORT OF THING.

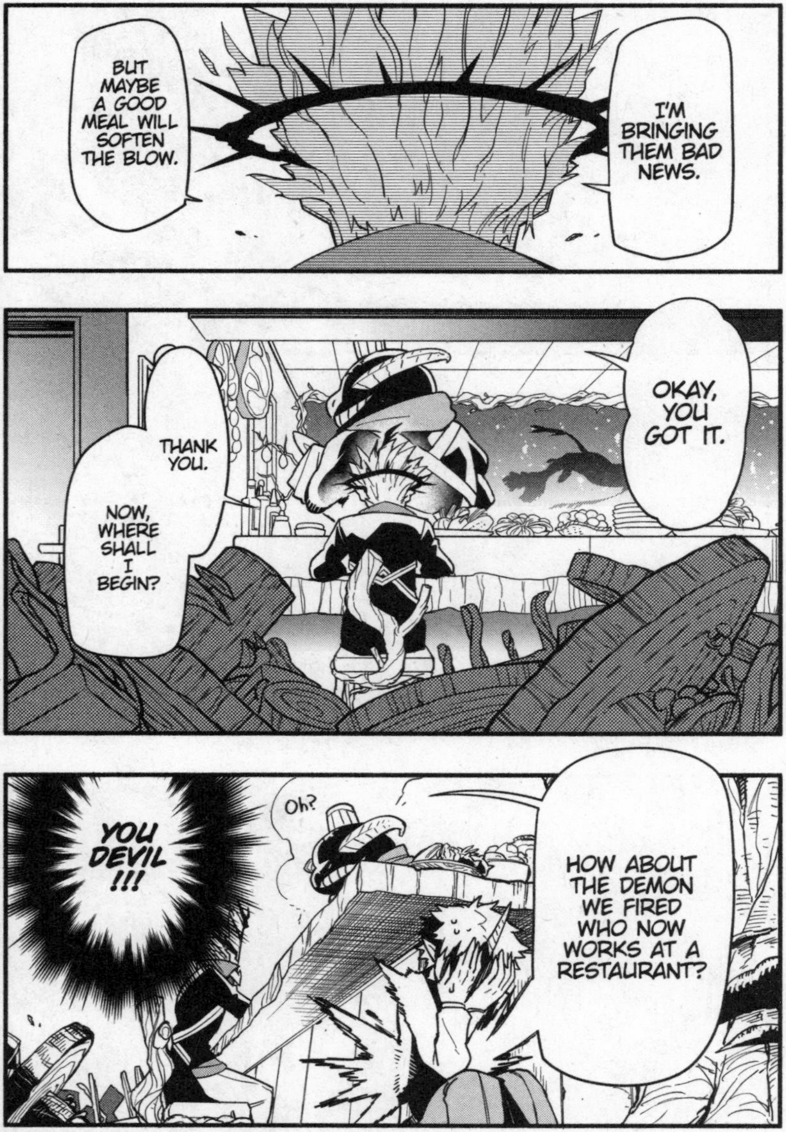
I'M BRINGING THEM BAD NEWS.
BUT MAYBE A GOOD MEAL WILL SOFTEN THE BLOW.
OKAY, YOU GOT IT.
THANK YOU.
NOW, WHERE SHALL I BEGIN?
HOW ABOUT THE DEMON WE FIRED WHO NOW WORKS AT A RESTAURANT?
Oh?
YOU DEVIL!!!

Sorry For My Familiar

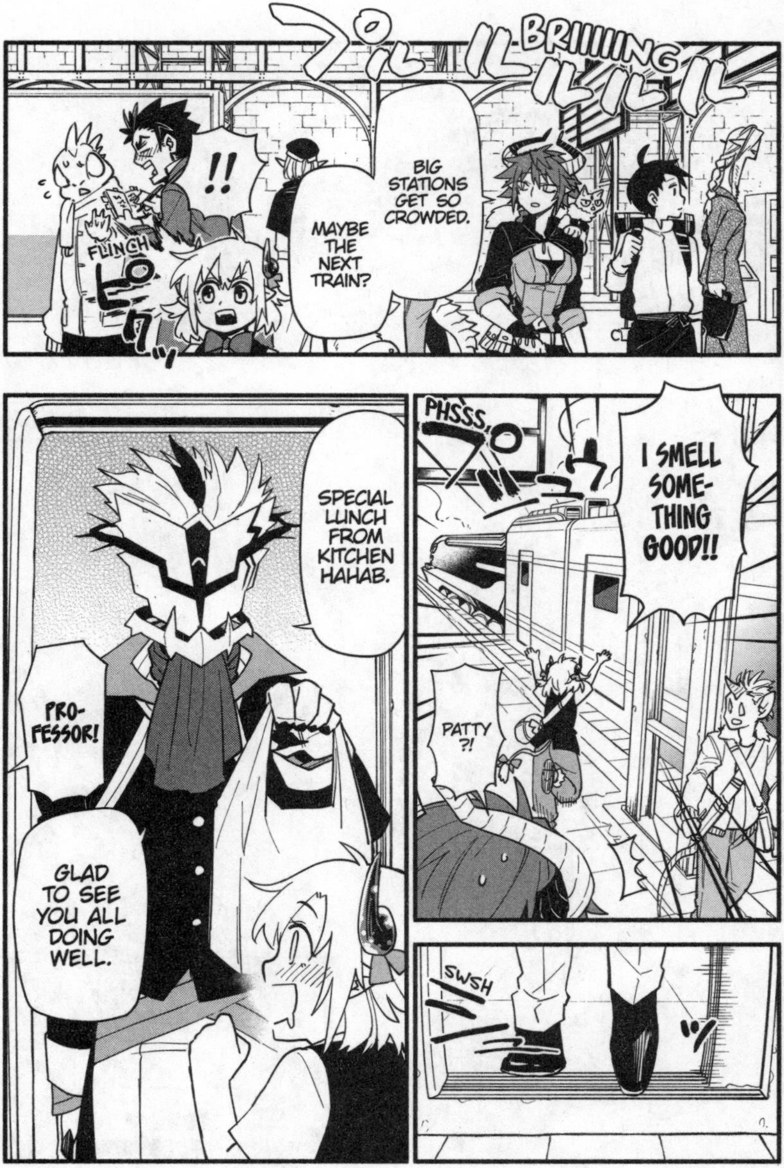
BRIIIIIING
BIG STATIONS GET SO CROWDED.
MAYBE THE NEXT TRAIN?
!!
FLINCH
PHSSS
I SMELL SOME-THING GOOD!!
PATTY ?!
SWSH
SPECIAL LUNCH FROM KITCHEN HAHAB.
PRO-FESSOR!
GLAD TO SEE YOU ALL DOING WELL.

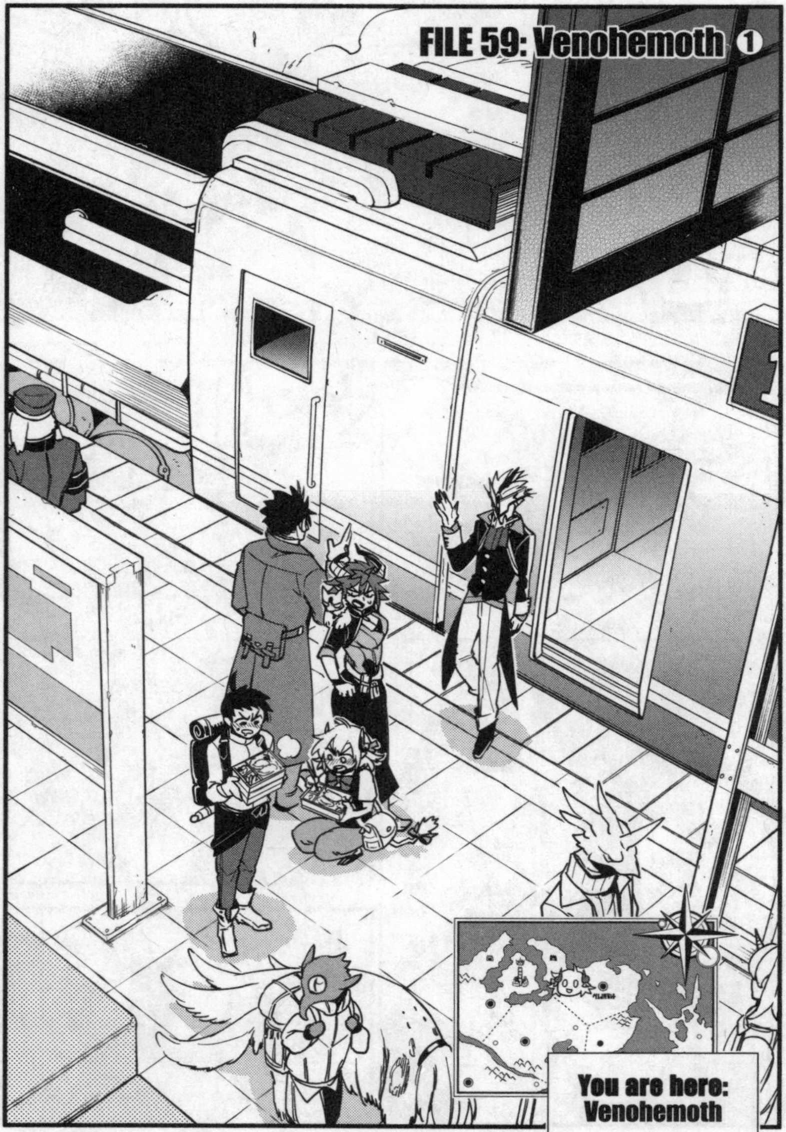
FILE 59: Venohemoth ①
You are here:
Venohemoth

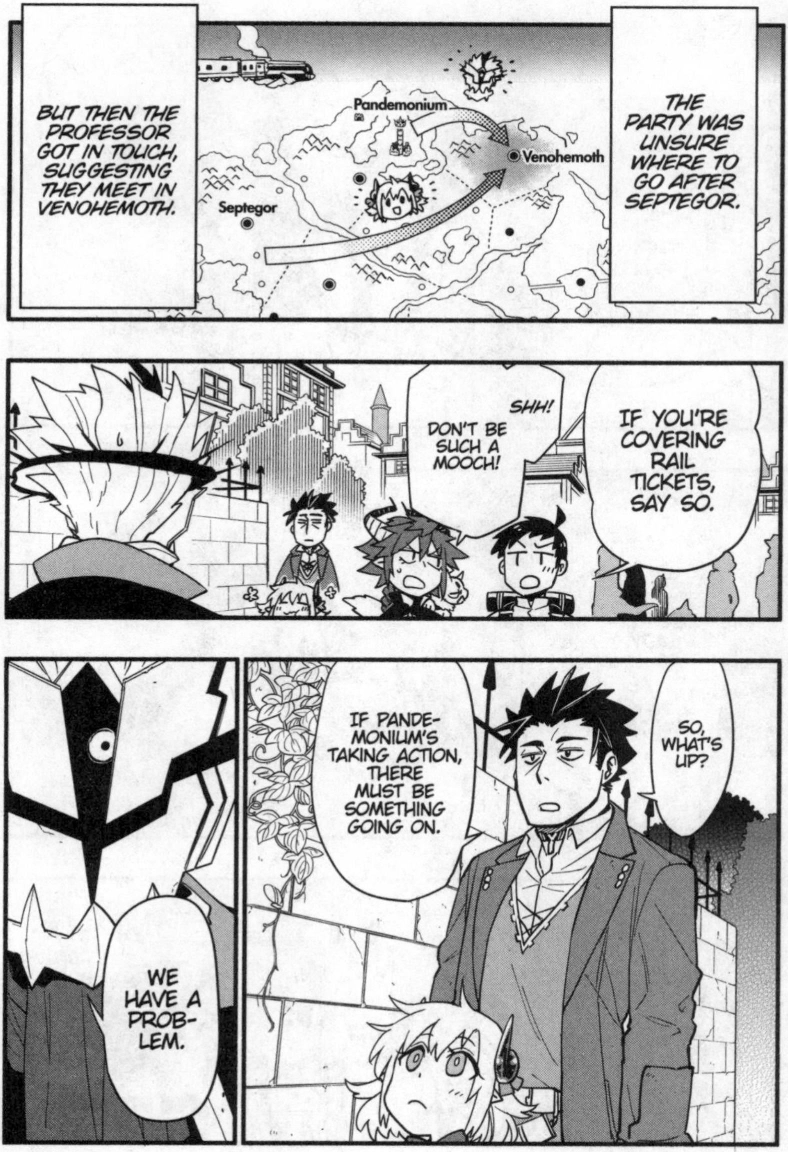
THE PARTY WAS UNSURE WHERE TO GO AFTER SEPTEGOR.
BUT THEN THE PROFESSOR GOT IN TOUCH, SUGGESTING THEY MEET IN VENOHEMOTH.
Pandemonium
Venohemoth
Septegor
IF YOU'RE COVERING RAIL TICKETS, SAY SO.
SHH!
DON'T BE SUCH A MOOCH!
SO, WHAT'S UP?
IF PANDE-MONIUM'S TAKING ACTION, THERE MUST BE SOMETHING GOING ON.
WE HAVE A PROB-LEM.

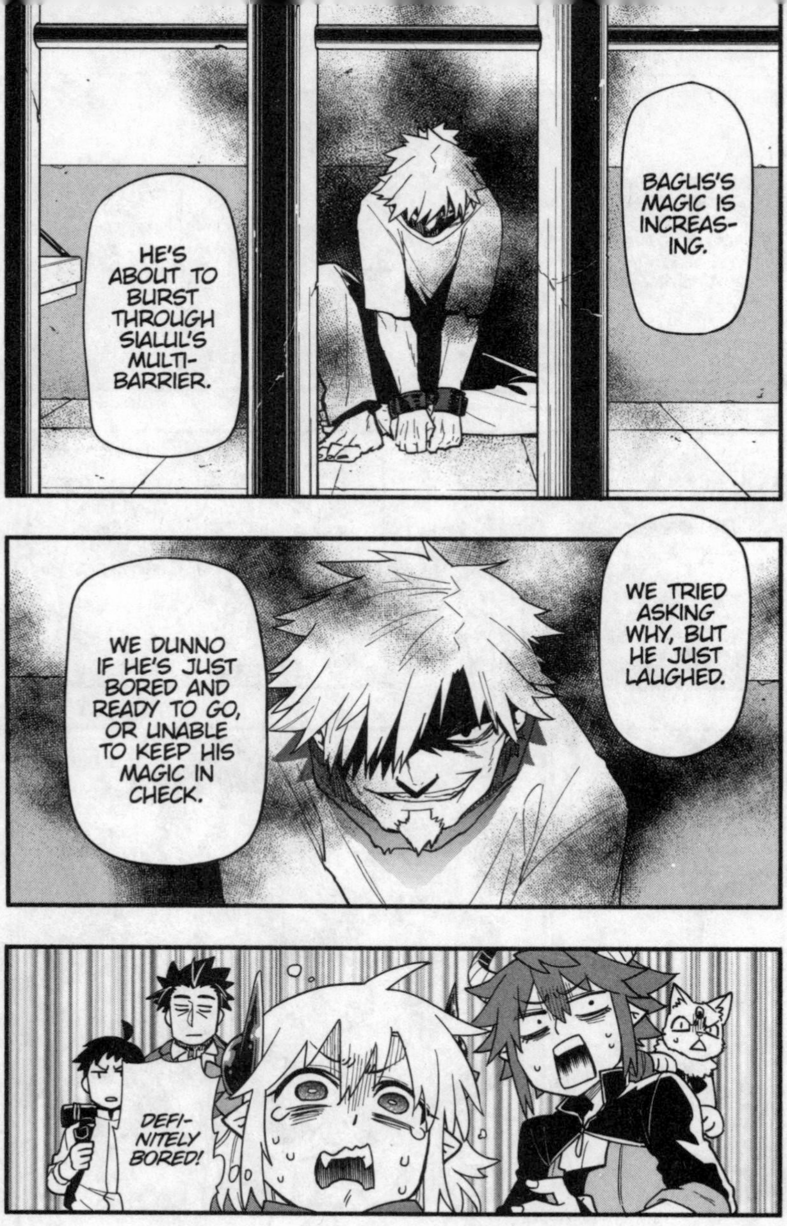
BAGLIS'S MAGIC IS INCREAS-ING.
HE'S ABOUT TO BURST THROUGH SIALUL'S MULTI-BARRIER.
WE TRIED ASKING WHY, BUT HE JUST LAUGHED.
WE DUNNO IF HE'S JUST BORED AND READY TO GO, OR UNABLE TO KEEP HIS MAGIC IN CHECK.
DEFI-NITELY BORED!

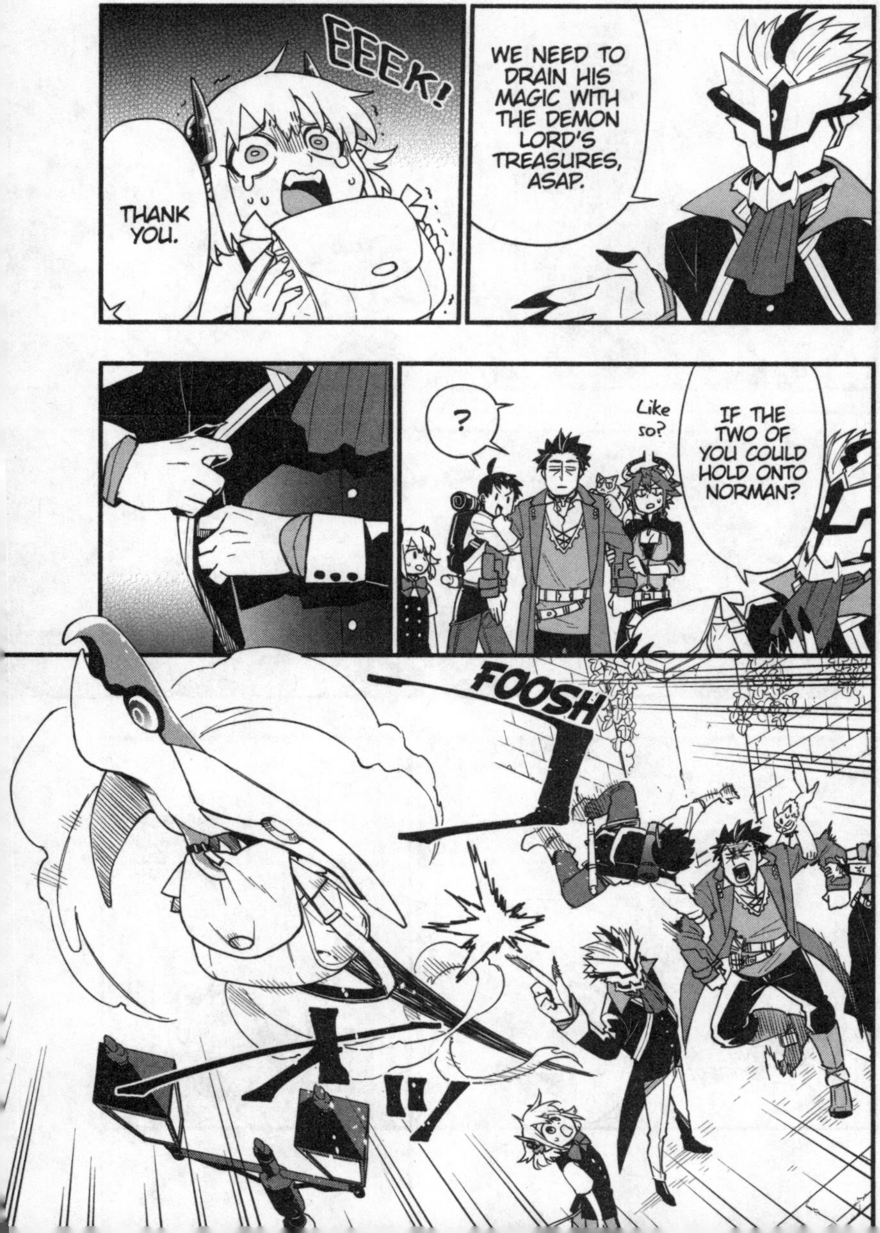
WE NEED TO DRAIN HIS MAGIC WITH THE DEMON LORD'S TREASURES, ASAP.
EEEEK!
THANK YOU.
IF THE TWO OF YOU COULD HOLD ONTO NORMAN?
Like so?
?
FOOSH

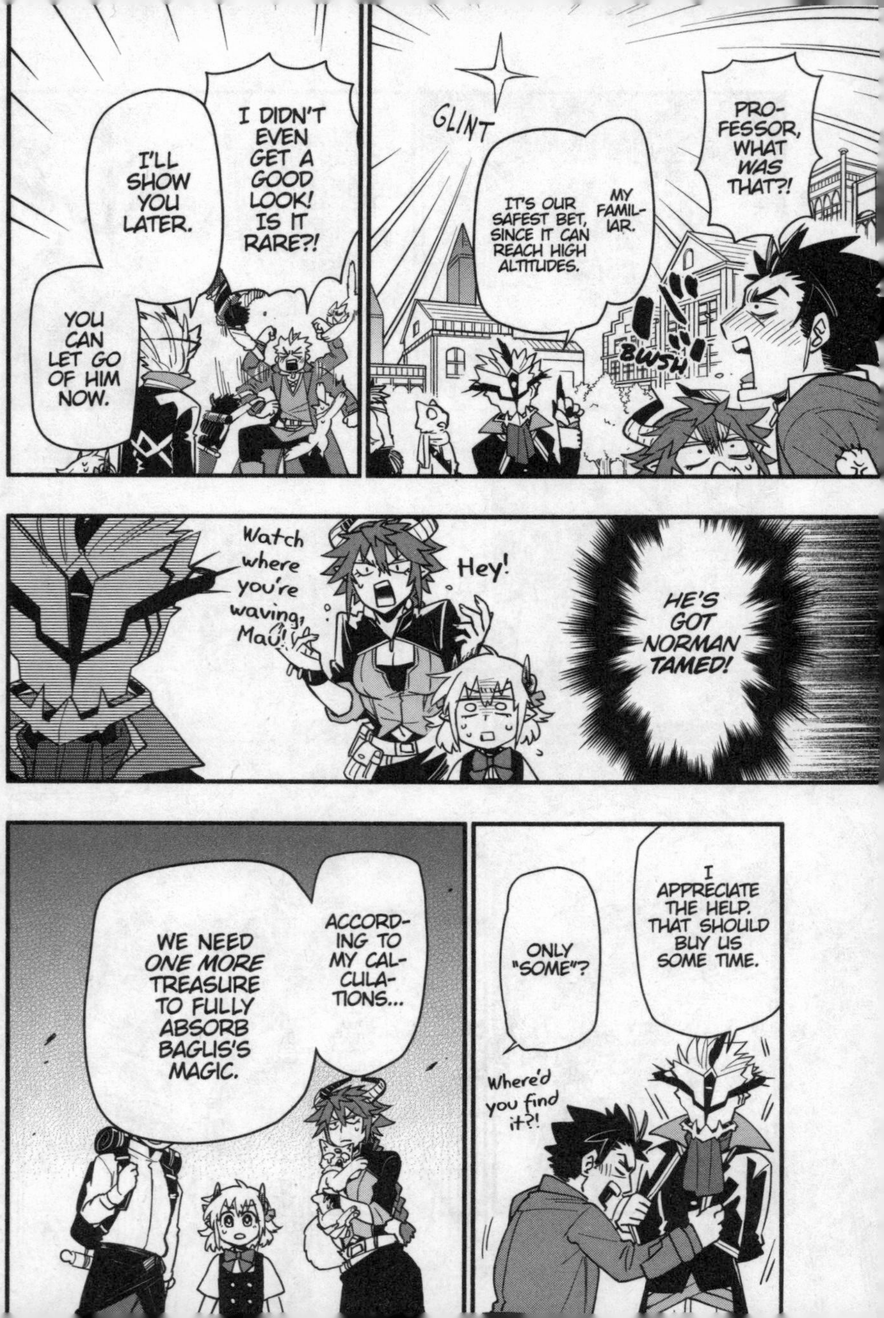
PRO-FESSOR, WHAT WAS THAT?!
GLINT
BWSH
MY FAMIL-IAR.
IT'S OUR SAFEST BET, SINCE IT CAN REACH HIGH ALTITUDES.
I DIDN'T EVEN GET A GOOD LOOK! IS IT RARE?!
I'LL SHOW YOU LATER.
YOU CAN LET GO OF HIM NOW.
HE'S GOT NORMAN TAMED!
Hey!
Watch where you're waving, Mau!
I APPRECIATE THE HELP. THAT SHOULD BUY US SOME TIME.
ONLY "SOME"?
Where'd you find it?!
ACCORD-ING TO MY CAL-CULA-TIONS...
WE NEED ONE MORE TREASURE TO FULLY ABSORB BAGLIS'S MAGIC.

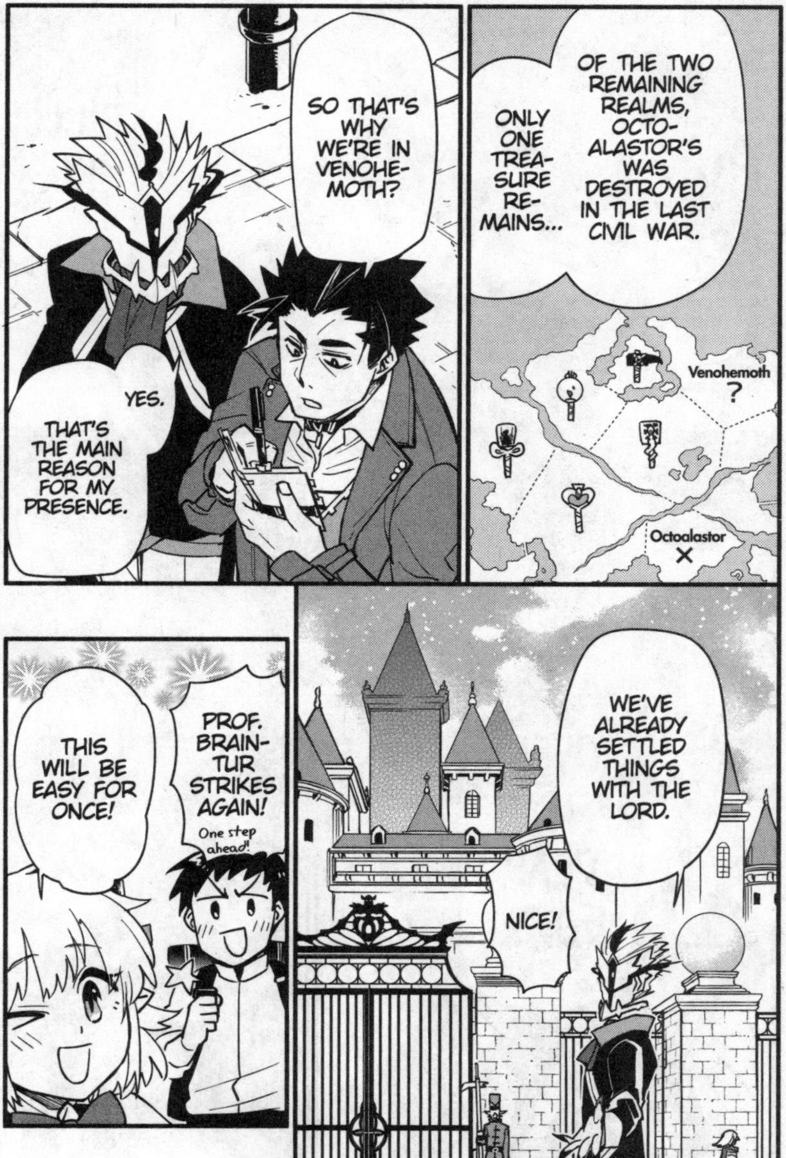
OF THE TWO REMAINING REALMS, OCTO-ALASTOR'S WAS DESTROYED IN THE LAST CIVIL WAR.
ONLY ONE TREASURE REMAINS...
Venohemoth
?
Octoalastor
×
SO THAT'S WHY WE'RE IN VENOHEMOTH?
YES.
THAT'S THE MAIN REASON FOR MY PRESENCE.
WE'VE ALREADY SETTLED THINGS WITH THE LORD.
NICE!
PROF. BRAINTUR STRIKES AGAIN!
One step ahead!
THIS WILL BE EASY FOR ONCE!

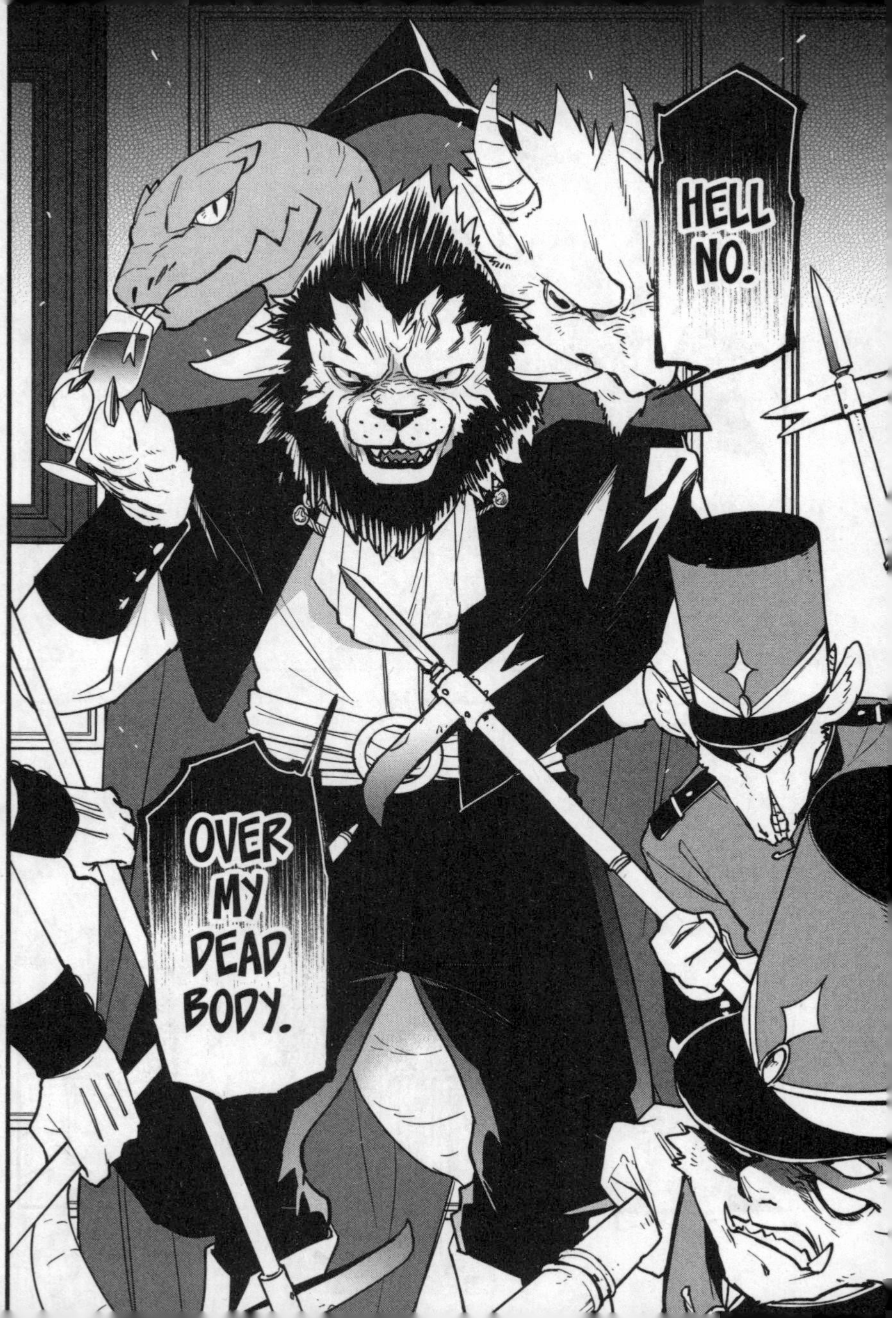
HELL NO.
OVER MY DEAD BODY.

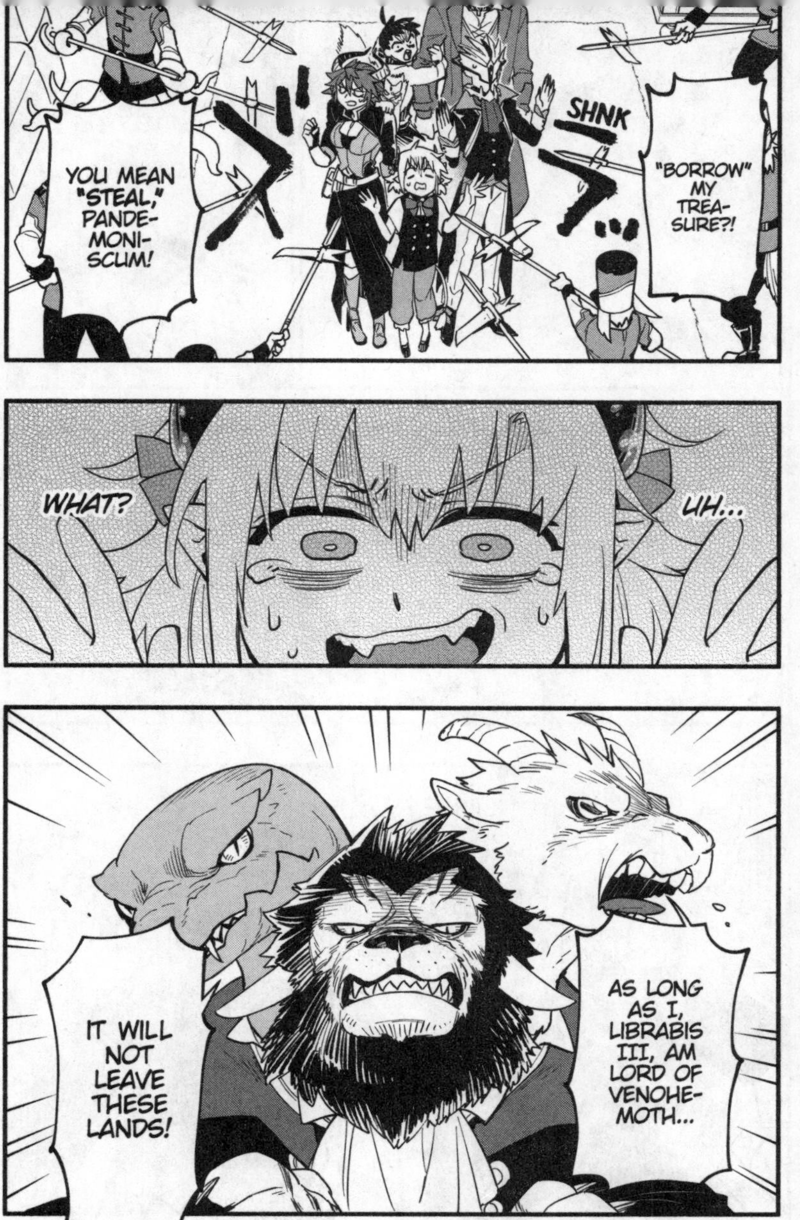
"BORROW" MY TREASURE?!
SHNK
YOU MEAN "STEAL," PANDEMONISCUM!
UH...
WHAT?
AS LONG AS I, LIBRABIS III, AM LORD OF VENOHEMOTH...
IT WILL NOT LEAVE THESE LANDS!

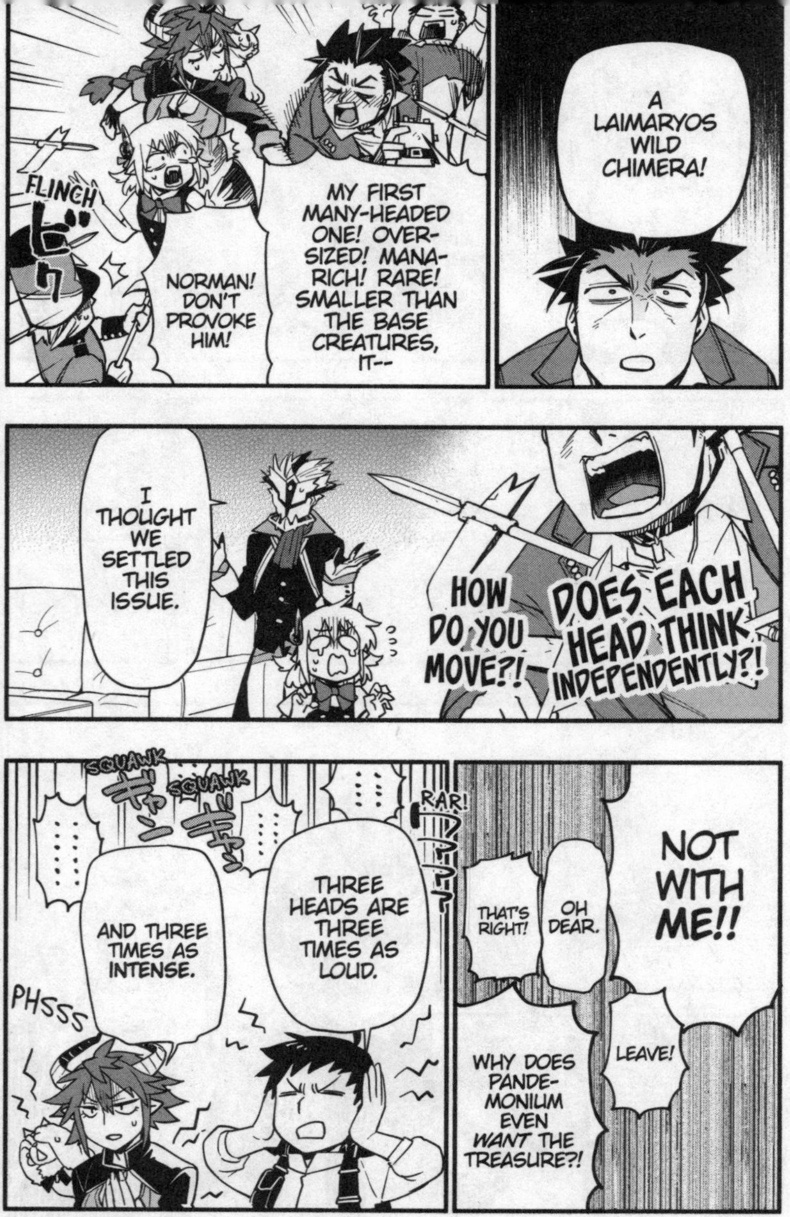
A LAIMARYOS WILD CHIMERA!
MY FIRST MANY-HEADED ONE! OVER-SIZED! MANA-RICH! RARE! SMALLER THAN THE BASE CREATURES, IT--
NORMAN! DON'T PROVOKE HIM!
FLINCH
DOES EACH HEAD THINK INDEPENDENTLY?!
HOW DO YOU MOVE?!
I THOUGHT WE SETTLED THIS ISSUE.
NOT WITH ME!!
OH DEAR.
THAT'S RIGHT!
LEAVE!
WHY DOES PANDE-MONIUM EVEN *WANT* THE TREASURE?!
RAR!
THREE HEADS ARE THREE TIMES AS LOUD.
SQUAWK
SQUAWK
AND THREE TIMES AS INTENSE.
PHSSS

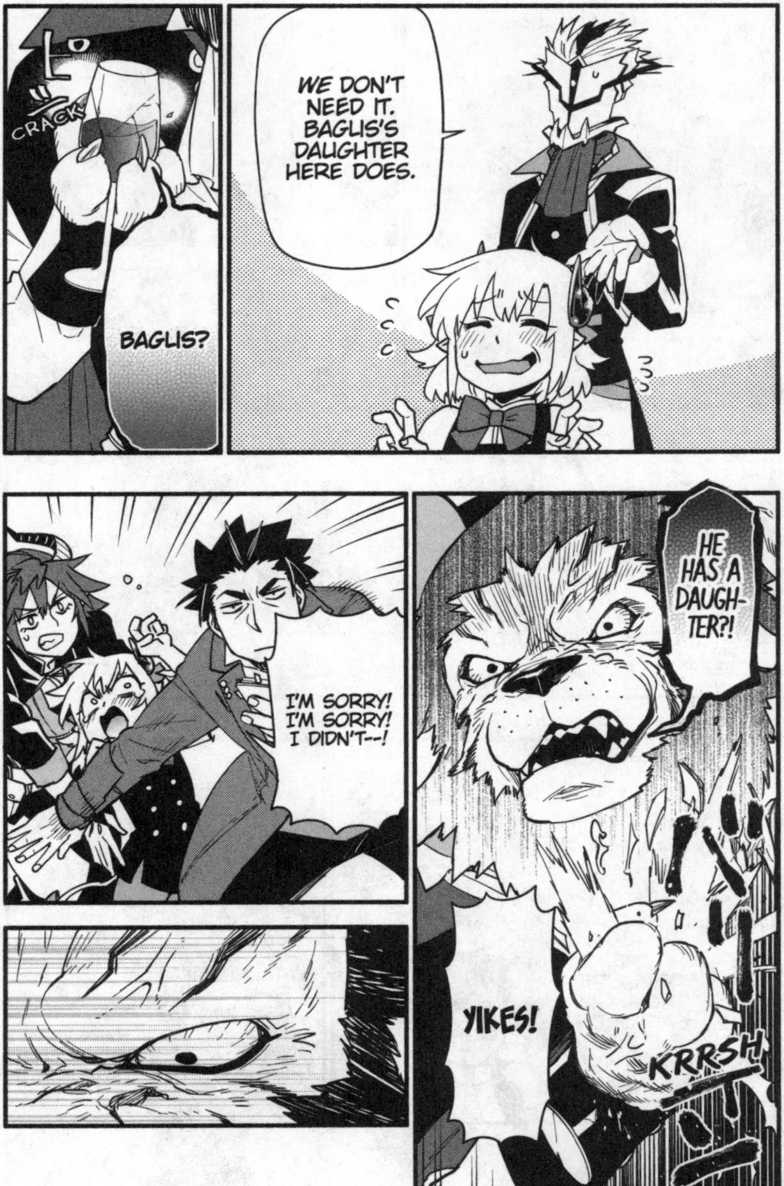
CRACK
BAGLIS?
WE DON'T NEED IT. BAGLIS'S DAUGHTER HERE DOES.
I'M SORRY! I'M SORRY! I DIDN'T--!
HE HAS A DAUGH-TER?!
YIKES!
KRRSH

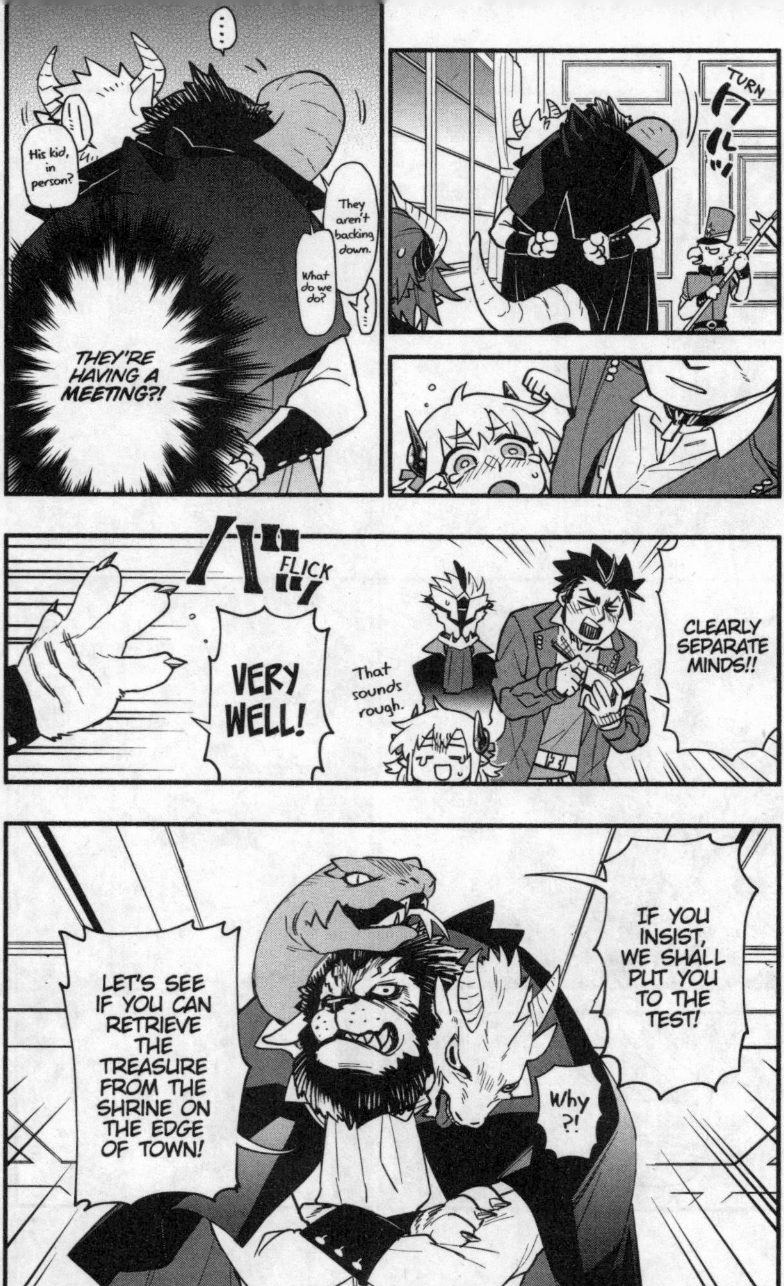

TURN
...
They aren't backing down.
What do we do?
His kid, in person?
THEY'RE HAVING A MEETING?!
CLEARLY SEPARATE MINDS!!
That sounds rough.
VERY WELL!
FLICK
IF YOU INSIST, WE SHALL PUT YOU TO THE TEST!
Why?!
LET'S SEE IF YOU CAN RETRIEVE THE TREASURE FROM THE SHRINE ON THE EDGE OF TOWN!

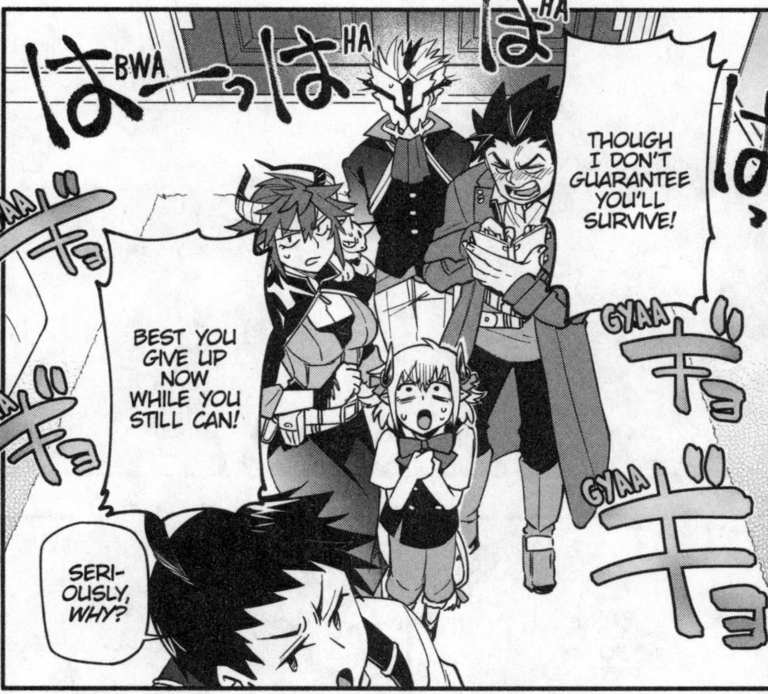
はーっははは
BWA HA HA HA!
THOUGH I DON'T GUARANTEE YOU'LL SURVIVE!
GYAA ギョ
GYAA ギョ
BEST YOU GIVE UP NOW WHILE YOU STILL CAN!
GYAA ギョ
GYAA ギョ
SERI-OUSLY, WHY?

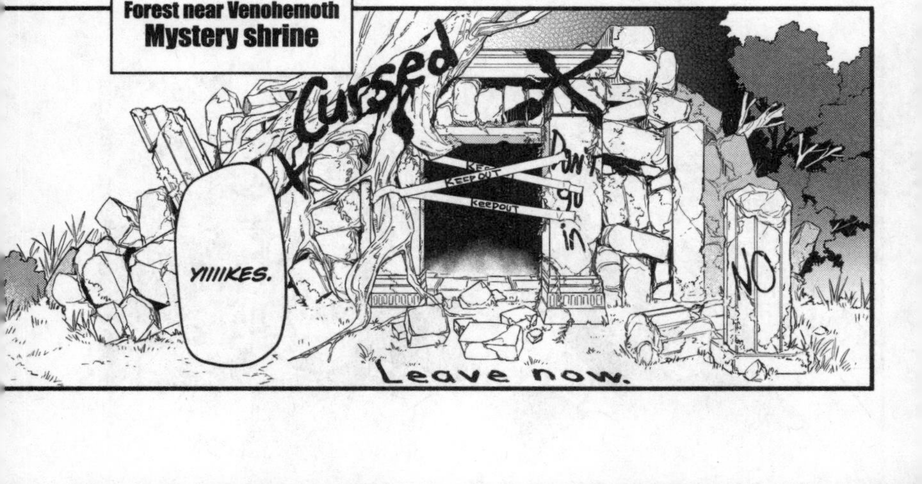
Forest near Venohemoth
Mystery shrine
Cursed
KEEP OUT
KEEP OUT
KEEP OUT
Don't go in
NO
YIIIIKES.
Leave now.

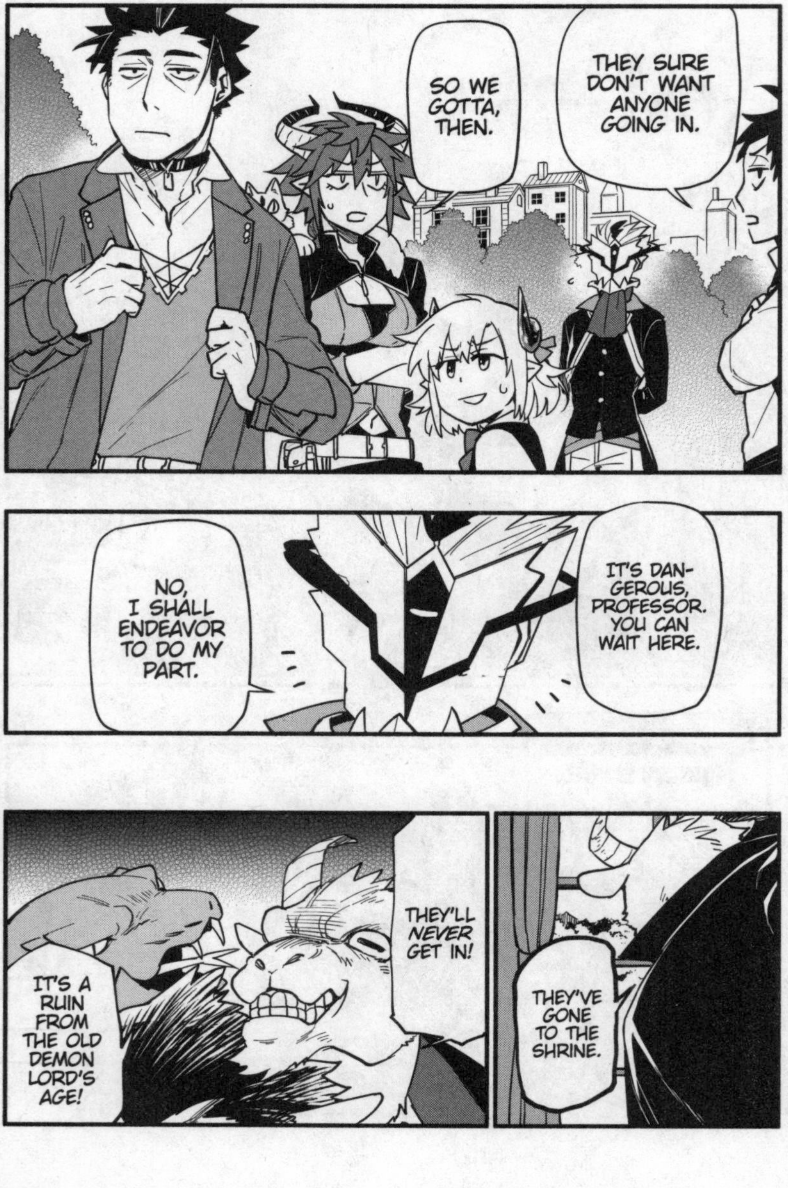
THEY SURE DON'T WANT ANYONE GOING IN.
SO WE GOTTA, THEN.
IT'S DAN-GEROUS, PROFESSOR. YOU CAN WAIT HERE.
NO, I SHALL ENDEAVOR TO DO MY PART.
THEY'VE GONE TO THE SHRINE.
THEY'LL *NEVER* GET IN!
IT'S A RUIN FROM THE OLD DEMON LORD'S AGE!

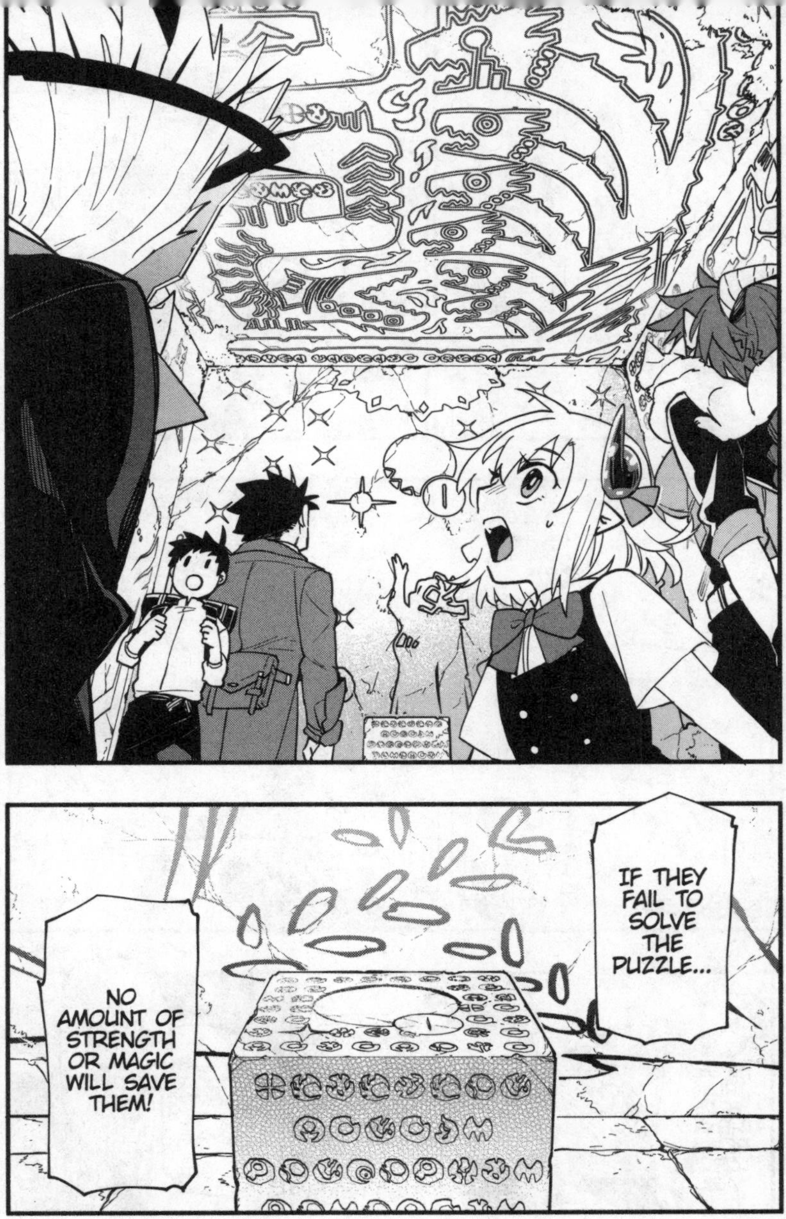
IF THEY FAIL TO SOLVE THE PUZZLE...
NO AMOUNT OF STRENGTH OR MAGIC WILL SAVE THEM!

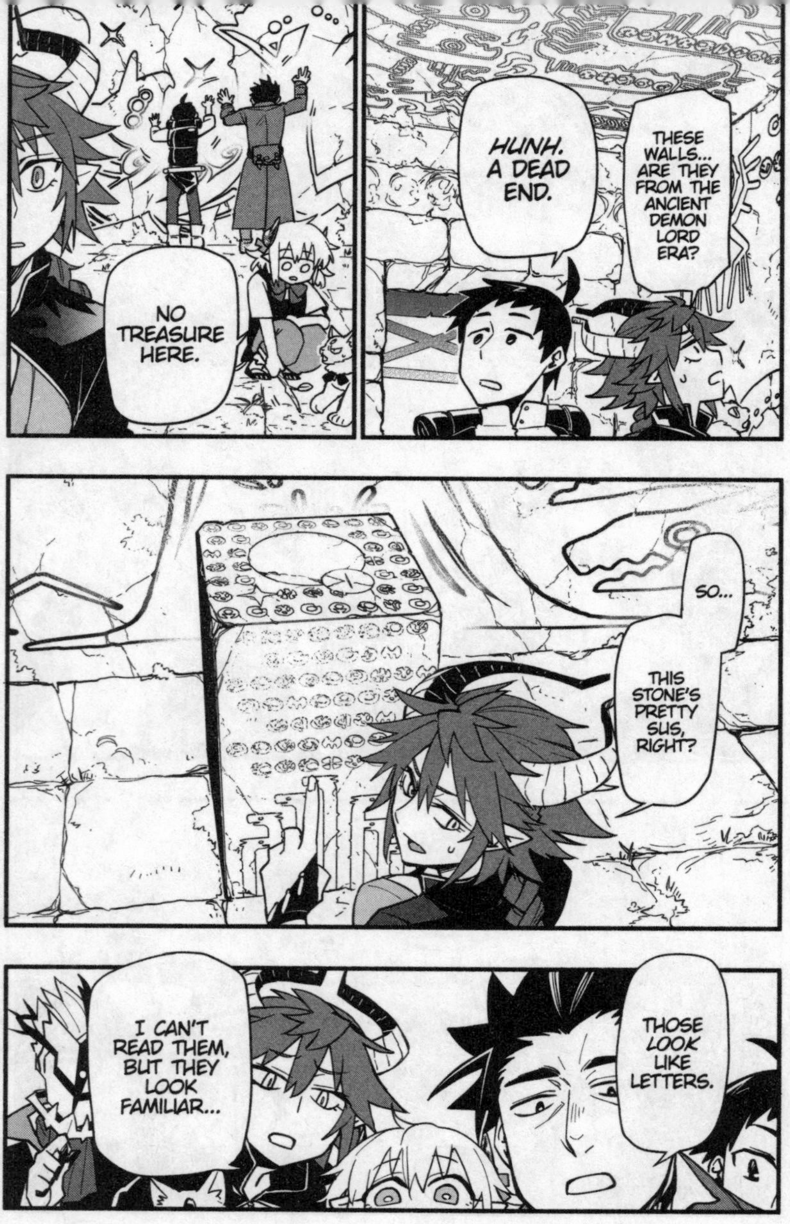
NO TREASURE HERE.
HUNH. A DEAD END.
THESE WALLS... ARE THEY FROM THE ANCIENT DEMON LORD ERA?
SO...
THIS STONE'S PRETTY SUS, RIGHT?
THOSE *LOOK* LIKE LETTERS.
I CAN'T READ THEM, BUT THEY LOOK FAMILIAR...

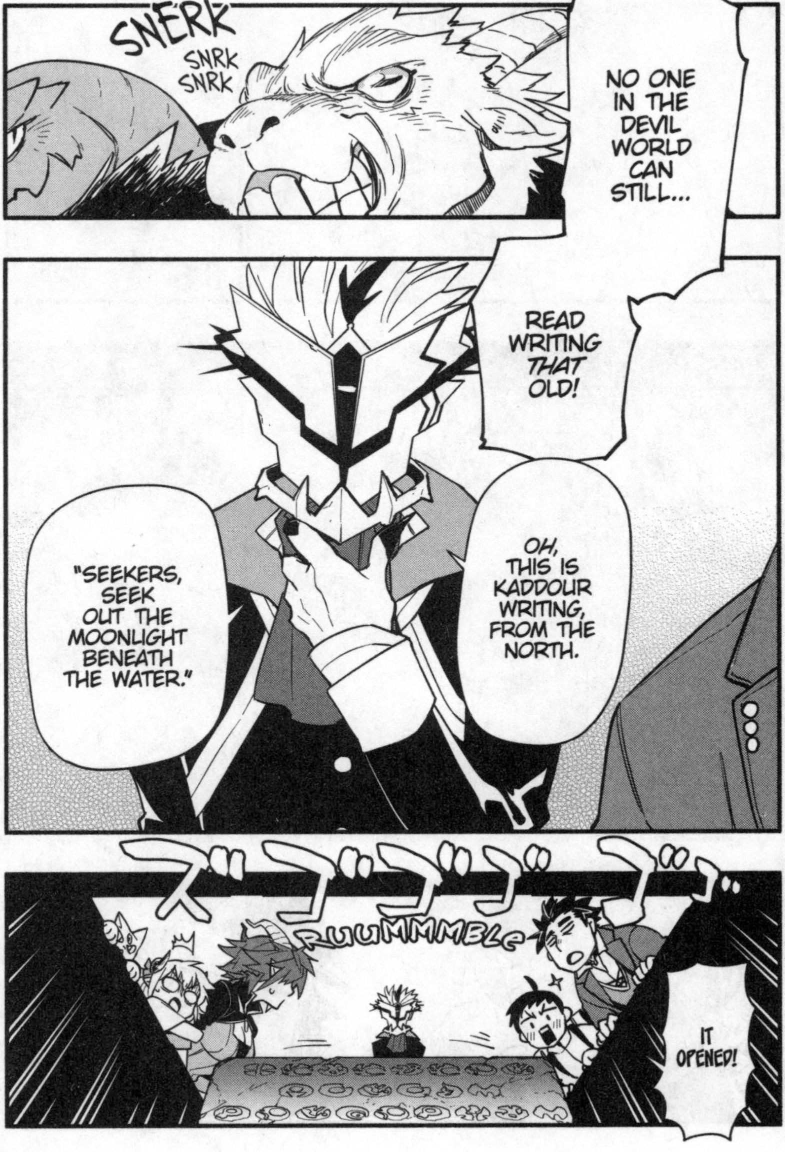

SNERK
SNRK SNRK
NO ONE IN THE DEVIL WORLD CAN STILL...
READ WRITING THAT OLD!
OH, THIS IS KADDOUR WRITING, FROM THE NORTH.
"SEEKERS, SEEK OUT THE MOONLIGHT BENEATH THE WATER."
RUUMMMBLE
IT OPENED!

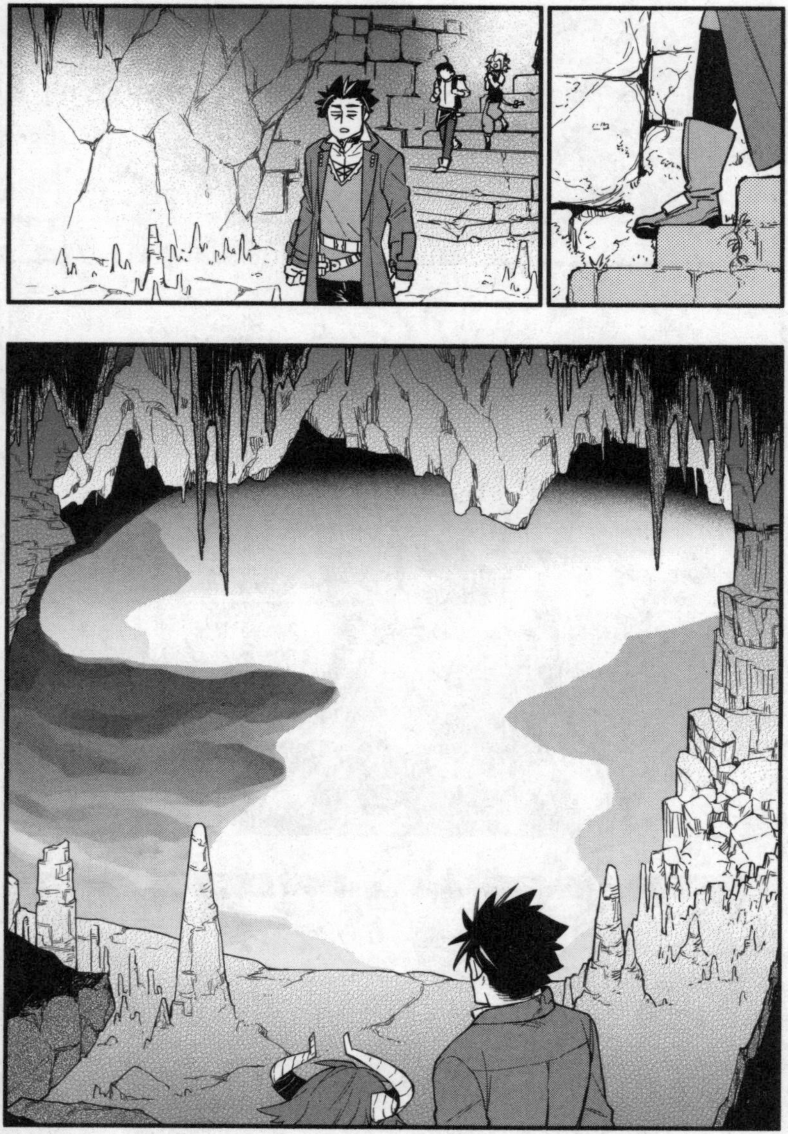

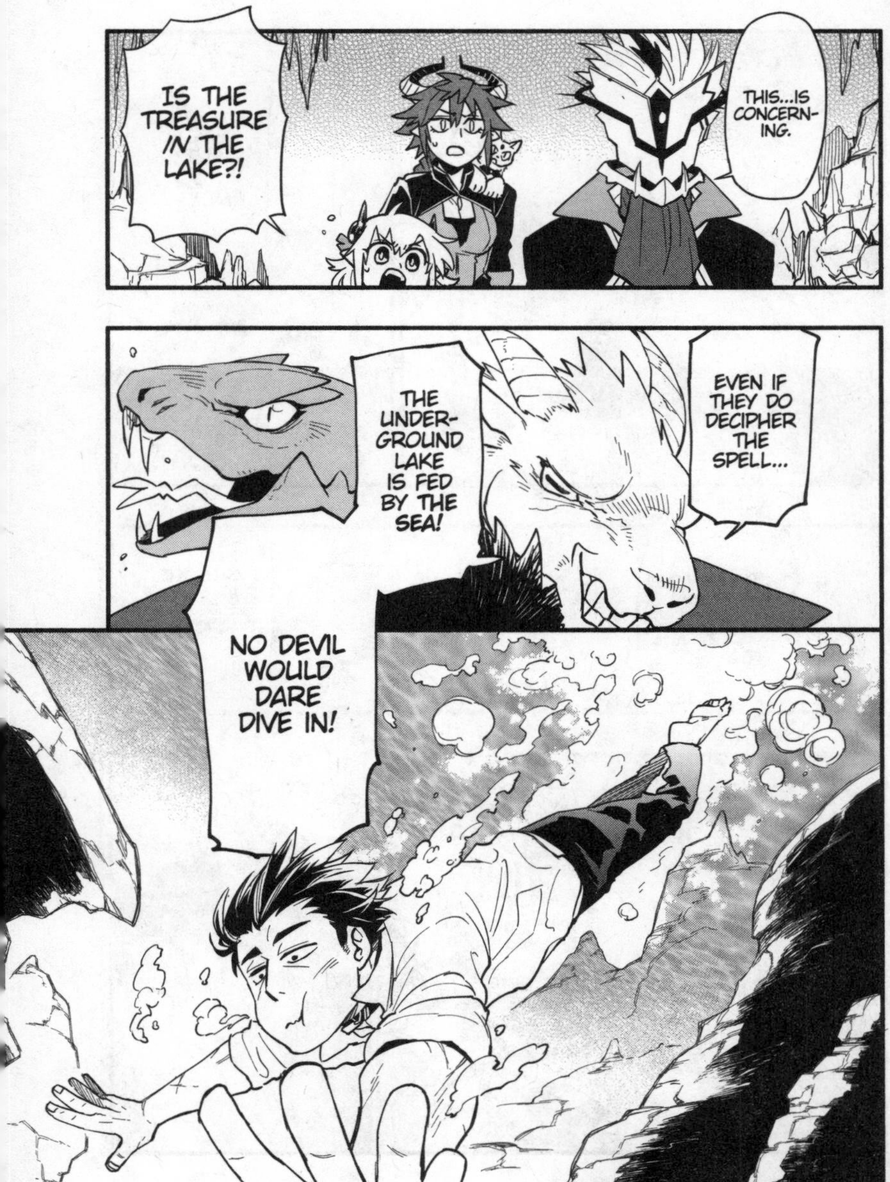
THIS...IS CONCERNING.
IS THE TREASURE IN THE LAKE?!
EVEN IF THEY DO DECIPHER THE SPELL...
THE UNDERGROUND LAKE IS FED BY THE SEA!
NO DEVIL WOULD DARE DIVE IN!

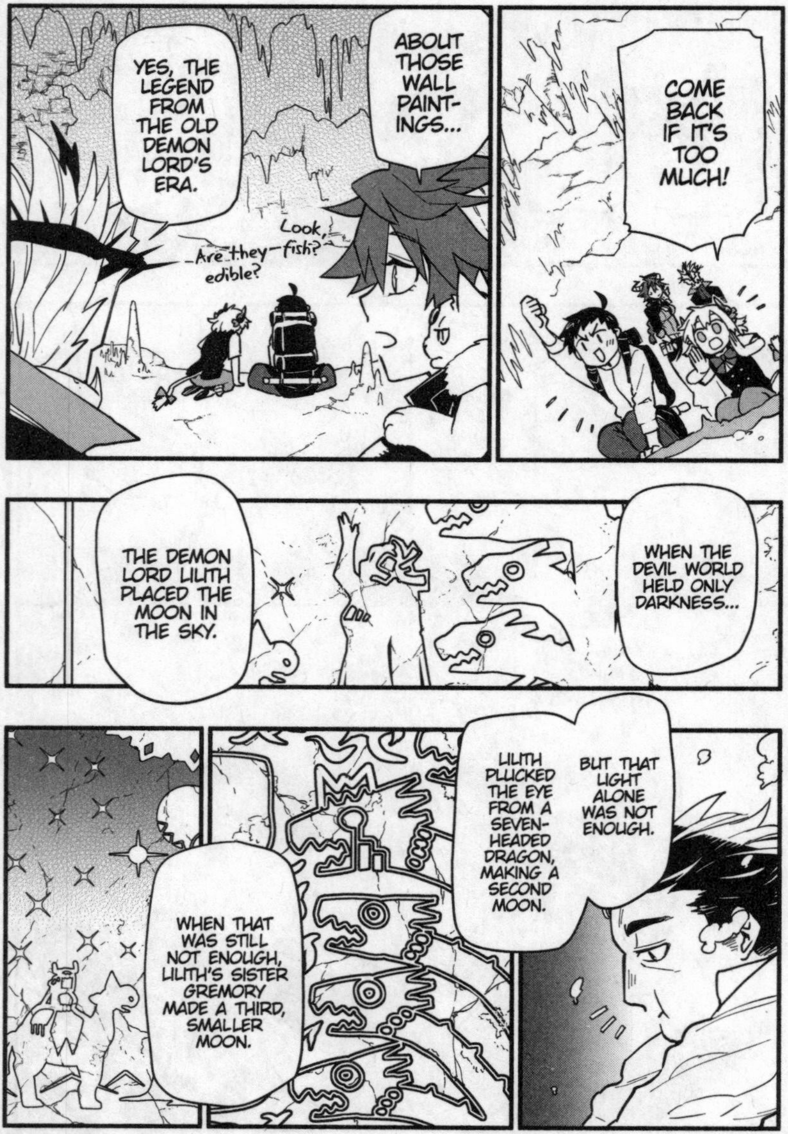
COME BACK IF IT'S TOO MUCH!
ABOUT THOSE WALL PAINT-INGS...
YES, THE LEGEND FROM THE OLD DEMON LORD'S ERA.
Look, fish?
Are they edible?
WHEN THE DEVIL WORLD HELD ONLY DARKNESS...
THE DEMON LORD LILITH PLACED THE MOON IN THE SKY.
BUT THAT LIGHT ALONE WAS NOT ENOUGH.
LILITH PLUCKED THE EYE FROM A SEVEN-HEADED DRAGON, MAKING A SECOND MOON.
WHEN THAT WAS STILL NOT ENOUGH, LILITH'S SISTER GREMORY MADE A THIRD, SMALLER MOON.

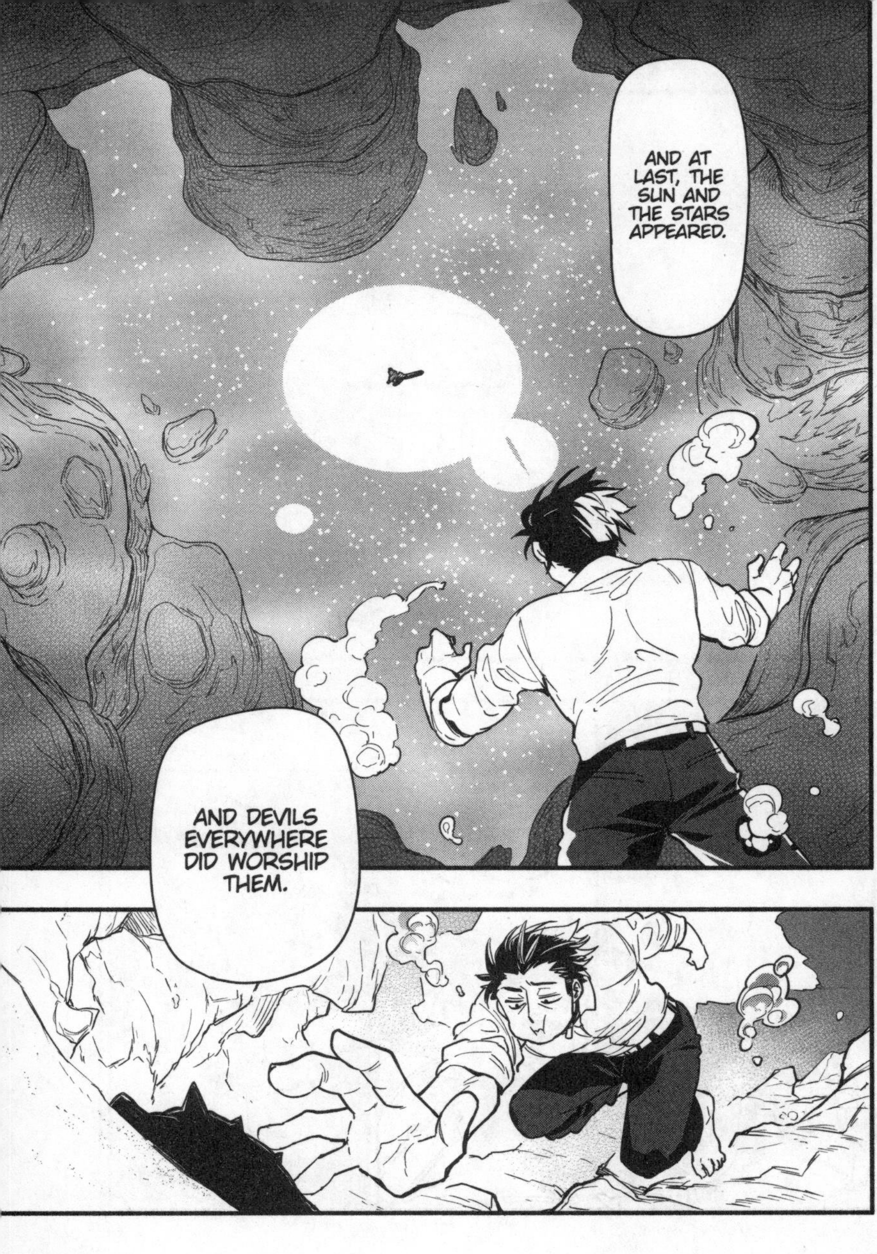
AND AT LAST, THE SUN AND THE STARS APPEARED.
AND DEVILS EVERYWHERE DID WORSHIP THEM.

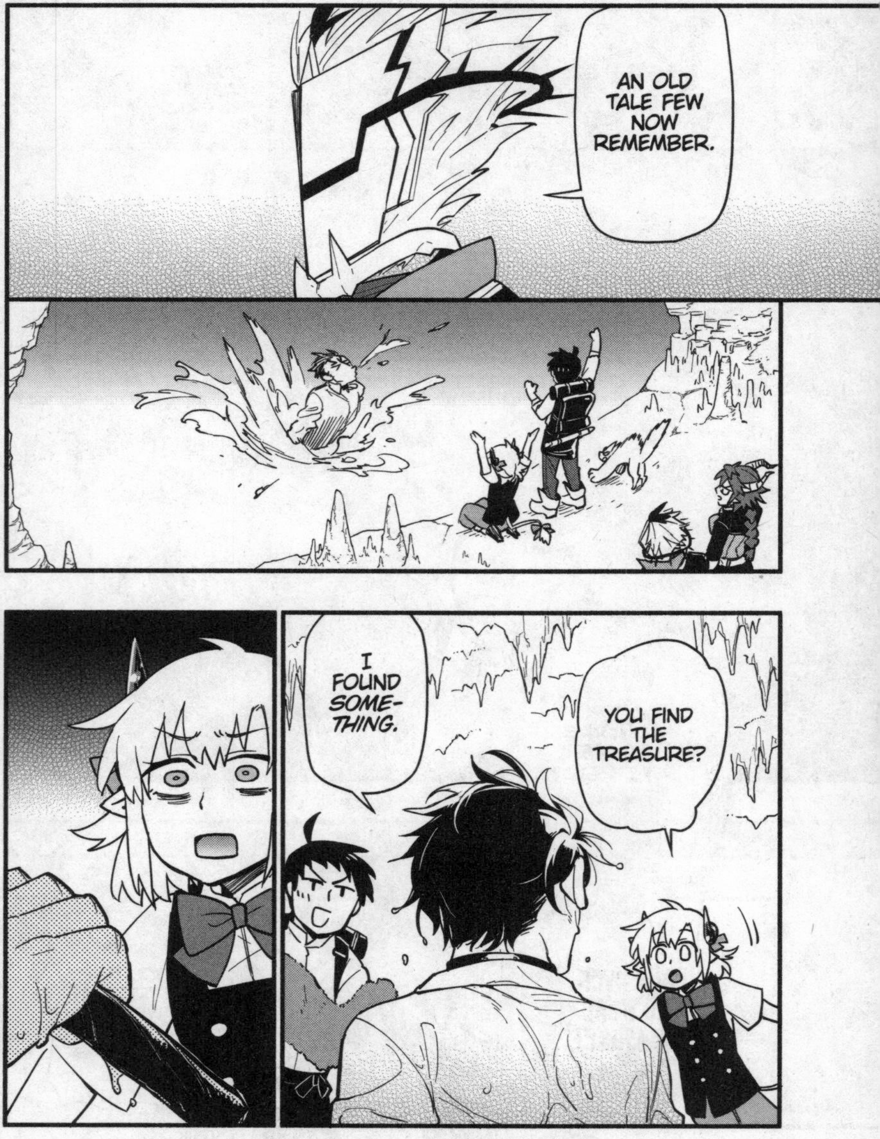
AN OLD TALE FEW NOW REMEMBER.
YOU FIND THE TREASURE?
I FOUND SOME-THING.

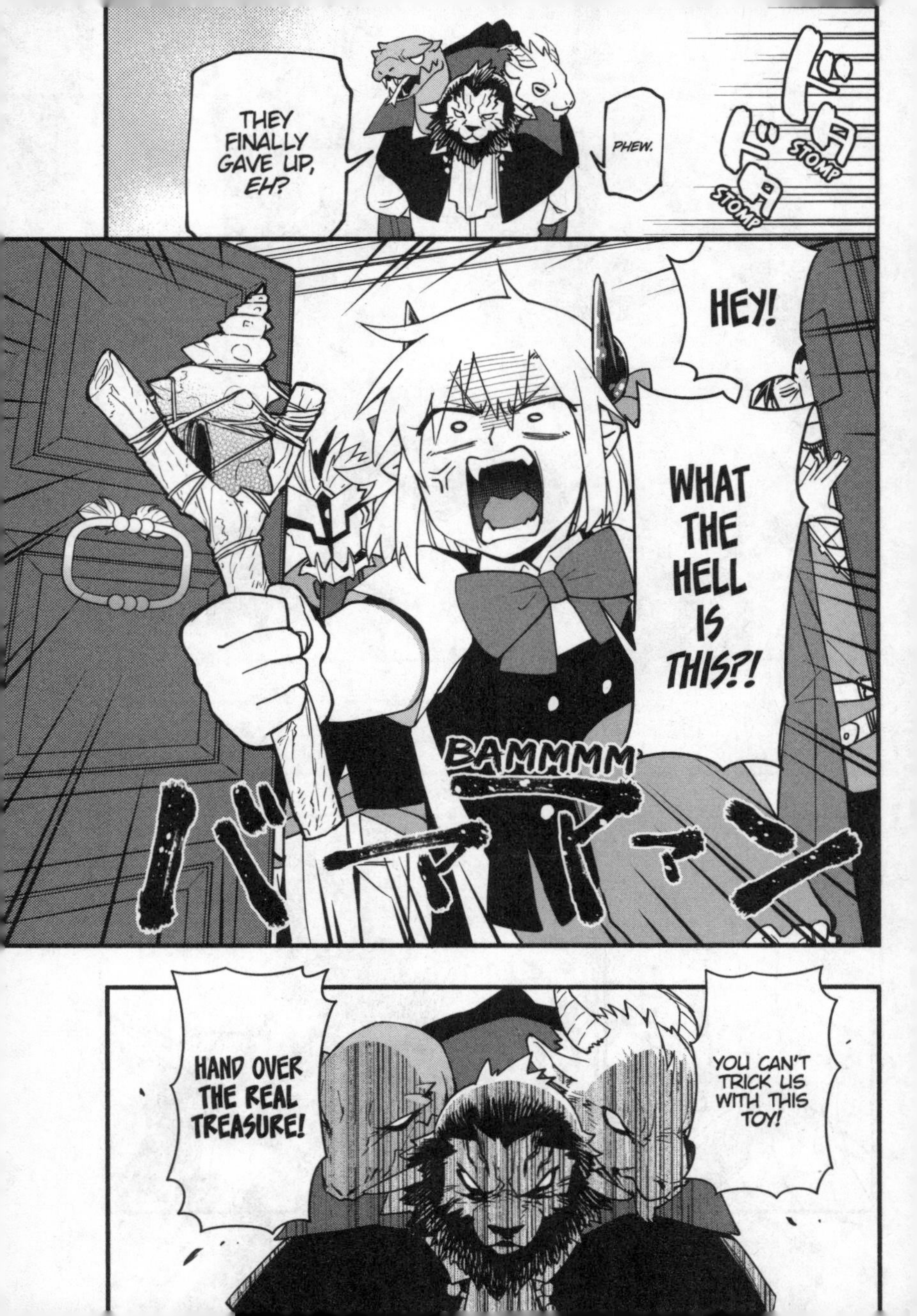
STOMP
STOMP
PHEW.
THEY FINALLY GAVE UP, EH?
HEY!
WHAT THE HELL IS THIS?!
BAMMMM
YOU CAN'T TRICK US WITH THIS TOY!
HAND OVER THE REAL TREASURE!

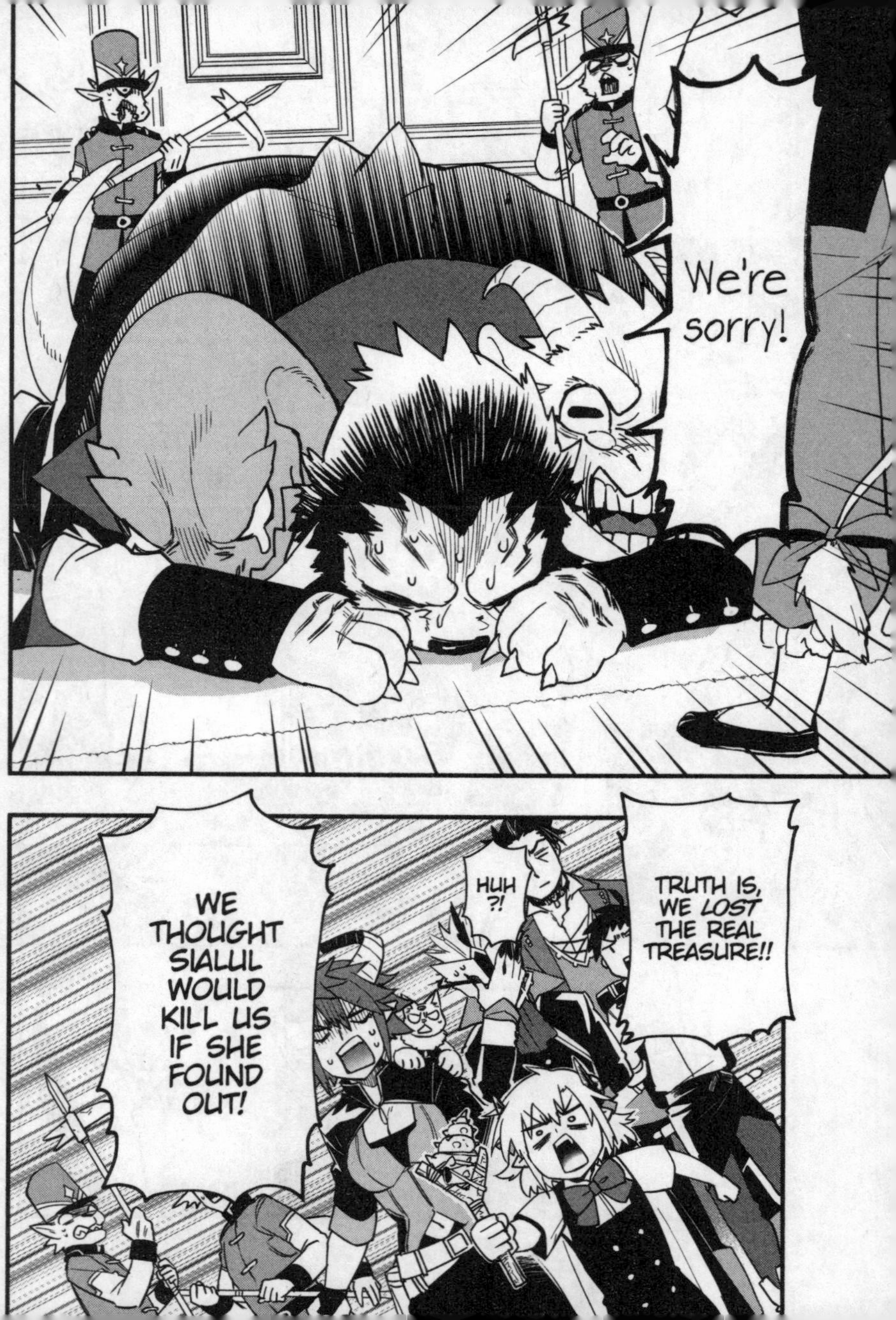
We're sorry!
TRUTH IS, WE LOST THE REAL TREASURE!!
HUH ?!
WE THOUGHT SIALUL WOULD KILL US IF SHE FOUND OUT!

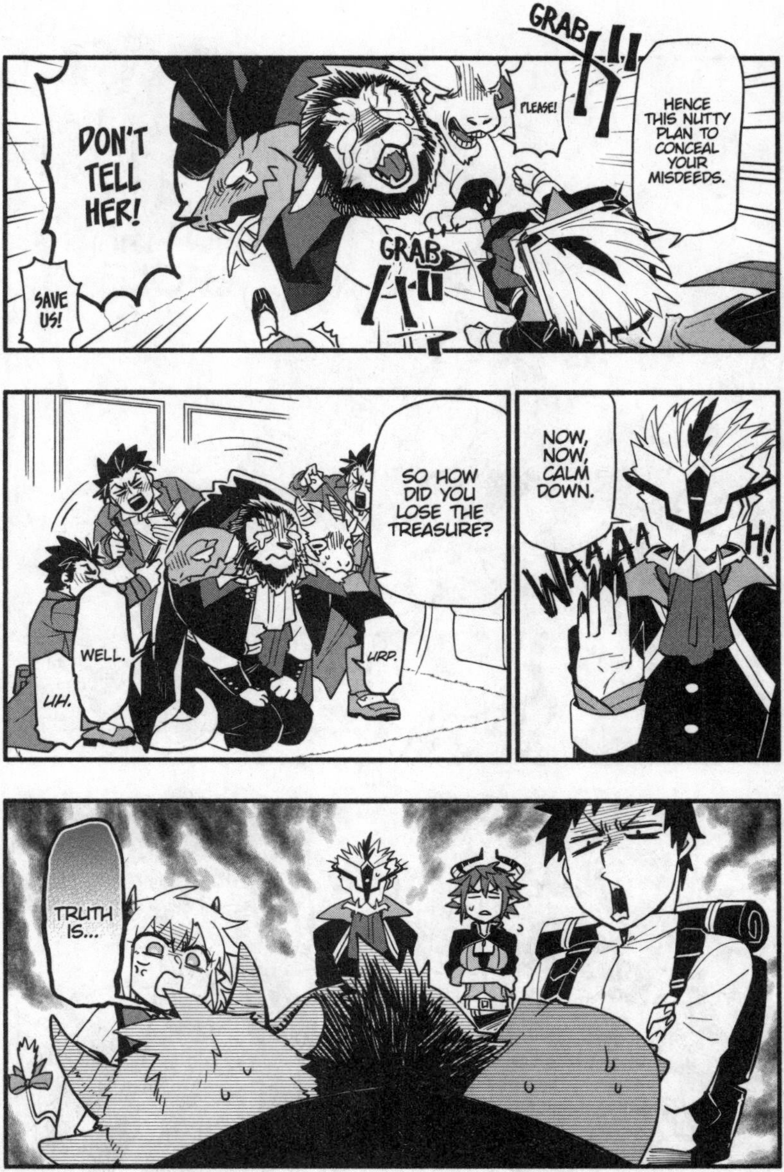
HENCE THIS NUTTY PLAN TO CONCEAL YOUR MISDEEDS.
GRAB!!
PLEASE!
GRAB!!
DON'T TELL HER!
SAVE US!
NOW, NOW, CALM DOWN.
WAAAAAH!
SO HOW DID YOU LOSE THE TREASURE?
URP.
WELL.
UH.
TRUTH IS...

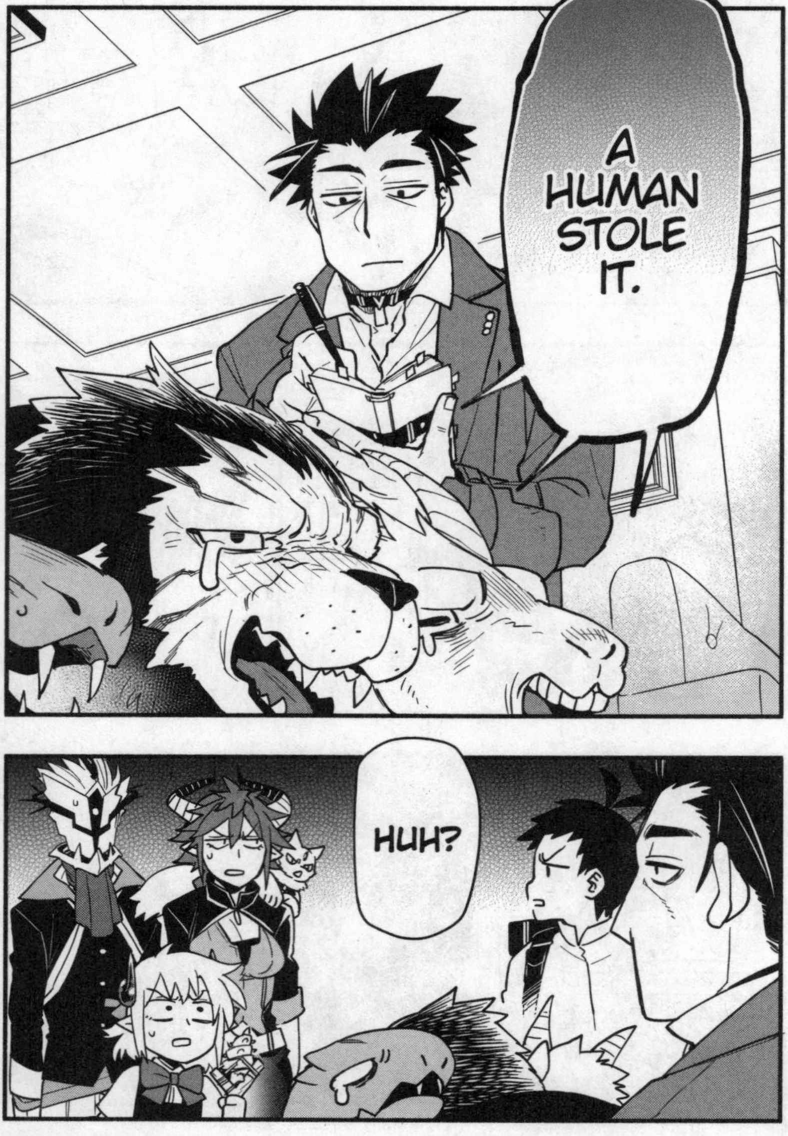
A HUMAN STOLE IT.
HUH?

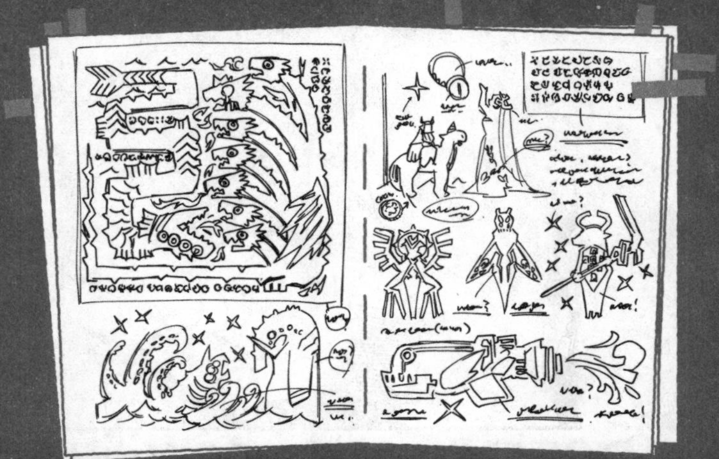

Sorry For My Familiar

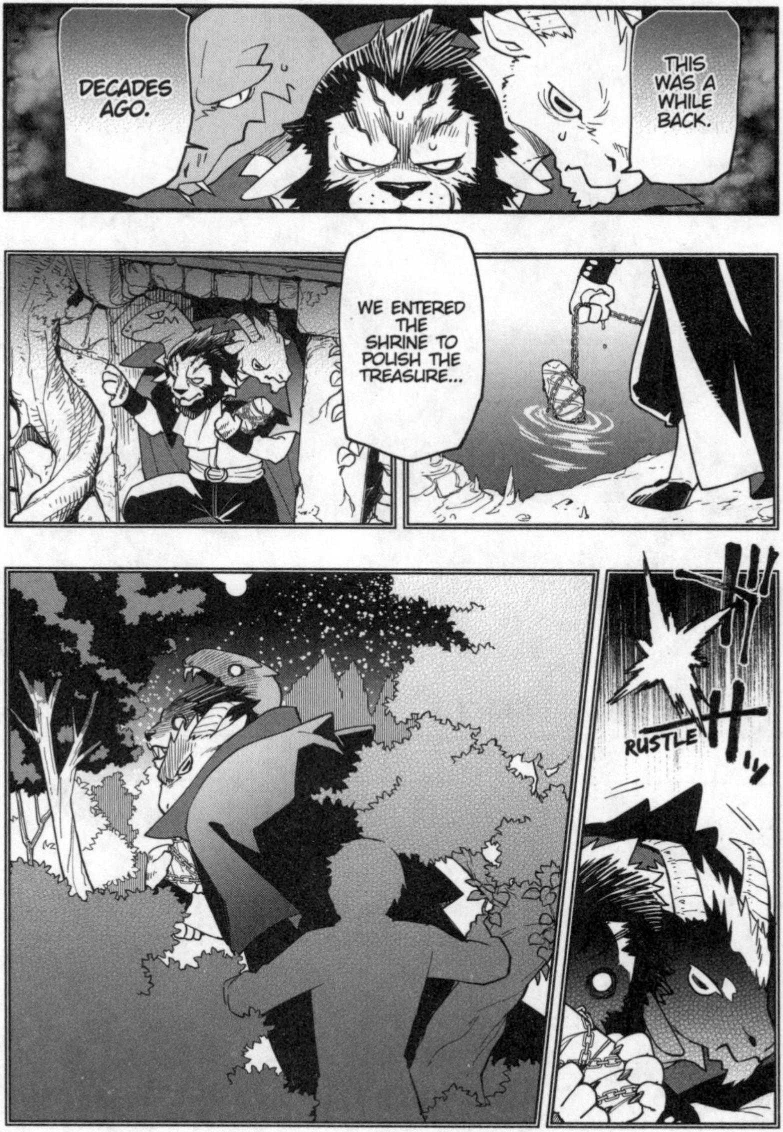
THIS WAS A WHILE BACK.
DECADES AGO.
WE ENTERED THE SHRINE TO POLISH THE TREASURE...
RUSTLE

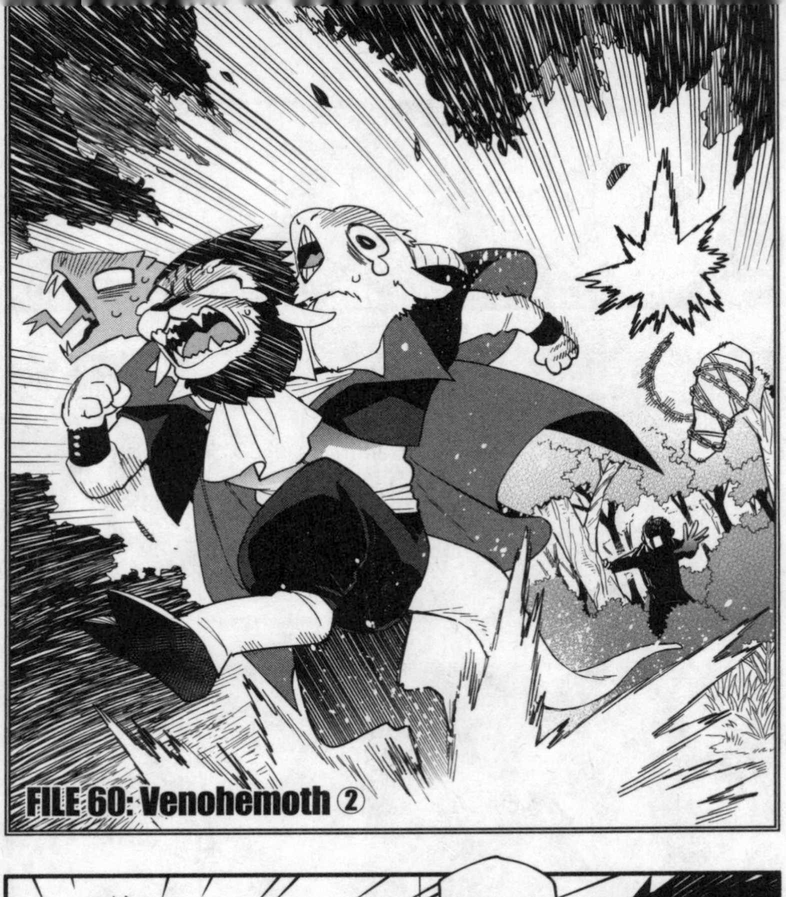
FILE 60: Venohemoth ②

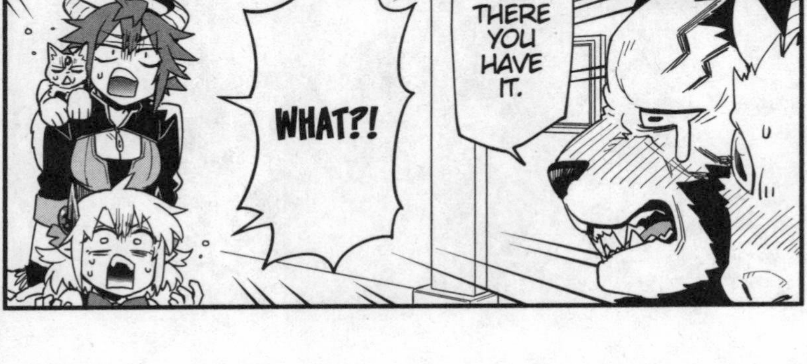
AND THERE YOU HAVE IT.
WHAT?!

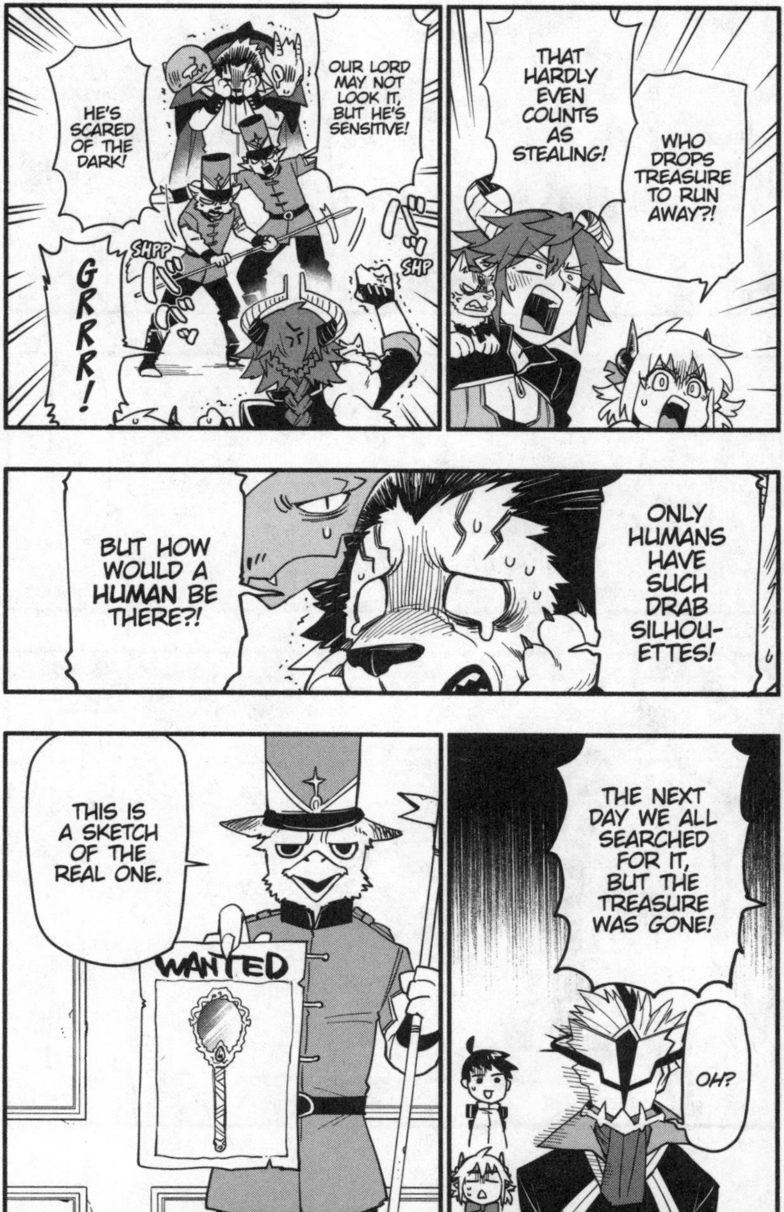
WHO DROPS TREASURE TO RUN AWAY?!
THAT HARDLY EVEN COUNTS AS STEALING!
OUR LORD MAY NOT LOOK IT, BUT HE'S SENSITIVE!
HE'S SCARED OF THE DARK!
SHP
SHPP
GRRR!
ONLY HUMANS HAVE SUCH DRAB SILHOU-ETTES!
BUT HOW WOULD A HUMAN BE THERE?!
THE NEXT DAY WE ALL SEARCHED FOR IT, BUT THE TREASURE WAS GONE!
OH?
THIS IS A SKETCH OF THE REAL ONE.
WANTED

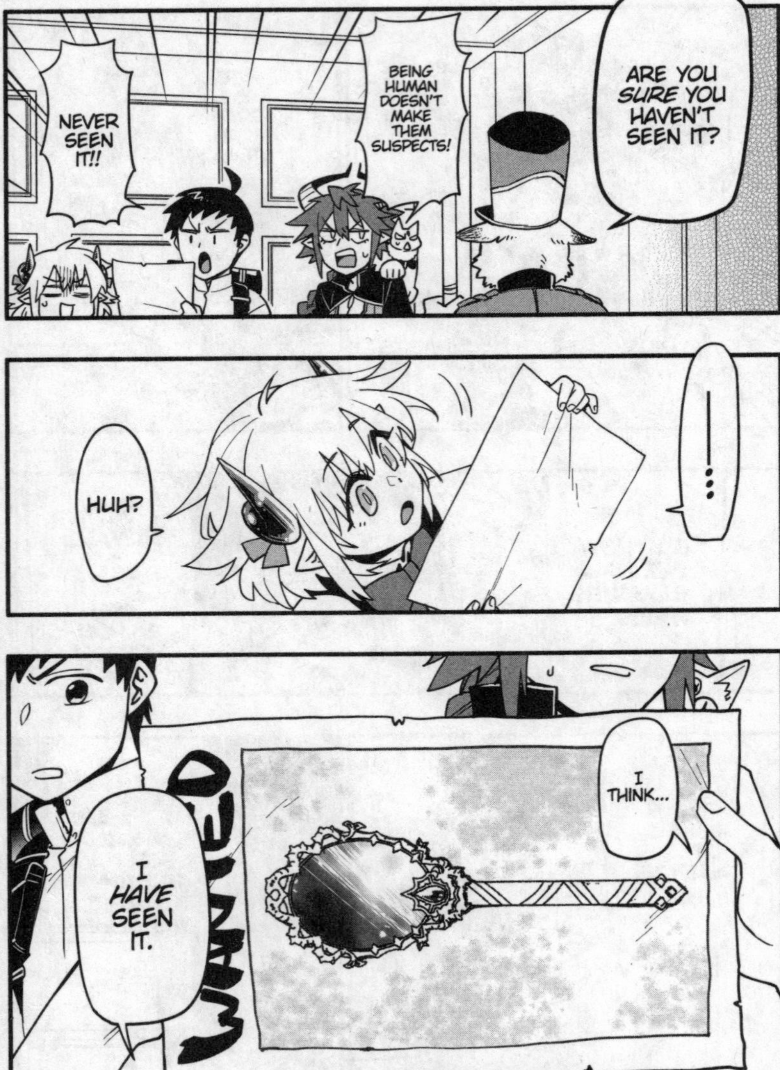
ARE YOU SURE YOU HAVEN'T SEEN IT?
BEING HUMAN DOESN'T MAKE THEM SUSPECTS!
NEVER SEEN IT!!
......
HUH?
I THINK...
I HAVE SEEN IT.

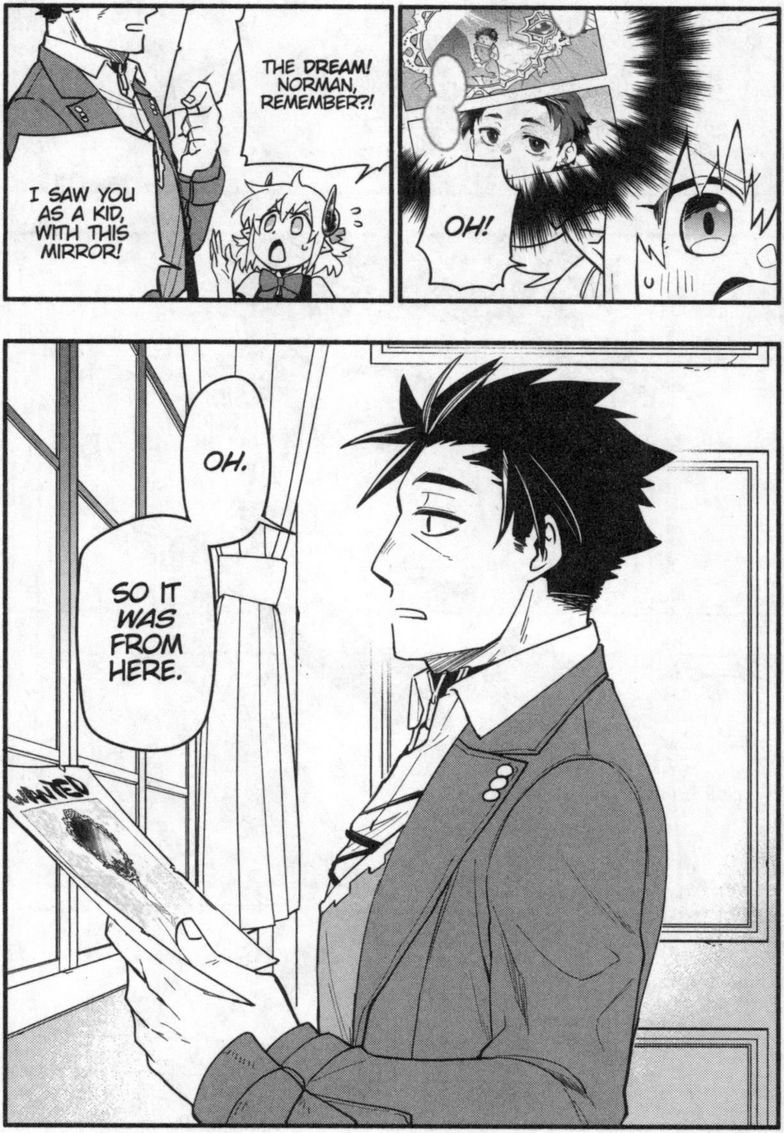
THE DREAM! NORMAN, REMEMBER?!
I SAW YOU AS A KID, WITH THIS MIRROR!
OH!
OH.
SO IT WAS FROM HERE.

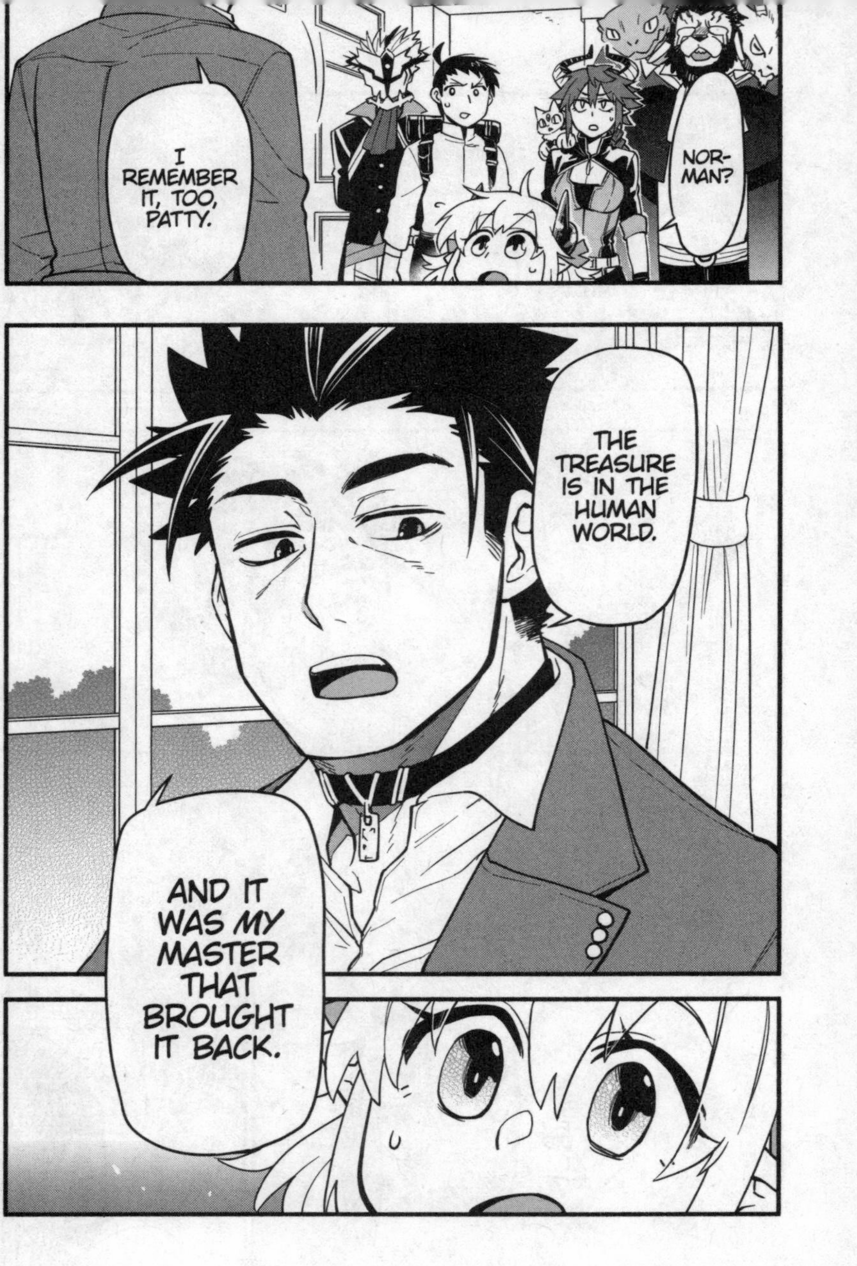
NOR-MAN?
I REMEMBER IT, TOO, PATTY.
THE TREASURE IS IN THE HUMAN WORLD.
AND IT WAS *MY* MASTER THAT BROUGHT IT BACK.

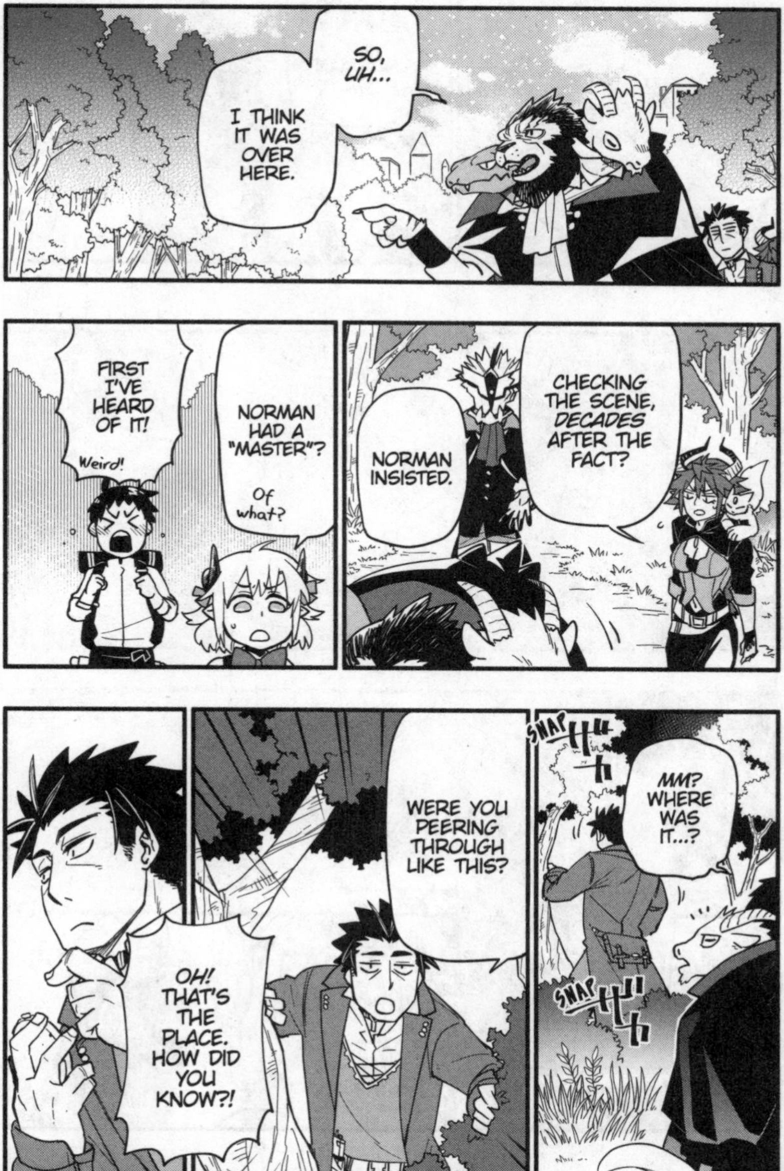
SO, UH...
I THINK IT WAS OVER HERE.
CHECKING THE SCENE, DECADES AFTER THE FACT?
NORMAN INSISTED.
NORMAN HAD A "MASTER"?
Of what?
FIRST I'VE HEARD OF IT!
Weird!
SNAP
MM? WHERE WAS IT...?
SNAP
WERE YOU PEERING THROUGH LIKE THIS?
OH! THAT'S THE PLACE. HOW DID YOU KNOW?!

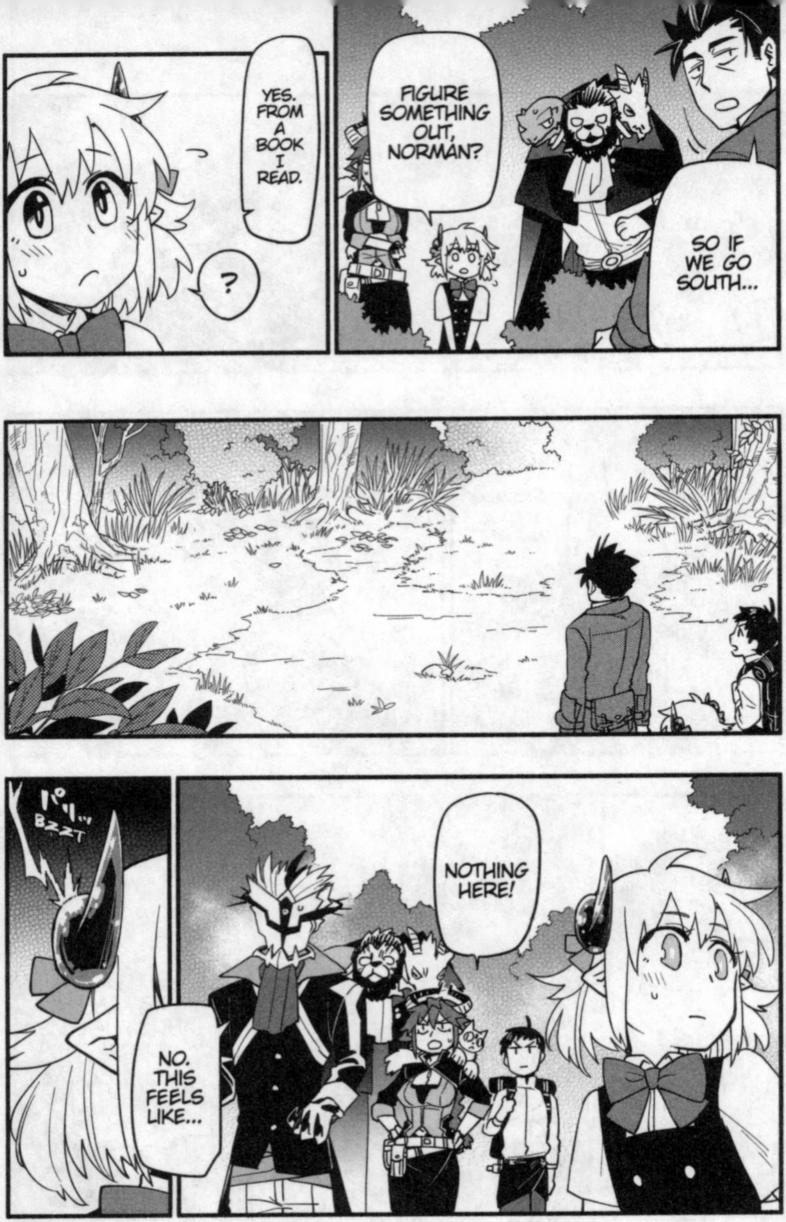
SO IF WE GO SOUTH...
FIGURE SOMETHING OUT, NORMAN?
YES. FROM A BOOK I READ.
?
NOTHING HERE!
パリッ
BZZT
NO. THIS FEELS LIKE...

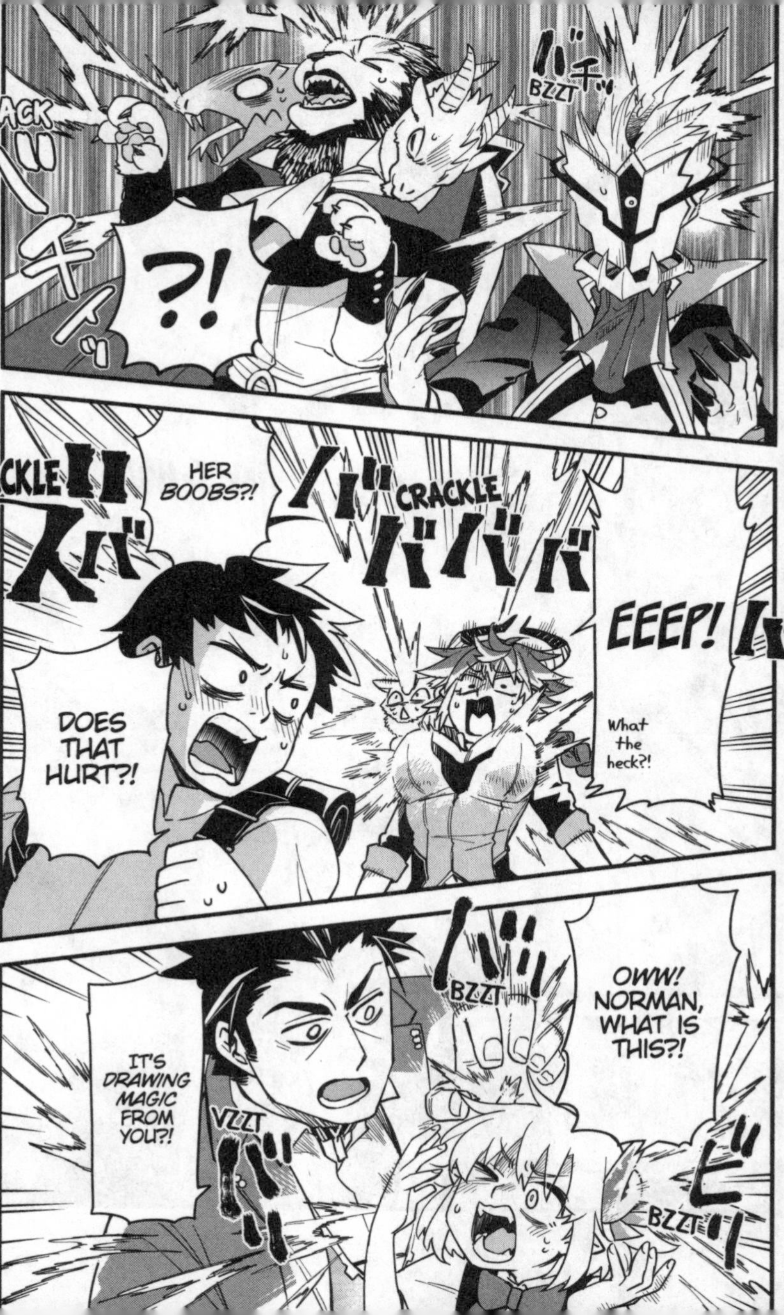

バチッ
BZZT
CRACK
バチィッ
?!
CRACKLE
スパ
HER BOOBS?!
CRACKLE
バババババ
EEEP!
What the heck?!
DOES THAT HURT?!
バリ
BZZT
OWW! NORMAN, WHAT IS THIS?!
IT'S DRAWING MAGIC FROM YOU?!
VZZT
ビ
BZZT

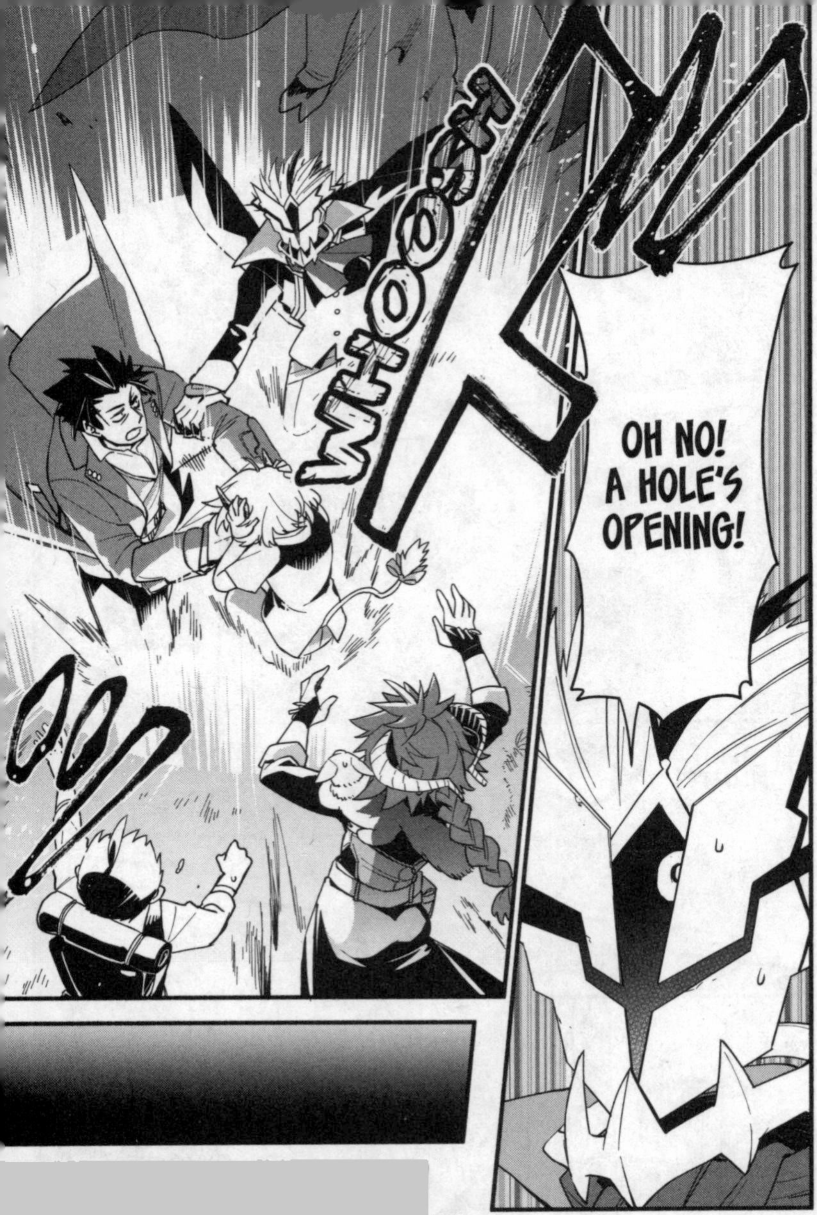
WHOOOSH
OH NO! A HOLE'S OPENING!

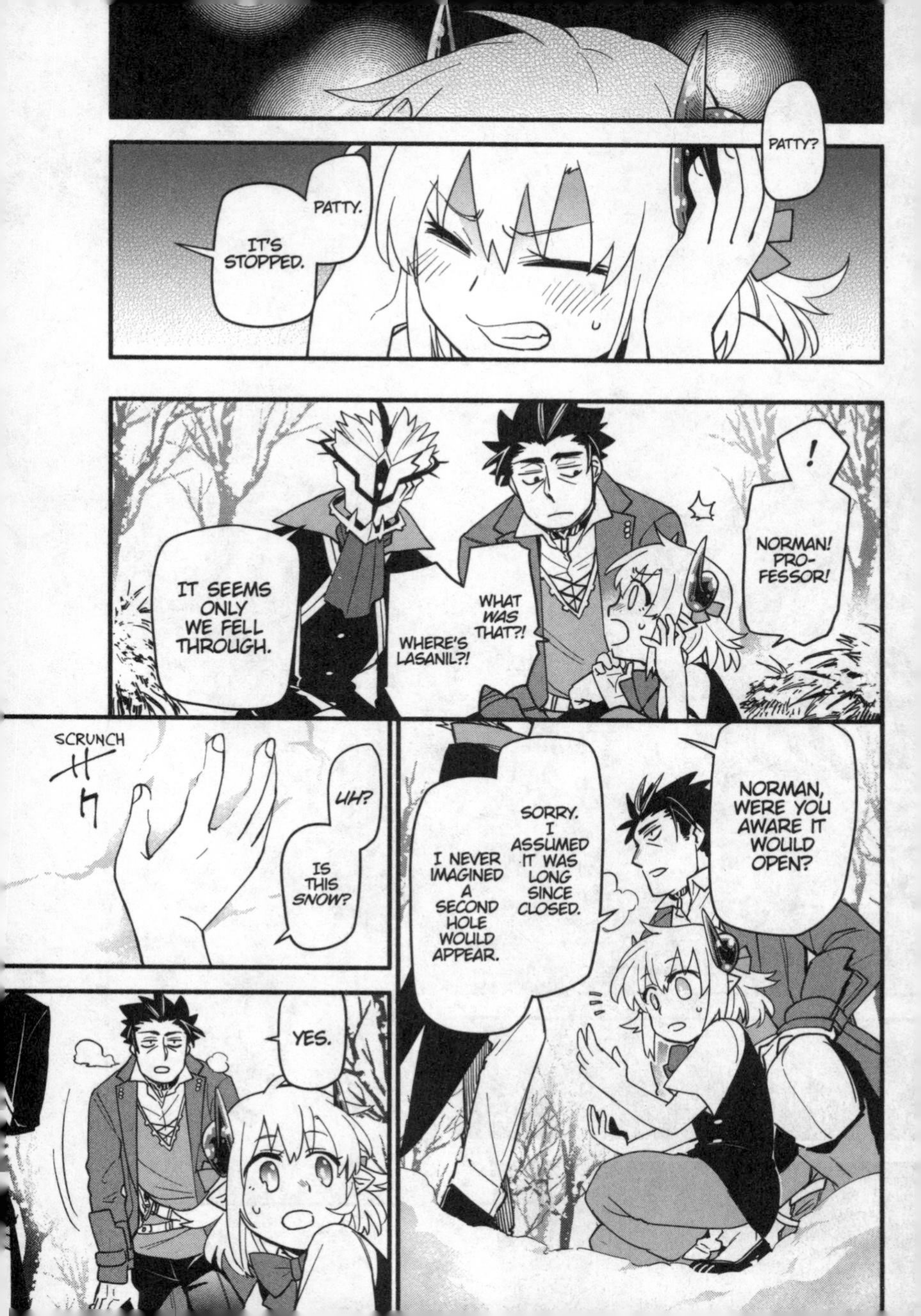
PATTY?
PATTY.
IT'S STOPPED.
NORMAN! PRO-FESSOR!
WHAT WAS THAT?!
WHERE'S LASANIL?!
IT SEEMS ONLY WE FELL THROUGH.
SCRUNCH
UH?
IS THIS SNOW?
NORMAN, WERE YOU AWARE IT WOULD OPEN?
SORRY. I ASSUMED IT WAS LONG SINCE CLOSED.
I NEVER IMAGINED A SECOND HOLE WOULD APPEAR.
YES.

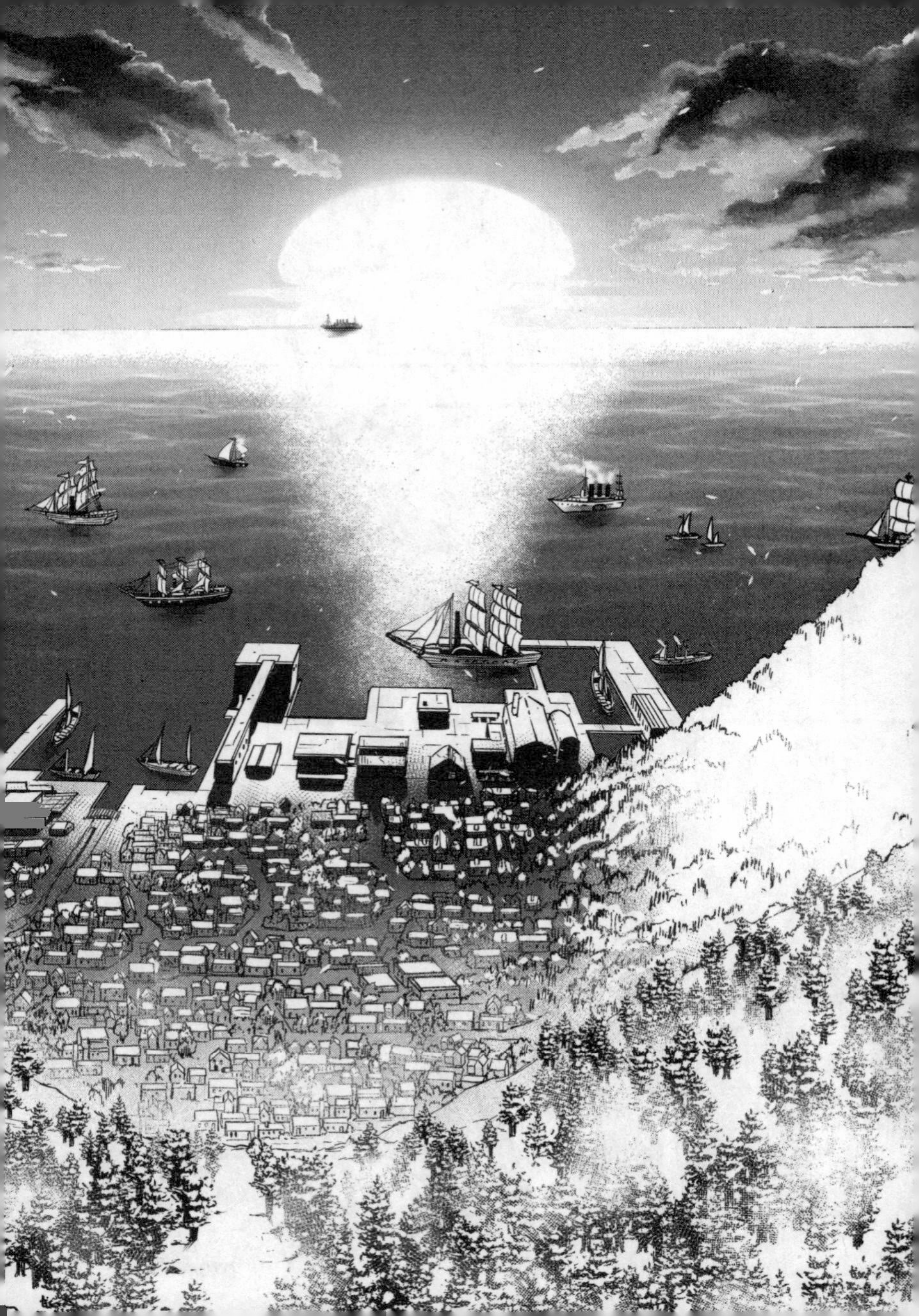

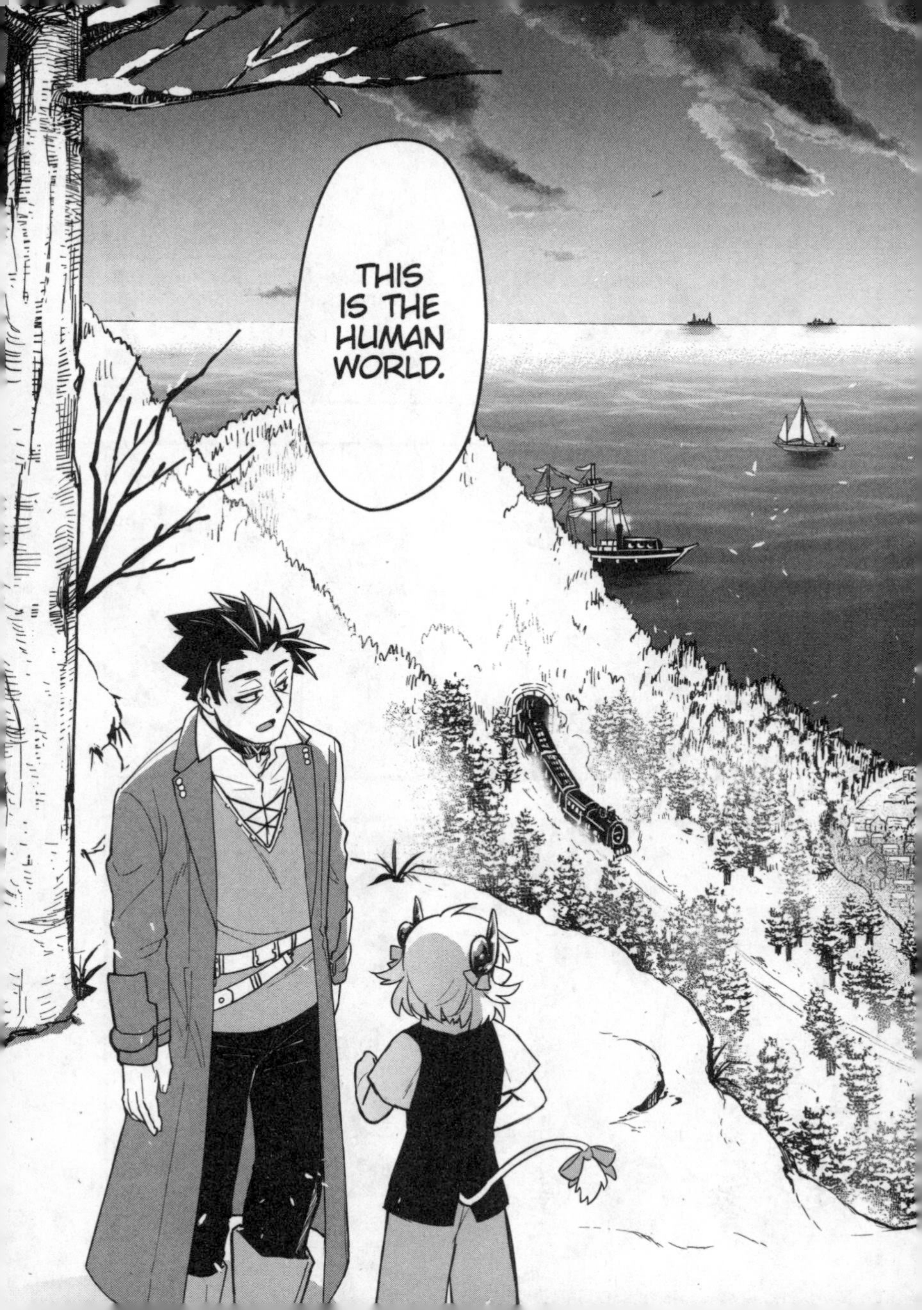
THIS IS THE HUMAN WORLD.

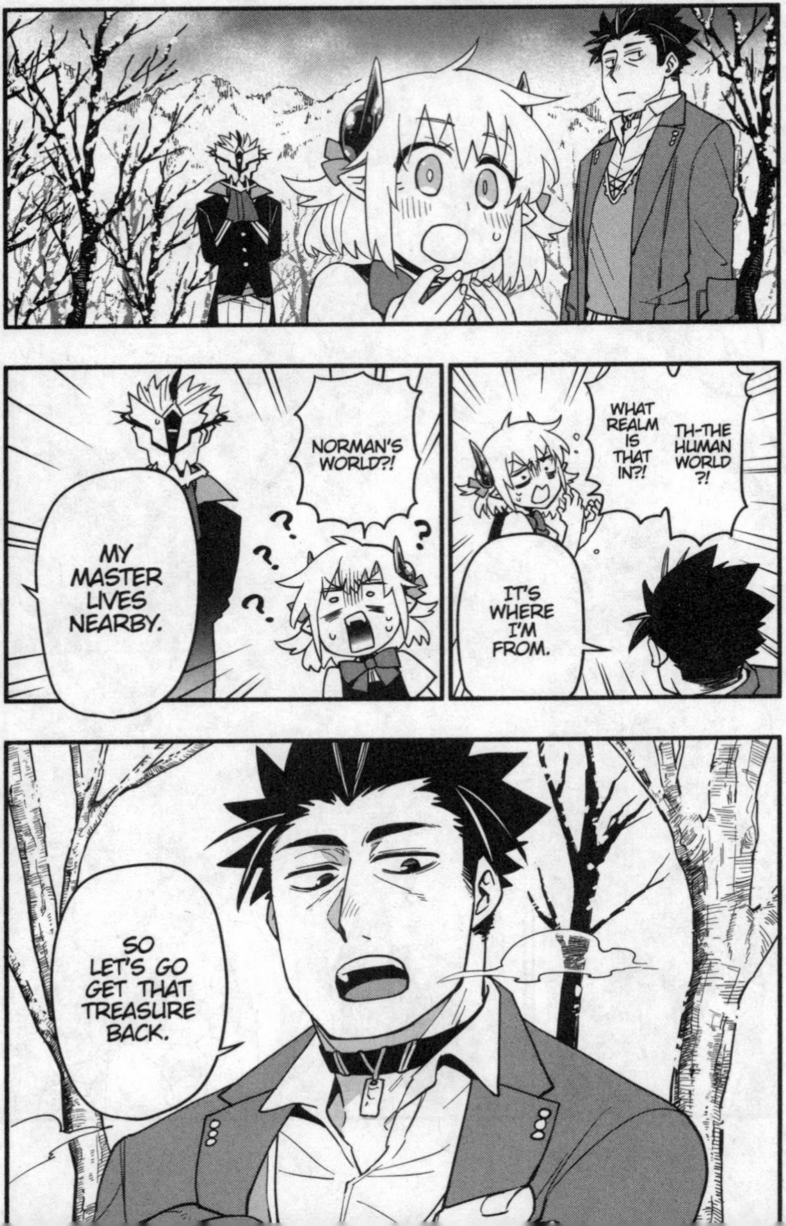
WHAT REALM IS THAT IN?!
IT'S WHERE I'M FROM.
TH-THE HUMAN WORLD?!
NORMAN'S WORLD?!
MY MASTER LIVES NEARBY.
SO LET'S GO GET THAT TREASURE BACK.

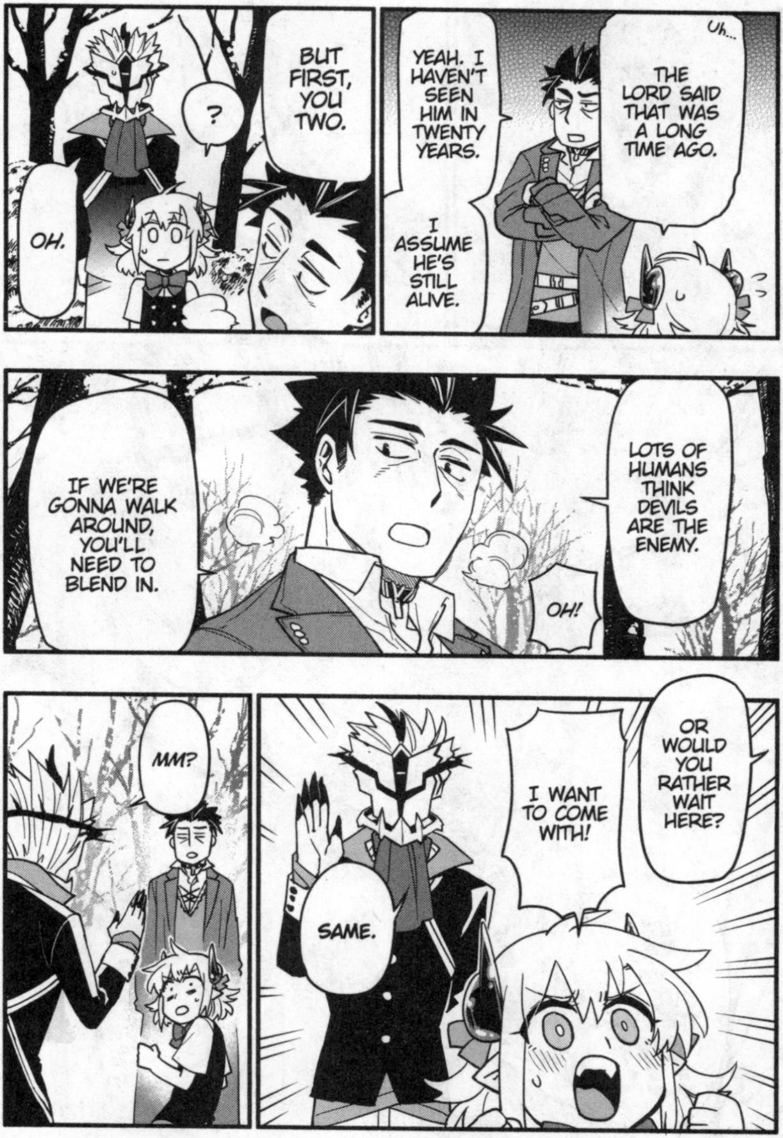
Uh...
THE LORD SAID THAT WAS A LONG TIME AGO.
YEAH. I HAVEN'T SEEN HIM IN TWENTY YEARS.
I ASSUME HE'S STILL ALIVE.
BUT FIRST, YOU TWO.
?
OH.
LOTS OF HUMANS THINK DEVILS ARE THE ENEMY.
OH!
IF WE'RE GONNA WALK AROUND, YOU'LL NEED TO BLEND IN.
OR WOULD YOU RATHER WAIT HERE?
I WANT TO COME WITH!
SAME.
MM?

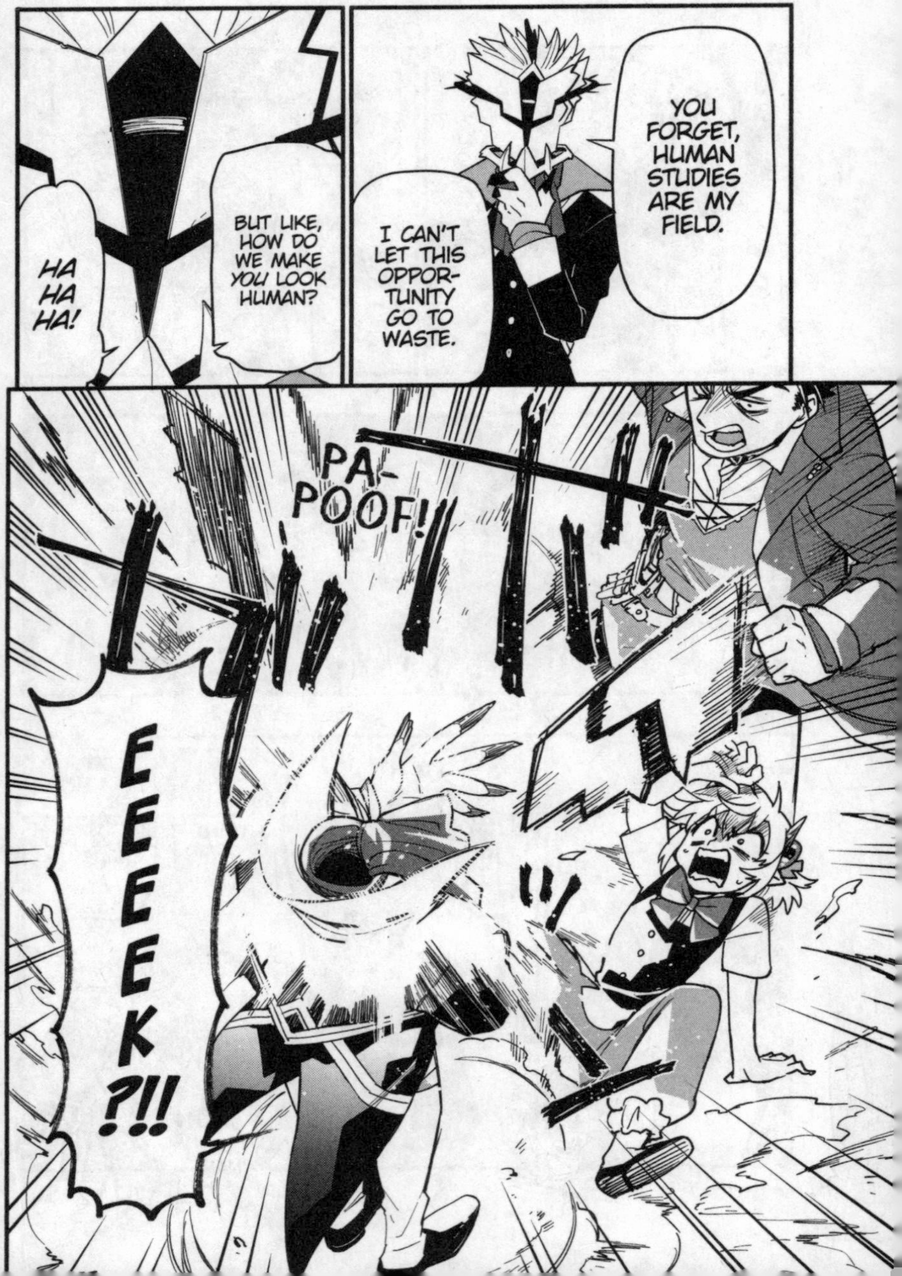
YOU FORGET, HUMAN STUDIES ARE MY FIELD.
I CAN'T LET THIS OPPOR-TUNITY GO TO WASTE.
BUT LIKE, HOW DO WE MAKE YOU LOOK HUMAN?
HA HA HA!
PA-POOF!
!!
EEEEK?!!

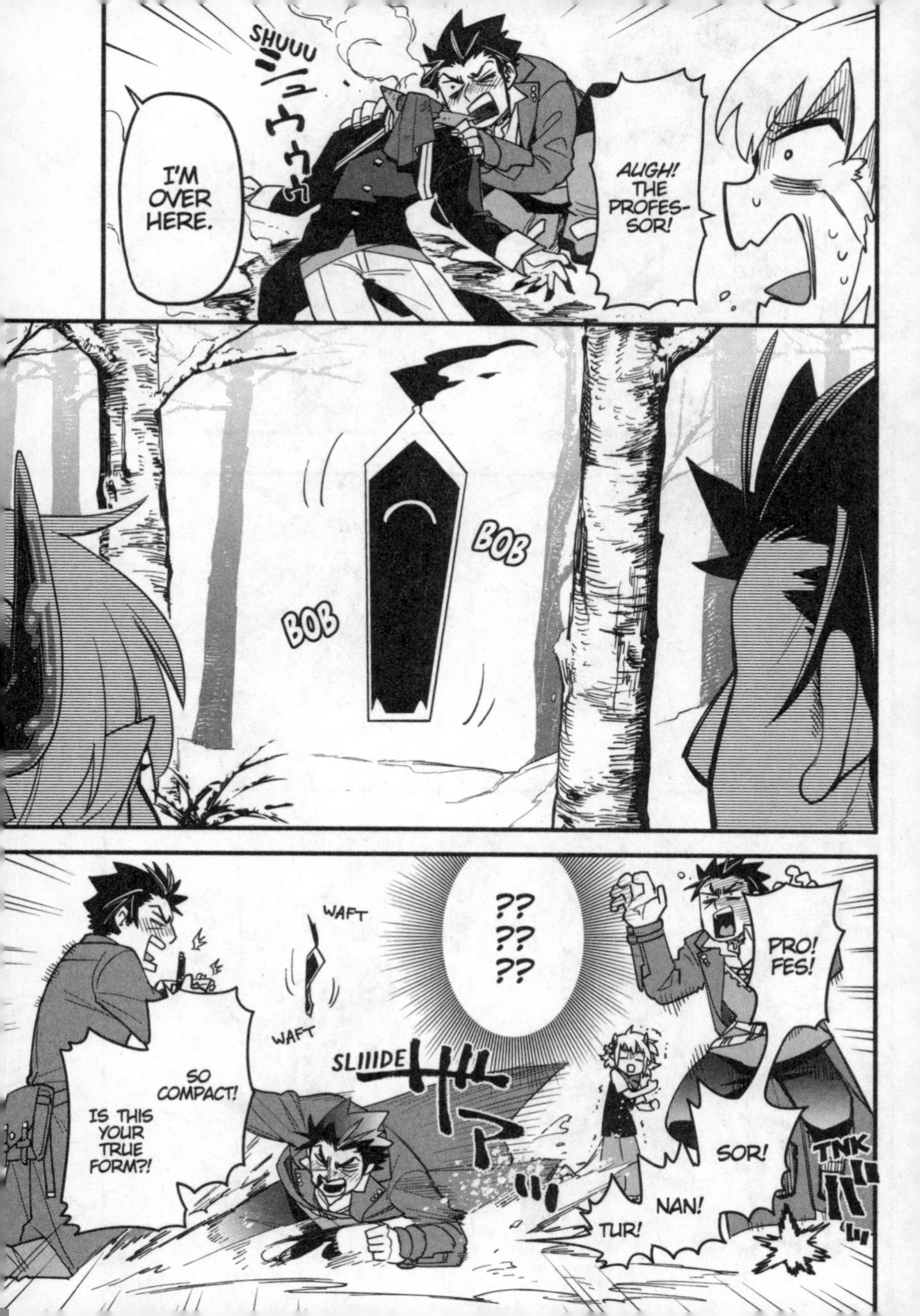

AUGH! THE PROFES-SOR!
SHUUU
I'M OVER HERE.
BOB
BOB
PRO! FES!
SOR!
NAN!
TUR!
TNK
??
??
??
WAFT
WAFT
SLIIIDE
SO COMPACT!
IS THIS YOUR TRUE FORM?!

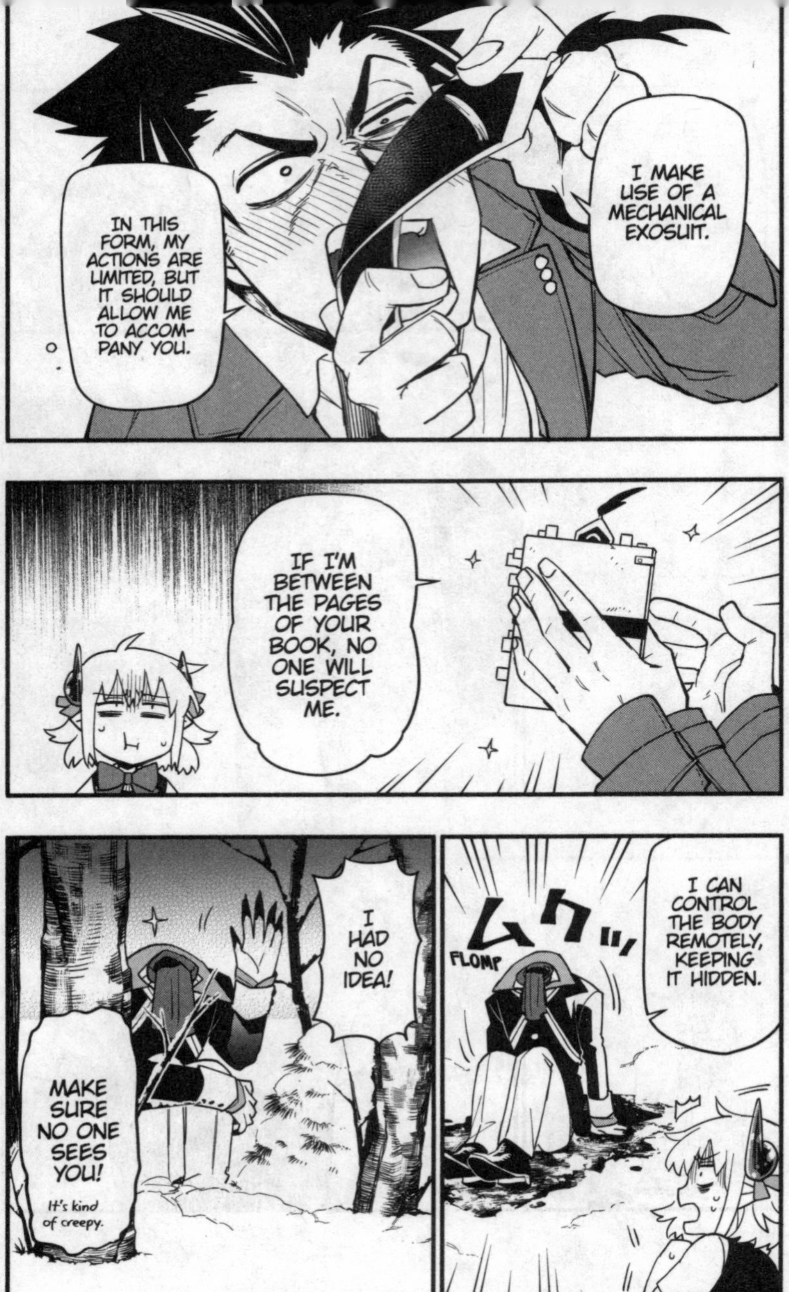

I MAKE USE OF A MECHANICAL EXOSUIT.
IN THIS FORM, MY ACTIONS ARE LIMITED, BUT IT SHOULD ALLOW ME TO ACCOMPANY YOU.
IF I'M BETWEEN THE PAGES OF YOUR BOOK, NO ONE WILL SUSPECT ME.
I CAN CONTROL THE BODY REMOTELY, KEEPING IT HIDDEN.
ムク
FLOMP
I HAD NO IDEA!
MAKE SURE NO ONE SEES YOU!
It's kind of creepy.

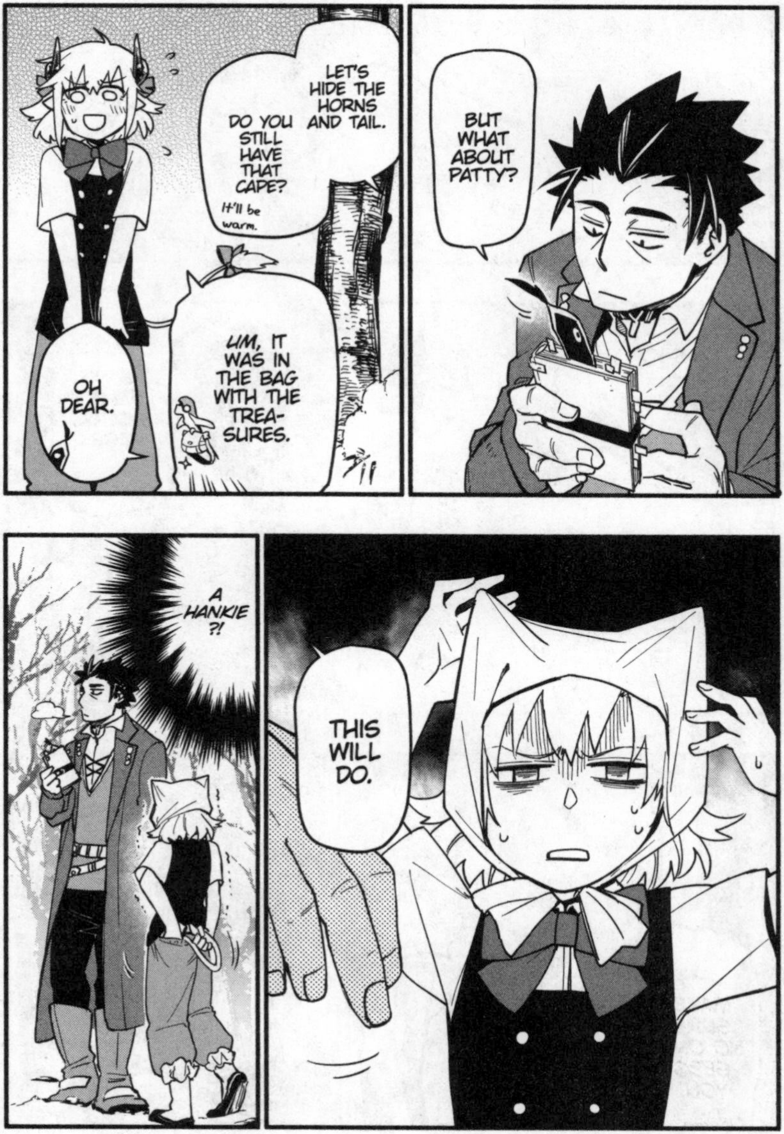

BUT WHAT ABOUT PATTY?
LET'S HIDE THE HORNS AND TAIL.
DO YOU STILL HAVE THAT CAPE?
It'll be warm.
UM, IT WAS IN THE BAG WITH THE TREA-SURES.
OH DEAR.
THIS WILL DO.
A HANKIE ?!

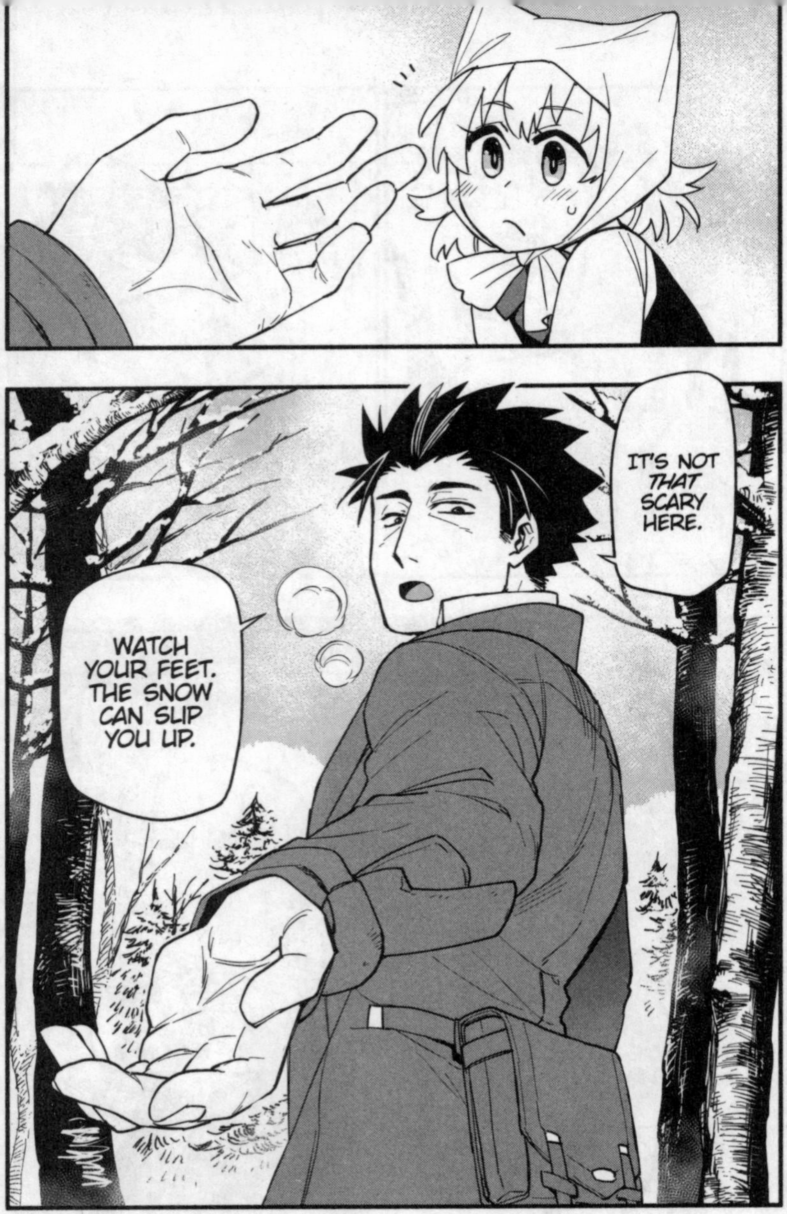
IT'S NOT *THAT* SCARY HERE.
WATCH YOUR FEET. THE SNOW CAN SLIP YOU UP.

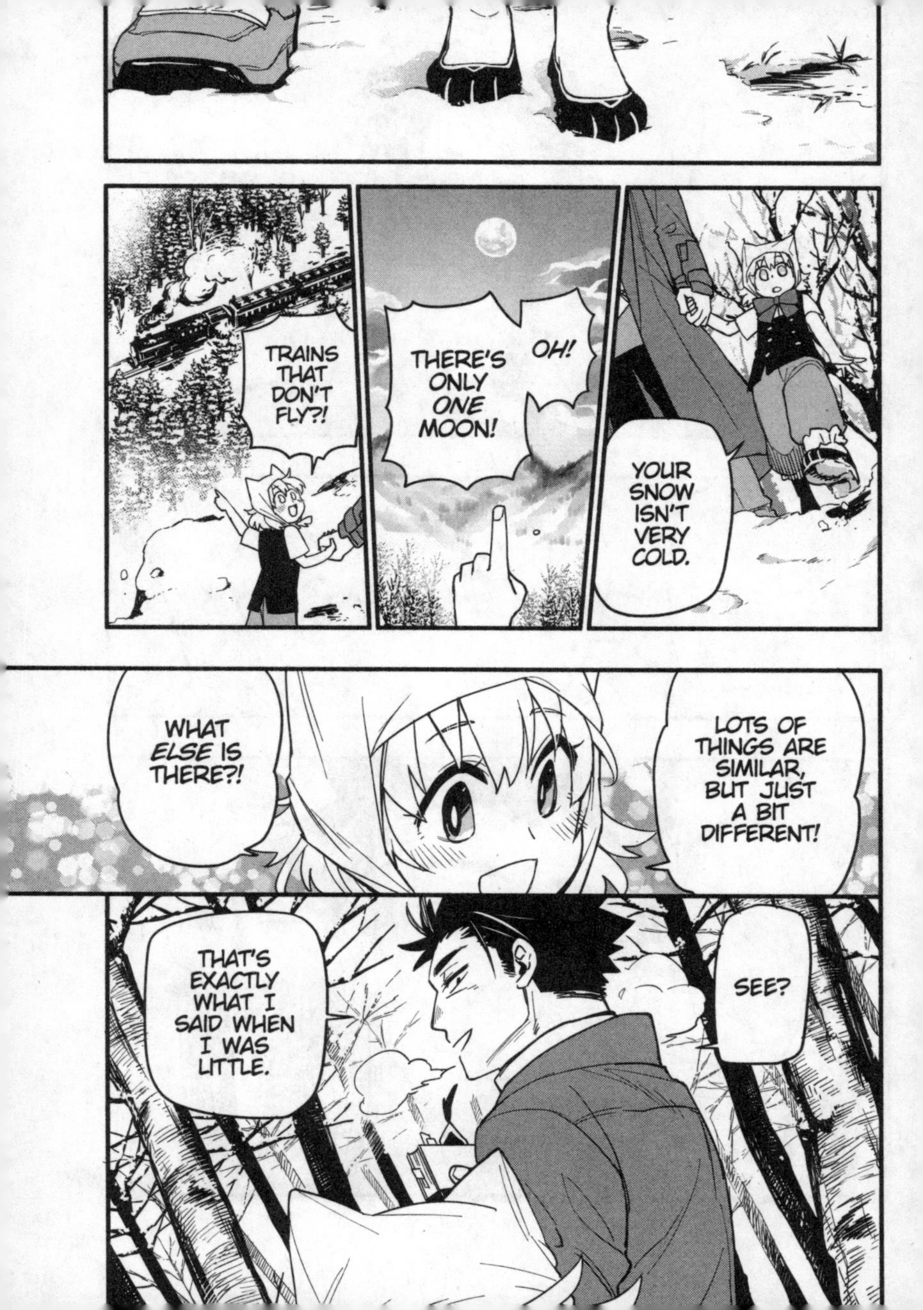
TRAINS THAT DON'T FLY?!
OH!
THERE'S ONLY ONE MOON!
YOUR SNOW ISN'T VERY COLD.
WHAT ELSE IS THERE?!
LOTS OF THINGS ARE SIMILAR, BUT JUST A BIT DIFFERENT!
THAT'S EXACTLY WHAT I SAID WHEN I WAS LITTLE.
SEE?

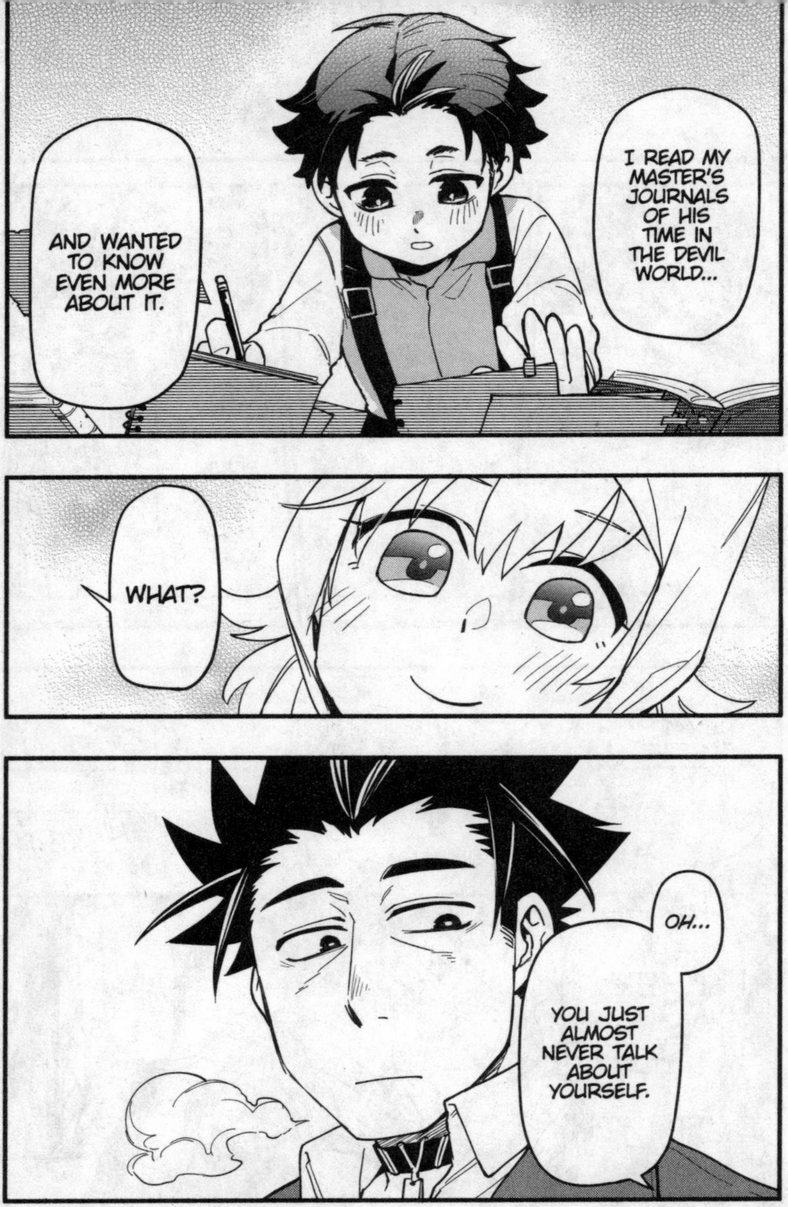
I READ MY MASTER'S JOURNALS OF HIS TIME IN THE DEVIL WORLD...
AND WANTED TO KNOW EVEN MORE ABOUT IT.
WHAT?
OH...
YOU JUST ALMOST NEVER TALK ABOUT YOURSELF.

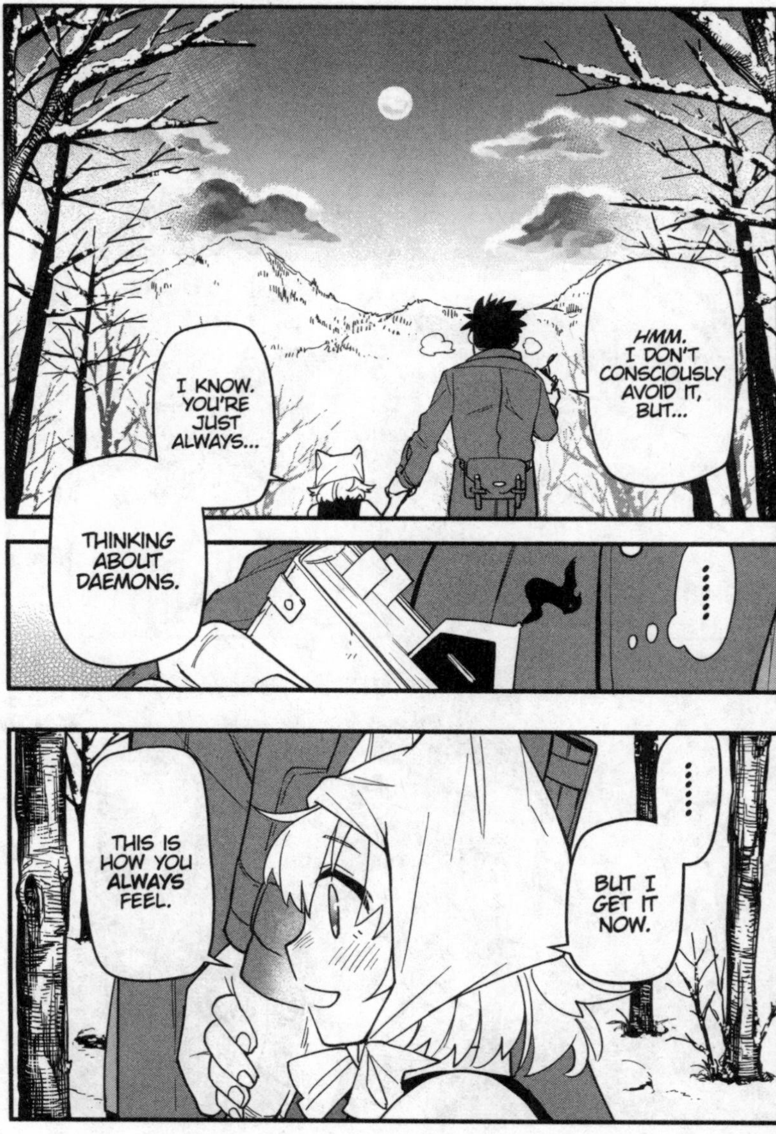
HMM. I DON'T CONSCIOUSLY AVOID IT, BUT...
I KNOW. YOU'RE JUST ALWAYS...
THINKING ABOUT DAEMONS.
......
......
BUT I GET IT NOW.
THIS IS HOW YOU ALWAYS FEEL.

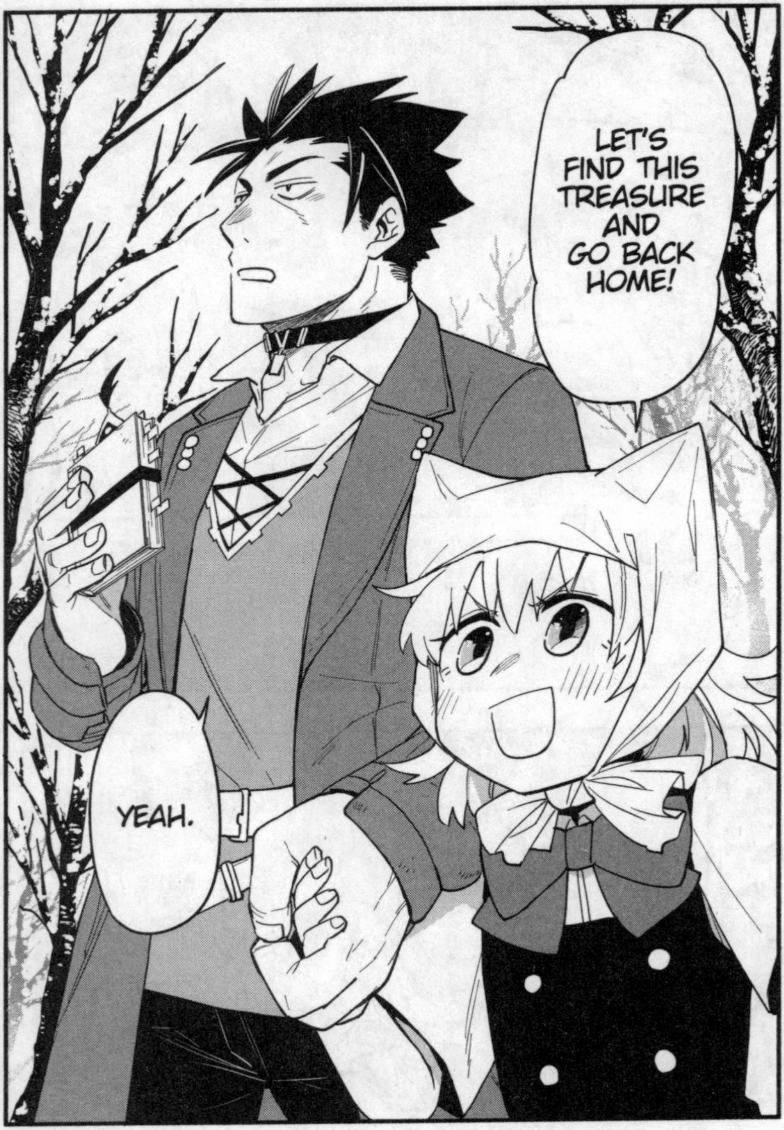
LET'S FIND THIS TREASURE AND GO BACK HOME!
YEAH.

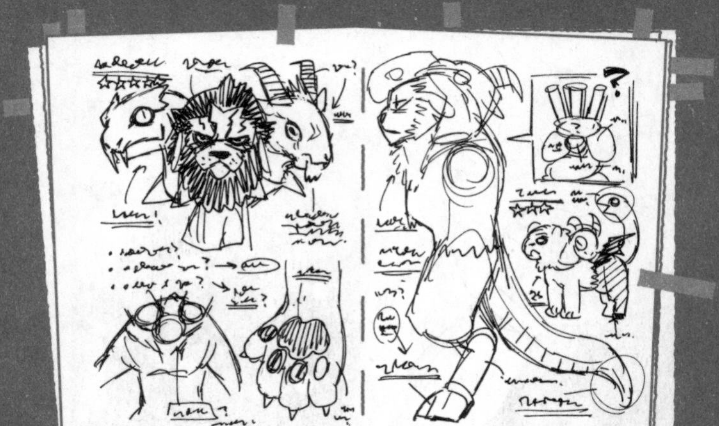

Sorry For My Familiar

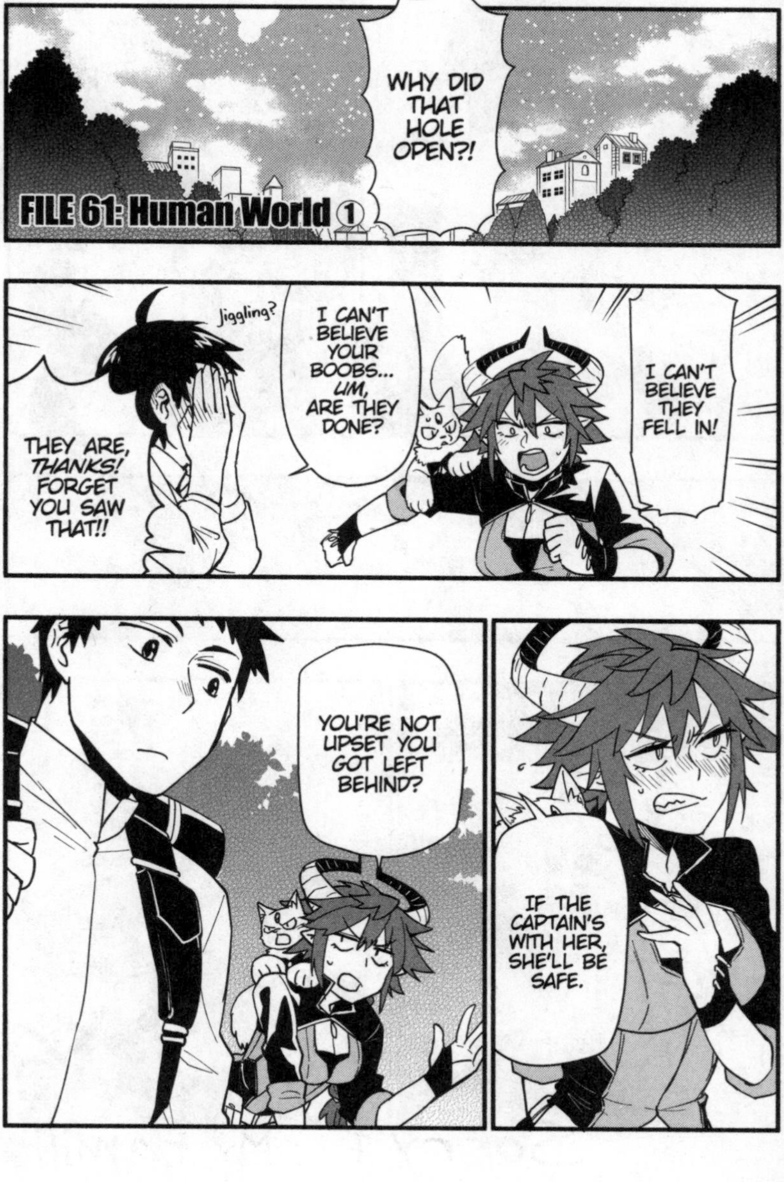
FILE 61: Human World ①
WHY DID THAT HOLE OPEN?!
I CAN'T BELIEVE THEY FELL IN!
I CAN'T BELIEVE YOUR BOOBS... UM, ARE THEY DONE?
jiggling?
THEY ARE, THANKS! FORGET YOU SAW THAT!!
IF THE CAPTAIN'S WITH HER, SHE'LL BE SAFE.
YOU'RE NOT UPSET YOU GOT LEFT BEHIND?

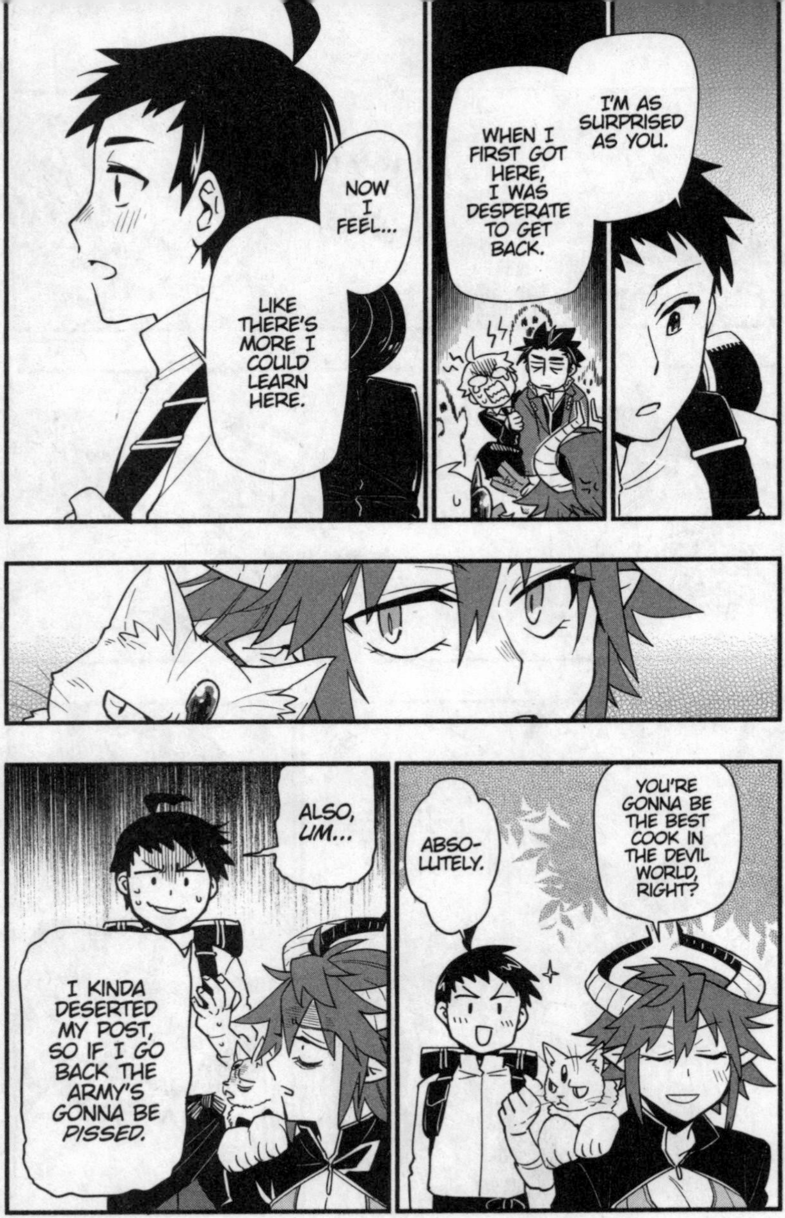
I'M AS SURPRISED AS YOU.
WHEN I FIRST GOT HERE, I WAS DESPERATE TO GET BACK.
NOW I FEEL...
LIKE THERE'S MORE I COULD LEARN HERE.
YOU'RE GONNA BE THE BEST COOK IN THE DEVIL WORLD, RIGHT?
ABSO-LUTELY.
ALSO, UM...
I KINDA DESERTED MY POST, SO IF I GO BACK THE ARMY'S GONNA BE *PISSED.*

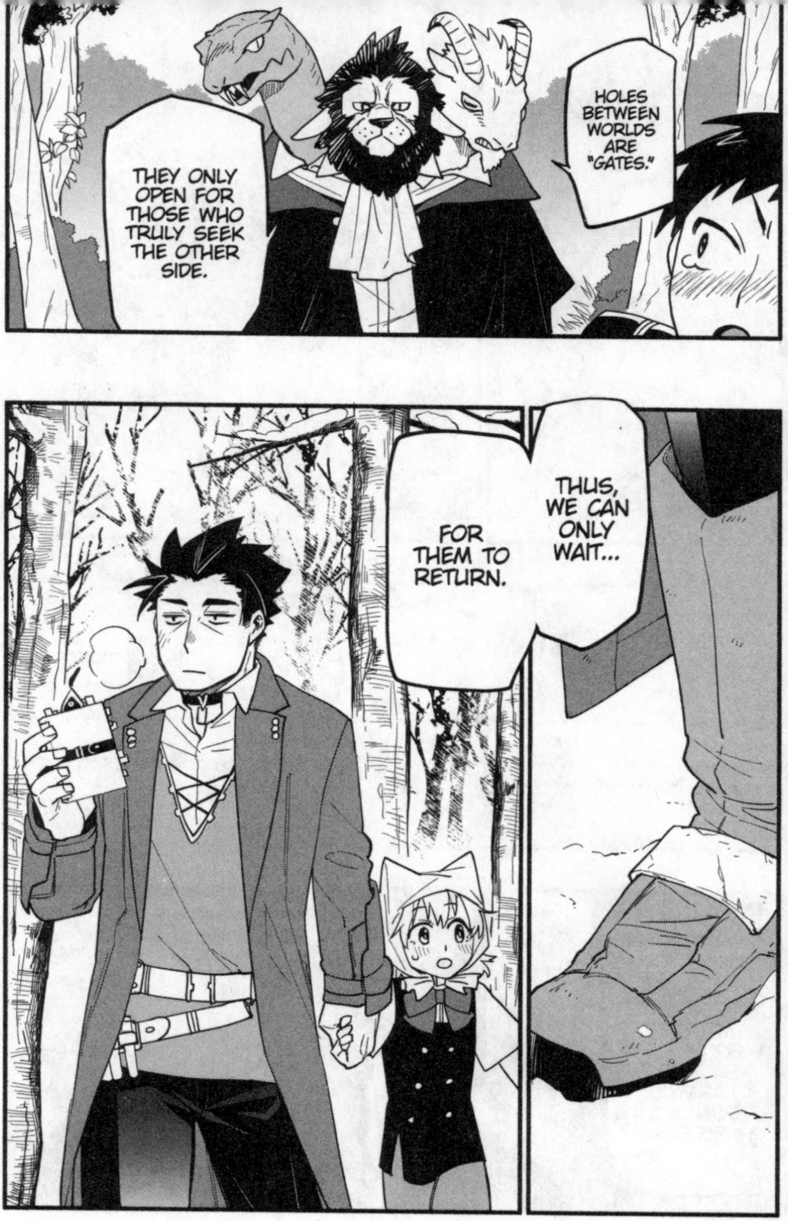
HOLES BETWEEN WORLDS ARE "GATES."
THEY ONLY OPEN FOR THOSE WHO TRULY SEEK THE OTHER SIDE.
THUS, WE CAN ONLY WAIT...
FOR THEM TO RETURN.

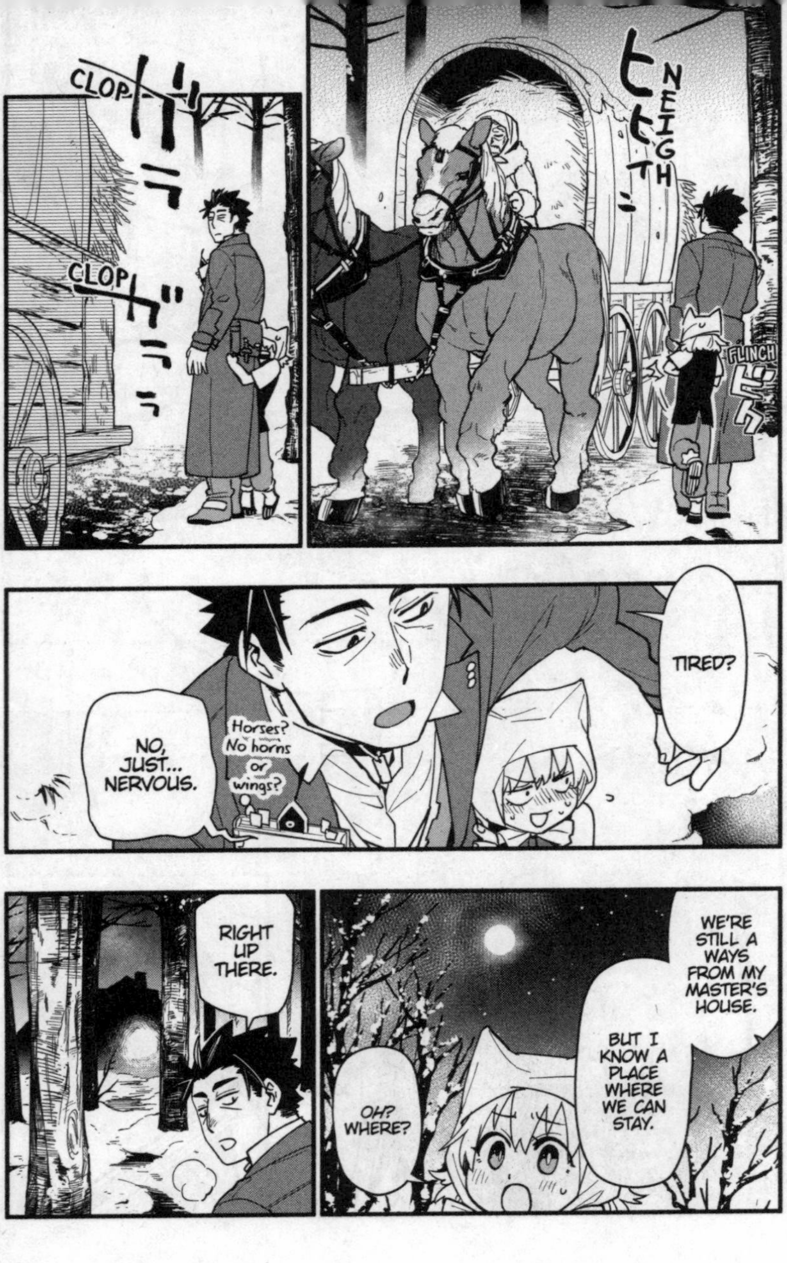
NEIGH
FLINCH
CLOP
CLOP
TIRED?
NO, JUST... NERVOUS.
Horses? No horns or wings?
WE'RE STILL A WAYS FROM MY MASTER'S HOUSE.
BUT I KNOW A PLACE WHERE WE CAN STAY.
OH? WHERE?
RIGHT UP THERE.

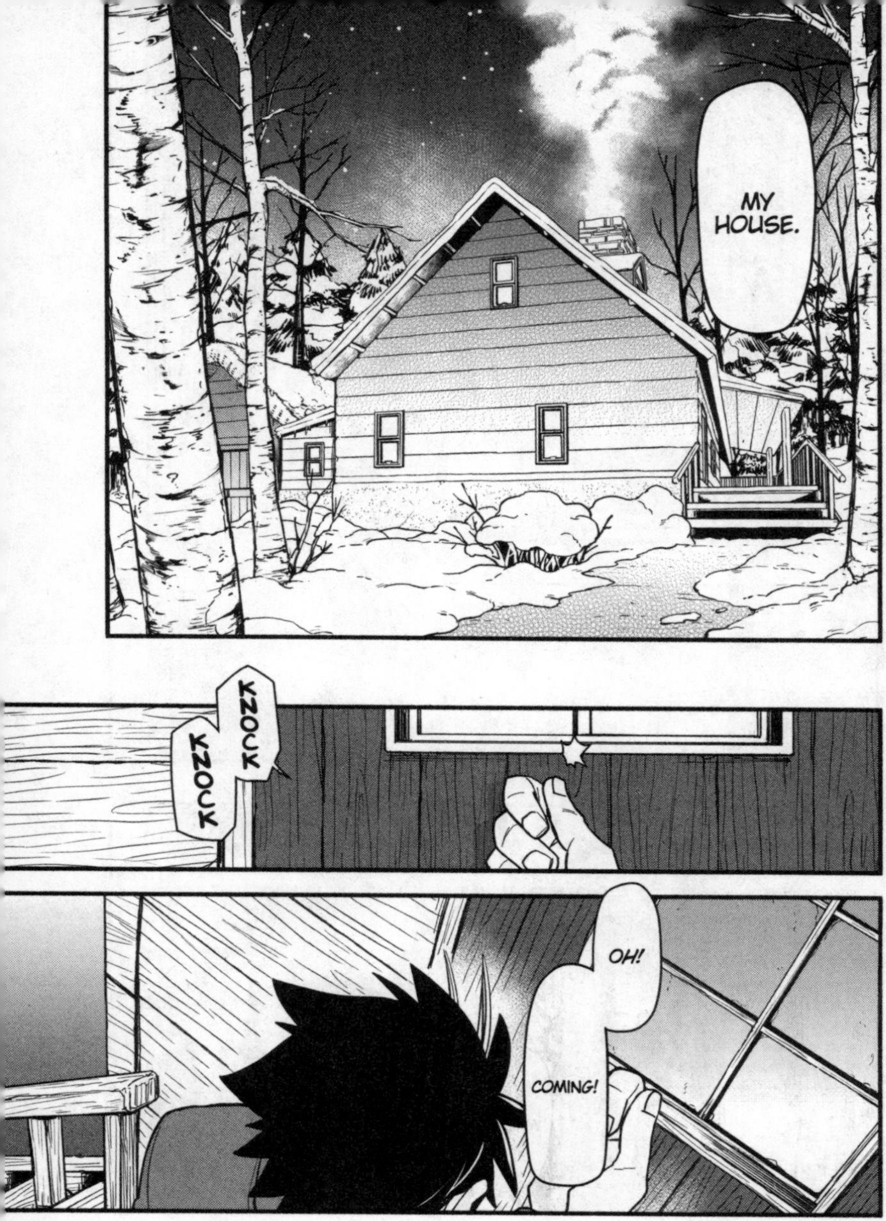
MY HOUSE.
KNOCK
KNOCK
OH!
COMING!

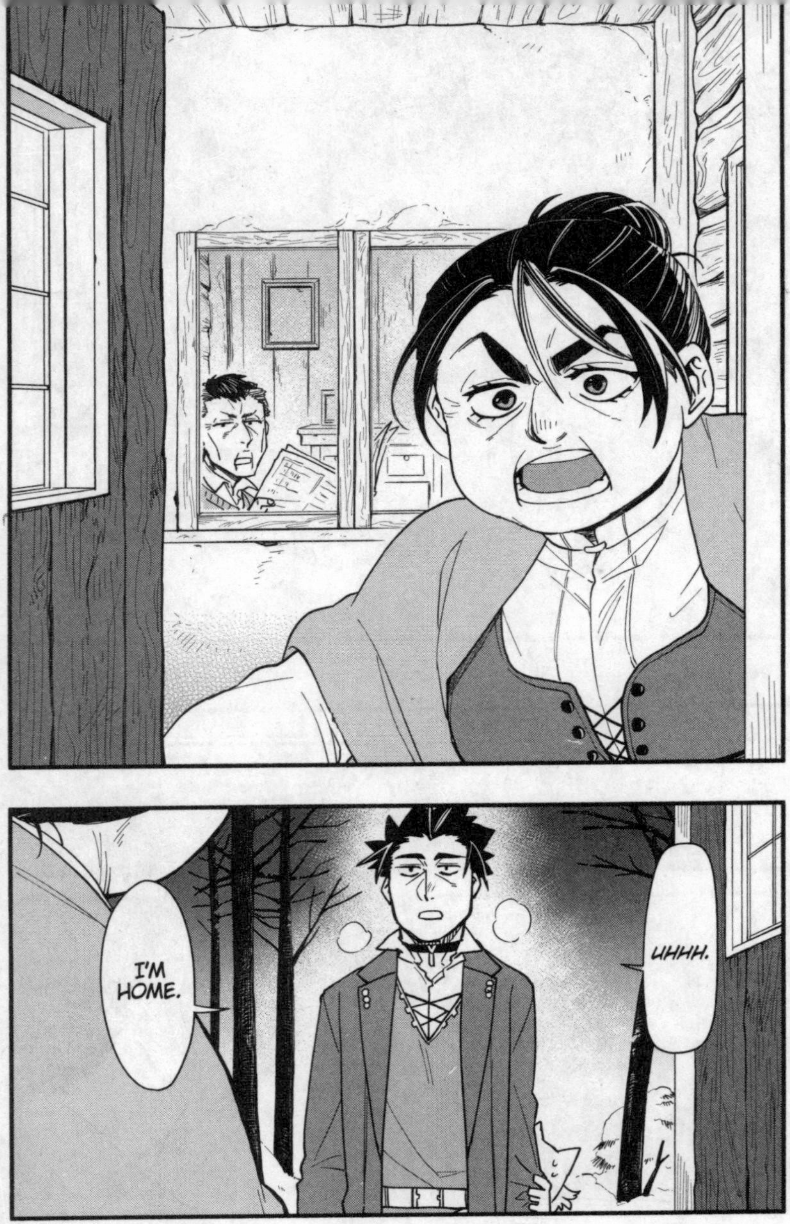
UHHH.
I'M HOME.

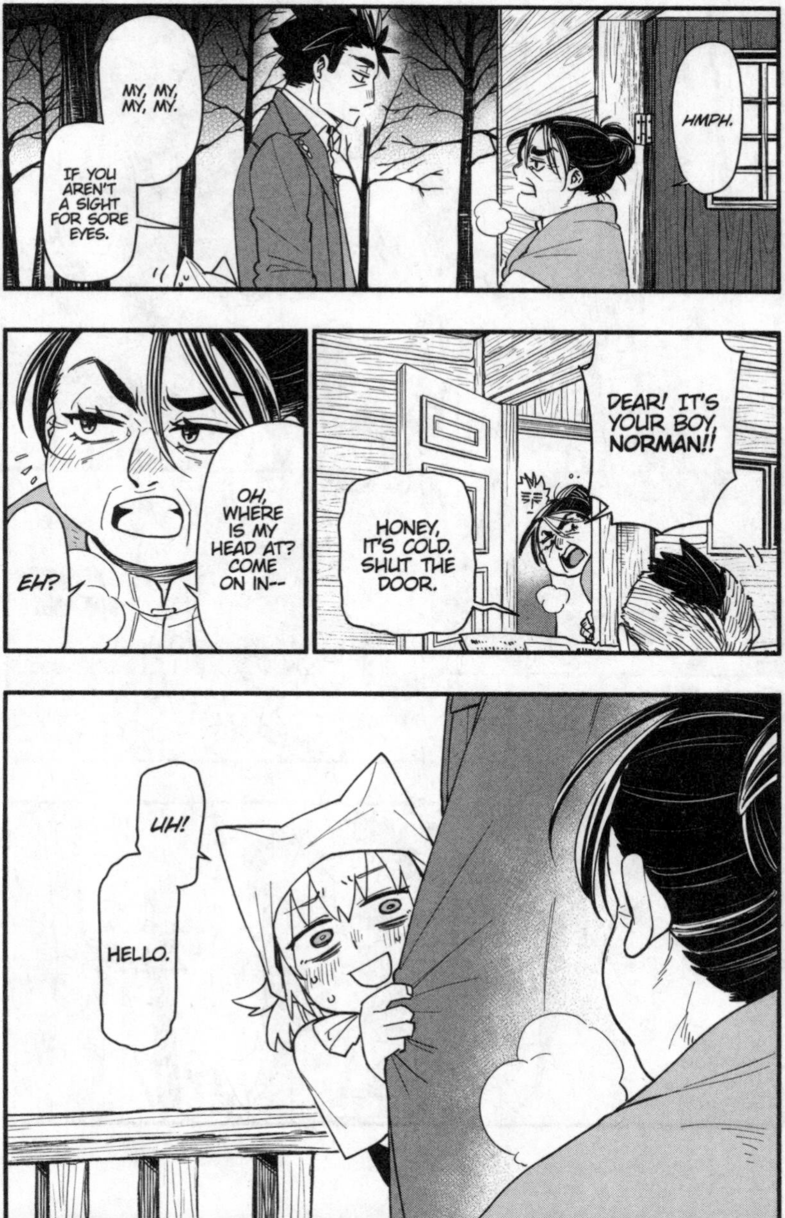
HMPH.
MY, MY, MY, MY.
IF YOU AREN'T A SIGHT FOR SORE EYES.
DEAR! IT'S YOUR BOY, NORMAN!!
HONEY, IT'S COLD. SHUT THE DOOR.
OH, WHERE IS MY HEAD AT? COME ON IN--
EH?
UH!
HELLO.

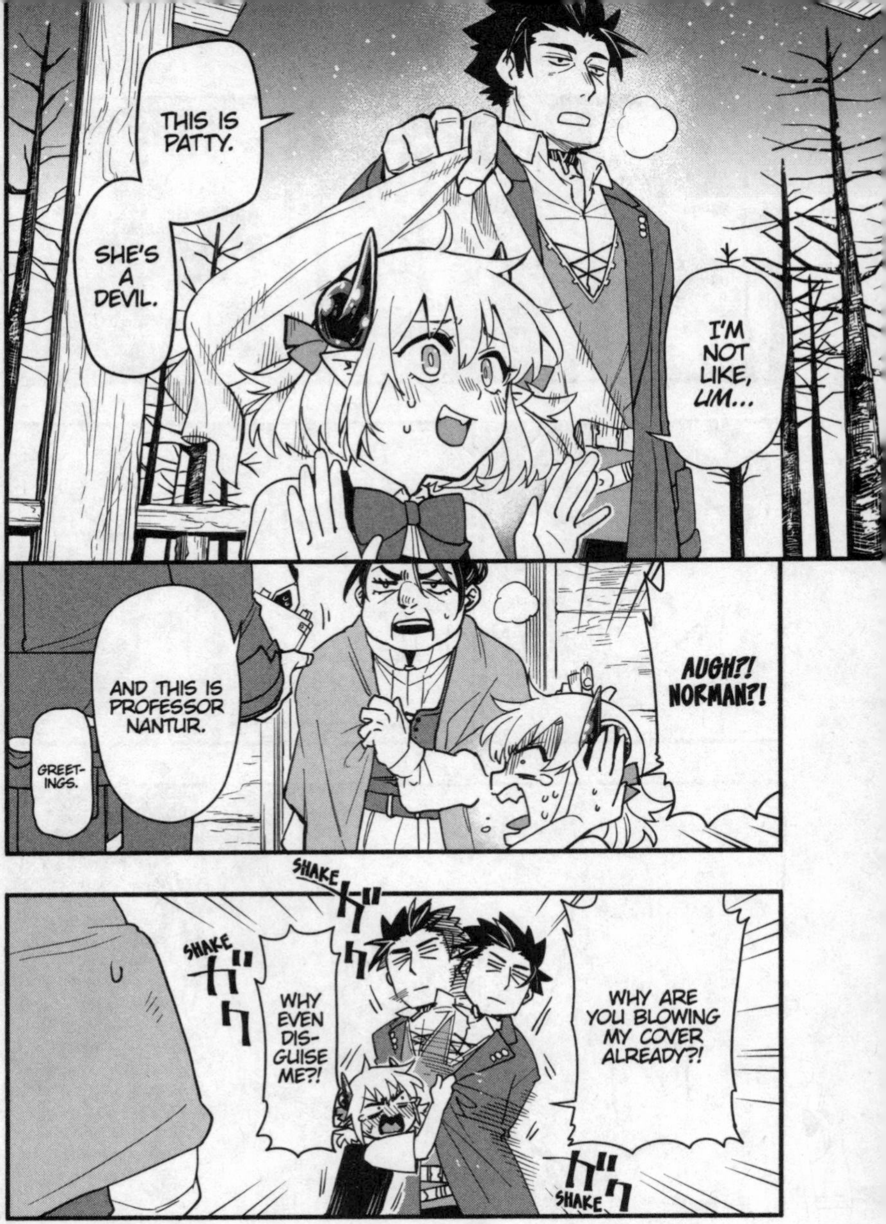
THIS IS PATTY.
SHE'S A DEVIL.
I'M NOT LIKE, UM...
AND THIS IS PROFESSOR NANTUR.
GREET-INGS.
AUGH?! NORMAN?!
SHAKE ガク
WHY ARE YOU BLOWING MY COVER ALREADY?!
SHAKE ガク
WHY EVEN DISGUISE ME?!
ガク SHAKE

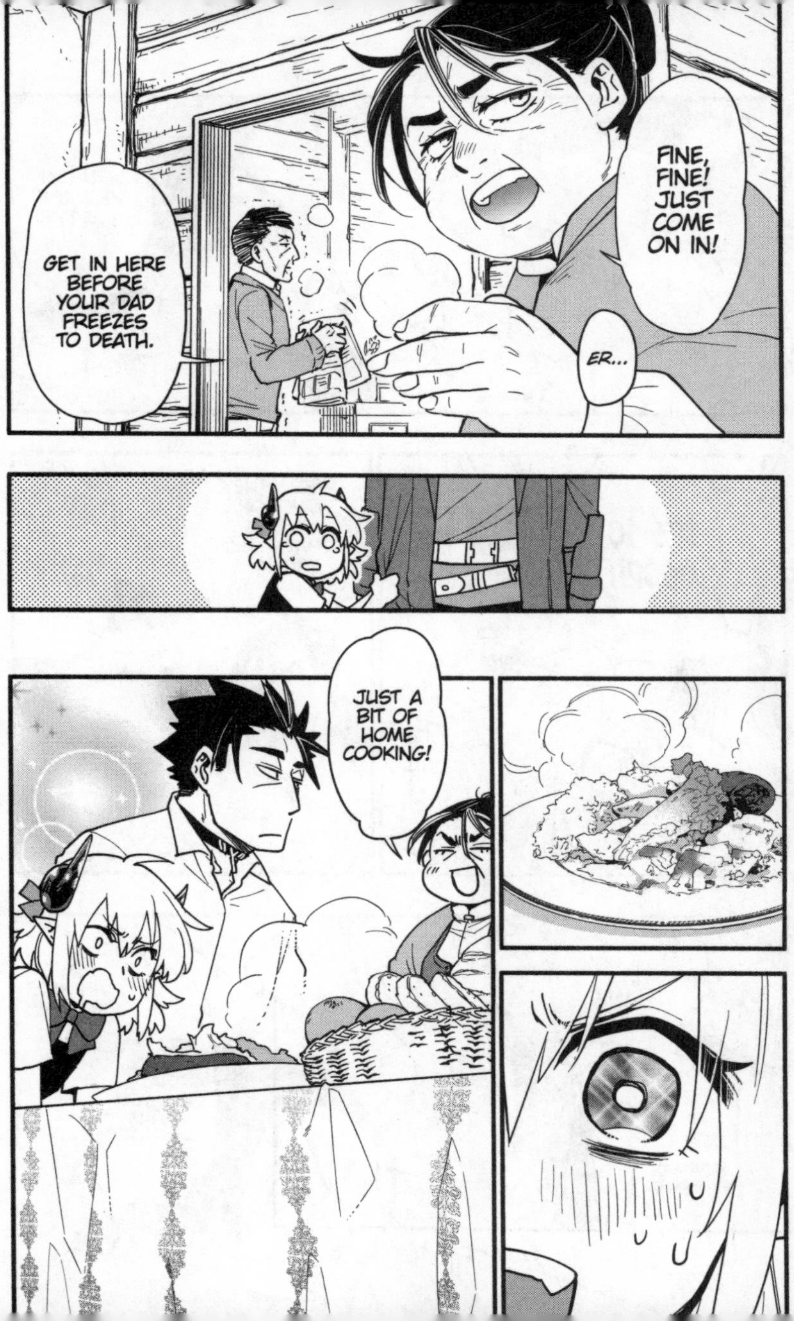
FINE, FINE! JUST COME ON IN!
ER...
GET IN HERE BEFORE YOUR DAD FREEZES TO DEATH.
JUST A BIT OF HOME COOKING!

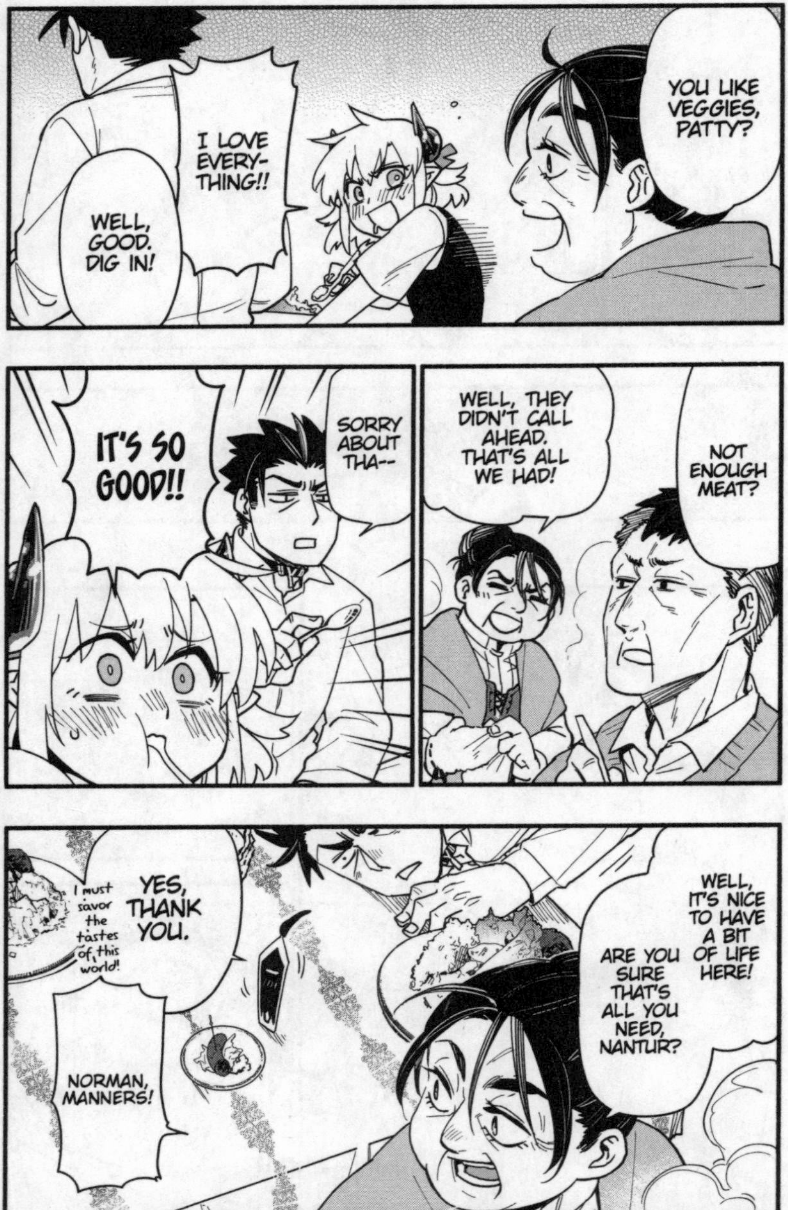
YOU LIKE VEGGIES, PATTY?
I LOVE EVERY-THING!!
WELL, GOOD. DIG IN!
NOT ENOUGH MEAT?
WELL, THEY DIDN'T CALL AHEAD. THAT'S ALL WE HAD!
SORRY ABOUT THA--
IT'S SO GOOD!!
WELL, IT'S NICE TO HAVE A BIT OF LIFE HERE!
ARE YOU SURE THAT'S ALL YOU NEED, NANTUR?
YES, THANK YOU.
I must savor the tastes of this world!
NORMAN, MANNERS!

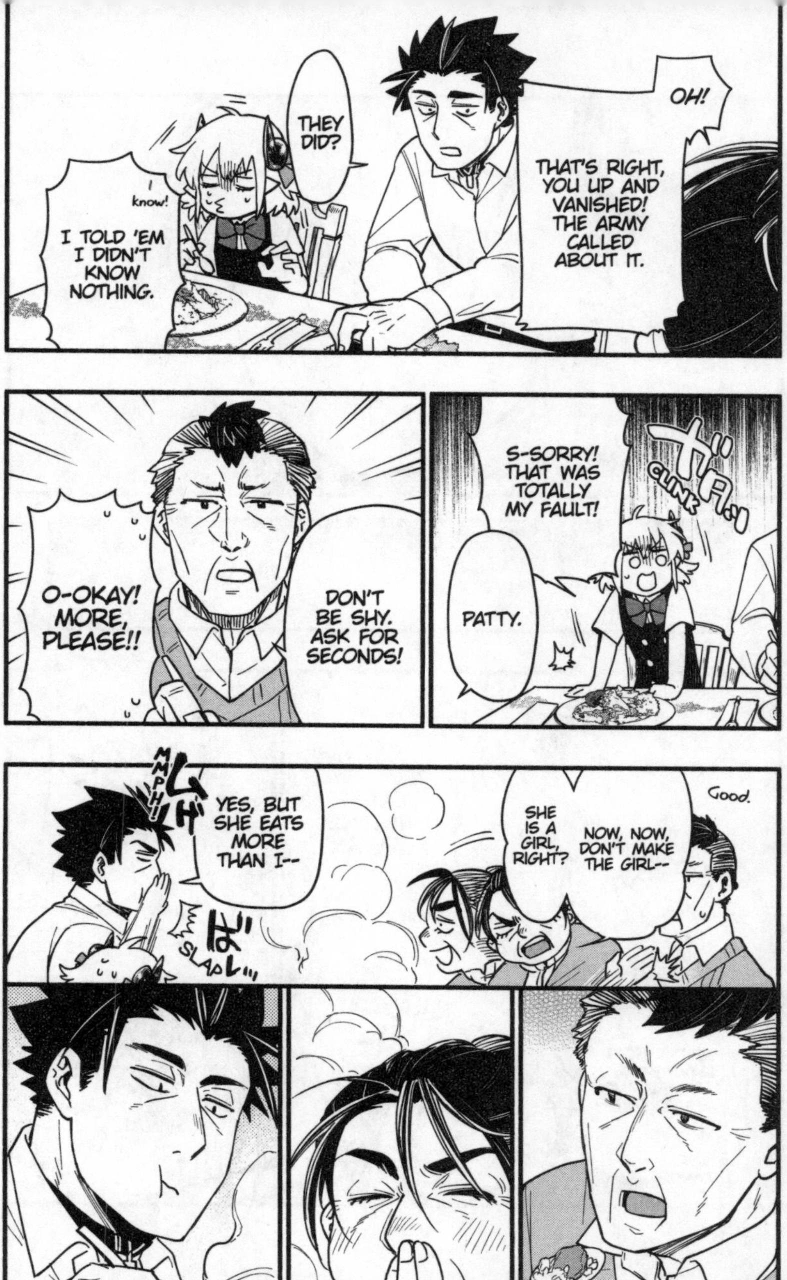
OH!
THAT'S RIGHT, YOU UP AND VANISHED! THE ARMY CALLED ABOUT IT.
THEY DID?
I TOLD 'EM I DIDN'T KNOW NOTHING.
I know!
S-SORRY! THAT WAS TOTALLY MY FAULT!
CLINK
PATTY.
DON'T BE SHY. ASK FOR SECONDS!
O-OKAY! MORE, PLEASE!!
Good.
NOW, NOW, DON'T MAKE THE GIRL--
SHE IS A GIRL, RIGHT?
YES, BUT SHE EATS MORE THAN I--
MMPH!
SLAP

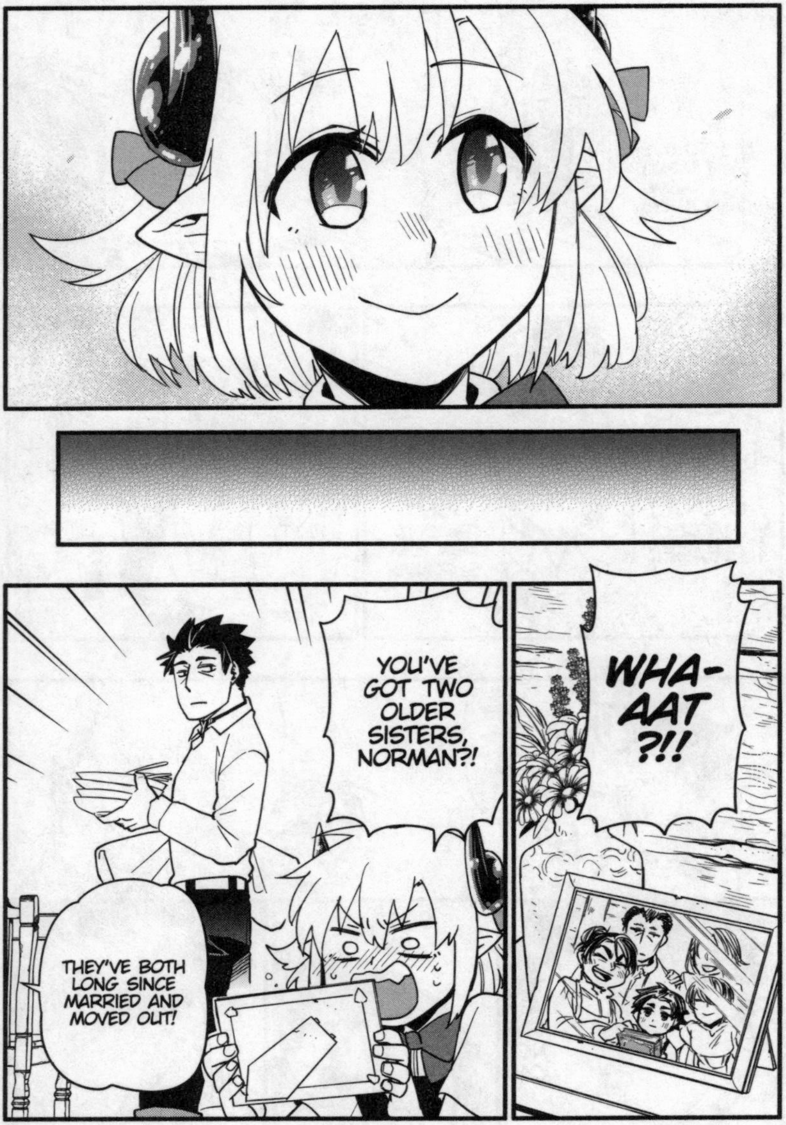

WHA-AAT?!!
YOU'VE GOT TWO OLDER SISTERS, NORMAN?!
THEY'VE BOTH LONG SINCE MARRIED AND MOVED OUT!

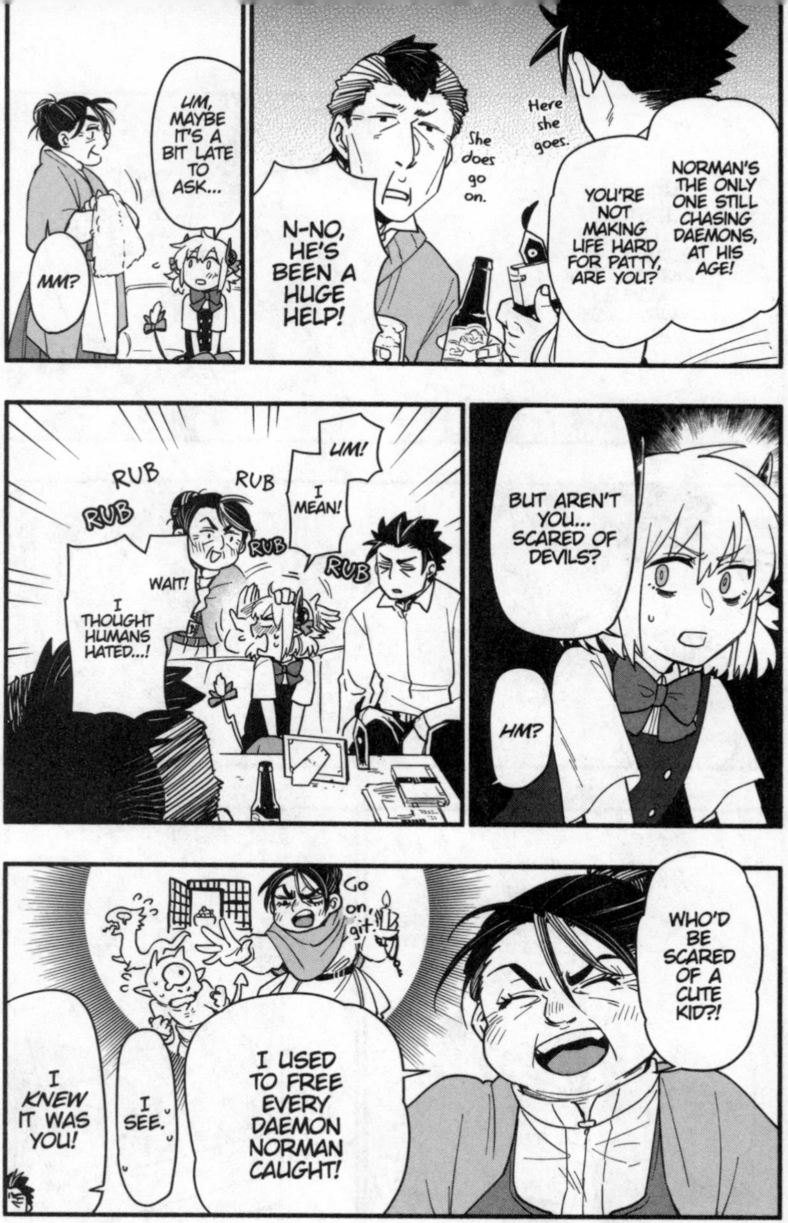
UM, MAYBE IT'S A BIT LATE TO ASK...
MM?
NORMAN'S THE ONLY ONE STILL CHASING DAEMONS, AT HIS AGE!
YOU'RE NOT MAKING LIFE HARD FOR PATTY, ARE YOU?
Here she goes.
She does go on.
N-NO, HE'S BEEN A HUGE HELP!
RUB
RUB
RUB
RUB
RUB
UM! I MEAN!
WAIT! I THOUGHT HUMANS HATED...!
BUT AREN'T YOU... SCARED OF DEVILS?
HM?
WHO'D BE SCARED OF A CUTE KID?!
I USED TO FREE EVERY DAEMON NORMAN CAUGHT!
Go on, git!
I SEE.
I KNEW IT WAS YOU!

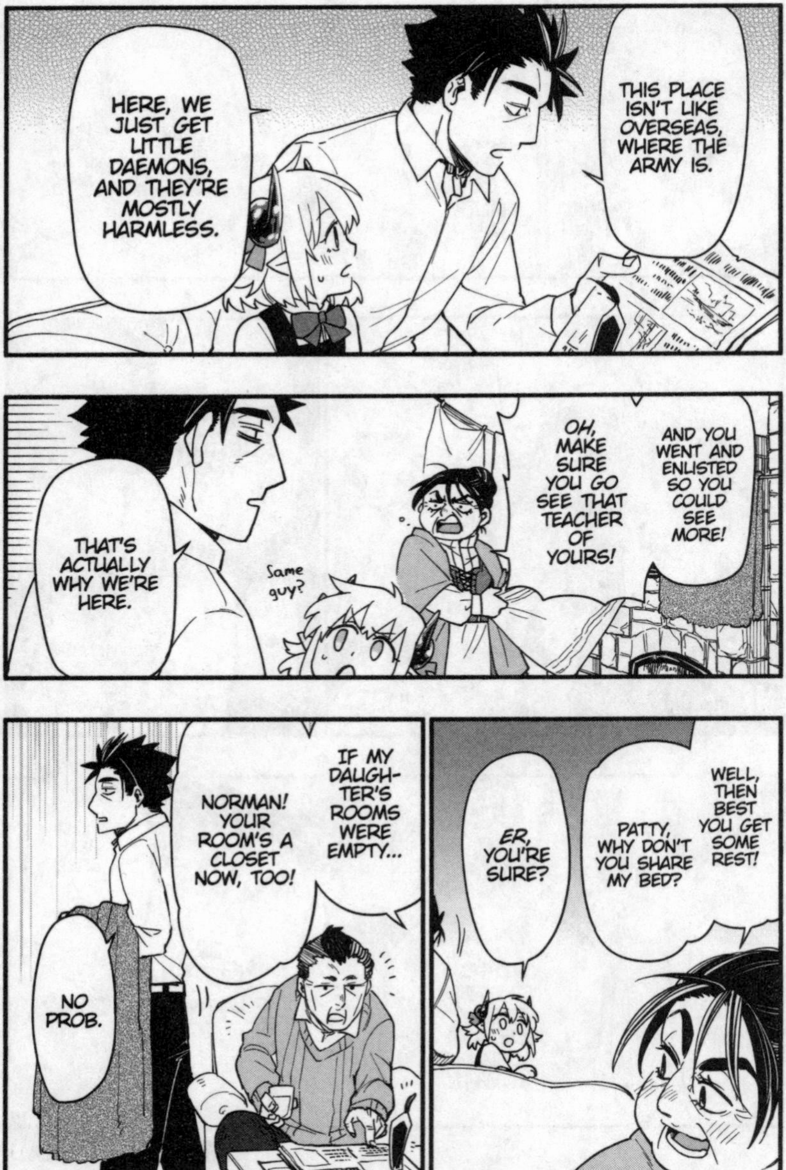
THIS PLACE ISN'T LIKE OVERSEAS, WHERE THE ARMY IS.
HERE, WE JUST GET LITTLE DAEMONS, AND THEY'RE MOSTLY HARMLESS.
AND YOU WENT AND ENLISTED SO YOU COULD SEE MORE!
OH, MAKE SURE YOU GO SEE THAT TEACHER OF YOURS!
Same guy?
THAT'S ACTUALLY WHY WE'RE HERE.
WELL, THEN BEST YOU GET SOME REST!
PATTY, WHY DON'T YOU SHARE MY BED?
ER, YOU'RE SURE?
IF MY DAUGH-TER'S ROOMS WERE EMPTY...
NORMAN! YOUR ROOM'S A CLOSET NOW, TOO!
NO PROB.

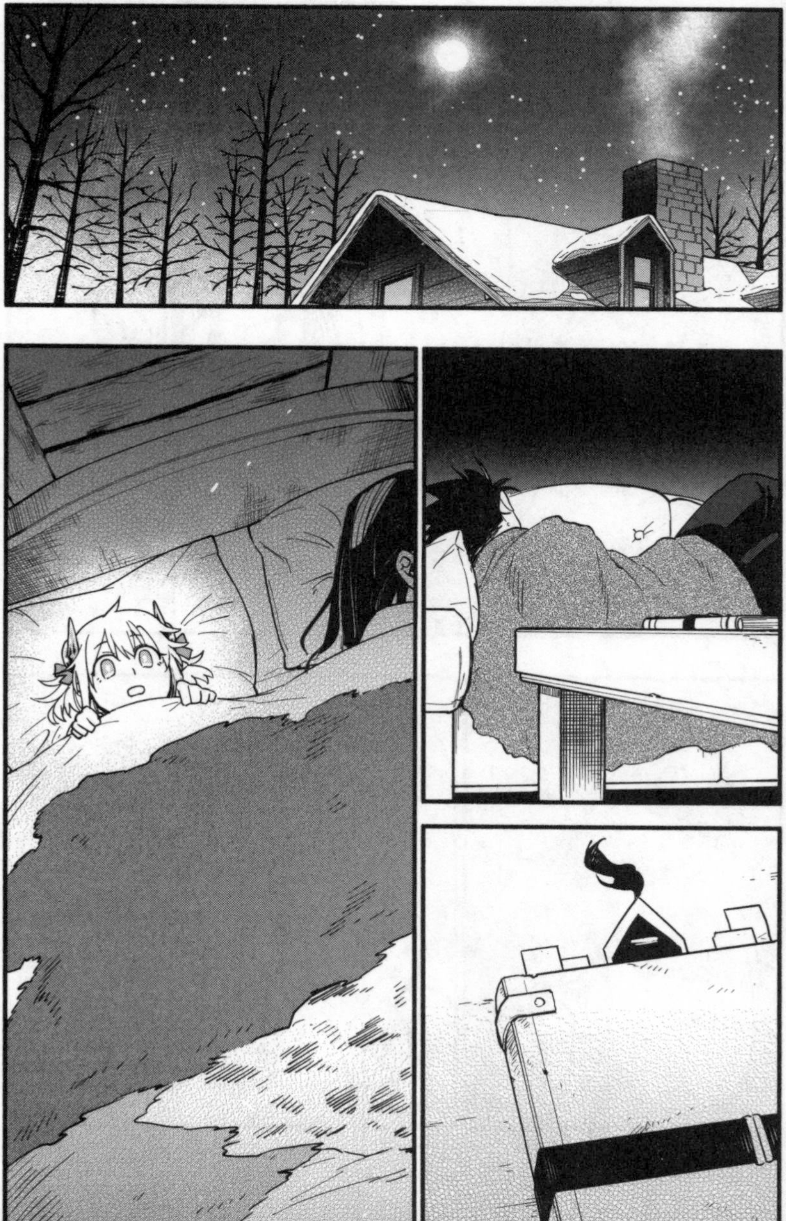

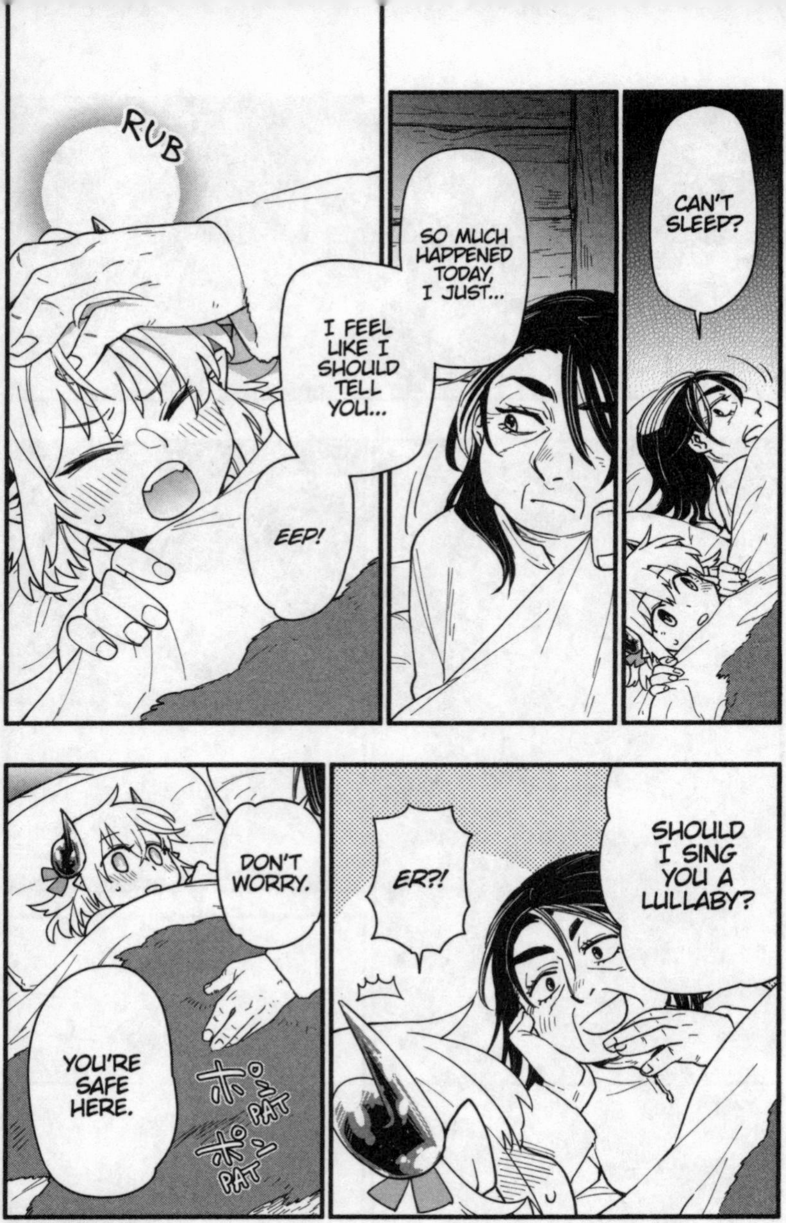
CAN'T SLEEP?
SO MUCH HAPPENED TODAY, I JUST...
I FEEL LIKE I SHOULD TELL YOU...
RUB
EEP!
SHOULD I SING YOU A LULLABY?
ER?!
DON'T WORRY.
YOU'RE SAFE HERE.
ポン PAT
ポン PAT

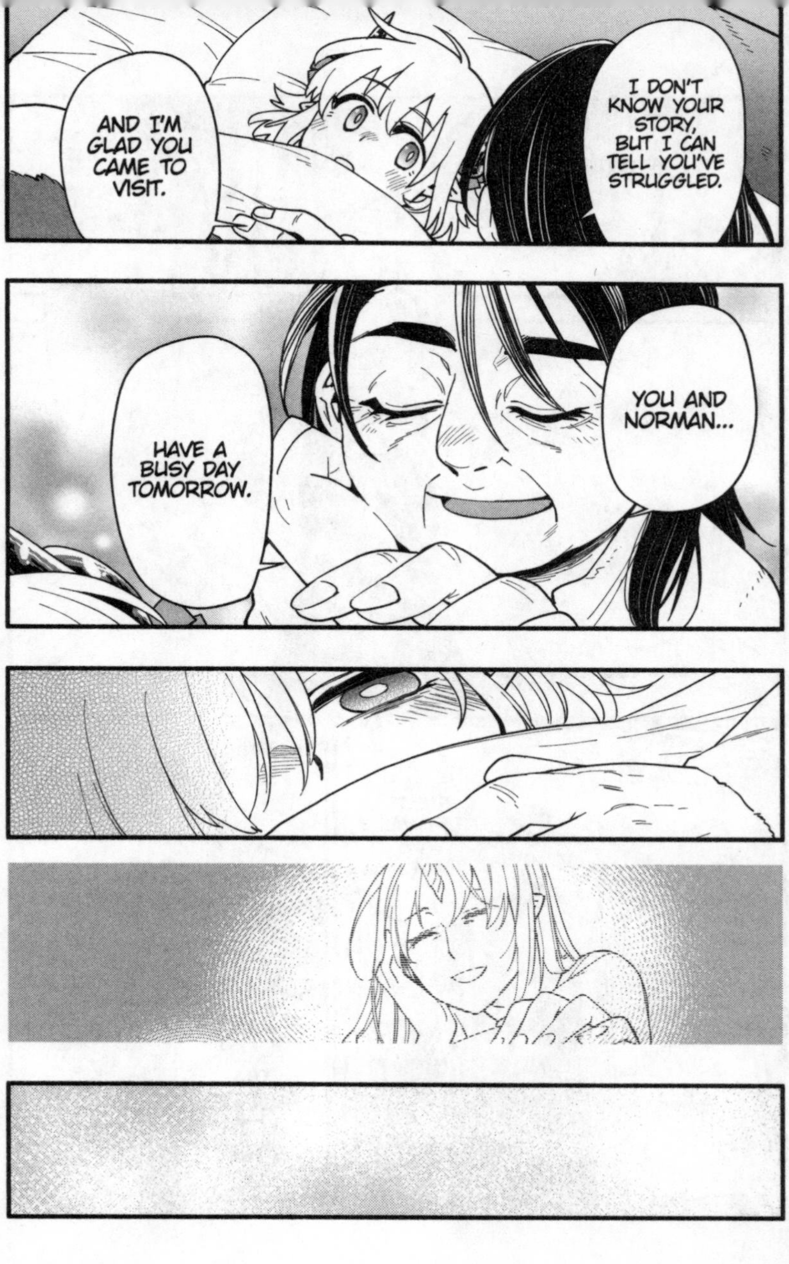
I DON'T KNOW YOUR STORY, BUT I CAN TELL YOU'VE STRUGGLED.
AND I'M GLAD YOU CAME TO VISIT.
YOU AND NORMAN...
HAVE A BUSY DAY TOMORROW.

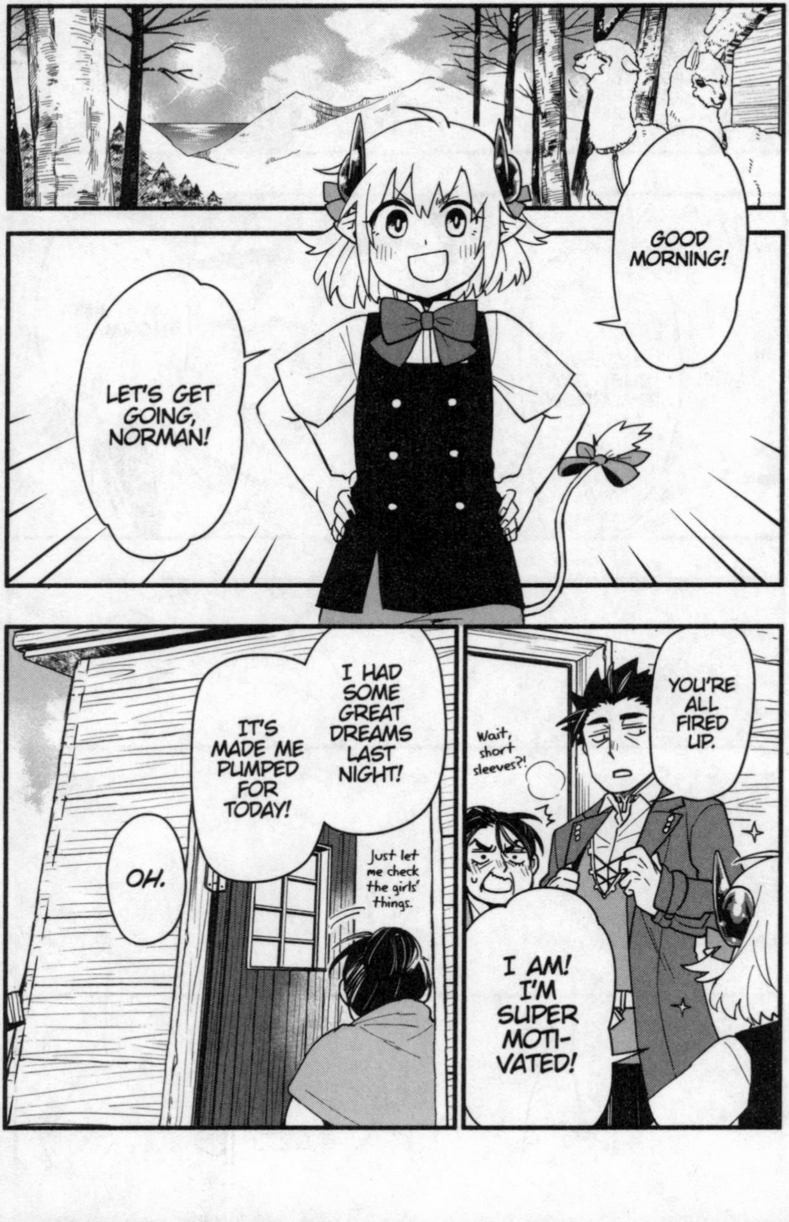
GOOD MORNING!
LET'S GET GOING, NORMAN!
YOU'RE ALL FIRED UP.
Wait, short sleeves?!
I AM! I'M SUPER MOTI-VATED!
I HAD SOME GREAT DREAMS LAST NIGHT!
IT'S MADE ME PUMPED FOR TODAY!
Just let me check the girls' things.
OH.

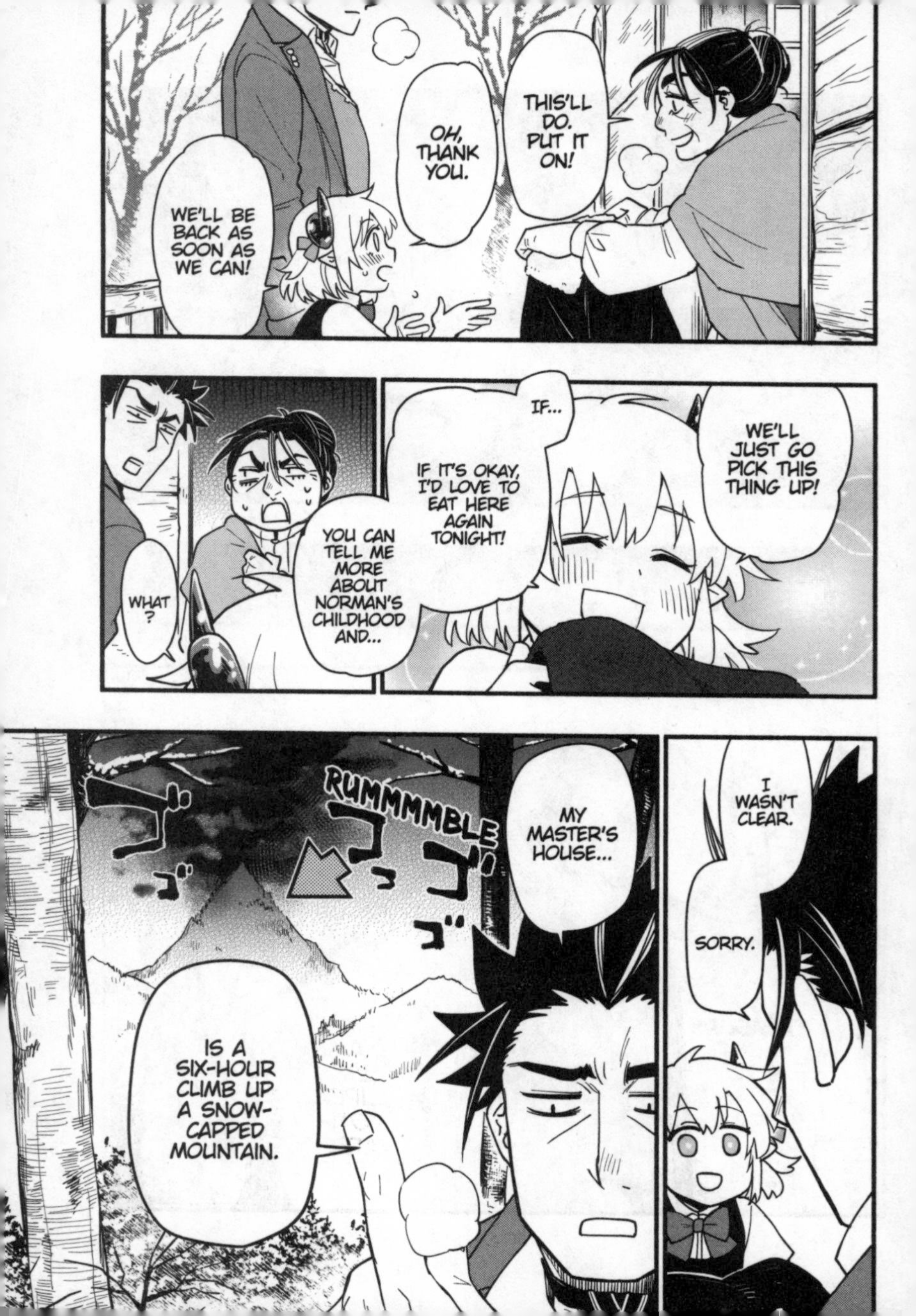
THIS'LL DO. PUT IT ON!
OH, THANK YOU.
WE'LL BE BACK AS SOON AS WE CAN!
WE'LL JUST GO PICK THIS THING UP!
IF...
IF IT'S OKAY, I'D LOVE TO EAT HERE AGAIN TONIGHT!
YOU CAN TELL ME MORE ABOUT NORMAN'S CHILDHOOD AND...
WHAT?
I WASN'T CLEAR.
SORRY.
MY MASTER'S HOUSE...
RUMMMMBLE
IS A SIX-HOUR CLIMB UP A SNOW-CAPPED MOUNTAIN.

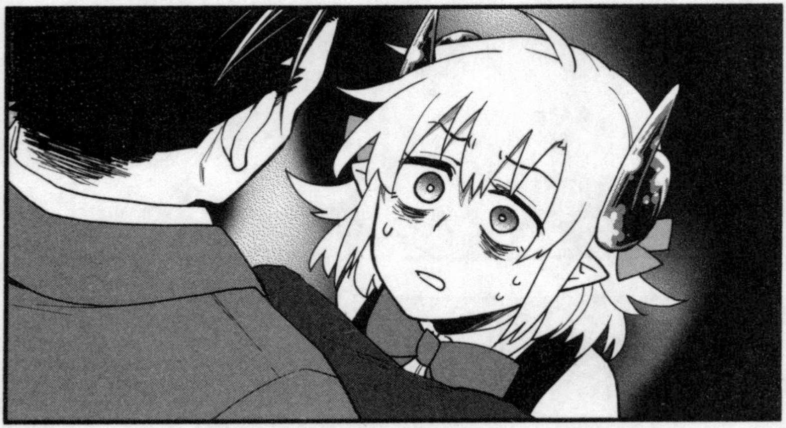

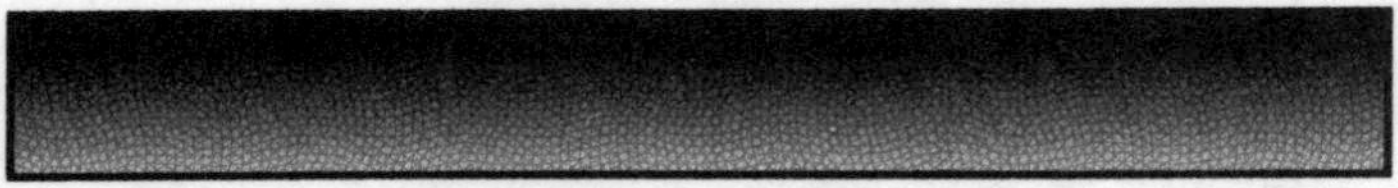

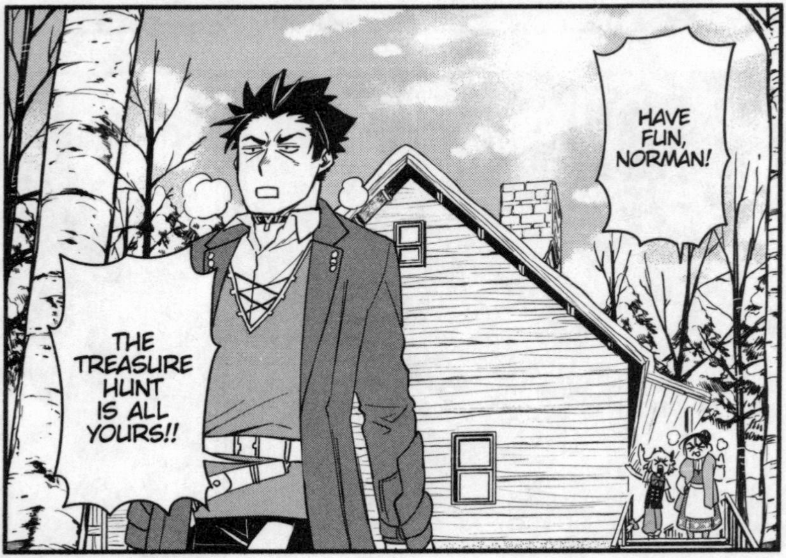
HAVE FUN, NORMAN!
THE TREASURE HUNT IS ALL YOURS!!

Sorry For My Familiar

FILE 62: Human World ②

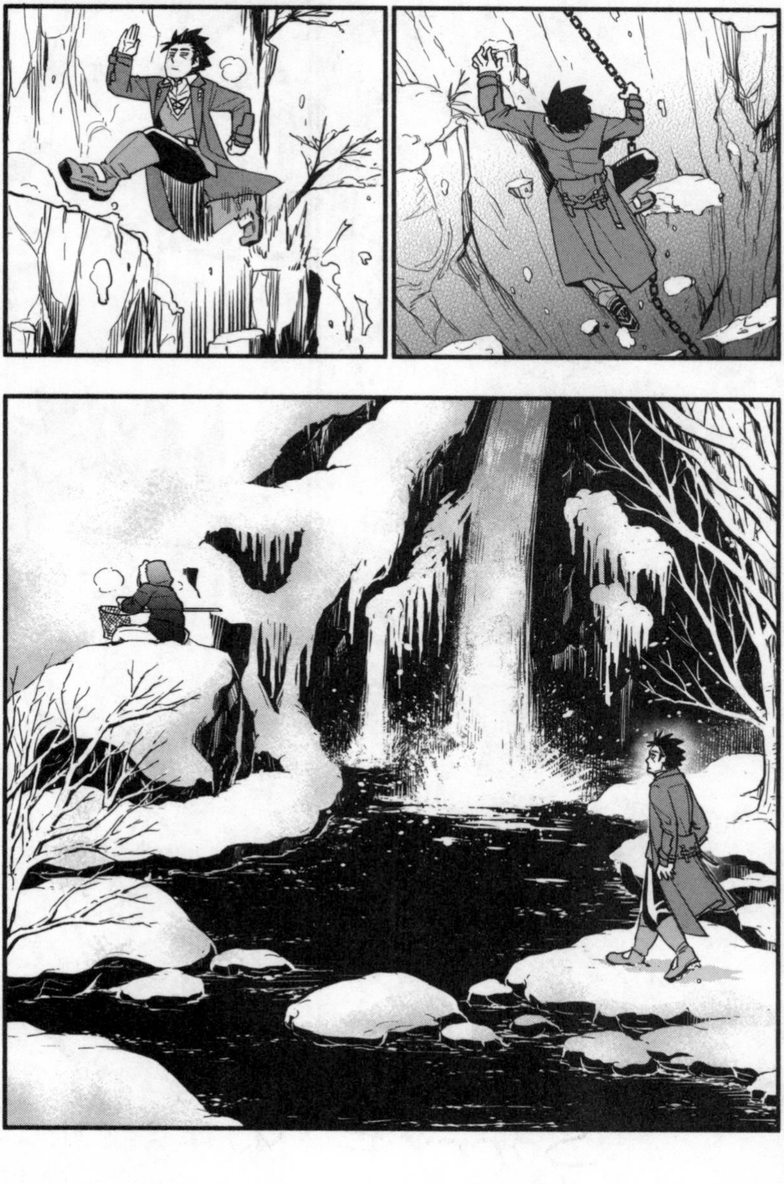

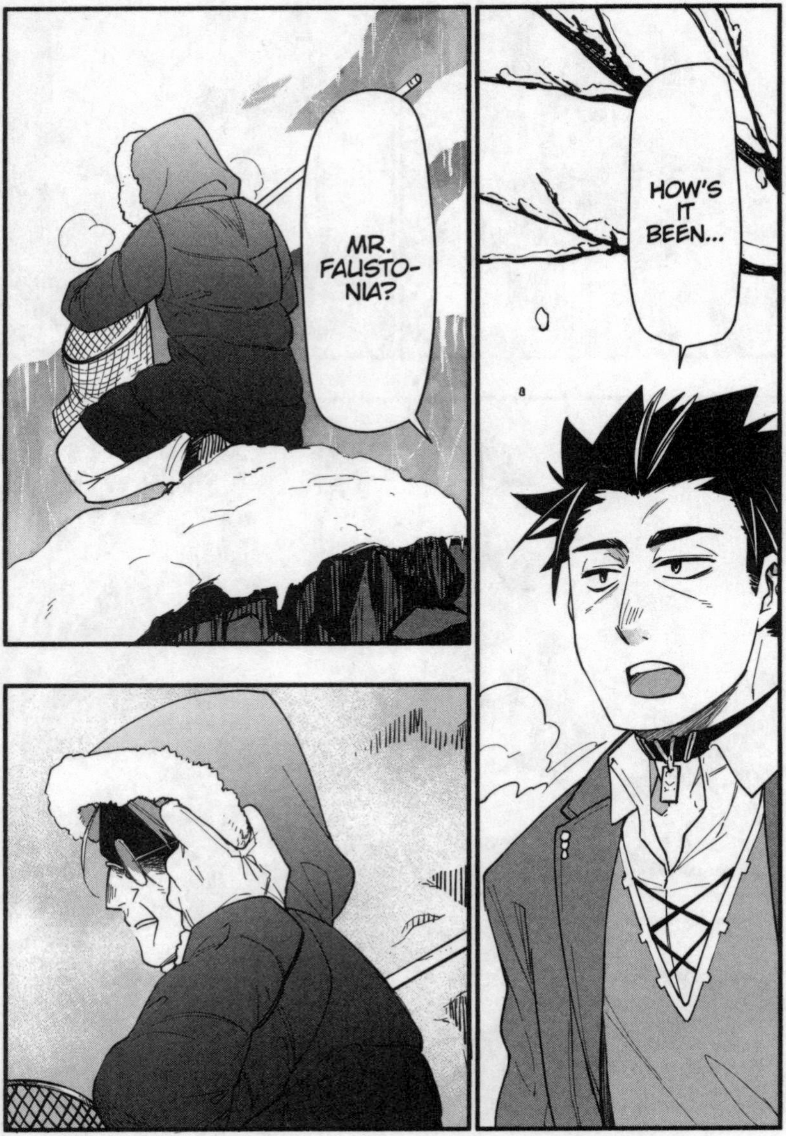
HOW'S IT BEEN...
MR. FAUSTONIA?

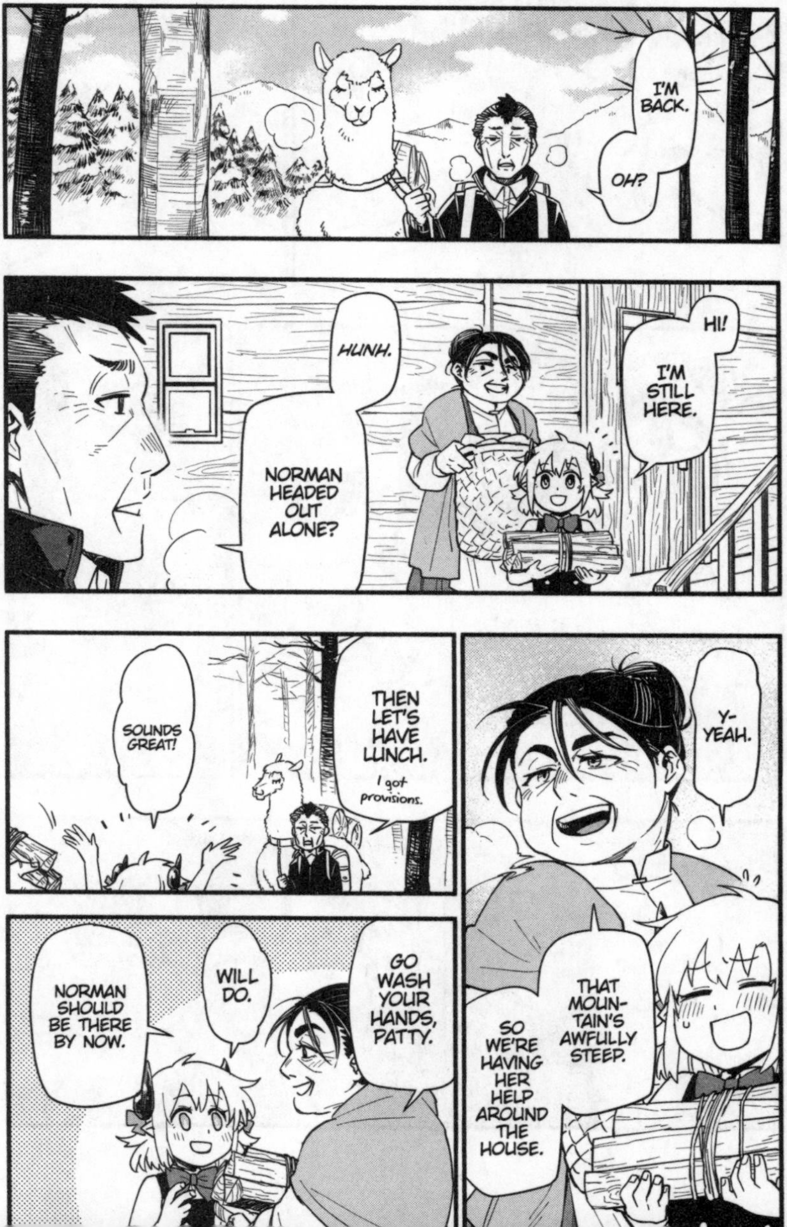
I'M BACK.
OH?
HI!
I'M STILL HERE.
HUNH.
NORMAN HEADED OUT ALONE?
Y-YEAH.
THAT MOUNTAIN'S AWFULLY STEEP.
SO WE'RE HAVING HER HELP AROUND THE HOUSE.
THEN LET'S HAVE LUNCH.
I got provisions.
SOUNDS GREAT!
GO WASH YOUR HANDS, PATTY.
WILL DO.
NORMAN SHOULD BE THERE BY NOW.

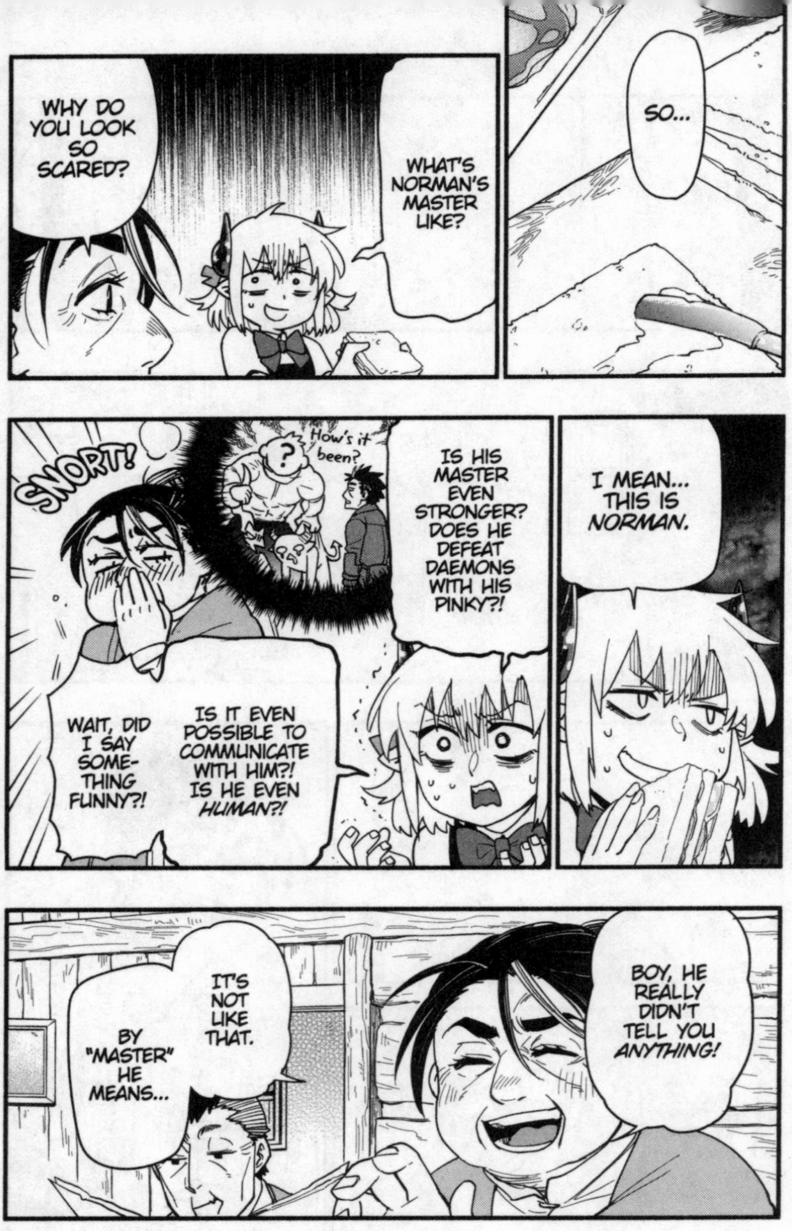
SO...
WHAT'S NORMAN'S MASTER LIKE?
WHY DO YOU LOOK SO SCARED?
I MEAN... THIS IS *NORMAN.*
IS HIS MASTER EVEN STRONGER? DOES HE DEFEAT DAEMONS WITH HIS PINKY?!
How's it been?
SNORT!
IS IT EVEN POSSIBLE TO COMMUNICATE WITH HIM?! IS HE EVEN *HUMAN?!*
WAIT, DID I SAY SOME-THING FUNNY?!
BOY, HE REALLY DIDN'T TELL YOU *ANYTHING!*
IT'S NOT LIKE THAT.
BY "MASTER" HE MEANS...

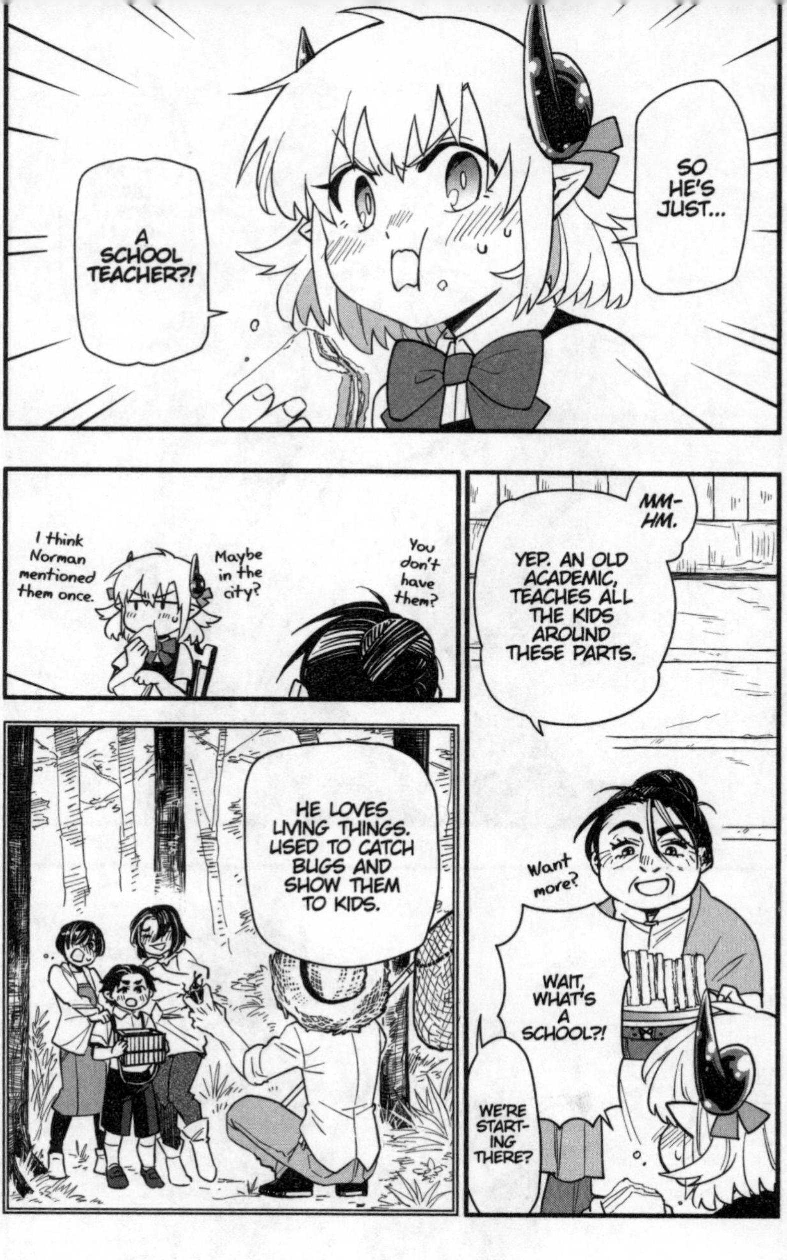
SO HE'S JUST...
A SCHOOL TEACHER?!
MM-HM.
YEP. AN OLD ACADEMIC, TEACHES ALL THE KIDS AROUND THESE PARTS.
You don't have them?
Maybe in the city?
I think Norman mentioned them once.
HE LOVES LIVING THINGS. USED TO CATCH BUGS AND SHOW THEM TO KIDS.
Want more?
WAIT, WHAT'S A SCHOOL?!
WE'RE STARTING THERE?

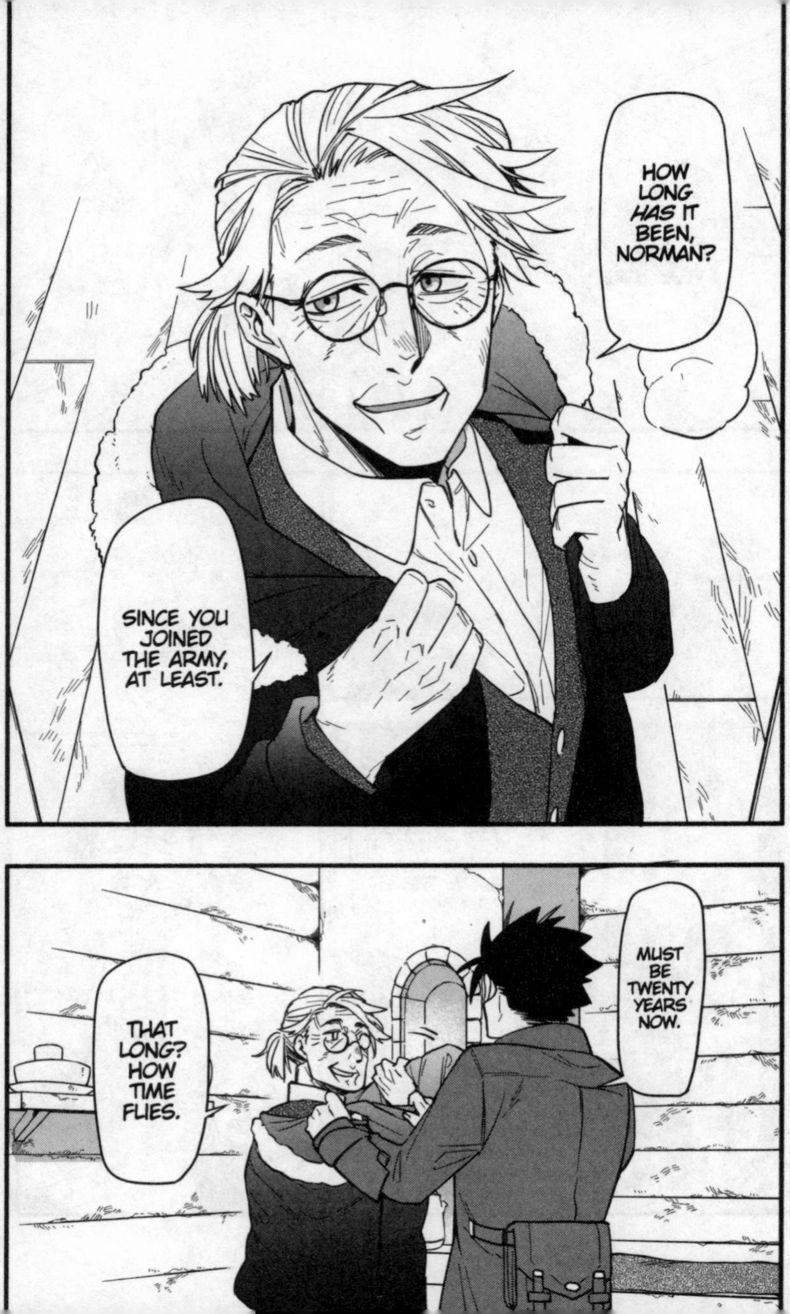
HOW LONG *HAS* IT BEEN, NORMAN?
SINCE YOU JOINED THE ARMY, AT LEAST.
MUST BE TWENTY YEARS NOW.
THAT LONG? HOW TIME FLIES.

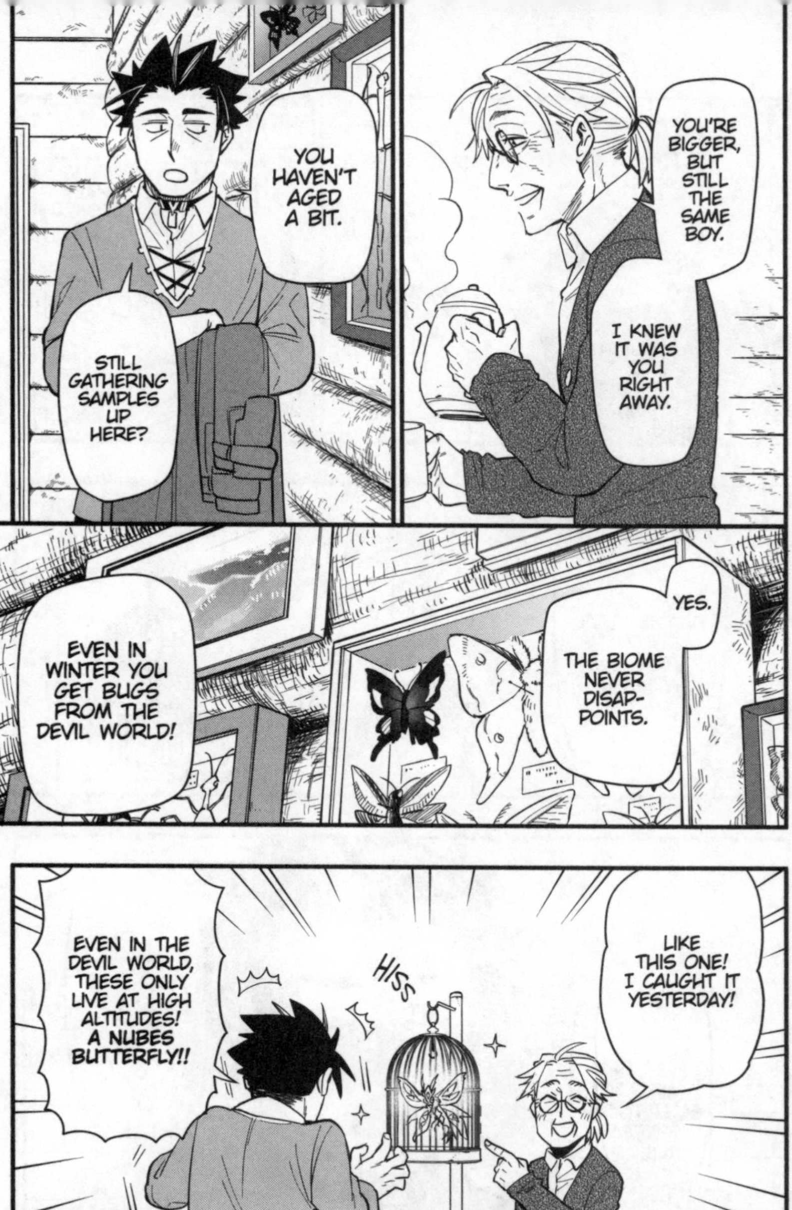
YOU'RE BIGGER, BUT STILL THE SAME BOY.
I KNEW IT WAS YOU RIGHT AWAY.
YOU HAVEN'T AGED A BIT.
STILL GATHERING SAMPLES UP HERE?
YES.
THE BIOME NEVER DISAP-POINTS.
EVEN IN WINTER YOU GET BUGS FROM THE DEVIL WORLD!
LIKE THIS ONE! I CAUGHT IT YESTERDAY!
HISS
EVEN IN THE DEVIL WORLD, THESE ONLY LIVE AT HIGH ALTITUDES! A NUBES BUTTERFLY!!

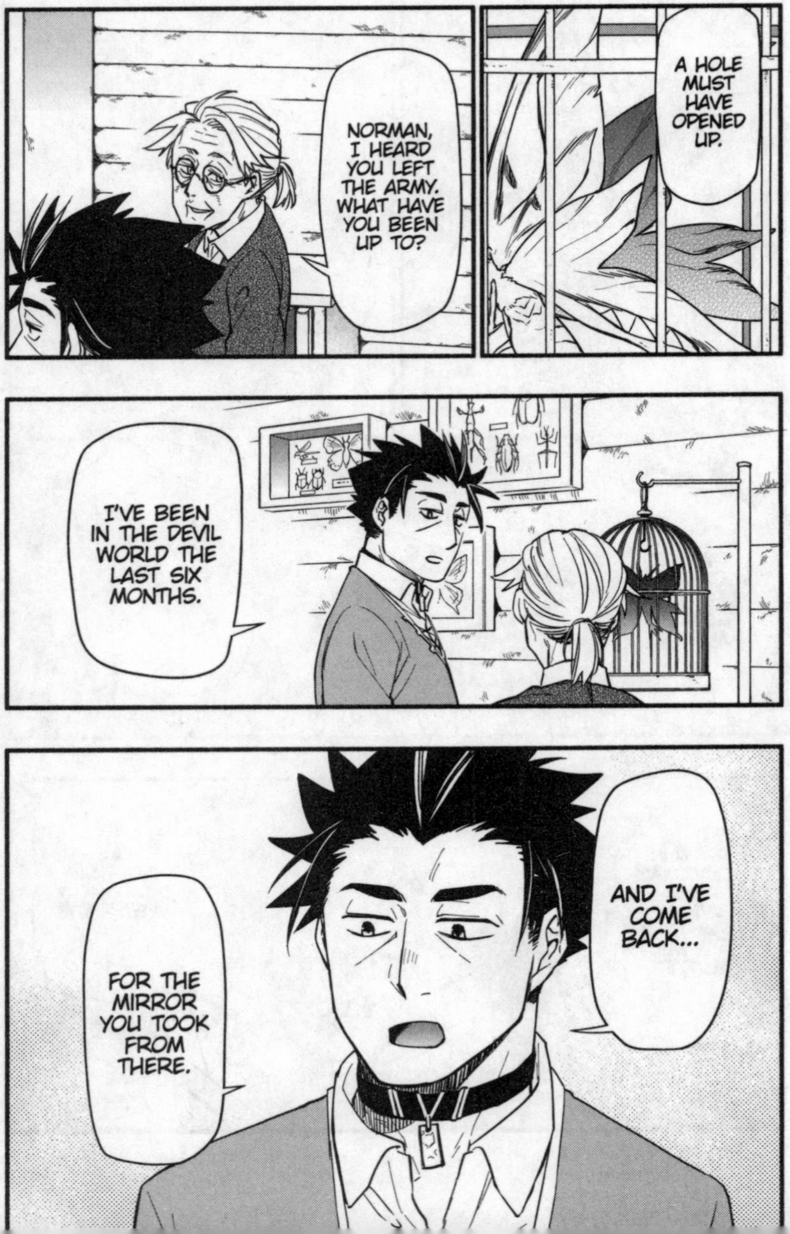
A HOLE MUST HAVE OPENED UP.
NORMAN, I HEARD YOU LEFT THE ARMY. WHAT HAVE YOU BEEN UP TO?
I'VE BEEN IN THE DEVIL WORLD THE LAST SIX MONTHS.
AND I'VE COME BACK...
FOR THE MIRROR YOU TOOK FROM THERE.

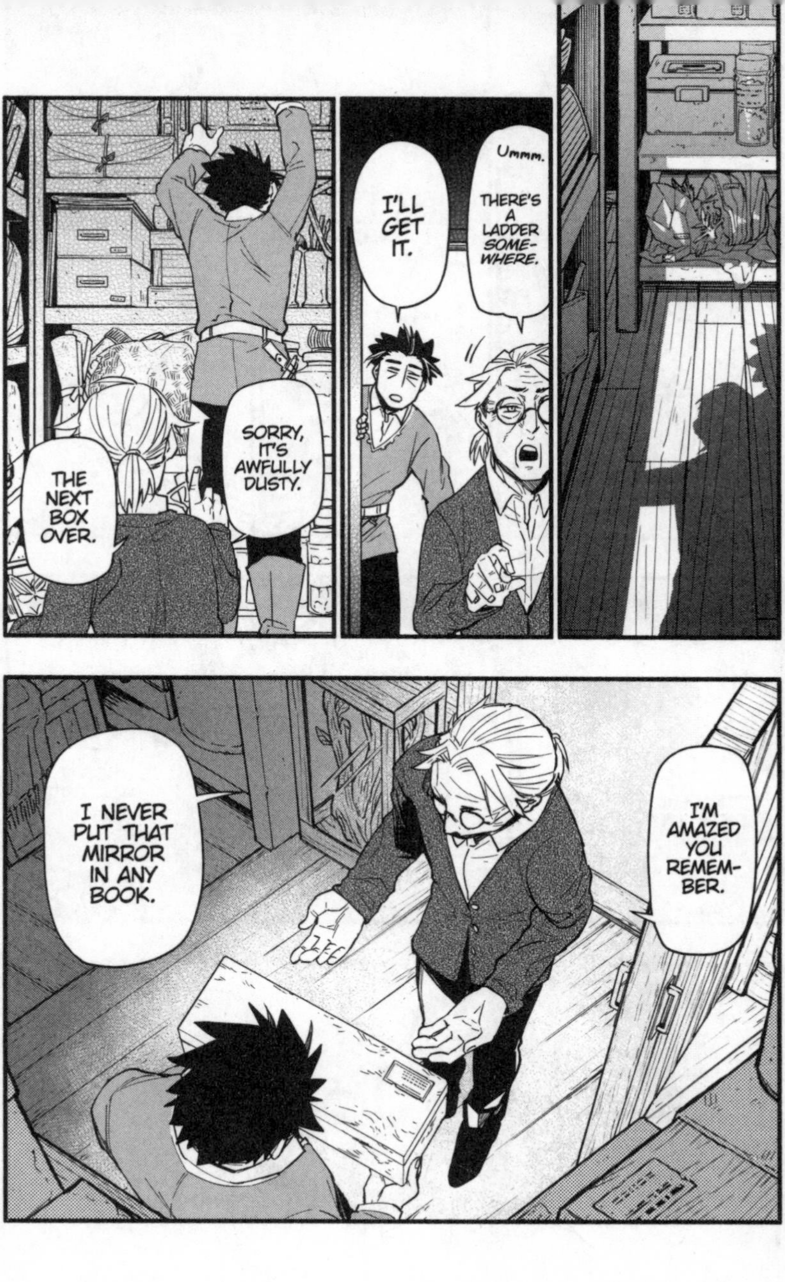
Ummm.
THERE'S A LADDER SOME-WHERE.
I'LL GET IT.
SORRY, IT'S AWFULLY DUSTY.
THE NEXT BOX OVER.
I'M AMAZED YOU REMEM-BER.
I NEVER PUT THAT MIRROR IN ANY BOOK.

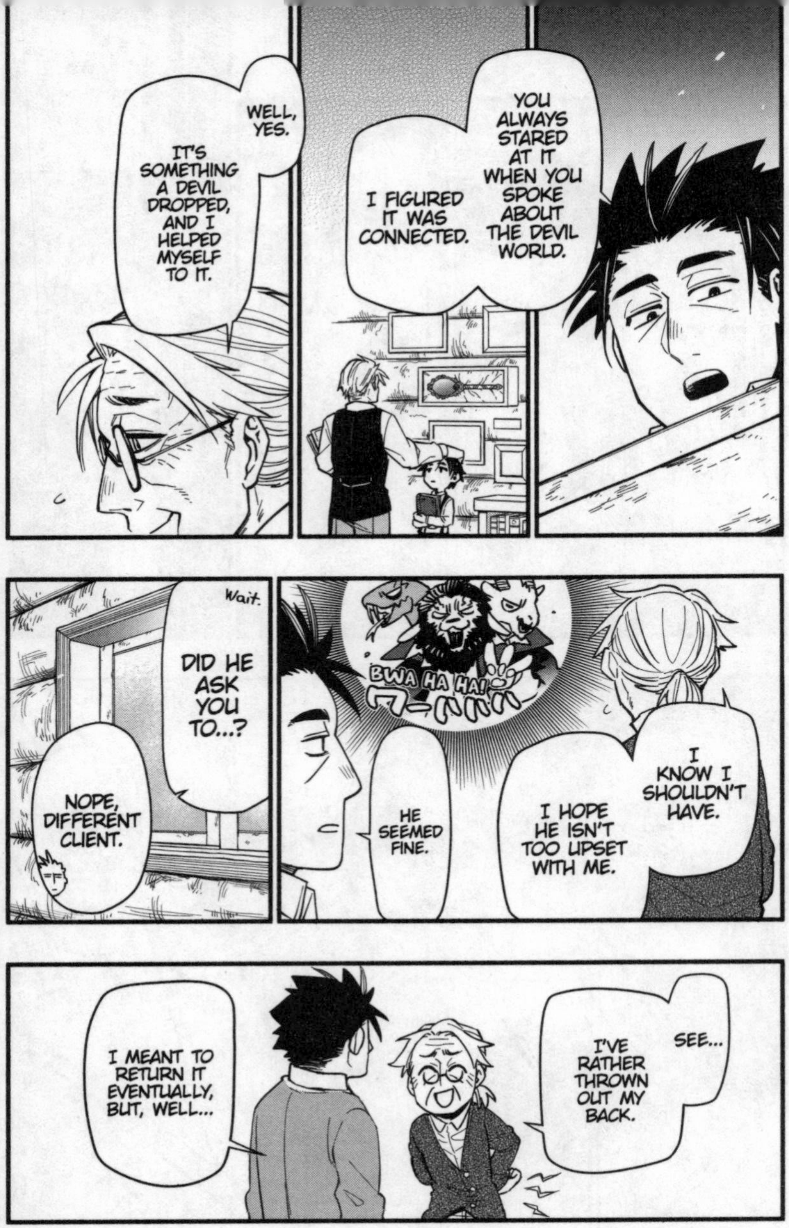
YOU ALWAYS STARED AT IT WHEN YOU SPOKE ABOUT THE DEVIL WORLD.
I FIGURED IT WAS CONNECTED.
WELL, YES.
IT'S SOMETHING A DEVIL DROPPED, AND I HELPED MYSELF TO IT.
I KNOW I SHOULDN'T HAVE.
I HOPE HE ISN'T TOO UPSET WITH ME.
BWA HA HA!
ワーハハハ
HE SEEMED FINE.
Wait.
DID HE ASK YOU TO...?
NOPE, DIFFERENT CLIENT.
SEE...
I'VE RATHER THROWN OUT MY BACK.
I MEANT TO RETURN IT EVENTUALLY, BUT, WELL...

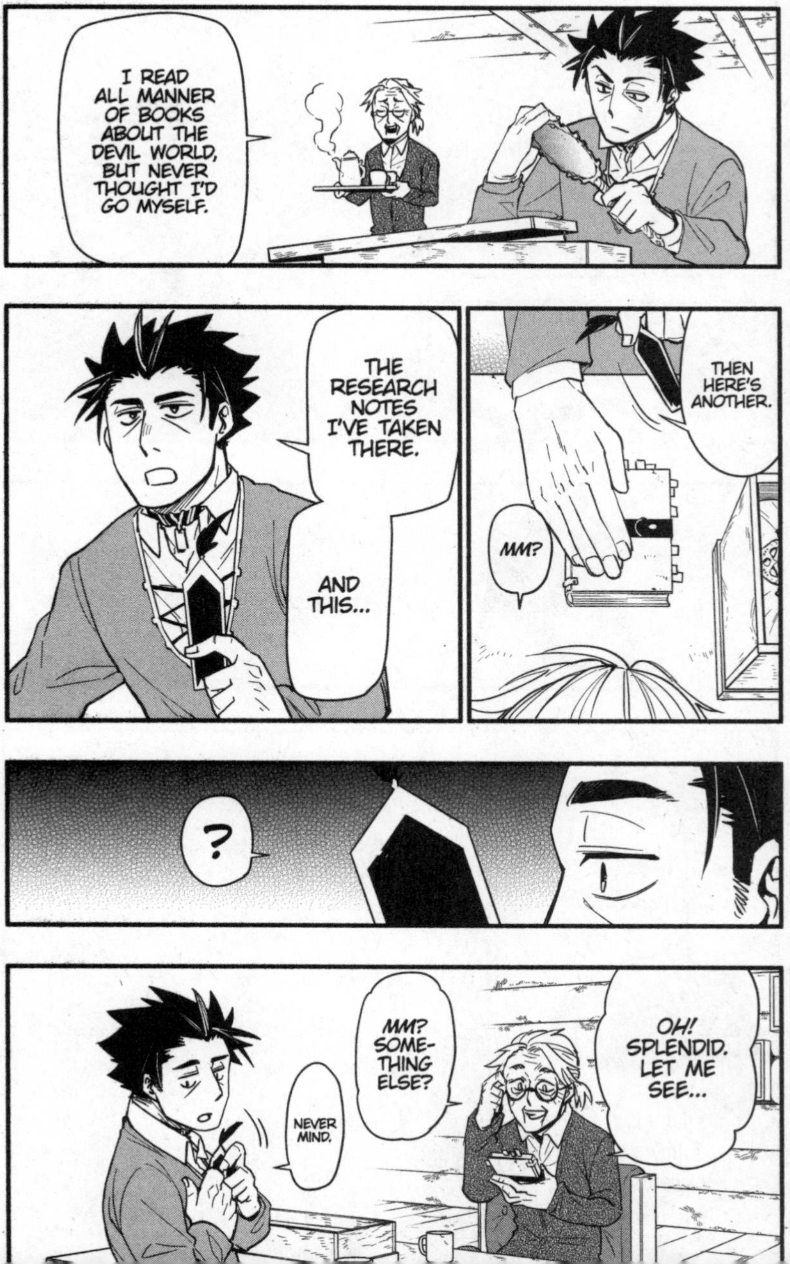
I READ ALL MANNER OF BOOKS ABOUT THE DEVIL WORLD, BUT NEVER THOUGHT I'D GO MYSELF.
THEN HERE'S ANOTHER.
MM?
THE RESEARCH NOTES I'VE TAKEN THERE.
AND THIS...
?
OH! SPLENDID. LET ME SEE...
MM? SOME-THING ELSE?
NEVER MIND.

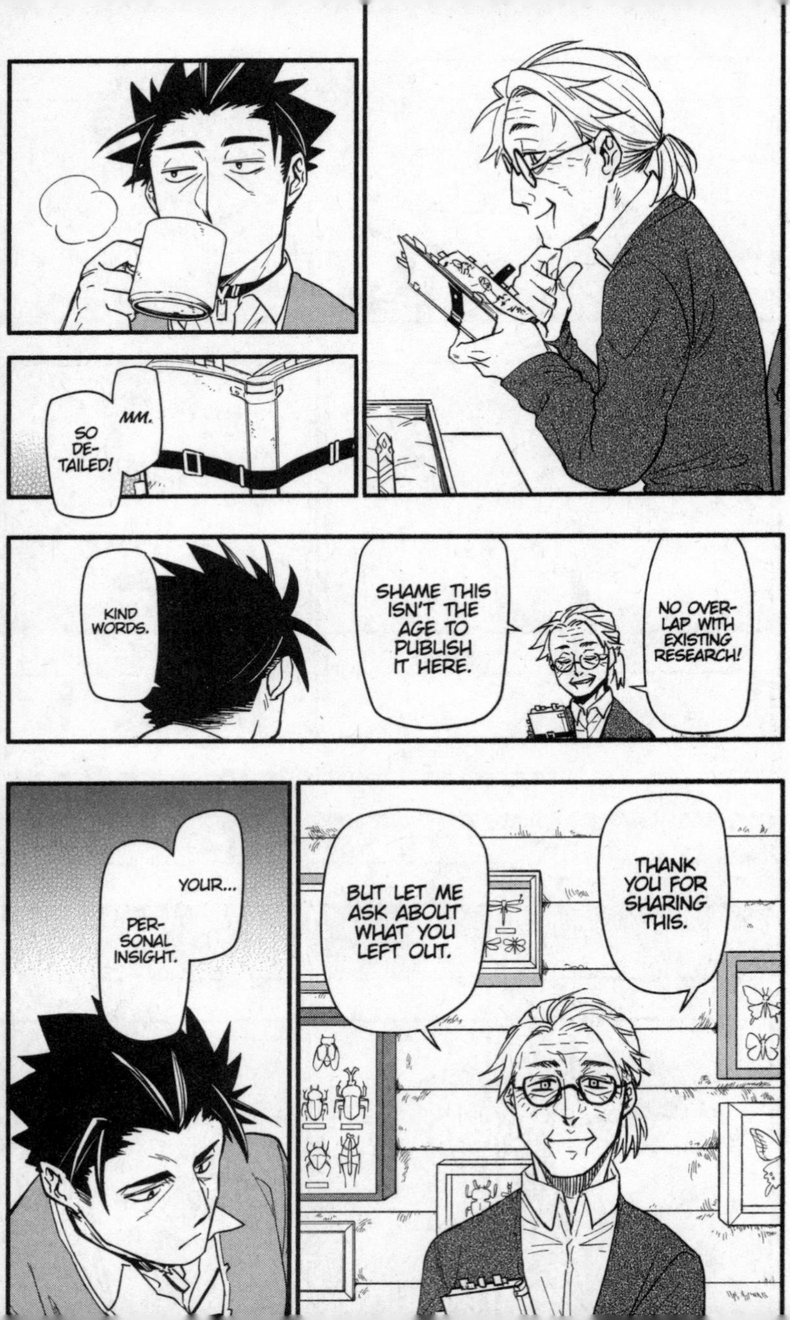
MM.
SO DE-TAILED!
NO OVER-LAP WITH EXISTING RESEARCH!
SHAME THIS ISN'T THE AGE TO PUBLISH IT HERE.
KIND WORDS.
THANK YOU FOR SHARING THIS.
BUT LET ME ASK ABOUT WHAT YOU LEFT OUT.
YOUR...
PER-SONAL INSIGHT.

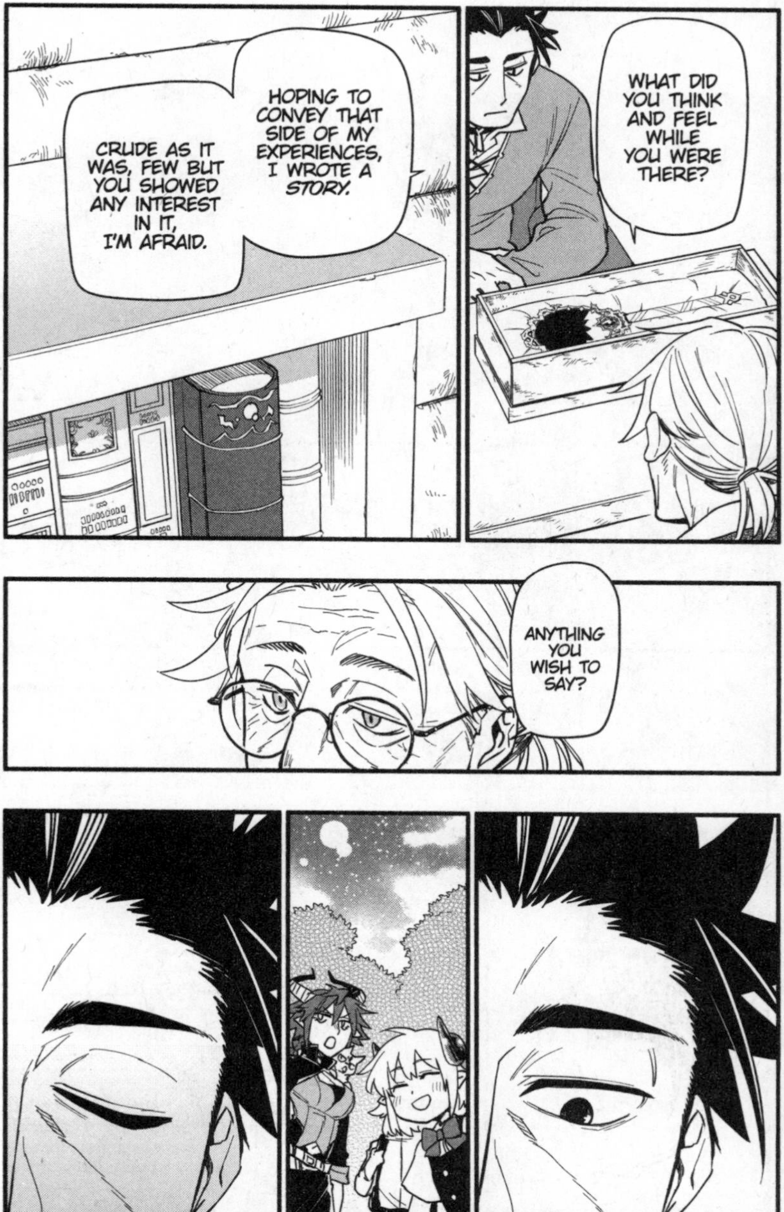
CRUDE AS IT WAS, FEW BUT YOU SHOWED ANY INTEREST IN IT, I'M AFRAID.
HOPING TO CONVEY THAT SIDE OF MY EXPERIENCES, I WROTE A *STORY.*
WHAT DID YOU THINK AND FEEL WHILE YOU WERE THERE?
ANYTHING YOU WISH TO SAY?

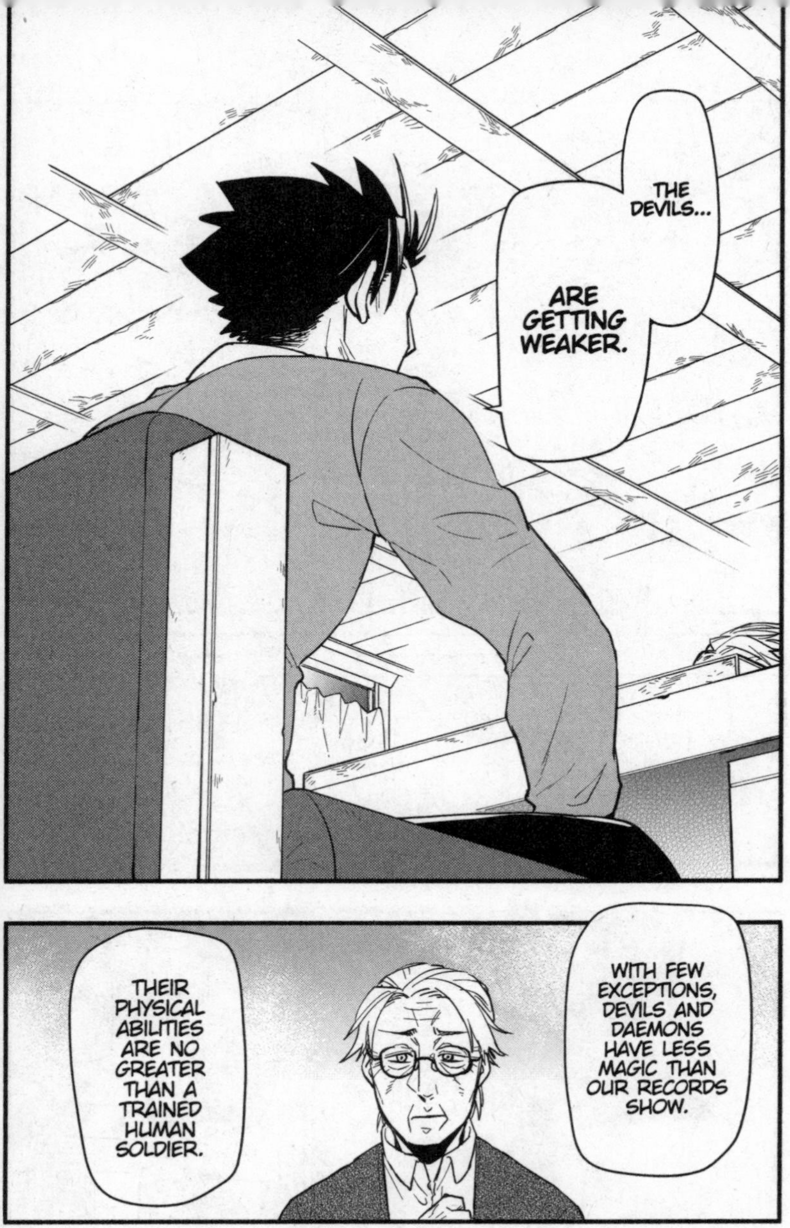
THE DEVILS...
ARE GETTING WEAKER.
WITH FEW EXCEPTIONS, DEVILS AND DAEMONS HAVE LESS MAGIC THAN OUR RECORDS SHOW.
THEIR PHYSICAL ABILITIES ARE NO GREATER THAN A TRAINED HUMAN SOLDIER.

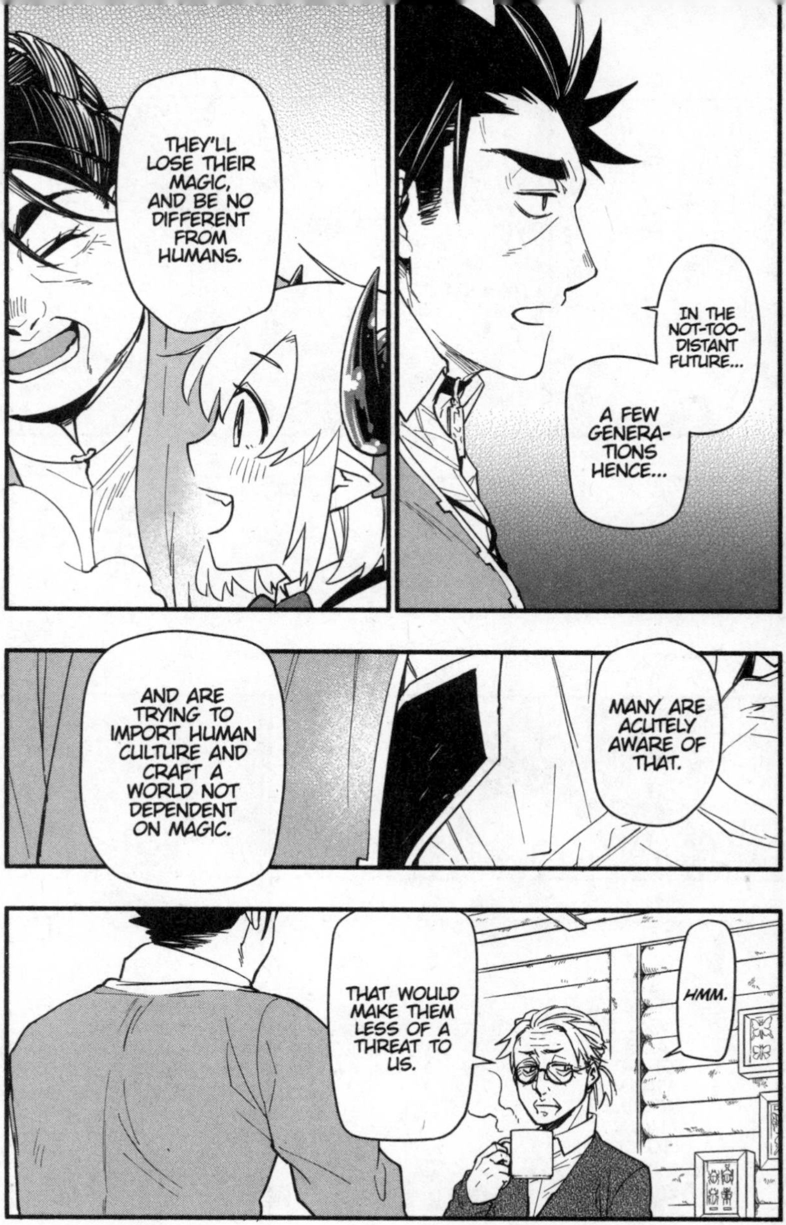
IN THE NOT-TOO-DISTANT FUTURE...
A FEW GENERATIONS HENCE...
THEY'LL LOSE THEIR MAGIC, AND BE NO DIFFERENT FROM HUMANS.
MANY ARE ACUTELY AWARE OF THAT.
AND ARE TRYING TO IMPORT HUMAN CULTURE AND CRAFT A WORLD NOT DEPENDENT ON MAGIC.
HMM.
THAT WOULD MAKE THEM LESS OF A THREAT TO US.

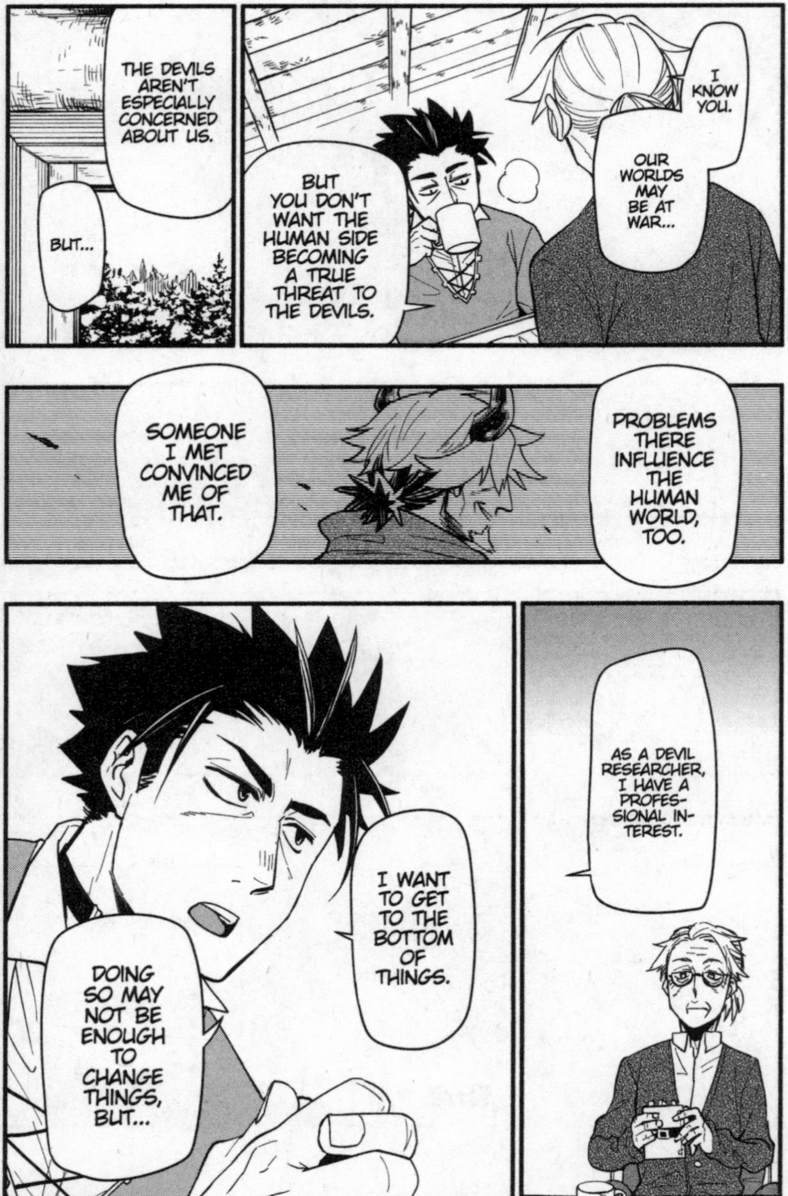
I KNOW YOU.
OUR WORLDS MAY BE AT WAR...
BUT YOU DON'T WANT THE HUMAN SIDE BECOMING A TRUE THREAT TO THE DEVILS.
THE DEVILS AREN'T ESPECIALLY CONCERNED ABOUT US.
BUT...
PROBLEMS THERE INFLUENCE THE HUMAN WORLD, TOO.
SOMEONE I MET CONVINCED ME OF THAT.
AS A DEVIL RESEARCHER, I HAVE A PROFES-SIONAL IN-TEREST.
I WANT TO GET TO THE BOTTOM OF THINGS.
DOING SO MAY NOT BE ENOUGH TO CHANGE THINGS, BUT...

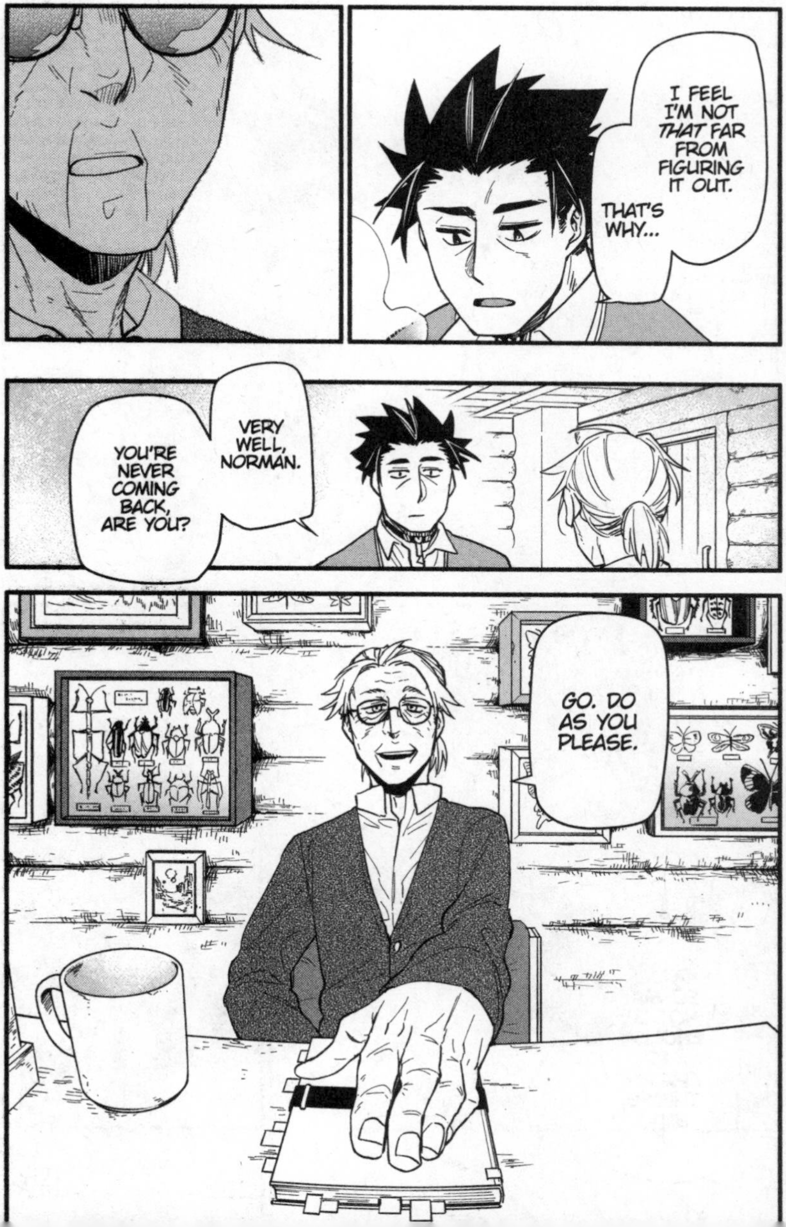
I FEEL I'M NOT *THAT* FAR FROM FIGURING IT OUT.
THAT'S WHY...
VERY WELL, NORMAN.
YOU'RE NEVER COMING BACK, ARE YOU?
GO. DO AS YOU PLEASE.

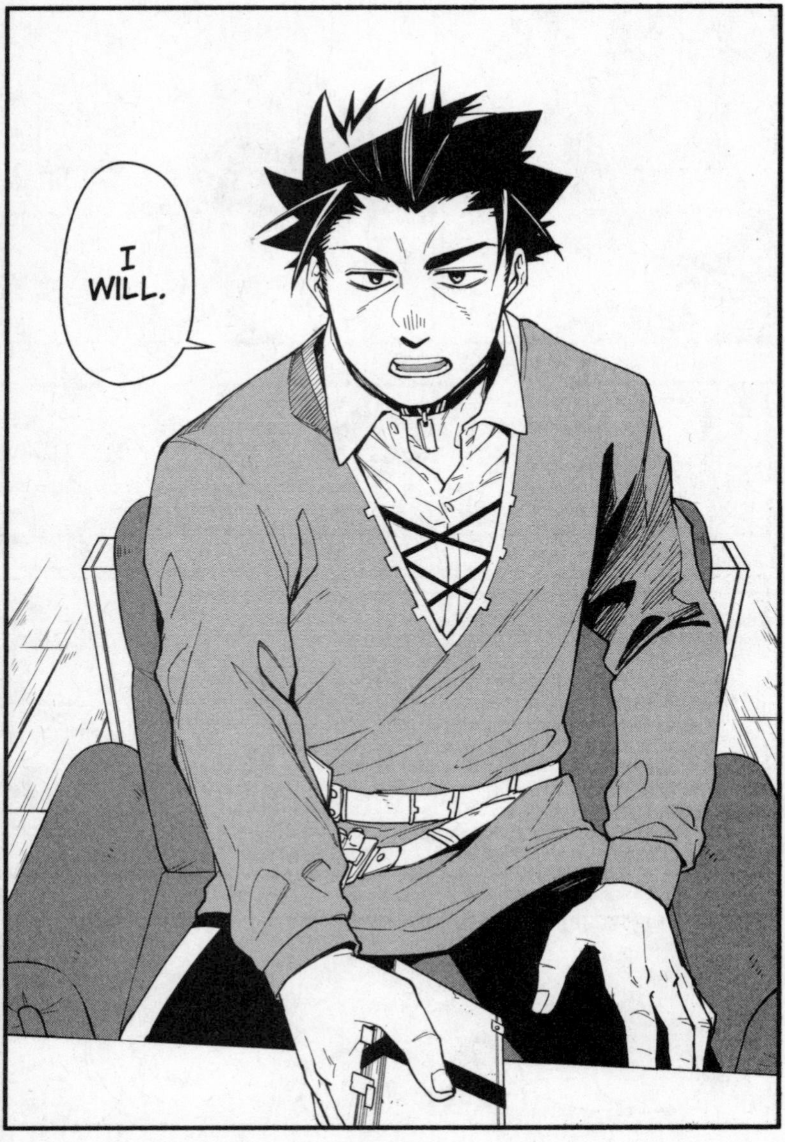
I WILL.

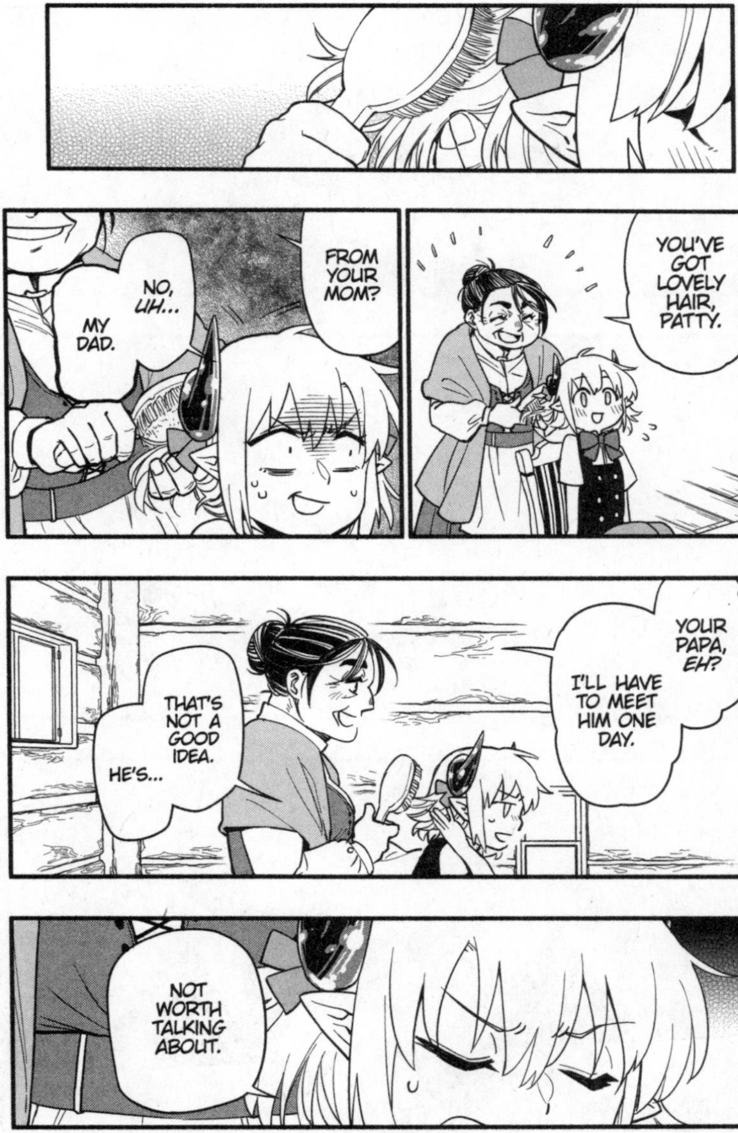

YOU'VE GOT LOVELY HAIR, PATTY.
FROM YOUR MOM?
NO, UH...
MY DAD.
Oh!
YOUR PAPA, EH?
I'LL HAVE TO MEET HIM ONE DAY.
THAT'S NOT A GOOD IDEA.
HE'S...
NOT WORTH TALKING ABOUT.

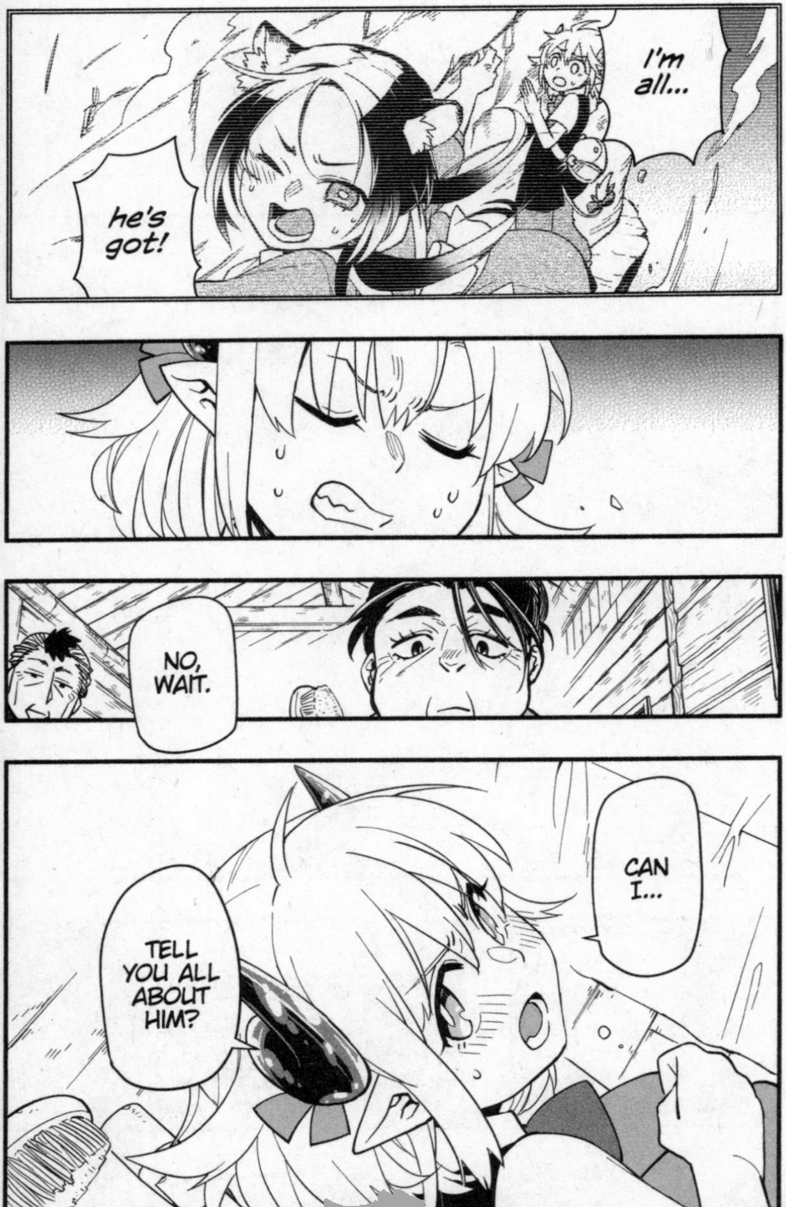
I'm all...
he's got!
NO, WAIT.
CAN I...
TELL YOU ALL ABOUT HIM?

Sorry For My Familiar

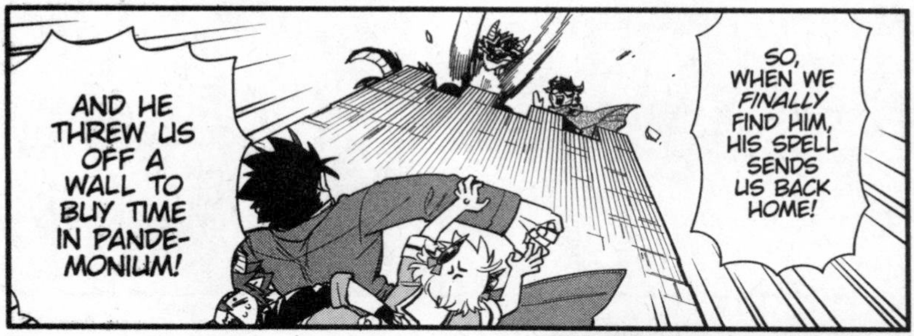
SO, WHEN WE *FINALLY* FIND HIM, HIS SPELL SENDS US BACK HOME!
AND HE THREW US OFF A WALL TO BUY TIME IN PANDE-MONIUM!

FILE 63: Human World ③

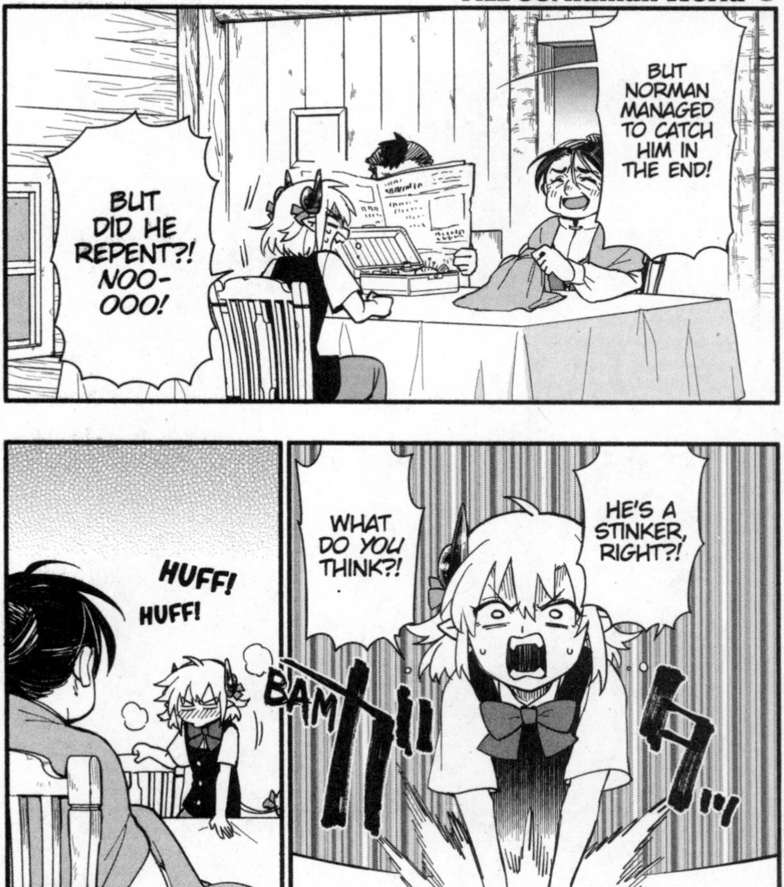
BUT NORMAN MANAGED TO CATCH HIM IN THE END!
BUT DID HE REPENT?! *NOO-OOO!*
HE'S A STINKER, RIGHT?!
WHAT DO *YOU* THINK?!
BAM
HUFF!
HUFF!

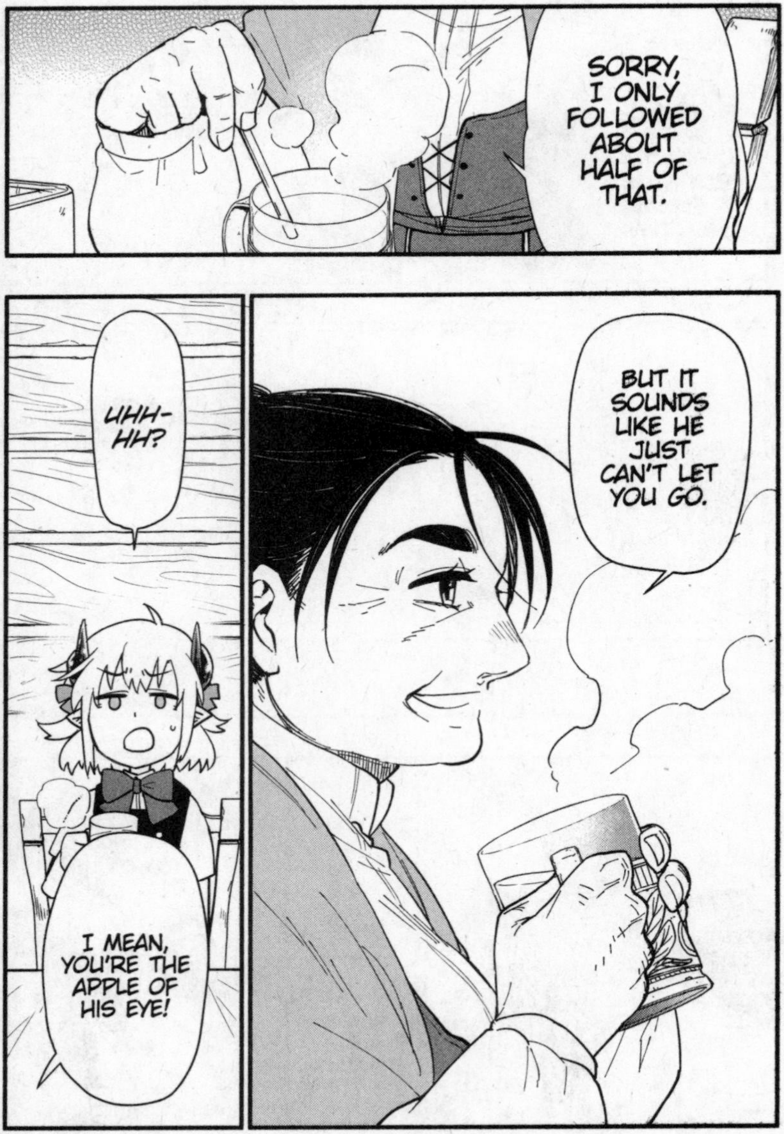
SORRY, I ONLY FOLLOWED ABOUT HALF OF THAT.
BUT IT SOUNDS LIKE HE JUST CAN'T LET YOU GO.
UHH-HH?
I MEAN, YOU'RE THE APPLE OF HIS EYE!

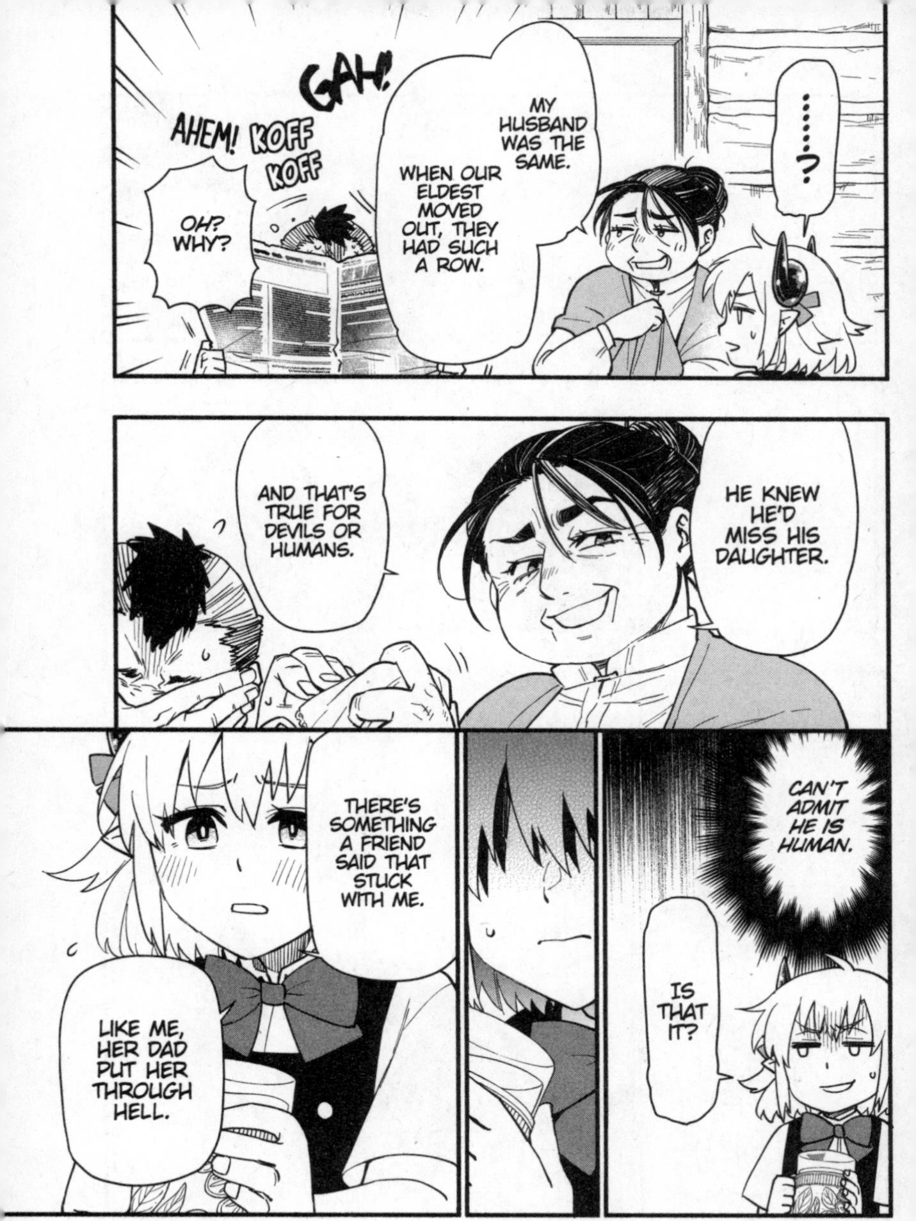
......?
MY HUSBAND WAS THE SAME.
WHEN OUR ELDEST MOVED OUT, THEY HAD SUCH A ROW.
GAH!
AHEM! KOFF KOFF
OH? WHY?
HE KNEW HE'D MISS HIS DAUGHTER.
AND THAT'S TRUE FOR DEVILS OR HUMANS.
CAN'T ADMIT HE IS HUMAN.
IS THAT IT?
THERE'S SOMETHING A FRIEND SAID THAT STUCK WITH ME.
LIKE ME, HER DAD PUT HER THROUGH HELL.

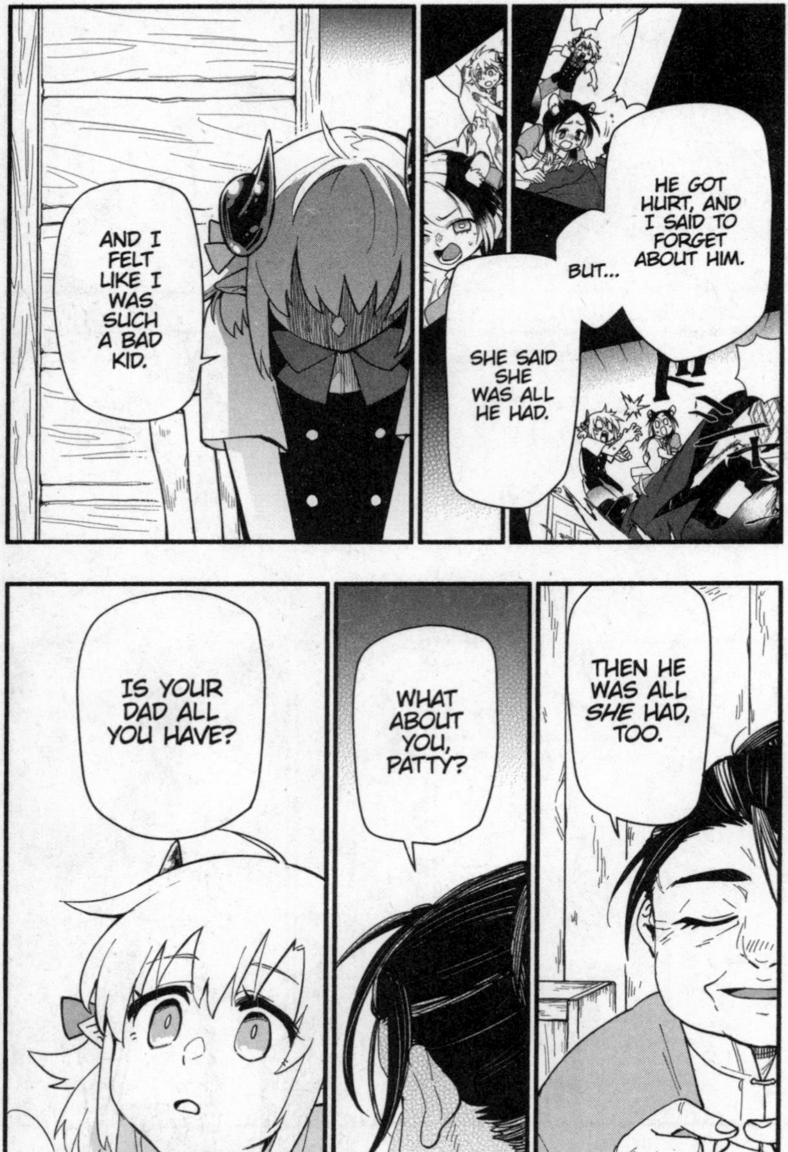
HE GOT HURT, AND I SAID TO FORGET ABOUT HIM.
BUT...
SHE SAID SHE WAS ALL HE HAD.
AND I FELT LIKE I WAS SUCH A BAD KID.
THEN HE WAS ALL *SHE* HAD, TOO.
WHAT ABOUT YOU, PATTY?
IS YOUR DAD ALL YOU HAVE?

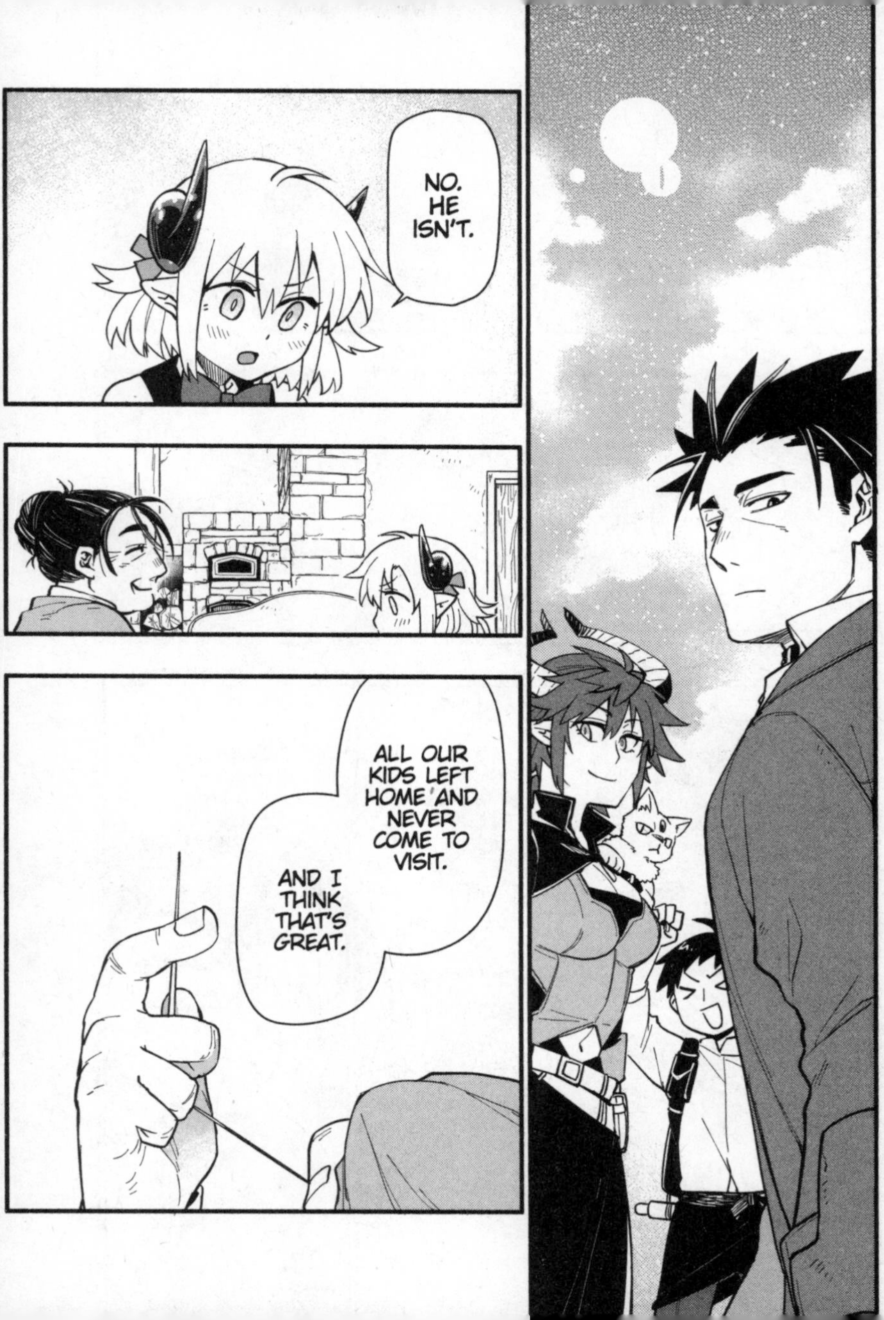
NO. HE ISN'T.
ALL OUR KIDS LEFT HOME AND NEVER COME TO VISIT.
AND I THINK THAT'S GREAT.

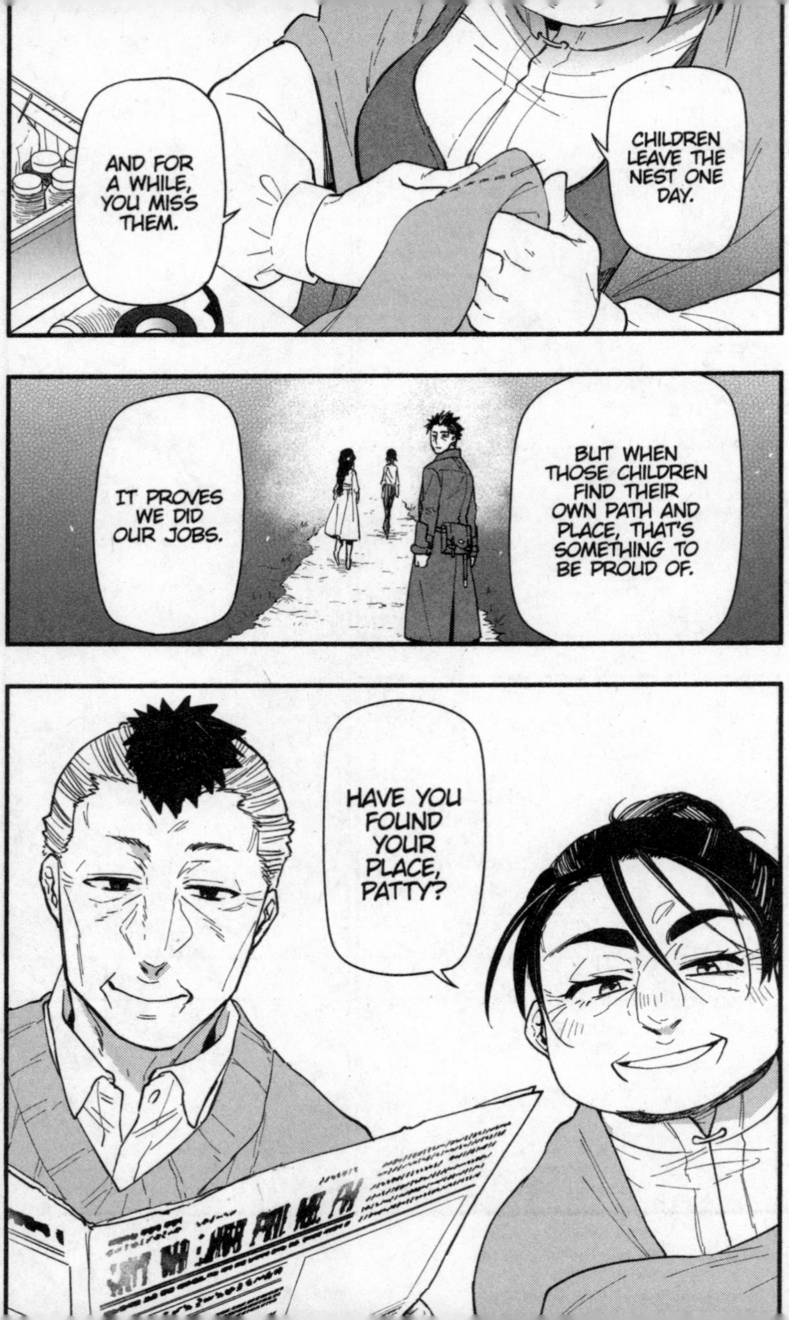

CHILDREN LEAVE THE NEST ONE DAY.
AND FOR A WHILE, YOU MISS THEM.
BUT WHEN THOSE CHILDREN FIND THEIR OWN PATH AND PLACE, THAT'S SOMETHING TO BE PROUD OF.
IT PROVES WE DID OUR JOBS.
HAVE YOU FOUND YOUR PLACE, PATTY?

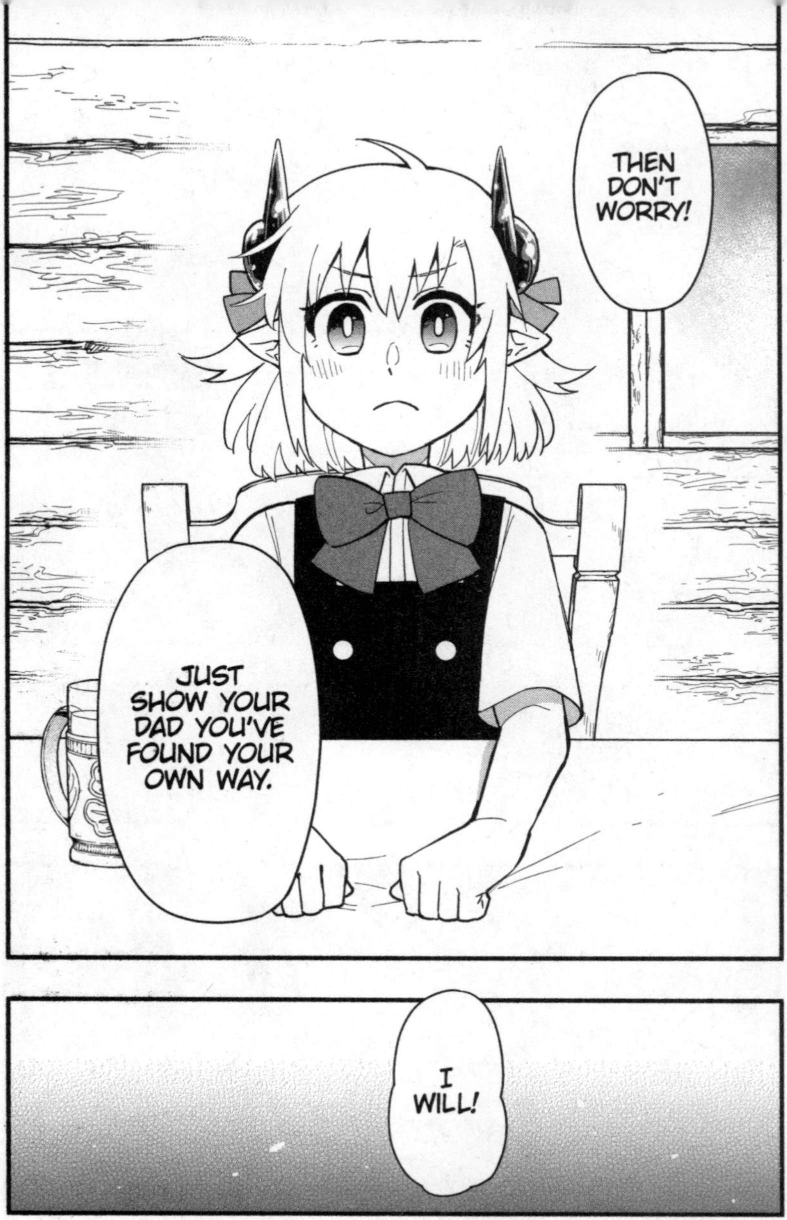
THEN DON'T WORRY!
JUST SHOW YOUR DAD YOU'VE FOUND YOUR OWN WAY.
I WILL!

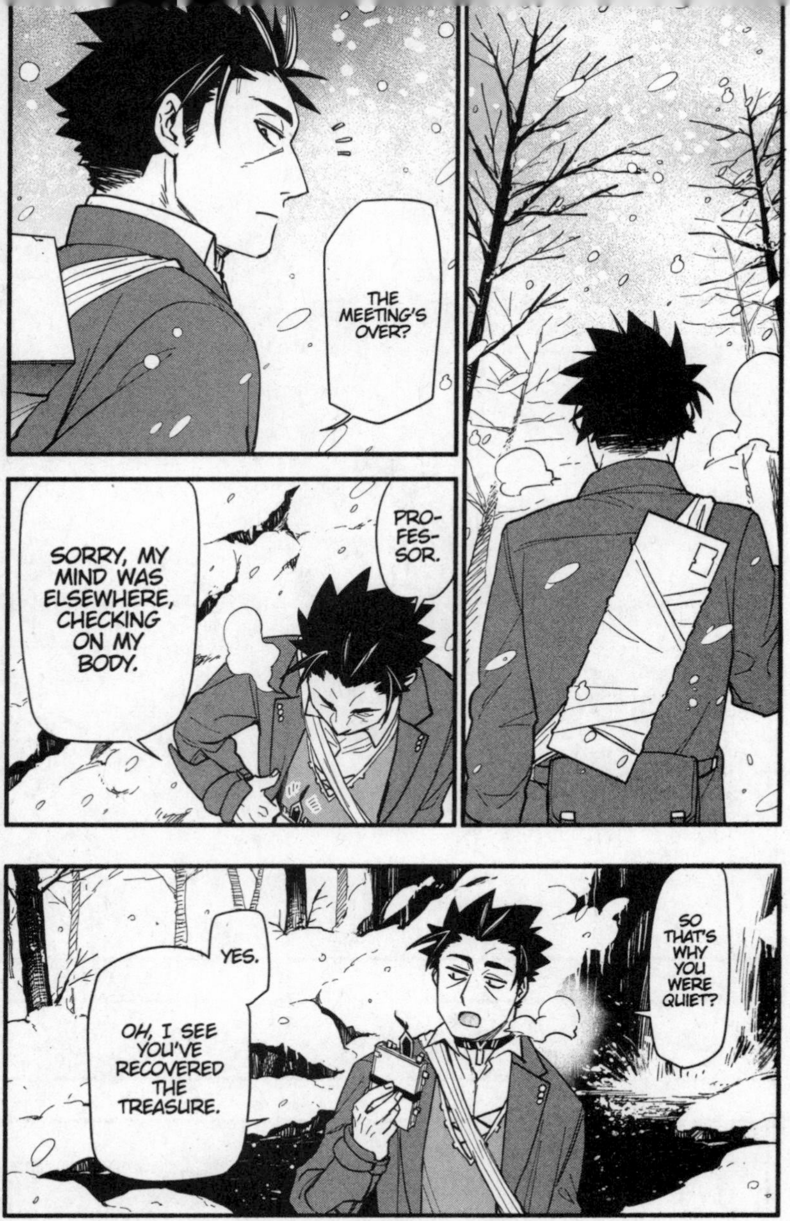
THE MEETING'S OVER?
PRO-FES-SOR.
SORRY, MY MIND WAS ELSEWHERE, CHECKING ON MY BODY.
SO THAT'S WHY YOU WERE QUIET?
YES.
OH, I SEE YOU'VE RECOVERED THE TREASURE.

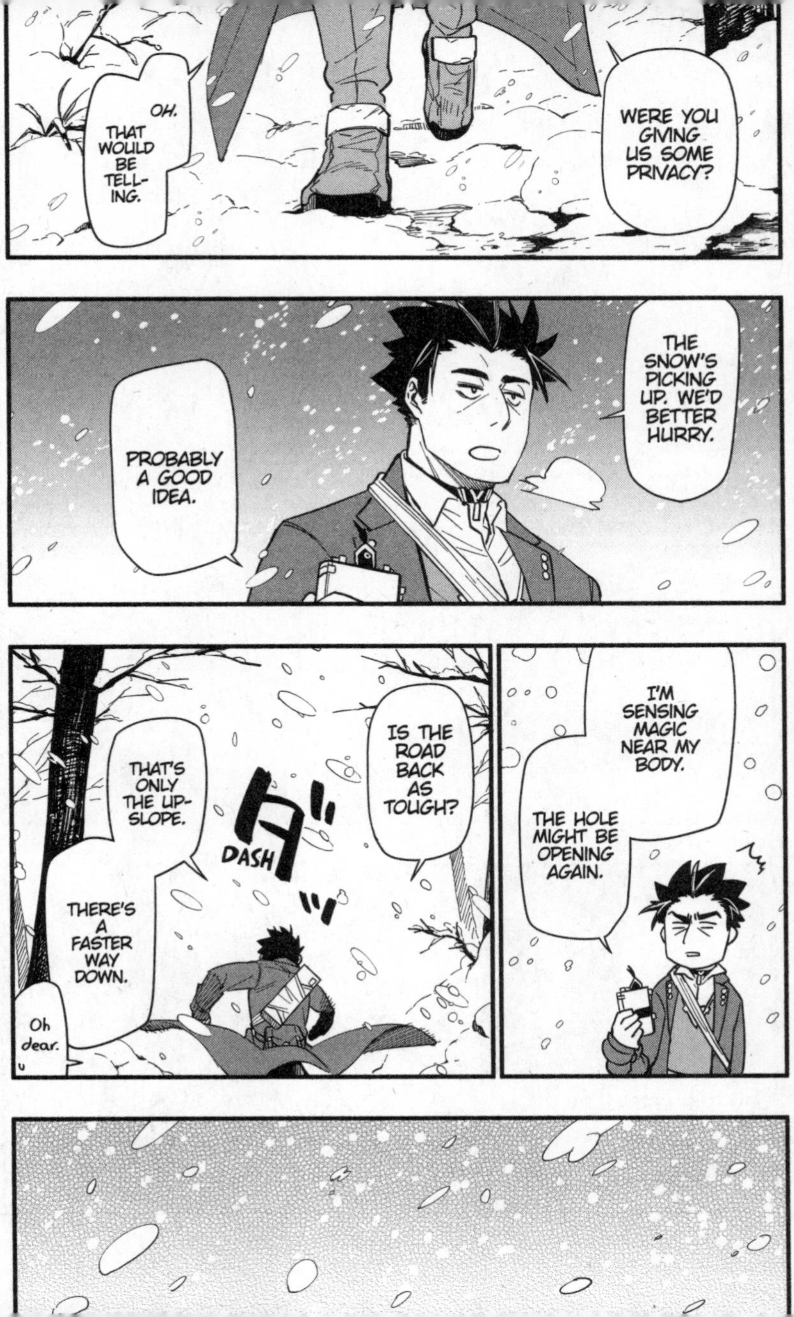
WERE YOU GIVING US SOME PRIVACY?
OH. THAT WOULD BE TELL-ING.
THE SNOW'S PICKING UP. WE'D BETTER HURRY.
PROBABLY A GOOD IDEA.
I'M SENSING MAGIC NEAR MY BODY.
THE HOLE MIGHT BE OPENING AGAIN.
IS THE ROAD BACK AS TOUGH?
THAT'S ONLY THE UP-SLOPE.
DASH
THERE'S A FASTER WAY DOWN.
Oh dear.

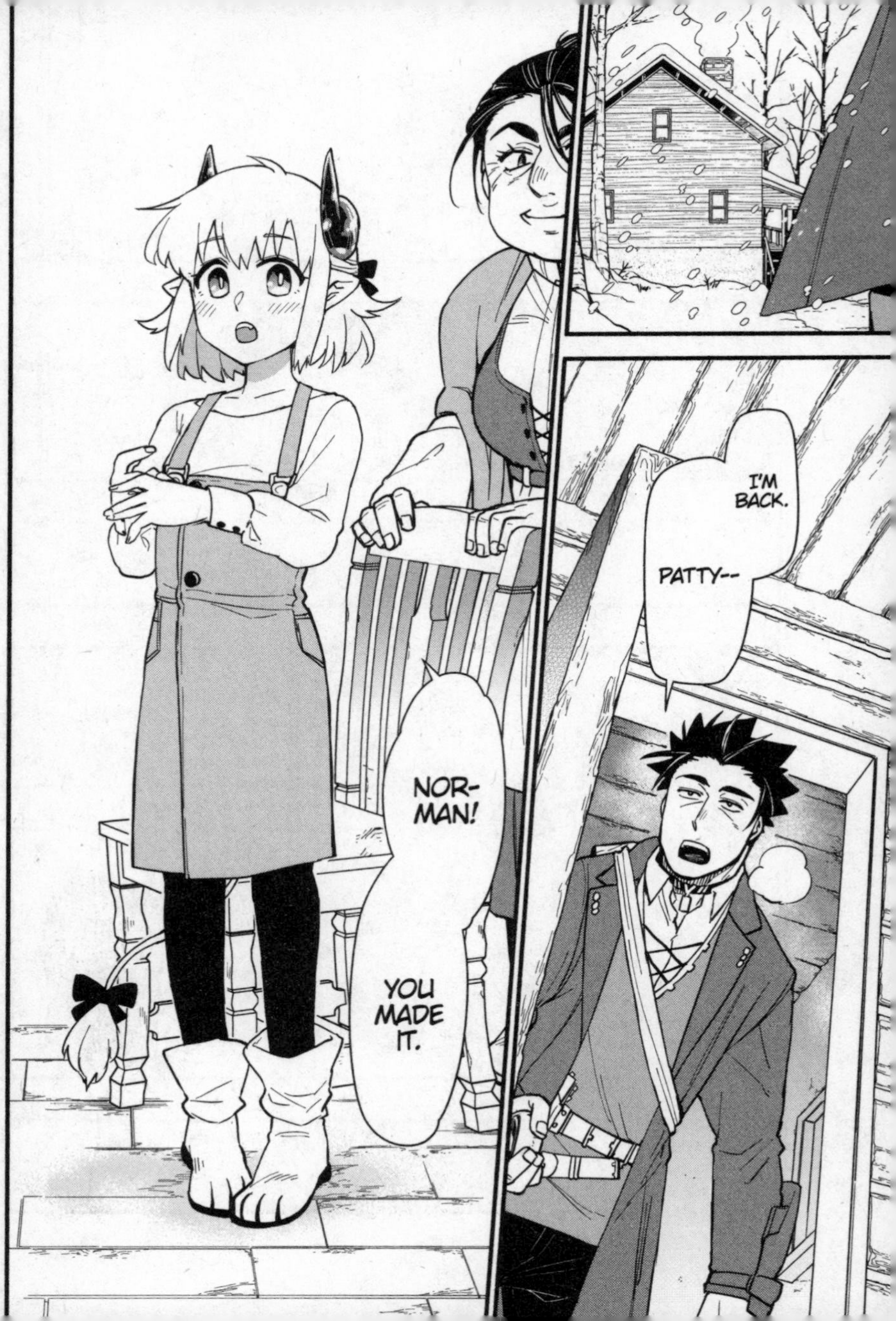
I'M BACK.
PATTY--
NOR-MAN!
YOU MADE IT.

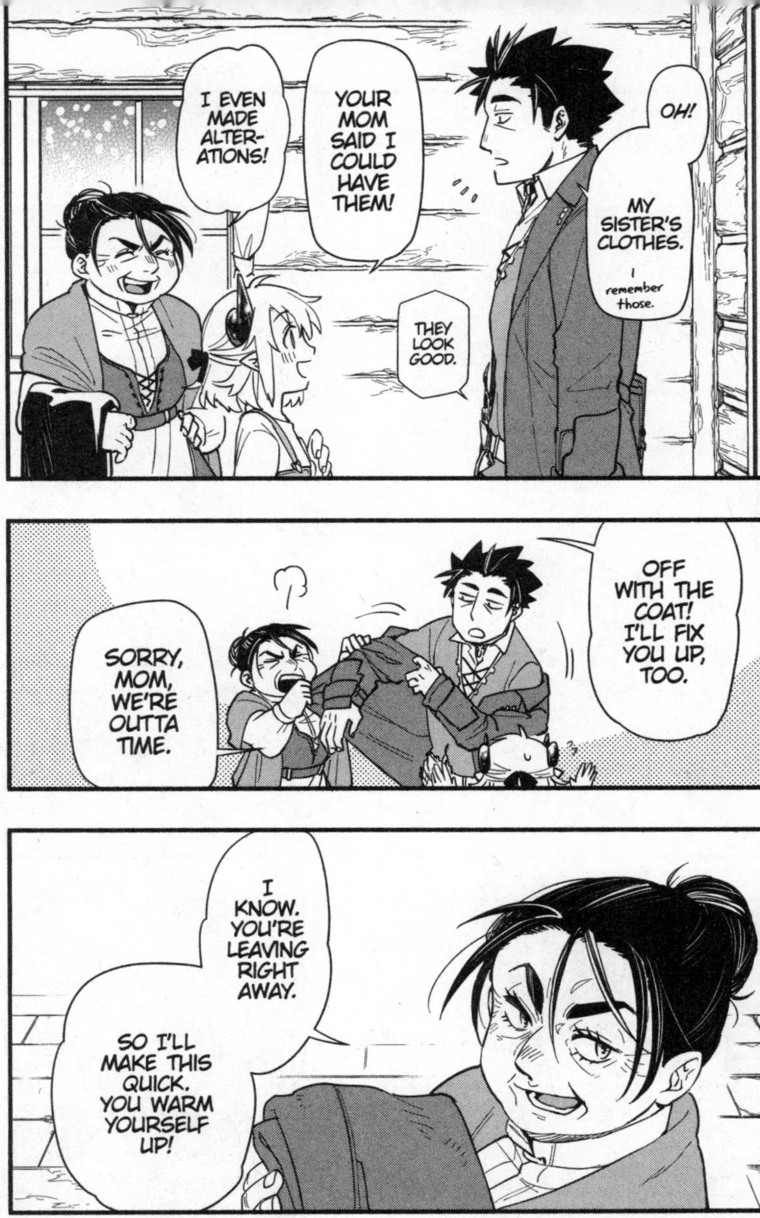
I EVEN MADE ALTER-ATIONS!
YOUR MOM SAID I COULD HAVE THEM!
OH!
MY SISTER'S CLOTHES.
I remember those.
THEY LOOK GOOD.
SORRY, MOM, WE'RE OUTTA TIME.
OFF WITH THE COAT! I'LL FIX YOU UP, TOO.
I KNOW. YOU'RE LEAVING RIGHT AWAY.
SO I'LL MAKE THIS QUICK. YOU WARM YOURSELF UP!

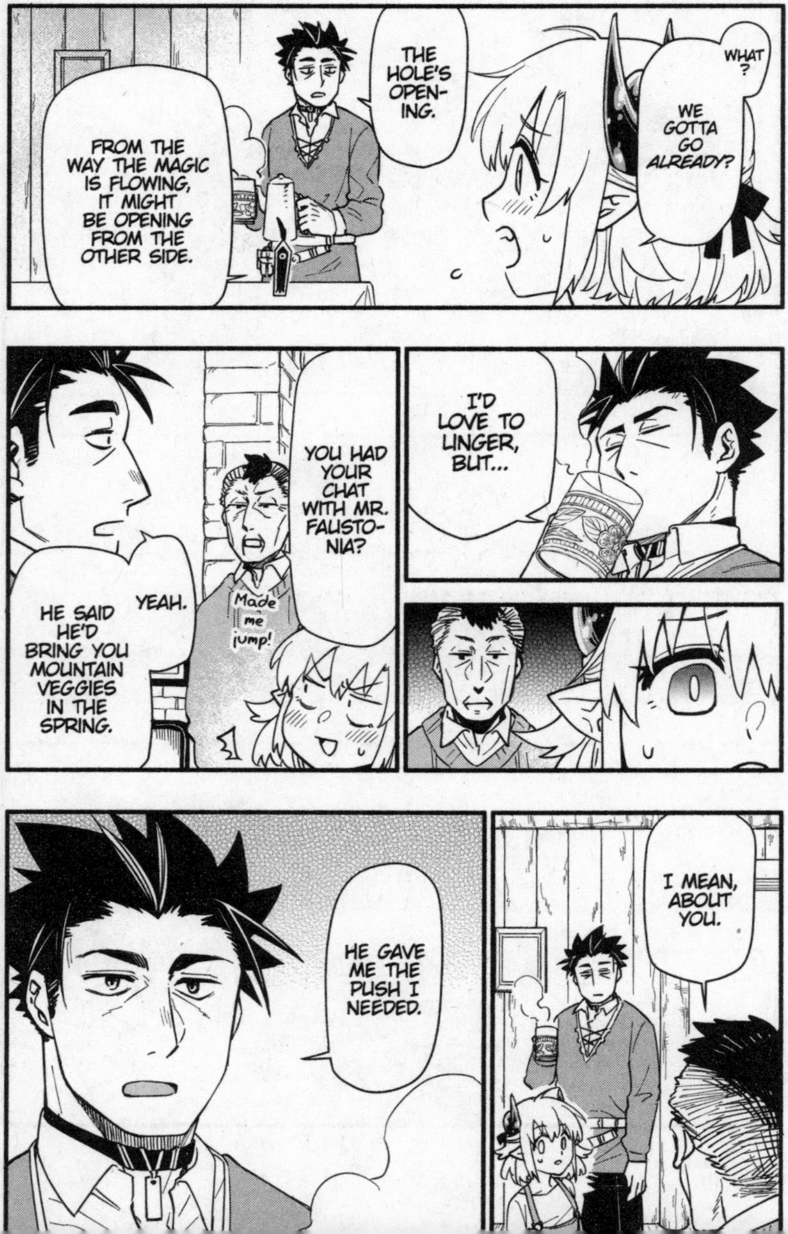
WHAT?
WE GOTTA GO ALREADY?
THE HOLE'S OPEN-ING.
FROM THE WAY THE MAGIC IS FLOWING, IT MIGHT BE OPENING FROM THE OTHER SIDE.
I'D LOVE TO LINGER, BUT...
YOU HAD YOUR CHAT WITH MR. FAUSTO-NIA?
YEAH.
HE SAID HE'D BRING YOU MOUNTAIN VEGGIES IN THE SPRING.
Made me jump!
I MEAN, ABOUT YOU.
HE GAVE ME THE PUSH I NEEDED.

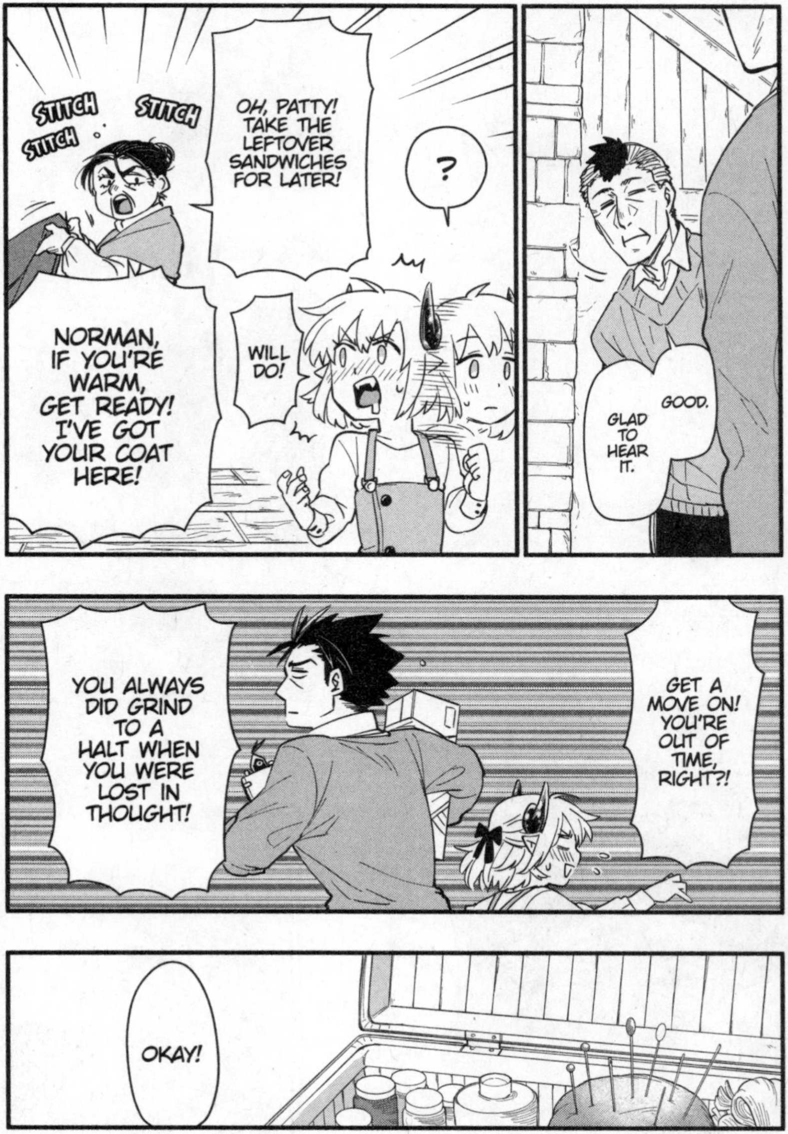
STITCH
STITCH
STITCH
OH, PATTY! TAKE THE LEFTOVER SANDWICHES FOR LATER!
?
WILL DO!
NORMAN, IF YOU'RE WARM, GET READY! I'VE GOT YOUR COAT HERE!
GOOD.
GLAD TO HEAR IT.
GET A MOVE ON! YOU'RE OUT OF TIME, RIGHT?!
YOU ALWAYS DID GRIND TO A HALT WHEN YOU WERE LOST IN THOUGHT!
OKAY!

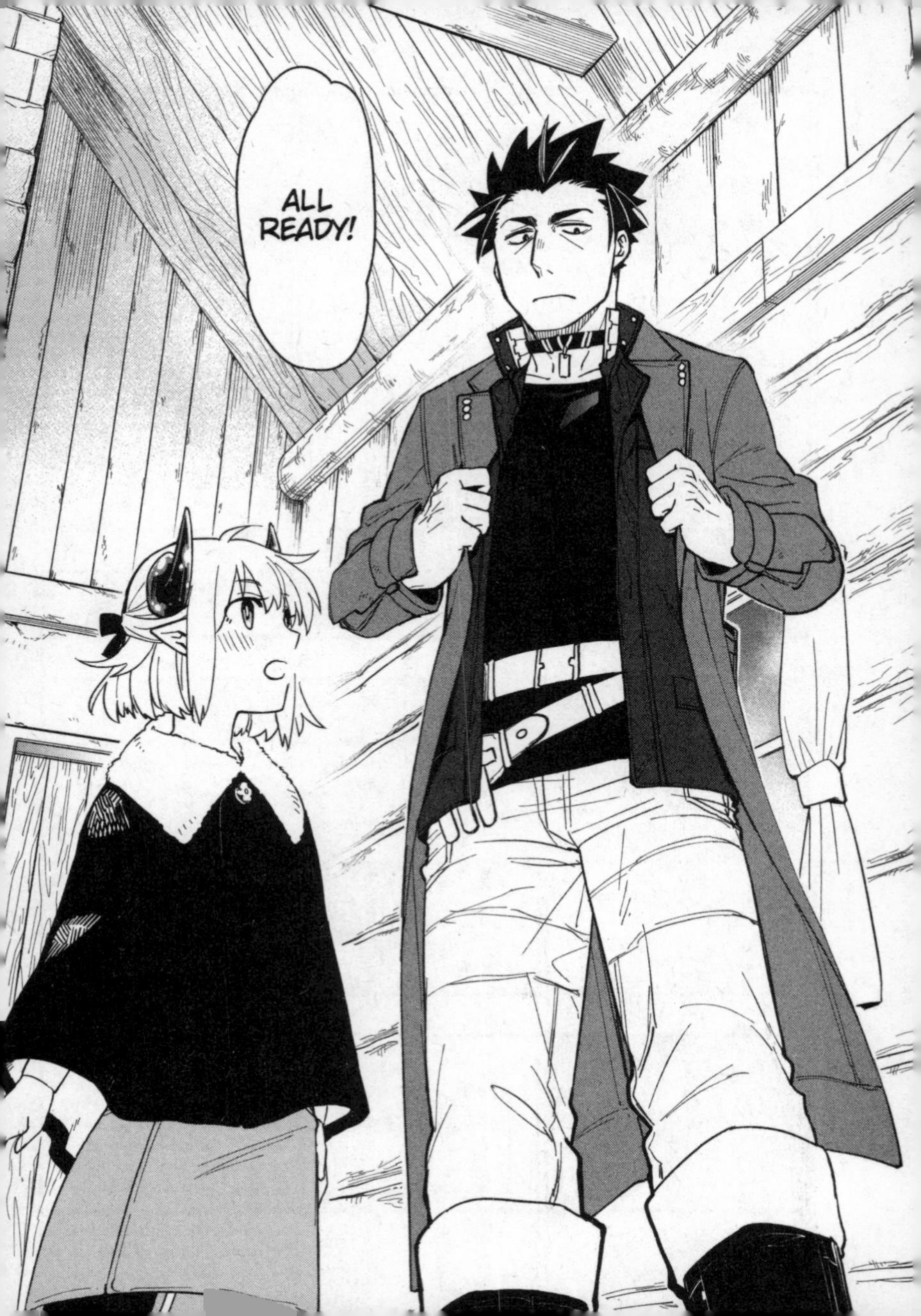
ALL READY!

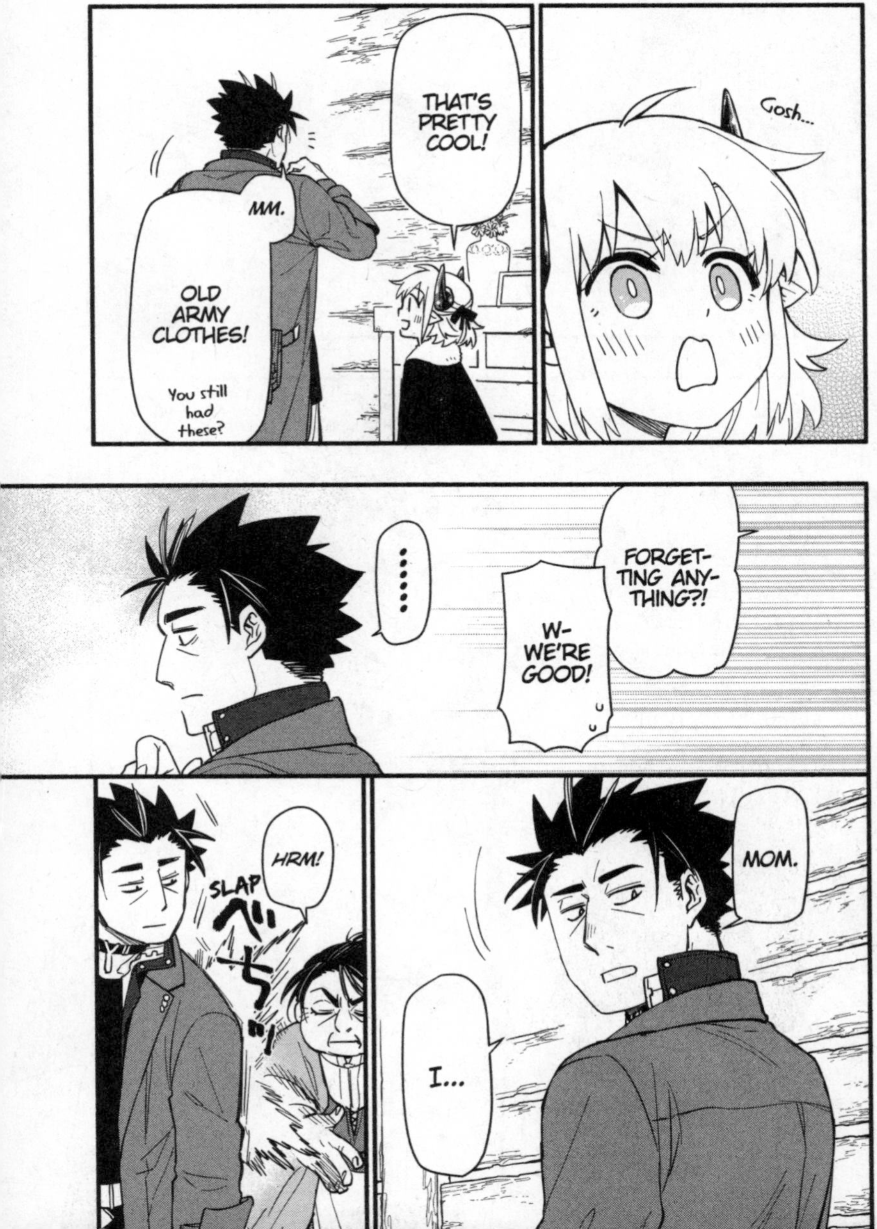
Gosh...
THAT'S PRETTY COOL!
MM.
OLD ARMY CLOTHES!
You still had these?
FORGETTING ANYTHING?!
W-WE'RE GOOD!
......
MOM.
I...
HRM!
SLAP

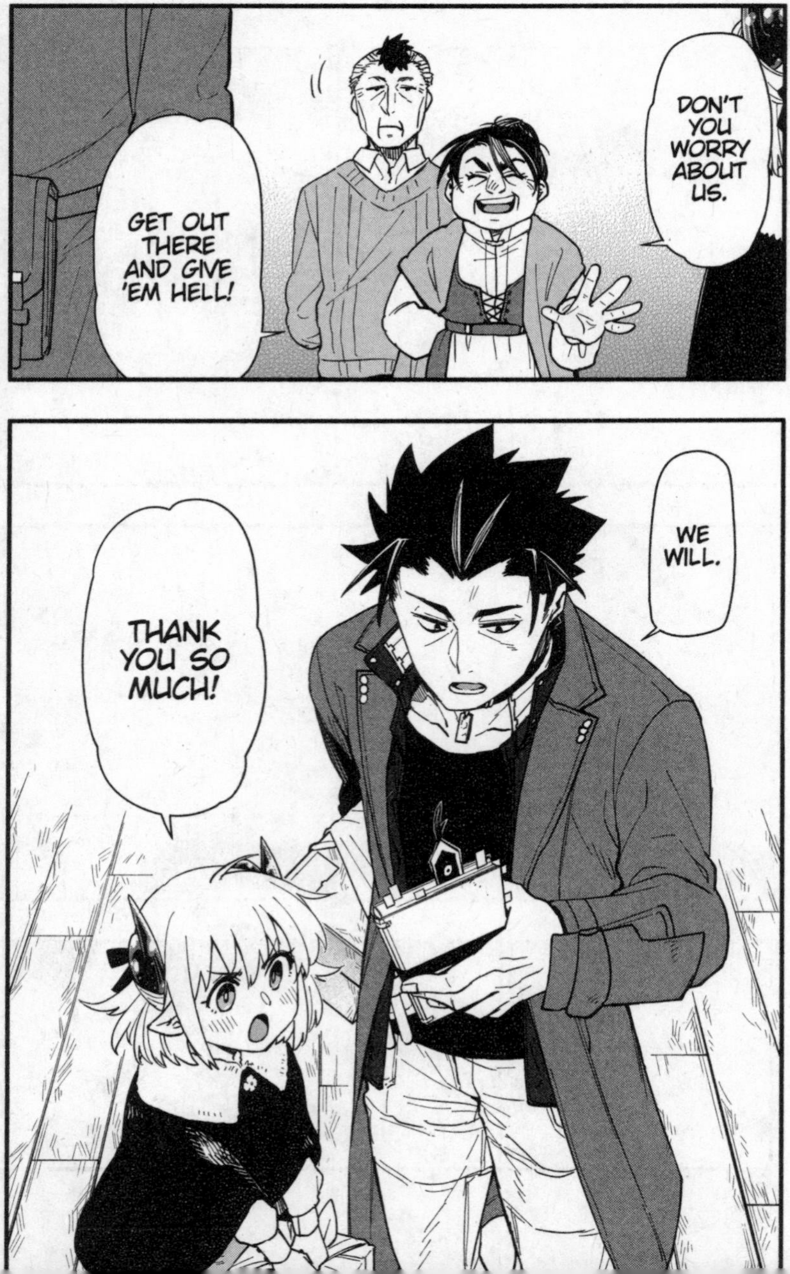
DON'T YOU WORRY ABOUT US.
GET OUT THERE AND GIVE 'EM HELL!
WE WILL.
THANK YOU SO MUCH!

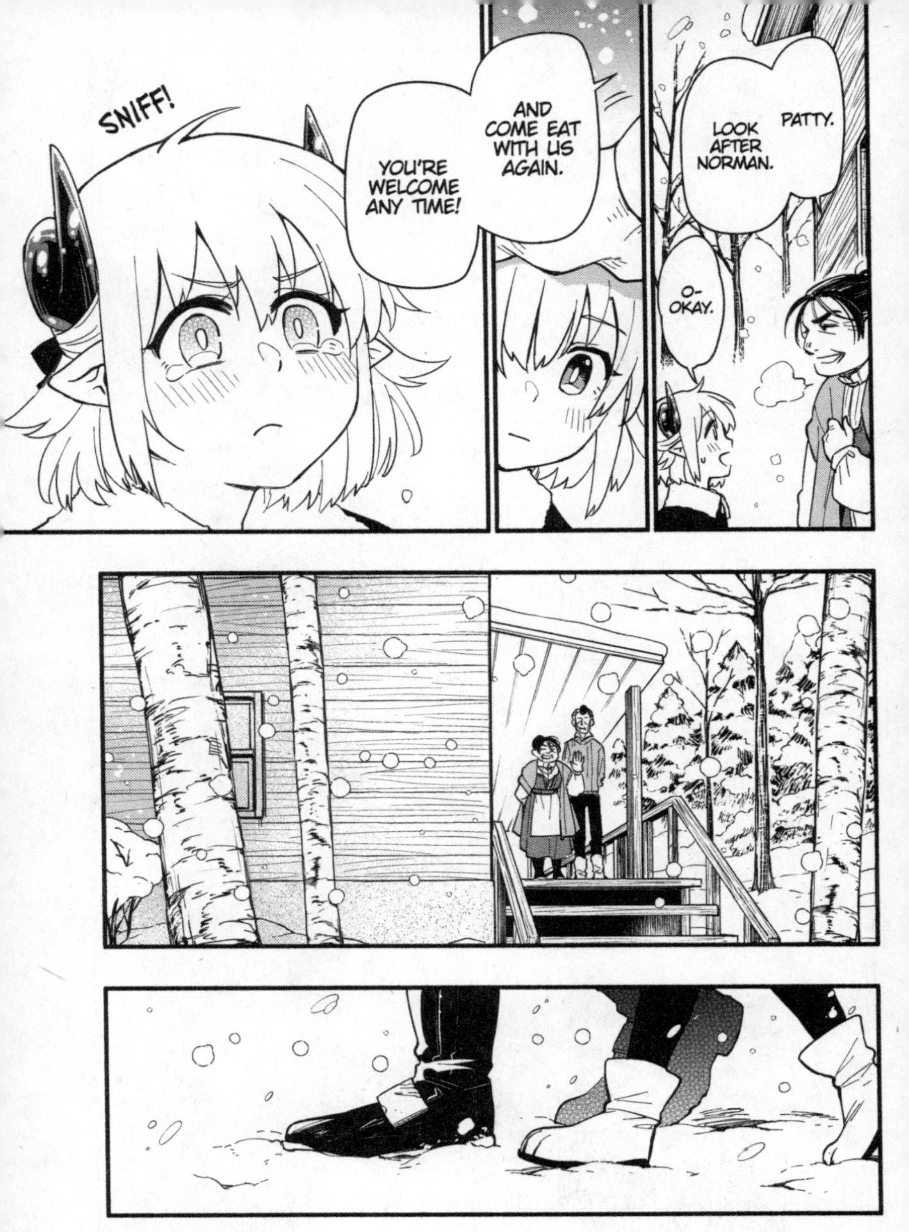
PATTY.
LOOK AFTER NORMAN.
O-OKAY.
AND COME EAT WITH US AGAIN.
YOU'RE WELCOME ANY TIME!
SNIFF!

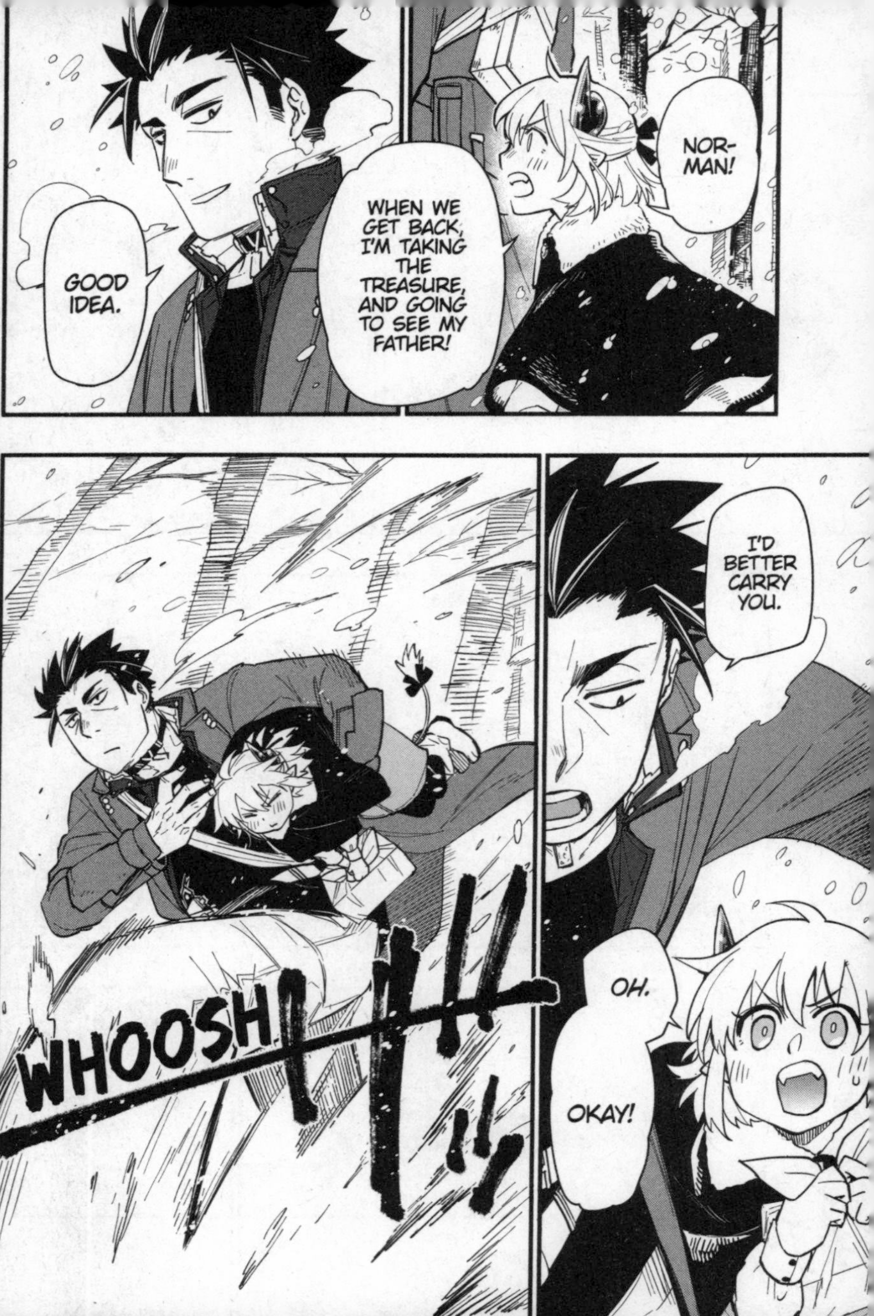
NOR-MAN!
WHEN WE GET BACK, I'M TAKING THE TREASURE, AND GOING TO SEE MY FATHER!
GOOD IDEA.
I'D BETTER CARRY YOU.
OH.
OKAY!
WHOOSH!!

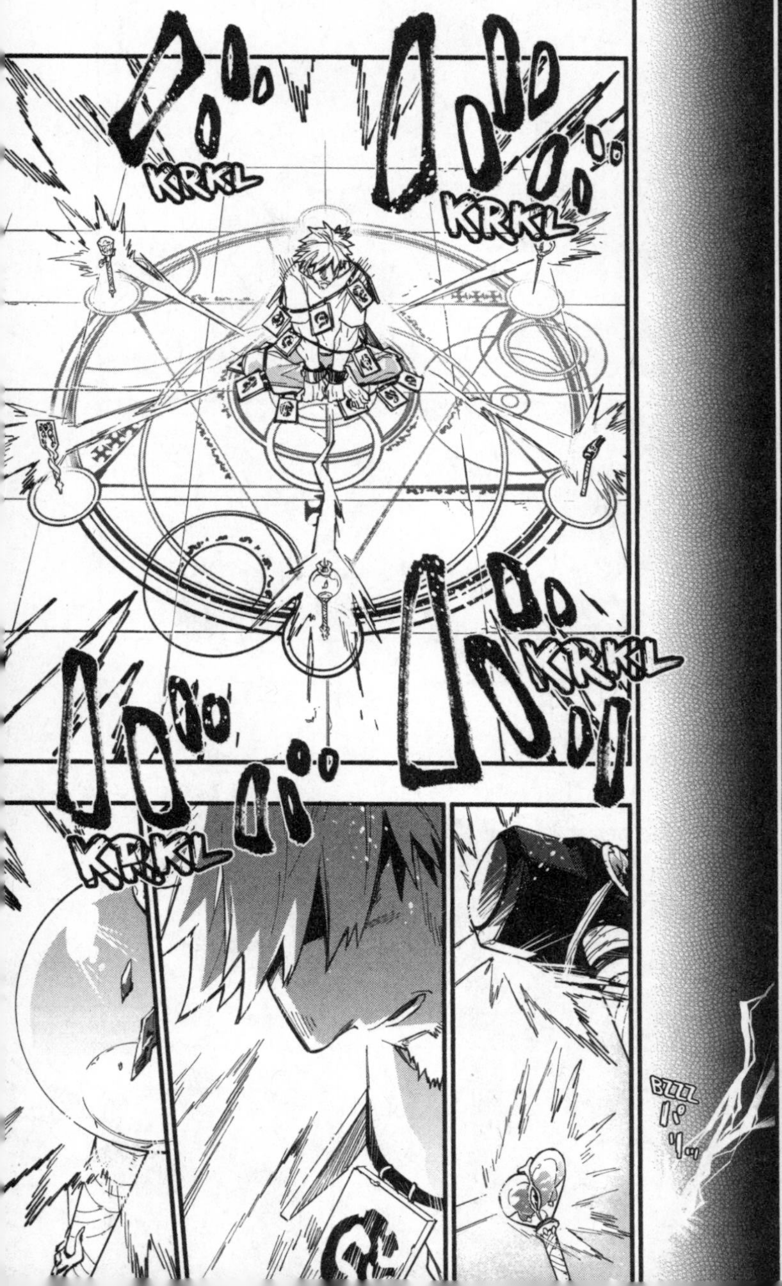
KRKL
KRKL
KRKL
KRKL
BZZZ

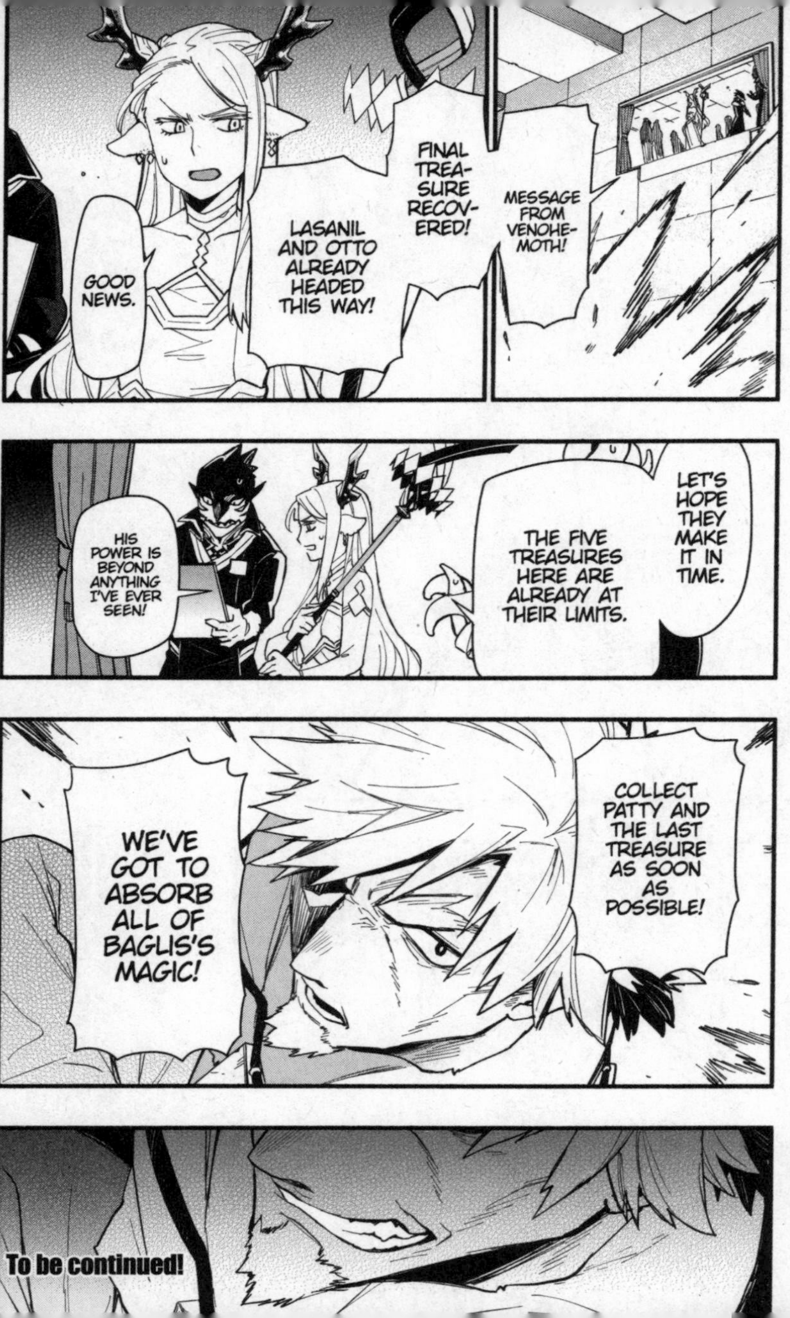
MESSAGE FROM VENOHEMOTH!
FINAL TREASURE RECOVERED!
LASANIL AND OTTO ALREADY HEADED THIS WAY!
GOOD NEWS.
LET'S HOPE THEY MAKE IT IN TIME.
THE FIVE TREASURES HERE ARE ALREADY AT THEIR LIMITS.
HIS POWER IS BEYOND ANYTHING I'VE EVER SEEN!
COLLECT PATTY AND THE LAST TREASURE AS SOON AS POSSIBLE!
WE'VE GOT TO ABSORB ALL OF BAGLIS'S MAGIC!
To be continued!

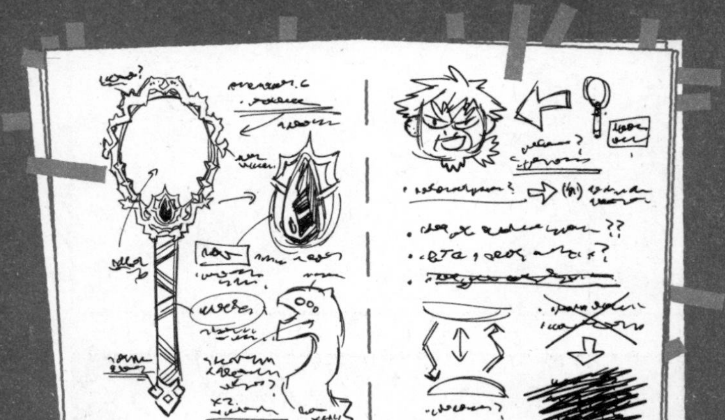

Sorry For My Familiar

SPECIAL
The Secret of Lasanil's Top♥

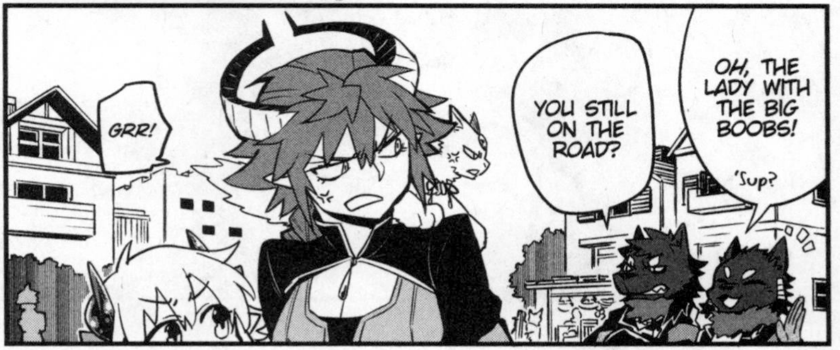
GRR!
YOU STILL ON THE ROAD?
OH, THE LADY WITH THE BIG BOOBS!
'Sup?

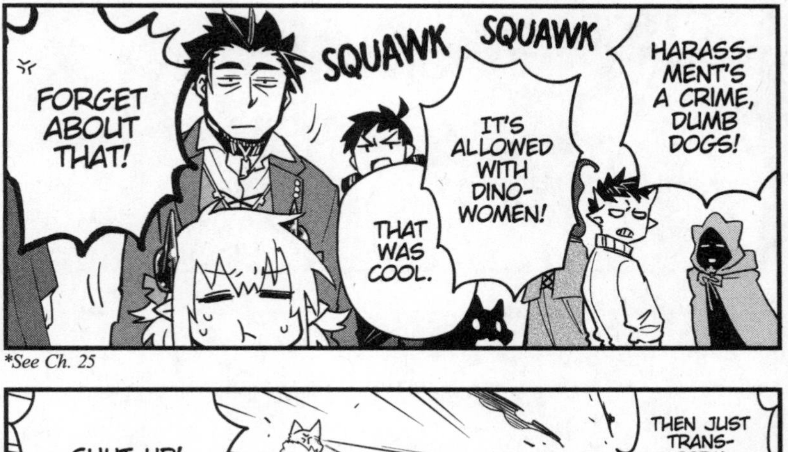
FORGET ABOUT THAT!
SQUAWK
SQUAWK
IT'S ALLOWED WITH DINO-WOMEN!
THAT WAS COOL.
HARASS-MENT'S A CRIME, DUMB DOGS!

*See Ch. 25

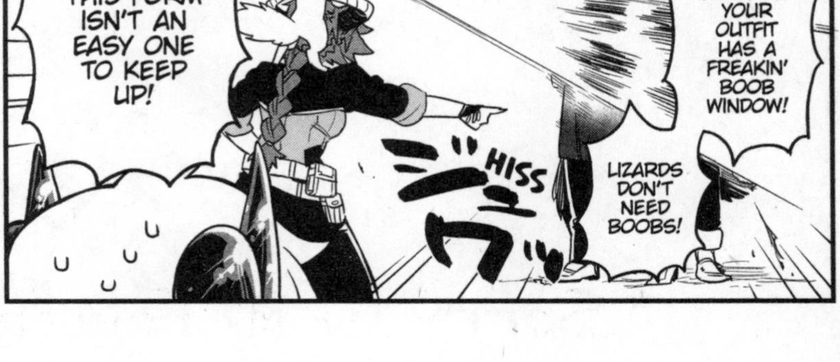
SHUT UP! THIS FORM ISN'T AN EASY ONE TO KEEP UP!
HISS
THEN JUST TRANS-FORM ALREADY! YOUR OUTFIT HAS A FREAKIN' BOOB WINDOW!
LIZARDS DON'T NEED BOOBS!

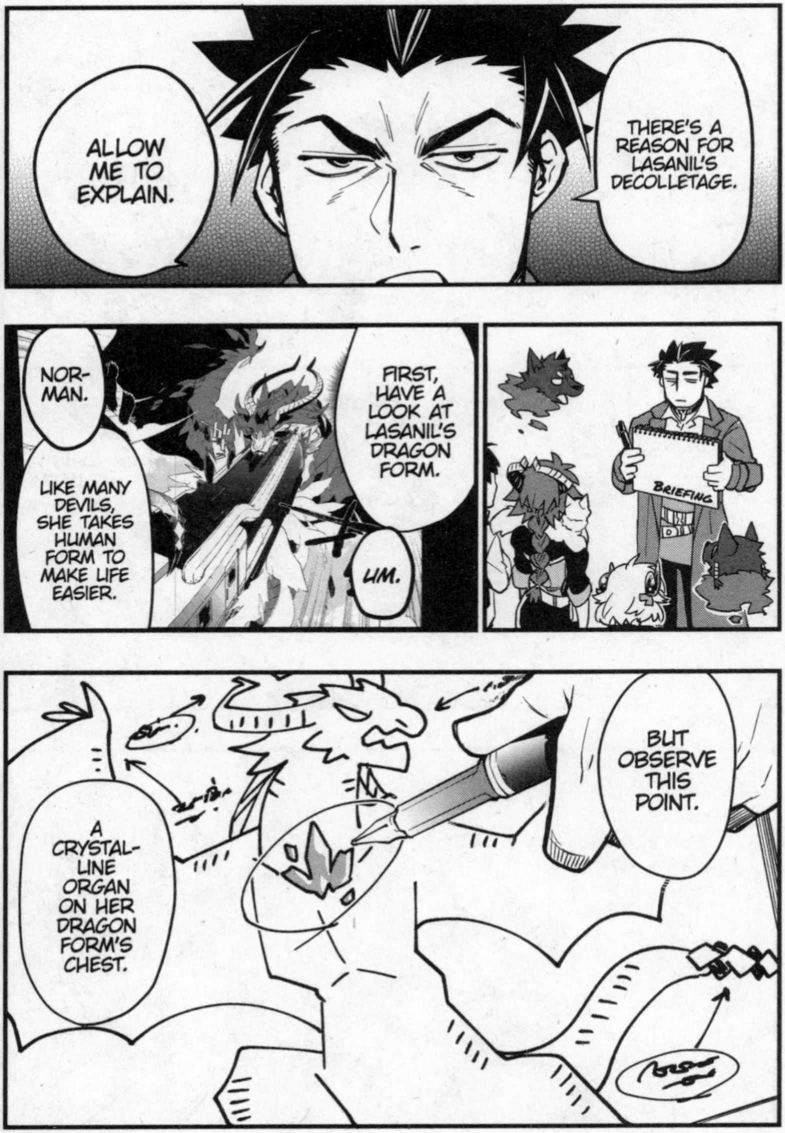

THERE'S A REASON FOR LASANIL'S DECOLLETAGE.
ALLOW ME TO EXPLAIN.
BRIEFING
FIRST, HAVE A LOOK AT LASANIL'S DRAGON FORM.
NOR-MAN.
UM.
LIKE MANY DEVILS, SHE TAKES HUMAN FORM TO MAKE LIFE EASIER.
BUT OBSERVE THIS POINT.
A CRYSTAL-LINE ORGAN ON HER DRAGON FORM'S CHEST.